GOLDEN AS THE NIGHT

BROOKE ERINS

Identifiers:
ISBN: 9780645403725 (paperback)
ISBN: 678064503749 (ebook)

For everyone who loves to lose themselves in another world.

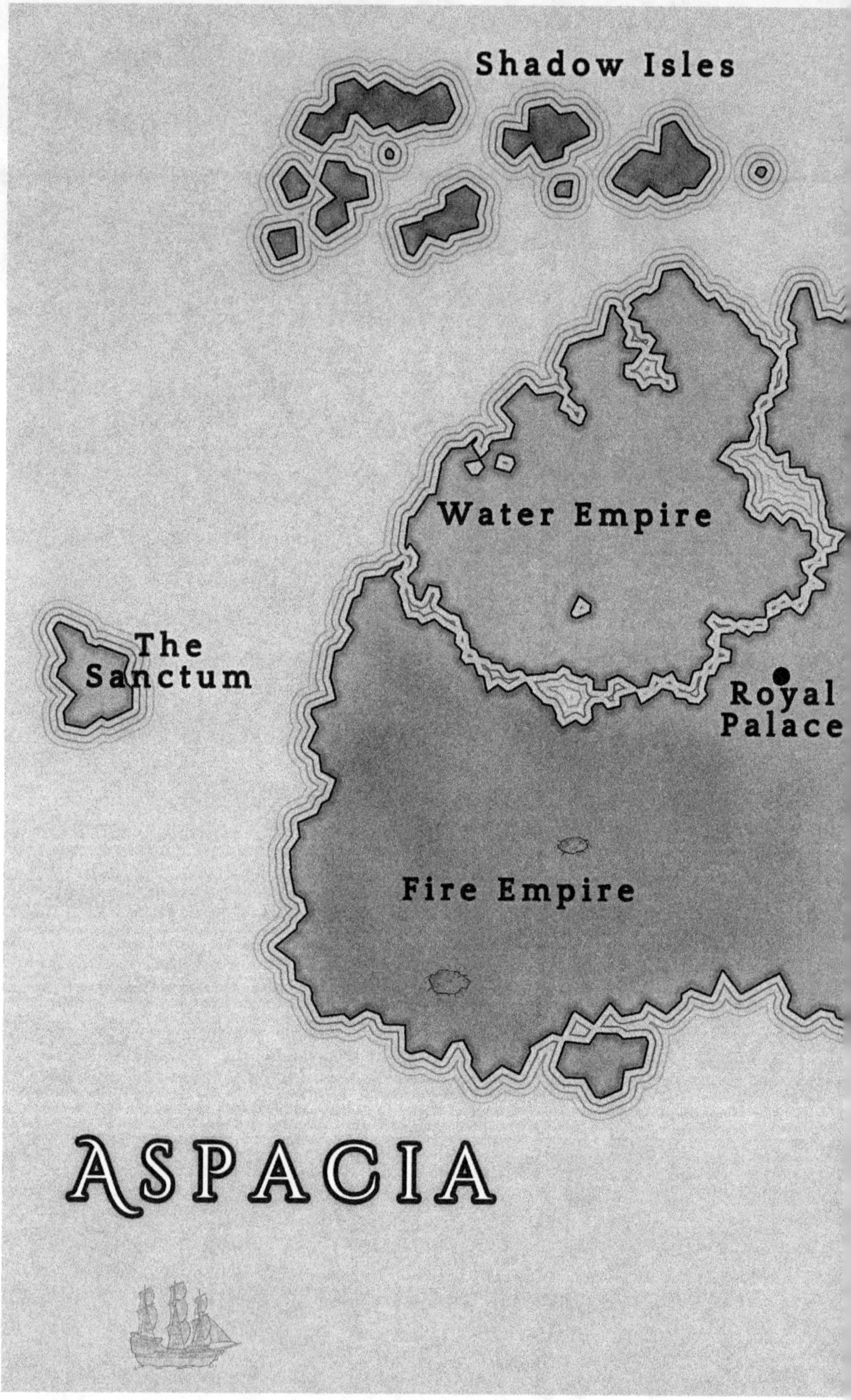

Shadow Isles
Water Empire
The
Sanctum
Royal
Palace
Fire Empire
ASPACIA

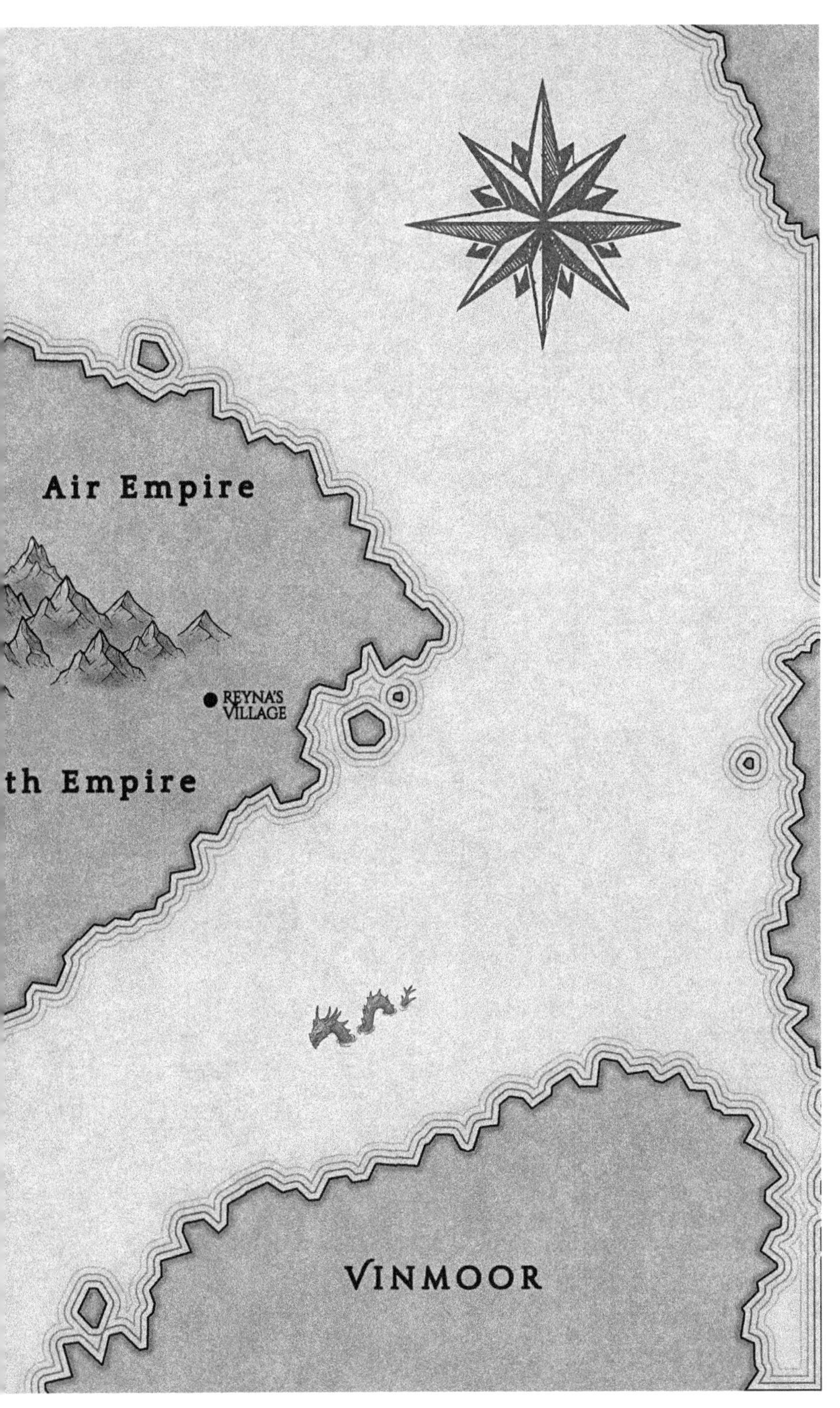

Air Empire
th Empire
REYNA'S
VILLAGE
VINMOOR

1

I watch from the corner of a darkened room as my father places a firm hand on my mother's thin shoulder for the very last time. He pulls her tightly against his chest, her body but a fragment of his. They fit together like a puzzle, and now it will be forever unfinished. My lips tremble as my father meets her eyes, then grimaces as he tears his away. But I will not cry.

My father walks towards my brother and I with a demanding stride, kneeling down before me so I see every last scar on his hardened face. So full of memories, his saddened smile brimming with love. But I will not cry.

Pollo stands over me, his hands gripping my shoulders tightly. My brother watches the tall man as he kisses his cheek, then mine, for the very last time. But I will not cry.

My mother sobs through her hands clasped at her mouth, muffling a sorrow that would continue for endless years. My father runs a soft finger down my face, my eyes meeting his identically green ones in a saddened stare.

"This is not goodbye, Reyna. We will meet again," my father says. His voice is gravel on a silken sheet. "I've left you something I should've given you a long time ago. It's in your shed. Take care of it for me." He walks from our small living room to the front door, opening it without looking back at the family who depend on him. He pauses only slightly, and then he is gone.

I wrench my shoulders from Pollo's grasp, pulling myself away and sprinting to follow the only person who has ever believed in me. But a child's hope is stronger than a king's orders... Right?

"Reyna! Come back!" I hear my brother call from inside the house, amongst the sobs my mother can no longer hold in. But I do not slow my pace. I am through the front door and onto the winding dirt path that connects our ramshackle excuse of a house to the street. My feet press into the dirt as I run, and I scan through the tall trees and wild shrubbery for the carriage.

And there it is. Parked outside our house on the street paved with patchy cobblestones, with two golden horses ready to pull it away. Their manes shine in the sun as they ignore my screams for my father, oblivious to the world that's being ripped from beneath my feet. The beasts take off, pulling the golden carriage behind them.

"Father! Wait! Don't go!" I scream, chasing the carriage through the streets, but it does not slow. I'm going to need to try something else. I continue sprinting until we are in the centre of our small village, the golden carriage sticking out like a sore thumb amongst the run-down, grey buildings and wooden shacks.

I find exactly what I'm searching for lying on the side of the path, and hurl the decent-sized rock at the back of the carriage. It hits its mark with a loud bang.

If I cared, I would notice the dozen pairs of eyes lifted in surprise, watching me from the shopfronts and alleyways. The carriage immediately halts, and two Royal Guards dressed in elaborate golden armour jump out from inside. They are followed by another, familiar man.

I continue running until I am in my father's arms once more, and crash into him so forcefully that I hope he will never leave me again. I can only imagine what the guards are seeing: a pathetic, weak child with unruly raven hair and tattered clothes causing them more trouble than she's worth. But I would do anything to see him one last time, even if he said we will meet again one day. But part of me knows we may never get that chance. My father wipes my streaming tears from my freckled face, looking down at me the same way he did before.

"Reyna, it will be okay. I promise. You are so much tougher than you could ever know. Be strong for me. For your mother and brother. They're going to need you," he says, his rough voice somehow as soft as a melody to my ears.

"But what if I never find it? How will I be strong?" I say, my lip trembling and voice shaking. I should've gotten my powers a few years ago, or at least have seen some sign of them. But no. Nothing. And despite still being young, I am already attracting the wrong kinds of attention. The attention that often leaves me lying bruised in the street with cruel, taunting words replaying in my mind,

"My words still stand, whether you have magic in your veins or not. You are my greatest gift," he says, and kisses me on the forehead. He stands, and I grab onto his waist, not wanting him to go. The guards step forward hesitantly, but my father waves them away.

"Reyna, you've got to let me go. Remember what I taught you. I love you, my warrior," he says, trailing his fingers through mine before he steps back into the carriage.

I don't bother resuming my chase when the golden horses begin trotting away once more. I don't even bother to watch as they disappear beyond the outskirts of the village. I turn my back on the carriage, on the town, and begin walking back to my home where I know Pollo will be waiting, trying to console my mother. It will be no use.

Today, I make myself a silent promise: I will never love again. They will only leave and break my heart into even smaller pieces than my father has done by abandoning us. Leaving us for the king, to become a Royal Guard. I can feel the fragments of my heart splitting apart, and I'm not sure if they can ever be put back together. His words rattle around in my mind for the remainder of the walk home. When I approach the chipped, decaying wooden door, it is silent.

I decide not to go in and face whatever lies inside my home. I'm not sure if I will be able to stand the defeated look on my mother's face, the sight of my brother shedding a rare, silent tear. Besides, the words my father spoke finally reach me: It's in your shed. Look after it for me.

I walk through our small, dying garden, past the gate leading to our field of crops, until my eyes find the weathered tin garden shed in the far corner of our property. It is covered in rust, almost hidden behind tangled vines and unruly bushes, but it is mine. The one place where I am the most powerful in the room. I carefully step over the plants and twist the handle, and the door opens with a loud scream of metal against metal.

There, in the dim light shining through the small window, is a box made of dark, red wood that wasn't there the last time I was here. It sits alone on the shelf, its shiny surface out of place amongst the dust and cobwebs. This must be what my father left for me. I reach out with hesitant hands, brushing my fingers over the smooth wood, and notice the swirling engravings atop the lid. I push it open with my thumbs, and inside lies the most beautiful blade I've ever seen. Actually, the only proper blade I've ever seen.

I carefully lift it from its velvet encasement, marvelling at the smooth handle that matches the outside of the box. The sharp, silver blade gleams in the rays of light inside the rusted shed. I picture my father in one of the golden suits of armour the men from the carriage wore, and even though I am mad at him, I can't help but feel... inspired. To wield such power, to carry such strength—that would be exactly what my father asked of me.

Be strong for me.

His words rattle around inside my mind as I try to piece together the thought forming inside of me like a whirling hurricane. I know what my father wants me to do. And so, I make myself my second promise of the day: one day, when I am grown, I will become a Royal Guard. One day I will make him proud. I will never have to love, never have to feel. Only serve.

The guard manning the entrance nods in greeting, beckoning our carriage forward to the checkpoint. The peeling interior is a stark contrast to that of the golden carriage all those years ago. I listen intently as our driver produces mine and my brother's student paperwork, which the guard takes and reads over. He waves a hand towards the overgrown brick gatehouse, gesturing for another guard to release the lock on the tall iron gate.

I've been waiting for this moment with open arms for as long as I can remember, and finally, I am here. Ever since the day my father gave me my dagger when I was a child, I've known the path I need to follow leads me here. To the Sanctum.

I notice the flecks of grey in his eyes as he stands waiting. Green eyes—an Earth Keeper, like me. His uniform comprises heavy leather armour, with two longswords crossed at his back. The Sanctum's emblem is embroidered onto his dark grey shirt—a square divided into quarters with a golden four-pointed star in the centre.

I watch from inside the carriage as a shimmering veil lifts from the ground to the top of the gates. They swing open.

Pollo grins from beside me, giving the guard a too-friendly wave as we pass, but the man simply rolls his eyes. Pollo, my black-sheep older brother, is in his third year at the Sanctum. His wavy brunette hair is tied at the back of his head. I know why he's grinning so menacingly: he's back on his turf. He may be a reckless, rule breaking ass with an eye for the dark side, but he is fiercely loyal to my family. I never have to doubt his true motives, even when his behaviour wavers because of his own poor judgement or greedy desire. His purple eyes shine with pride as we continue down the winding brick road. I turned eighteen last month, and any hope I have of my powers developing is lost. But I'm done wallowing in my shame: there are other ways to be powerful in Aspacia. Maybe one day, I will be able to take my place alongside my father in the Royal Guard. One day, I will figure out what exactly those other ways to be powerful are.

The first few buildings of the Sanctum's premises come into view and I gasp. I've heard stories of how intriguing the grounds of the Sanctum are, but nothing could prepare me for this. Winding, dark towers, walls laden with mossy brick, and gardens as lush as the king's express the power and wealth the Sanctum holds. Residing on a small island to the west of our lands, the Sanctum has been an important institution in the Keeper world for centuries. It is the only educational institution for Keepers to develop their elemental abilities.

When my father married my mother, a wave of controversy shook our small village in the Earth Empire. My mother is an Air Keeper, and my father is an Earth Keeper. Marrying across Empires isn't unheard of, but rare and extremely frowned upon. Most couples just don't do it, no matter how much they love each other, because of the constant ridicule they face. And sometimes the ridicule turns into broken bones and cries from the centre of the Town Square. My parents have always been careful—they don't go out into the town together, they take turns working on the farm, to try to make our village forget their treachery. Though not everyone has forgotten.

The carriage pulls into a parking space in front of Air House. The purple Air insignia—a cloud with three neat lines signalling wind—is everywhere on this quarter of the Sanctum. It's on the walls, painted on each tile on the ground, and on every banner. Even the flames of the metal torches lighting the small courtyard are purple.

"Are you nervous?" Pollo asks. I give a small nod, but refrain from fear of being mocked. "It's okay, I know how it feels. I bugged out the first time I saw this place," he begins, understandingly. He ditches his usually confident and cocky persona and continues.

"Remember everything we told you though, Reyna. Everything looks amazing, sometimes even beautiful. But everything is there to hide something else, and nothing is as it seems," he says, his gaze suddenly serious. I think back to all the discussions and warnings my mother and Pollo had given me over the summer to prepare for my attending school here.

"I know," I say as I roll my eyes. "Thanks for the super warm welcome," I say, jumping out of the carriage and heading to the back to retrieve my luggage. The Sanctum has a sturdy reputation of being a safe school for young Keepers, so I'm not worried for my safety despite their warnings. Despite being powerless. I know how to wield a knife, how to win a fight, although I know that the threats my family is most worried about have more to do with what lies outside the Sanctum.

A few Air Keepers pass us by—their purple eyes finding Pollo and I across the front entrance to Air house.

"Pollo! Who's that you're with? New hustle? Nice, man," a tall blond man sneers at us with a dark smile as he approaches.

"Knock it off, Wex. This is my little sister, Reyna," Pollo replies with a grin as he lifts some more suitcases out of the carriage.

I follow suit and begin helping the carriage driver unload our luggage from the back compartment. Pollo and Wex slap each other on the back in greeting as Wex gives me a nod, his sparkling eyes dragging over me.

"That's too bad… although, good news for me," he says, squaring his shoulders. There's something devious hiding behind those eyes… Something I can't quite put my finger on.

My wonderings are answered when Wex suddenly has his strong, muscular arms around my waist. Before I can even call out, he scoops me up and jumps high into the air. I scream and slap at his arms around me, but it is no use. His grip is tight, and we are already hovering about ten feet above the ground.

"Put me down! Now!" I scream. I'm not particularly afraid of heights, but this was uncalled for. Typical Air Keepers—always abusing their power. My dark hair is whipping around me as I frantically stare up at Wex, who is having way too much fun and is way too close to me.

"What's that? You want me to put you down? All right," he sneers. The air Wex is using to keep us afloat changes. It feels less… heavy. He releases his arms from me, and I am sent free falling to the ground.

I squeeze my eyes shut in terror, not wanting to look to my guaranteed demise as I hurtle downwards. But the feeling of my bones breaking against the ground never comes. I am suspended mid-air by a different gust of wind coming from below me. I glance down, and Pollo is there. His hands are open wide, and a channel of air slowly lowers me the remaining few meters to the ground. Wex floats down and grins a devilish smile.

"Lucky save, Pollo. Next time your sister won't have anyone there to catch her," he calls out to us before sauntering off, followed by his small posse of Air Keepers. What a jerk. I immediately make a mental note to stay away from Air House as much as possible.

"Are you okay?" Pollo asks with a teasing grin, sticking out his lower lip.

I can't even begin to imagine why he is friends with a guy like that. Yet, perhaps I can. Pollo has always had a need to prove himself to everyone around him, whether or not they are good people. I can see him buddying up to Wex in his first year and sticking by his side ever since.

"Shut up," I retort, jabbing him in the side with my elbow. I can imagine this kind of thing happening all the time at this school. I'm not about to let one little Air Keeper ruin any chance I have of being seen as the strong, future Royal Guard I know I can be. I just need to find my power first, and perhaps I've found a good target for when I do.

"You're welcome," he grins.

I want to slap the smug expression off of his face. "I don't need your help," I say.

"It sure seemed like it, but all right, my bad," he says sarcastically. I huff as I pull a few more suitcases out of the carriage.

I packed lightly, but would still need Pollo's help to carry my suitcases across the campus to the Earth House. As soon as we unpack our bags from the black carriage, the driver pulls away, leading the horses out of the Air House lot and back towards the exit. So much for any help with all this luggage.

I know my parents scrounged up what little money they had together to get us here, so I try not to be ungrateful for the dismal service and bumpy ride here. Pollo is already on it though, both hands hauling our black suitcases off the ground. I give him a nudge and an appreciative grin, and he returns the gesture.

Immediately, I forget the teasing and he is straight back to his dedicated, loyal self. I know I can never stay mad at him, especially when he might be my ticket to actually making some friends at this place. Pollo may be a teasing, people-pleasing ass, but I know he has built countless connections with the Keepers here at the Sanctum. He wouldn't shut up about all of the friends he wants to catch up with on the ride here.

We walk in silence past Air House and towards the centre of the Sanctum. Well, at least *I* am silent. Pollo is trying to give me more advice about life at the Sanctum, but I can't help but drown him out as my eyes turn to my surroundings.

"Always keep away from the pond near Water House—it's full of water sprites," I hear Pollo say through the daze in my head.

It is about five o'clock now, and the sky is turning a wondrous shade of pink. The tall pine trees surrounding the Sanctum sway in the breeze as a peaceful evening settles in. The Sanctum is bustling with students and teachers, and even some parents with their teary-eyed teenagers linger nearby, whispering saddened goodbyes.

There's no way I'd bring my mother here at all, let alone on my first day. I already have a big enough target on my back—I'm just hoping no one takes advantage of me being powerless. Target practice for rogue fireballs or giant crashing waves doesn't exactly sound like something I want to be a part of. I nudge the thought away, not letting it consume me once more. One reason brought me here, and one reason only. I keep my head up high as we walk, refusing to let my own thoughts get me down.

This is the beginning of one year without home. One year at the Sanctum to learn all we can about our powers and the Keeper world. And in my case, to learn all I can about becoming a Royal Guard before the Royal Tournament commences in just over two weeks' time.

Pollo and I walk through the Central Gardens, passing luscious beds of sculpted plants, dozens of species of trees, and flowers of every colour. Tall white pillars circle the gardens, and in the distance I hear a small gushing fountain. The gentle breeze of the late-summer air kisses my cheeks as we walk side by side through the gardens, following the grassy, paved path. A lone, giant black bird flies overhead. It's dark wings spread out in contrast with the setting sun.

We soon reach Earth House and I bid my brother goodbye for now. I will see him around, but most likely not each day as we are in different Houses. He gives me one last, worried glance before turning away and heading back through the Central Gardens.

I examine Earth House's foyer: green replaces Air House's purple insignias. Instead of the cloud with wind that Air House uses, Earth House has an intricate fern leaf. I recognise the symbol from some of our more important buildings back home in the Earth Empire. Green torch flames, paintings, carpets and tapestries reside in the building's entry alone. I take a deep breath, and enter the building from the side of the gardens.

2

As I wait alone inside the building, a familiar feeling rushes over me. I can't help the nervousness and fear as it bubbles up inside me, taking over my mind with all the self-doubt I've been repressing for as long as I can remember. This is the part I'm not looking forward to: making new friends. I've never been good at it; the only friend I had back home was Pollo. It's difficult to make friends when you spend all of your free time actively avoiding people and pushing them away.

And it doesn't help that the other children pushed you into the dirt and called you obscene names because of your missing power. It's easier to just be alone, as lonely as that may be. At least that way, I won't get hurt.

Since I was eight, I was forced to work alongside my brother on our small patch of land to grow crops and support our family. I would grow tomatoes, wheat, lettuce and other vegetables, and sell them every Saturday at our village market. It wasn't particularly easy, considering I wasn't able to grow crops using my power like my family can, but I made do. I had to learn how to do things the way a mortal would—with blood, sweat and tears. Lots of tears.

My father is a Guard in the Royal Palace, just as I one day wish to be, so he is forced to live within the Palace walls. I haven't seen him since the day he abandoned my family and left us alone to fend for ourselves.

My mother is often ill with what the apothecary told us is 'a sickness of the mind', leaving Pollo and I to support ourselves and her. Most days, she doesn't leave her tattered old armchair by the window of our small house. And when Pollo left for the Sanctum two years ago, the duty of taking care of the farm and the house was left to me. He was reluctant to go but my mother insisted, saying it would bring her no greater joy.

It didn't seem to bring her any sort of happiness when she would still cry out for my brother and father at night, with only me to break her out of her nightmares. And when she woke, the nightmares were still true. Although she denies it, I know that if my father were home, my mother's sickness would go away.

I follow the stream of people entering Earth House towards a small meeting hall past the foyer of the building. A range of people, all with green eyes, take their seats on the eclectic sofas, armchairs, futons and benches around the room. I stay standing in the corner instead of awkwardly finding a spot in a group of people I don't know. Thankfully, before long a bell sounds from the front of the room as a tall, ash-haired man who looks to be in his mid-thirties clears his throat. The remaining students find a seat or spot to stand out of the way.

"All right, all right, quiet down. Let's get started. Welcome back to the Sanctum, Earth Keepers," he starts, and I note the range of ages in the room.

There are people here who seem as though they are in their fifth year, and some who must be in their first. The latter are easily found by the unsure looks on their faces. Mine included.

"And welcome to our newest Earthies. I am Head Quill of Earth House, and we are honoured to have fresh Keeper blood in our midst this year. As always, at the beginning of the year, I like to remind students of our rules. There are only two, but they hold the utmost importance and result in severe punishment if broken." Head Quill scans the room.

"First, there will be no one outside of their dormitories after nine o'clock at night. Dark forces roam these woods, and I am responsible for your wellbeing whilst you are here at the Sanctum. Do not make me regret allowing your presence here—I can have you removed as quickly as you've arrived.

"Second, no form of magic is to be used outside of class by first-year students unless sanctioned by a professor. We don't want any accidents whilst you are still learning to wield your power."

I wonder what kinds of incidents the Sanctum has faced in the past. Who knows what could happen when untrained Keepers lose their tempers.

"Be mindful of your words and actions. We have ways of knowing what happens here at the Sanctum. That is all," Head Quill finishes.

What ways? Cameras? Spells? Spies? Who knows, the possibilities are endless.

I try not to let Head Quill's words get under my skin—besides, I have nothing to hide. But I can't shake the feeling that those two rules are going to be broken multiple times this year by yours truly.

After Head Quill finishes welcoming Earth House back, I follow his instructions and head off to find my room. I count the flights of stairs as I climb, nudging my way through the stream of Earthies doing the same as I am. One, two, three, four… seriously? It's not until I get up to the sixth floor that I see my name on the list of students tacked to the front door of the dorms. I don't recognise any of the other names and sigh internally with relief. I don't know if I could last a year with one of the Keepers from my village. They're all worthless bullies with an agenda against me.

This is it, I think to myself. No second impressions. These are my people this year. I knock twice on the door, and a few moments later, it swings open from the other side. A hazy green room full of pot plants, creeping vines, and small veggie plants lays before me. The small room has two plush sofas on either side of it, an armchair by the large window, and a colourful wicker rug in the middle.

"Hi," I say shyly to the figure in the doorway. Before me stands a small, slender girl with dark red hair and green eyes. She is gorgeous. Her hair falls in loose curls past her shoulders, and she is giving me a half-grin, half-smirk expression that is difficult to read.

"Hey. I'm Prisma, second year. You must be Reyna," she says, green eyes staring at me in question. I must let my confusion form on my face, because she speaks again. "You're the only first year on the sixth floor. There are others, but on the lower levels. Don't worry—you'll get used to the stairs… eventually," she trails off, as though she still hasn't accomplished her promise. Prisma motions me inside and locks the door once again behind me.

"Dexter, this is Reyna. Reyna, Dexter," she says.

Oh. I didn't realise the dorms are co-ed.

"Hi," I say in greeting. A pair of green eyes glance up from the book they were once buried in. It isn't until Dexter is actually looking at me he seems to take any notice of my arrival. The man before welcomes me warmly and I greet him in return. He has dark wavy hair and an intense gaze that utterly mesmerises me. He probably knows it, too.

Keepers have all inherited looks that lure in mortals so we can control them with our power. Although that part of our history is just that—history, some Keepers use their beauty and charm for similar reasons in our modern day society. I wonder what kind of crowd I'm getting into here… things could really go either way. I just hope I haven't been assigned a pair of extremists to spend my days with this year.

I know I was planning on making a great first impression with my new dorm mates, but this is a lot to take in for one day. The long journey here, the sheer beauty of the Sanctum, and all the new people seem to have drained my battery pretty fast. Prisma shows me my room—thank God, we each get our own within the dorm—and begins rattling off an itinerary.

"Tonight," she begins, "we will gather with the rest of the Keepers after dark in the Central Gardens for the Sanctum's annual 'End of Summer Ceremony'. The Heads of each House like to do it because of the centuries-old tradition—we like to go because of the afterparty."

She gives a small, testing smile, which I gather is to test how much of a partygoer I am.

"That sounds… like an exhausting end to an exhausting day. I think I'll pass," I reply. I'd usually love to go to a party like this—I'm excited to meet new people here. But the day truly has gotten away from me and I'm not sure I can keep my eyes open for much longer, which is unusual for me. Usually I have the opposite problem.

"What! You have to come. I know it's the first party of the year, but it's one of the best. Fire House knows how to throw down, and there isn't our usual nine o'clock curfew because of the ceremony," she says, practically begging me.

After some more persuasion, I finally agree on the terms that I am left alone until it's time to go, so I can rest and unpack. She nods and leaves me be.

When Prisma shuts the door behind her, I take in the small, dusty room that is now mine. A single bed, small bookshelf, desk and drawers are all that occupy the space. Much more than I am used to. Back home, I was lucky to win the fight against Pollo for a spot to sleep on our sofa. That was the only perk of him going to the Sanctum two year before me.

Thankfully, my suitcases were brought up by staff during Head Quill's speech—I don't think I would've survived the stairs with all of them. I unpack and spread the plain white blanket set I found neatly folded in the cupboard onto my bed. I place the only photo I have of my family on top of the wooden bookshelf. It is my favourite—we all seem so happy and carefree.

My mother's raven hair shines in the sunlight outside our house, whilst dad lifts a giggling Pollo onto his shoulders. I'm only a toddler here, but the smile on my rosy face is unmatched to this day. Pollo is three years older than me, and in this photo, he is the happiest I've ever seen him. It was before we ever had to question our world or what we are, before the responsibilities kicked in. Before I knew I was less than the others.

But all good times must end. Sometimes, your greatest gift is bound to be your downfall, and I certainly found mine.

I sigh as I continue unpacking until my suitcases are empty. I don't have many possessions—I only brought the things that mean most to me to the Sanctum. Finally, I lie back on my bed and shut my eyes for a moment.

I awake to a banging on my door when the guy from before with dark, wavy hair sticks his head into my room.

"You nearly ready? We're all about to head to the gardens," Dexter asks.

I wearily search for my watch as I force my eyes open. "Crap," I say, not realising I've been asleep for three hours. Usually sleep doesn't find me this easily, but the long day must've taken its toll on me.

"All good. I know moving day can be tiring. You don't have to come if…" he starts, but I cut him off.

"No, I'll be out in a minute." He gives a half smile as he shuts the door, and I hear footsteps retreating to the common area around the corner. He seems… nice. Friendly. I felt it the moment our eyes locked earlier, and suddenly I don't feel so alone.

I glare at myself in the mirror on the wall. My tangled hair looks as if a bird had made its nest in there. I never was a calm sleeper. I sigh as I quickly brush out the knots; my thick raven hair falling to my side in a wave of locks. I swipe some mascara and lip gloss on to make myself at least semi-presentable.

Everyone will be at this party, though I'm not sure how fancy it is going to be. I can't abandon my first-impression-plan. I decide on a simple outfit: jeans and a black sweater. It will have to do, and I know I will feel most at ease in something I would usually wear. I tuck the small dagger my father gave me into the waistband of my pants. It has an intricate swirling pattern on its dark, wooden handle, and its blade was surely forged in the famous hearths of the Fire Empire.

On that same day, I swore I would never have a family of my own. I've seen and felt the pain first hand of leaving behind your family to follow a dream. I will never make a man do that for me, as my father did to us. Especially when I become a Royal Guard alongside the man that left us.

Prisma and Dexter are waiting for me in the lounge area. I am relieved to see they have similar attire to me, sporting pants and tops that are casual yet presentable.

"Ready," I say as I swing my small black purse over my shoulder. Prisma links her arm with mine and leads me to the door.

As we walk, various other dorms join the growing stream of people descending the stairs. A crowd of green eyes chatter along as we all make our way towards the Central Garden for the ceremony.

"Oh, I nearly forgot. Here," Prisma says as she thrusts something small and hard into my palm.

I turn the object over in my hand and realise it is a small, elaborate key with a fern leaf and the number 'six' on it.

"I was going to give it to you later, but take it in case you get back earlier than us… or later." She winks and gives a small suggestive grin. "We all have one. It's yours." I nod in thanks and place the key into my purse for safekeeping, though I plan on staying with Prisma and Dexter tonight. Prisma tells me she's from a small village in the Earth Empire, not too far from my own. She lives there with her two younger sisters and father when she isn't at the Sanctum, and together they run a small jewellery shop selling pieces made from crystals and other minerals. She sounds quite well off, as when she describes her home my mouth drops to the floor.

"We're particularly good at locating gems in the ground. I've taught myself to use my power to find them," Prisma says, a gleam of pride flashing in her eyes. She rolls back the sleeve of her white shirt, revealing a small, dainty bracelet. When I look more closely, I see it is made of gold and dotted with small, green stones.

"Do you mind if I hang out with you tonight? I don't know anyone else," I say to Prisma, trying to sound as least pathetic as possible. When I scan the eyes of the Keepers in the crowd around me, I find very few friendly faces. Their hard eyes stare through me with icy glares, as if I had done something to personally offend them.

"Of course! Although I must admit, I'm surprised. I would've thought the daughter of the King's Royal Guard would be ripe with friends. But sure, stick with our little band of misfits," she says, motioning over to Dexter.

He walks in front of us, laughing with some other Earth Keepers over who knows what. That's another part of myself that I try to keep under wraps. Sure, it's an honour for my father to be one of King Zale's guards, but I worry it will make me somewhat of a target here at the Sanctum. Especially when people begin finding out about my lack of power, which I can safely assume Prisma is yet to hear about.

People might get the wrong idea—that my brother and I come from money and hold some sort of sway with the royals, when it couldn't be further than the truth. The money my father makes mainly goes towards his own uniform and weapon expenses, and what little is left is sent home to put clothes on our backs.

Looks like it's too late to keep my family history away from the hundreds of ears at this school—I'm sure they all know it if Prisma does. Who knows, maybe it will be a good thing to arrive with a powerful reputation, especially when that is the only type of power I wield. So long as I manage to avoid being manipulated or taken advantage of.

We proceed to the Central Gardens, and my eyes widen at the sight before me. Pollo and I walked through them earlier today, but they are a whole other level of glorious in the evening.

The grassy middle area has colourful flower arrangements and tall, white lamp posts illuminating the space. Tables of refreshments line the back of the area. If any mortals were present, they might think someone was about to get married due to the beautiful scene around us. The benches part down the middle, and at the front lies a small stage with a glossy white curtain behind it. The night air is a soft breeze on the back of my neck as I take a seat between Dexter and Prisma on a bench.

A loud horn sounds, signalling the beginning of the ceremony. Most of the professors sit to the left of us, and the four Sanctum Heads sit on the decorative wooden stage in front of us. Looking around the space, I'd say there are about four hundred students present in the expansive garden.

"Welcome back, students, professors and staff. We hope you had a safe, relaxing summer break full of training and development," begins Head Vespertine.

Each Head gives a short welcome speech following Head Vespertine, Head of Fire House. Head Montero of Water House gives her speech on the importance of friendship. She states that true power comes from the companions we keep and the enemies we hold closest.

Head Quill speaks next about Earth House's achievements on maintaining our beautiful surroundings here on the island, before trading places with the Fire Head once more.

"As most of you already know," Head Vespertine begins, "Prince Theon has been undertaking his studies here at the Sanctum for the past two years. This year, however, his sister, our beloved Princess Vera, will be beginning her first year of education with us. Please make both Prince Theon and Princess Vera feel a welcome part of our community."

Now those are some names I do know.

Theon Rhanes is the only son of our king; Aspacia's crown prince. I have had only one encounter with him, and it was dismal to say the least. The royal family visited the Earth Empire ten years ago as a part of their tour of Aspacia, to maintain their presence in the Empires. We were all called to Emperor Velynn's Manor in the heart of our Empire to greet the Royal family.

After the ceremony they hosted, the king spotted my father in the crowd. He must've been impressed by the man before him, because this is when King Zale invited my father to train to become a Royal Guard.

I remember the prince, a teenage boy at the time, standing tall next to his father, as if to mimic him. I guess he was trying to learn from his father's actions. I clearly remember the way his eyes found me in the sea of Earth Keepers, just as his father found my father. I remember the way his eyes raking over me made me feel—as if a fire had been set alight in my soul, calling me to him.

In that moment, knew that one day, I would be the one to protect them. To serve him. That he was going to be a great King. When our eyes met, I somehow sensed the kindness behind his features. That was before I learned he is quite possibly the least kind person in all of Aspacia.

Prince Theon and Princess Vera usually reside in the Royal Palace, and though it is my dream to one day join the royal guard, I no longer yearn for the day I'm required to guard the prince. He has a reputation I would not like to entangle with mine. There are rumours he spends his time amongst the company of many lovers, and always is the one to leave the room first. I know you can't believe everything you hear, but all rumours are born out of truth, and I have a personal informant in the Palace.

My father writes me letters from the Palace warning me of the prince and his future rule, telling me of his outlandish ways and venomous, intriguing words. He says the prince is a cold, unfeeling man, full of greed and sick with the powerful knowledge that one day he will be king.

Prince Theon emerges from somewhere at the front of the crowd, followed by Princess Vera. The two royal's golden eyes shine in the light projected from the lamps to the side of the gardens. Royal blood runs through their veins, meaning they have golden eyes caused by their unique celestial powers. Prince Theon's equally golden hair moves slightly in the soft breeze as he smiles and shakes Head Vespertine's hand.

Pollo has told me how the prince is treated here at the Sanctum, and I am honestly not surprised. Every effort is put in to assure his comfort and happiness—the Sanctum spares no expense for the Royal Family. I imagine the same will be done for Vera this year as she begins her higher education.

Prince Theon stands side by side with Head Vespertine on the stage, his sister next to him. He stares out at his audience: a sea of students eager to make his acquaintance at any cost necessary. If only they had a man inside the palace walls telling them what the prince is capable of. Maybe then they wouldn't be so blinded by his charm.

"Good evening, Keepers. It's an honour to be here," the prince says with a winning, fake smile, his loud voice booming across the gardens with no need for the microphone. The kindness I saw that day all those years ago lingers, but I won't be fooled again.

"I'm sure I will see some of you around in my classes, but otherwise, kindly stay out of our way. My sister and I are here to learn and leave as soon as possible." He sounds as though his family has forced him to come here, and he isn't intent on making any friends in the meantime.

You would think the future ruler of Aspacia would be more interested in making acquaintance with the people that he will rule one day, but I guess he takes after his father's selfish, power hungry ways. Princess Vera on the other hand stands there silently, her cheeks flushing at Prince Theon's words. Perhaps the feeling isn't mutual.

It seems just like the prince to brush the world off with a simple swish of his hand. Although, I doubt that will keep the gushing girls who are swooning in the front row away from him.

Just as the thought crosses my mind, his golden eyes meet mine in the sea of students and he holds my gaze intensely, just like all those years ago back in the Earth Empire. What the hell?

I stare him down, refusing to be the first to break the stare. Is this somehow because of the thought I just had? I thought his celestial power was transformation, not reading minds. Does he somehow remember me?

His stare is intense yet blank, and if he is thinking anything, it doesn't show on his face. Just as my own eyes are about to waver, he breaks the stare, giving me his trademark smirk. Knowing what I know about him, the prince was probably trying to locate his first conquest at the Sanctum.

I am just overreacting. He doesn't know me. He couldn't possibly know my connection to him through my father. He doesn't remember the way our eyes met in the crowd that day ten years ago.

"Thank you, Prince Theon. We are so glad you could join us this year," Head Vespertine says almost accusingly. "Prince Theon and Princess Vera will reside in—" He is cut off with a disapproving glare from the prince, as if to say, don't *you dare advertise my whereabouts.*

"Um, they will reside in a different location to the rest of you, as the Royal Family don't belong with any House," Head Vespertine continues cautiously.

A smug smile pulls at the prince's lips as he waltzes off the stage, past a bunch of swooning third years in the first row. He continues down the aisle and walks out of the gardens, out of sight. I guess that's his appearance for this evening.

Good riddance, I think to myself, more than happy to see him go. I don't know if he knows who I am, but I certainly don't intend on making his acquaintance.

3

Head Vespertine wraps up the End of Summer Ceremony by flicking his wrist at a giant bonfire in the middle of the Gardens. The enormous stack of logs blazes alight—a tower of fire so tall it creeps as high as the tops of the seven-floor residency buildings around it. A cheer erupts from the crowd, and I am pushed to the grassy ground as everyone around me jumps up and rushes over to the bonfire. They're no doubt in search of that so-called 'afterparty' Prisma mentioned earlier. The impact of the bodies forces my knees into the dirt, but Prisma notices and scoops an arm under mine to help me stand back up.

"Are you all right?" she asks, glaring at the crowd of people in front of us responsible for my tumble. They continue on to the fire. I watch as shadows from the blaze dance along the grey brick of the Sanctum's buildings, jumping and twirling with the fiery light.

"Yeah," I say. "I'm all good."

In fact, I am great. The rush of being here with so many of my kind instead of pushed to the side with Pollo is exhilarating. In fact, I'm not sure if I've ever seen so many Keepers my age in one place before.

School was a luxury I couldn't afford back home, both due to a lack of money and lack of talent.

Also, my parents weren't so convinced I would be able to take the daily beatings the other kids would no doubt lash out at me with. Not that staying at home stopped that. They found me even in the dead of night, sneaking through back alleys to try to get some sort of reprieve from my own four walls.

To them, I was and always will be a freak. An anomaly. My mother was hesitant to send me to the Sanctum, but I am eighteen now. I can make my own decisions, and I know I've made the right one. The only one. I didn't want to leave her, but I soon realised she was no better off with me there.

I had no intention of staying for the party, but this may be an excellent opportunity to get to know Prisma and Dexter better. To actually make some friends, before they too turn against me.

As I look around, streams of people are crashing forward into the open space around the bonfire. A band plays in the far corner of the Central Gardens, and the music booms so loudly that I'm not sure how anyone could possibly hear one another. Keepers are chatting or dancing in groups, and some even dare to stand by the raging bonfire with its towering blaze. Everything feels very cliquey.

I walk hesitantly towards the bonfire, but Prisma grabs my arm once again.

"What?" I ask. She grins and begins leading me in the opposite direction, with Dexter on my other side. "Where are we going? I thought you guys were keen to party?" I say, unsure of their motivations.

"Trust me," Prisma says, and we continue into the darkness of the forest.

We walk through the back entrance of the Central Gardens, and take a left towards Earth House. Confused but curious, I dredge on beside them. Perhaps they've changed their minds and just wanted to hang out back at the dorm. But why were they being so weird about it? They continue leading me along the brick path until it turns to dirt, well and truly past Earth House now.

Around me, I notice other Keepers heading in the same direction as us, lurking within the shadows of the buildings and trees as not to be seen. The trees in the darkness of the forest at night give me a dark, tingling chill up my spine. It is pitch black in front of us, and soon to be behind us also as we head deeper into the woods. I look to Prisma on my left for some sort of hint of what's happening, but her eyes remain trained straight ahead. Fine. I try Dexter instead, and when he notices my eyes on him, he gives a sly wink.

"Where are we going?" I try again, but Prisma's grip on my arm only tightens as she leads me forward.

"Just trust me," she repeats, but there is something in her green eyes, in the stiffness of her spine, that makes me doubt her.

In the distance, I hear voices coming from the trees. The few Keepers I'd noticed earlier were now a sizable crowd of faces lit by the moon. Finally, Prisma lets me go and she and Dexter disperse, mingling with the group of students that had also just gotten here. Here being the middle of nowhere deep in the forest late at night…

My teeth are chattering and I am left standing alone in the freezing, dark forest, without any explanation and unsure of what to do next. Should I try to sneak away? The stars shine brightly above, and I catch a glimpse of a large black bird circling the skies.

My skin crawls as I imagine what scenarios Prisma and Dexter have stupidly led me into. I turn as Dexter roars in laughter off to the right of us, amused by something that a tall, blonde Water Keeper has said. She giggles, and they turn away. I notice that every Keeper here is turning to face the same direction: south, out over the enormous cliff with the crashing ocean dozens of feet below. The air out here is wild— I have to wipe my hair from my face to see the sight before me. The smell of the ocean reaches me as quickly as one would fall from the top of this menacing height.

Suddenly, hands are pushing me forward and Prisma is nowhere to be seen. I haven't been here for even one day yet and this is the second time I've been pushed around like a rag doll. Do these people have no boundaries?

I push back, not allowing myself to be ordered around like a slab of meat, but there are too many arms, too many hands pushing at my back. I wish I had my powers at this moment. They push me until I am standing right on the edge of the cliff. I whirl around to face the group of about fifty Keepers who have made their way out to this creepy forest, and notice that about two dozen other students are also being pushed into place, just as I had. Each of them stands near the cliff, pushed daringly close to the edge.

I wait for their next move, and as the last of the screaming Keepers are forced to the edge, a familiar voice comes from the crowd. A tall man emerges, his blond hair shaped into a spiky style atop his head.

He wears simple jeans and a black shirt, with his thumbs stuffed into his pockets. Wex scans the crowd with a smug smile.

"Did you all really think it was going to be this easy?" he sneers.

I gasp in shock when I see he is flanked by my brother. The pair stand forward from the crowd now, self-approving smiles on their faces. A loud cheer erupts from the crowd, and I hear them yelling strings of words like *"Get them!"* and *"Suck it freshies!"*

I inspect the Keepers backed up to the edge of the cliff, and realise that we all must be first years. They look as worried as I feel, although I know my face is a blank slate. I've spent years mastering how to contort my features into emotionless, uncaring stone. It was necessary to my own sanity.

The walls I've built in my mind are holding in all the things I'm not strong enough yet to feel—they are ten feet high and reinforced with iron. In locking my feelings away, pushing them deep, down inside me, I've become numb to everything else. But it is a small price to pay for not having to feel. And sometimes, like now, it is a blessing.

I realise that this must be some kind of sick initiation prank to scare us into deferring from the Sanctum. It will not work. I am here to become powerful, to become a Royal Guard. And that is exactly what I am going to do.

"Welcome to the Sanctum," Wex speaks again, doing his best impression of Head Vespertine and his speech from earlier.

The crowd, now comprising more and more people, whoops and cheers in laughter. He grins, obviously pleased with himself and his pathetic joke. I look at Pollo pleadingly, but he does little to ease my nerves by refusing to make eye contact. He stands there, watching on with a face nearly as blank as mine.

Wex raises his hands and the air above the crowd stills, as if he had somehow given a signal for silence through wielding air. The crowd dies down, awaiting whatever is going to happen next.

A girl next to me shudders as the relentless wind, which I suspect Wex has something to do with, whips her short skirt high around her thighs. Thirsty Keepers watch from the crowd, their beady eyes now focussing all too closely on her. Disgusting, I think to myself. I am feeling mighty happy with my outfit choice right about now. She has no choice but to stand there in front of the crowd, grasping at her dress to try and cover herself.

"Let's see what the new year has brought us. First years, when I say go, you are to jump right off the edge of that cliff face," he exclaims with a dark, cheering voice.

Are you serious? A wave of shock ripples through the Keepers in question, as I let my jaw hang open without even realising it.

"You can use your power to save yourself from the sea, or… not." Wex grins. I cannot believe this is happening. Shouts of horror and worry arise from the crowd.

"Dude, this isn't how it goes," says Pollo, placing a hand on Wex's shoulder to turn him.

"I know," he replies, "but this year is different and you know it. If the rumours are true, this bunch is more than capable. Well… most of them, anyway." Wex eyes me, his cold, dark gaze trailing over my body, and I shudder.

I've been trying to prove to myself and everyone around me that not having power doesn't make me weak or helpless, but all I've faced since getting here is a cold, hard truth: at the Sanctum, your power is your strength. It is everything. And if it reflects the way the rest of the world is… I'm in deep shit.

The weight of my realisation is like a slap across the face. How will I survive this year without any power? It's like my dreams have been torn away from me, and I feel my body begin to tremble.

No. Not here. I can't fall apart now. I will not allow myself to prove them right. I straighten my back, standing tall against the repulsive man before me.

"What happens if we refuse?" asks a tall, thin boy to my left. A heavy silence settles over the crowd in anticipation of Wex's response. He rolls his shoulders back and narrows his eyes at the boy.

"If you refuse… then we can arrange someone to help you fall." Wex slowly walks closer to the boy, closing in on him as the boy moves so his heels are hanging off the edge. He moves so close that his toes are touching the boy's, then with one swift motion, he raises a finger and lays it on the boy's chest. Then pushes him off the edge.

An audible gasp comes from every single mouth in the crowd.

"Wex… You've gone too far," Pollo yells from the front of the crowd, retreating backwards. Not in fear. I know that about my brother. Out of need to protect the crowd of people from whatever will happen next. I have already made my assumptions on why Pollo hangs out with Wex, but this… this crosses a line that surely even he can't forgive.

I watch as Pollo's face contorts with the realisation of his friend's actions, his brow heavy with the betrayal. A glimpse of something else slips across his face… he seems entertained. Or is it humoured? It is difficult to tell in the dim light of the moon, but whatever I saw on my brother's face doesn't make sense.

There is no scream, no call for help from the boy as he plummets towards the ocean below. Mere feet before he meets his impending doom, a huge wave bursts out of the sea, meeting the boy's body with a hiss of sea spray. The boy rides the wave as it grows and grows, eventually bringing him all the way back up to the top of the cliff and into the spot he was standing in moments ago. He stands in place, drenched in salt water and trembling. But the smile on that boy's face could never be put into words—he had done as Wex had asked. He had saved himself with his Water Keeper abilities, and spared his life.

"Hmm, I guess this lot might not be totally useless after all. Good job, champ," Wex says to the boy as he slaps him on the shoulder.

The boy quickly scurries away into the crowd, away from Wex's tasting eyes. The sea of Keepers let him through; and I realise that he has earned his place in the Sanctum. Is this really what it is going to cost?

"So? Who's next?" Wex demands, eyeing the fearful line-up of first years. My heart sinks to the bottom of my body as I pray it's not me who he decides on to be his next victim. His eyes narrow when he notices me standing here, and he calls out my name. Of course.

"Reyna, how lovely to see you again," he says, grinning that smug smile of his.

I need to be strong. Calm. I can't let them all see me waver or they will always label me as weak. That's how it is in Aspacia—no second chances. I step forward, towards the crowd. I will my face to be plain; devoid of the emotions running through me right now. I need a plan, and fast.

All I know for certain is that to be seen as strong by the sizable crowd in front of me, I'm going to have to jump, not be pushed by the likes of Wex. There is no other way at this moment, even if my strength gets me killed.

Once again, I turn to Pollo. This time not for help—I can tell that he would never overstep Wex's demand. I curse him silently for being such a sheep. I stare at him so he can see my eyes. Remember what they look like, so they may haunt him in his dreams when I drown at the bottom of this cliff.

All the warnings he gave me, all the lectures… I thought I knew my brother better than this. I hold my hand up to him in an obscene gesture, and he grins slightly. Asshole. If this is my goodbye, I wouldn't have done it any differently.

"Well then, what will it be? Do you need a hand? I'd be happy to help." Wex winks, and I shudder at the thought of his manipulative hands on my body once again. I turn around so that I am facing out over the cliff. My body is trembling, but my face remains calm. What am I going to do? If I die today, I want it to be on my own terms, rather than have Wex push me off this cliff.

My knees go weak as I take a step forward and plummet off the edge, without so much as looking back at Wex and the crowd. I sail through the air, and when I glance up I can see the faces of first years peering over the edge in terror. I take a deep breath, and brace for the hard impact of the waves to hit my flailing body. But it never comes.

A thick, twisting vine encircles my waist, and I am lifted through the air. My feet slam into the side of the cliff, but the vine keeps pulling me up until I am at the top of the cliff once again.

How did I… No, it's not possible. That wasn't me. I know it for a fact.

I've read all the books, done all the theory I possibly could, and I know that when a Keeper uses their power, they need to concentrate on exactly what they want to happen. It feels like a rush through their skin; an exhilarating wind of energy. Pollo has described it to me before; he says it's as if you are flying but with two feet on the ground —your mind is ecstatic and you feel alive. That definitely didn't happen just then, and I let out a sigh of disappointment I didn't realise I was keeping in. If only it were me who brought those vines into existence.

I face the crowd of Keepers back at the top of the cliff—their eyes staring at me in awe.

"Well," Wex sneers at me, "it appears someone has finally found her power."

But my eyes are trained on Pollo. How could he allow this to happen to me? Why is he friends with such a cruel, cold man?

"Don't ever speak to me again," I hiss through my teeth at him, and I feel a pang of regret in my heart as the words leave my lips.

Maybe that was a bit harsh, but no. I could've died. Even though I've lived somehow, Pollo will not live this down. He deserves all the guilt I hope he is feeling right now. My own brother basically threw me off a cliff for the sake of maintaining his own stupid reputation he's spent his time here building.

I glare at Wex, then again at Pollo, hoping my eyes are giving them the intended effect, then storm off through the crowd.

A single question runs through my mind like a puzzle I can't quite solve: who saved me?

Don't get me wrong, I am very pleased to still be alive and not crushed into a pulp at the bottom of the ocean. But now I am in someone's debt, and I don't know the price they expect me to pay in return. I push through the crowd of people until I reach the other side, turning my back on the stupid initiation party and everyone at it.

"Reyna!" Prisma calls out from behind me, and I pause.

I turn and see her making her way towards me from the middle of the crowd. I am really not in the mood to speak to her right now after what she's done. I turn away and keep walking.

"Wait! Please, just wait a second!" she calls out, but I am already a dozen steps ahead of her. "Reyna, it needed to be done. Trust me. I wouldn't have brought you here if I didn't have to. I didn't know he was going to make you jump off a freaking cliff! Usually he just makes the first years show their abilities. But trust me, completing the initiation helped you." She pants, winded from trying to catch up to me.

I pause, wanting to hear her out for a second. Just one second.

"They never would've let it go, and if you didn't come here tonight they'd find some other, much worse, way to test you," she says. The sorrow in her eyes tells me she has seen such events before.

"So what, I guess I should thank you then?" I retort, clearly unhappy with her for bringing me here.

"Trust me, I'm telling the truth. I have no allegiance to Wex and his Airhead clan of psychos. I only did what's—"

"Best for me?" I cut her off.

"Yes," she replies, no longer yelling but using a soft, pleading voice. "Please, Reyna." she says, almost a whisper now. "I truly did you a favour. Now they can see how strong you are." She stands in front of me, face full of what looks like genuine worry and concern.

Why does she even care if I forgive or believe her? Why is she so desperate to be my friend? She doesn't even know me. If she did, she would know I am not strong at all. Not in the ways that matter here, anyway.

I give a slow nod, say "Okay," and turn to trek the remaining distance back to Earth House without looking back. Her stare burns into my back, but I need some space. I agreed with Prisma by saying 'okay', but I'm not exactly sure what part of what she said I'm agreeing with.

It's true, everyone on top of that cliff saw me use those vines to save myself and make my way back up to the top. But it was all a lie. I'm not so sure being powerful is a good thing at the Sanctum, but now they think that I actually do have some power within me. I won't be able to fake it again.

The walk back to my dorm is freezing and my sweater doesn't do much to block out the chill. It must be around midnight by now, and the path is devoid of people. Eventually I reach Earth House, slowly climb the six flights of stairs, and dig through my purse for the key. I fish it out, unlock the door, and step inside.

The small common area is completely pitch black, and I fumble for the light switch. Damn it, where was it again? I curse under my breath as I pad against the wall for a moment too long to not seem like a crazy person.

I hear a low laugh coming from the corner of the room.

"Who's there?" I ask, frozen in place with terror. A small lamp flickers on, and Dexter sits in a green armchair by the window with amusement written all over his face.

"Do you sit alone in the dark often?" I scowl, confused. Why is he back from the 'party' already?

"Sometimes," is all he offers as a reply. His sharp features are contorted in the dim light of the lamp.

"You didn't want to stay for the celebrations tonight? I didn't see you leave," I ask, treading carefully in this unfamiliar territory with him.

His lean, but muscular body sits back in the chair, and he wears his shirt with the top two buttons undone. He is handsome, in the way that all Keepers are, and his green eyes rake my body up and down before he speaks once more.

"I prefer not watching newbies fall to their deaths." He grins. "You obviously made it out all right," he says questioningly.

I nod, less convincingly than I hoped. "Barely. And not by myself." I figure there's no point in hiding the truth from him. He's going to find out sooner or later that I didn't just magically find my powers whilst falling through the air.

He simply nods, and gives me a slow, knowing smile. A little *too* knowing.

"It was you?" I ask, unsure how to proceed.

He gives me a single, slow nod, and leans back in the chair.

"Why?" I ask. He must've still been at the initiation when Wex threw me to what should've been my death.

"I couldn't have my new dorm mate falling to her death on the first day back. And besides, I like you. You're... different." If by different he means a total joke to the Keeper world, then yeah sure. I'm a fucking treasure. But my cheeks flush anyway at his words, and I curse myself for being so easy to read.

He grins before standing, his body towering above mine. He stares down at me, amused by my reaction to his words. Dexter stands so close to me that I can feel his soft breath on my cheek. I notice a golden ring encrusted with a small green stone on his finger. It's very similar to Prisma's bracelet.

His hands look soft and smooth, as though he's never had to work a day in his life. He clearly doesn't know the feeling of dirt under your fingernails or blisters from holding a shovel as well as I do. I open my mouth, about to ask about the ring, but he speaks first.

"Goodnight, Reyna," he says, giving me a half-smirk, then walks back to his room down the hall from mine. He slows to leave his door intentionally ajar.

An invitation, I realise with a start. One that I actually consider accepting... but no, that is not how I plan on ending my first day. As tempting as he might be. If this is the price he expects me to pay for saving me tonight, he's going to be disappointed.

I head towards my own room and close the door fully—noting that there isn't a lock on it. I will have to fix that if I want to maintain any shred of privacy in this place this year. I slip into my black, silky nightdress and climb under the covers. I almost feel bad for leaving Prisma at the party.

Almost.

As my eyelids get heavy, I replay the memory of her red hair swirling in the wind as she watches me fall towards the sea.

4

It's a Sunday morning. The air outside is heavy with the thick fog that seems to be permanently looming over the Sanctum. I open my eyes and embrace my first full day here. I will go to enrol in my classes later this morning, but for now: breakfast.

Feeling unnerved as I recall yesterday's near-death experience, I head for the bathroom to get ready for the day. I decide to postpone my thoughts of breakfast until I deal with my current state of mascara-smudged eyes and black tangled hair. The prince's glaring golden eyes sear into my memory as I drowsily make my way down the hallway.

As I approach the bathroom door, soft laughter sounds from within. Two distinctly separate voices speak to each other over the sound of running water. I begin tiptoeing back to my room, not wanting to face the two people I suspect are in there. I don't think I could handle a whole year with Dexter and Prisma after an awkward moment like finding them after a shower together.

Before I'm able to make my escape, Dexter rips the door open and smiles at me as he brushes past, running his fingers through his dark hair as he makes his way to the kitchen. I breathe out a breath I hadn't realised I was keeping in. I must've been hearing things; it's just him.

I go to step into the bathroom, but the door is swung open once again and a blonde girl stands before me, blocking my path. She smiles sheepishly as both of our cheeks flush red, and I recognise her as the girl Dexter was laughing with at the initiation last night. She opens her mouth, as if unsure whether to say something, but decides against it and hurries past. I roll my eyes, not in the mood to be running into my dorm-mate doing God knows what in the bathroom at eight o'clock in the morning. I quickly enter the bathroom, closing the door behind me, and am relieved to see this room actually has a lock on it. Relieved it wasn't Prisma in here with Dexter.

After a scalding hot shower, I sweep my dark hair into a high ponytail and swipe on some mascara. That will do. Besides, there's not much point trying to cover up when the canvas isn't much to begin with. My face is freckled and my skin tanned from years in the sun working on the farm. I pull on a pair of dark pants and a light green shirt, abandon the makeup, and head to the dining hall on the ground floor in search of food.

The dorms at the Sanctum have a room for each student, and a large dining and common area downstairs for Earth House to share, as well as each dorm having a small, shared lounge area that serves as an entryway and sitting room.

I descend the six flights of stairs with ease—I've always kept fit, especially when my chances against the village ruffians relied on it. As I scoop out some sugary cereal from the breakfast counter, I see Prisma and Dexter sitting across the room. Their faces are stern as they speak in hushed voices, Dexter hunches over his food. I pour some milk on my cereal and join them at one of the dark, wooden dining tables. Thankfully, Dexter's bathroom friend is nowhere to be seen.

"Morning," I say as I slide into one of the dark oak chairs at the dining table.

"Hey, Reyna. We were just talking about the prince." Prisma bats her lashes as she mentions him. "Have you met him?"

Ugh, great. More Prince talk. If only they knew the things the prince liked to do in the dark. I doubt word has made it past the castle gates of his taboo hobbies, but I decide to keep what I know to myself. Knowledge is power, and this might be useful later, so I shake my head softly. "No," I say, which isn't actually a lie.

Even from the far coast of the Earth Empire, tucked away in my small village, we all hear whispers of secrets from within the palace. My father and I figured out a code we could use in our letters to say all the things we wanted without fear of being caught.

He would capitalise letters to make a hidden code. He did the same for Pollo, and would often share the more scandalous events with only him—although Pollo would always tell me straight after he'd read them.

My father wrote to us a few years ago saying that Prince Theon hadn't been seen outside his room for nearly a week, but a constant stream of beautiful women came in and out frequently. The prince is a very attractive man, and with his power, it isn't surprising he courts so many ladies. But the issue is that when they come out, they are different from when they enter.

Bright, cheerful girls, excited to meet Prince Theon with enormous smiles on their faces, leave his room with tear stained cheeks and tangled hair. My father said that often, when completing his rounds of the palace, he would hear screams coming from the crown Prince's room. And not those caused by pleasure.

So no, I don't know the details, but I have plenty of reasons to suspect Prince Theon is bad news. Unfortunately, Aspacia is going to be stuck with him once King Zale steps down and passes down his crown.

Each member of the royal family is blessed with a different power that comes straight from the heavens, rather than an elemental source, making them the natural choice to lead Aspacia. King Zale can freeze time for a short while, and Princess Vera wields healing powers. Prince Theon can transform himself into different creatures. The rumour mill on the prince ran less rampant when the palace learned of his powers. It's hard to be treasonous when any passing mouse could be the prince himself. So the rumours stopped, although I doubt he stopped along with them.

"We are going over to the Academy to choose our classes soon. Wanna join?" Prisma's voice brings me out of my thoughts.

I quickly nod in response, not wanting them to ask me any questions about what I was thinking. I shovel the rest of my cereal into my mouth, and we make our way across the campus, now alive with bustling student bodies and chatter, and head to the Academy.

A wave of belonging washes over me as I step onto the threshold of the large building. The Academy was made from golden bricks, shining on the inside and outside, as if the sun's light were touching the surfaces from within. It glows in the morning light. Inside lies hundreds of students rushing about to different rooms.

I am required to take five different classes this year, and I need to find out as much as I can about finding my power once and for all, and how to be powerful even if that doesn't happen. Abjuration seems like a good place to start: a class that teaches me to protect myself may come in handy this year. Maybe I can learn about the secrets of our world whilst learning to defend myself from the dark forces that hide in the shadows.

"I'll catch up with you," I say to Prisma and Dexter as they nod and walk over to an Alchemy sign up stand across the large hall.

I pass the rooms branching off from the golden hall one by one, glancing inside to examine their different sign up stalls for classes. One for enchantment catches my eye, and I take a mental note to return after I find what I'm looking for. Maybe if I don't figure out how to use my powers, I'll still be able to do some enchantments and not be completely useless.

As I'm walking through the sea of Keepers, someone crashes against my shoulder, causing me to lose balance and almost topple over. I catch myself and glare around to find the person responsible. The books and sign-up flyers I was carrying are scattered on the floor around me, and I let out a frustrated huff. I whirl around and search the crowd, but the sea of Keepers continue to move past.

At once, my eyes lock with a tall, muscular man a few steps away, and I immediately know it is him. His strong arms hold a stack of books against his firm torso, and his gleaming amber eyes rake over my body. I try not to admire how utterly breathtaking he is whilst my fury bubbles beneath my skin.

His face is difficult to read, and he squares his shoulders as he stares. He looks a few years older than me, and from the way he holds himself it would be easy to assume he had chosen his classes a few times before today. The man stands with a demanding presence, navigating the crowd with ease.

When his eyes meet mine, he glances down at the pile of sign up flyers and textbooks now scattered across the floor. He shrugs once, giving an amused grin as if he couldn't care less, before walking in the opposite direction. My back stiffens at his indifference, and my temper only grows.

What kind of person doesn't take responsibility for their actions like that? How could he be so cruel? I'm beginning to believe in hate at first sight.

"Here, let me get those." I look up and Dexter is there, standing tall above me as I realise I am still crouched down amongst the crowd of Keepers. It's a wonder no one stepped on me. He gathers up the flyers and books, placing them on top of each other in a neat pile. He holds onto my arm to help me up and carries the stack of books as we continue walking.

"Thanks. I'm not sure how you even found me under the sea of feet." I laugh.

"I have the feeling I'd find you in any crowd," he says, hinting something in his eyes I can't quite put my finger on. "I'll see you later," he says, and before I know it, he is walking away in the opposite direction.

Why is he always leaving before I get the chance to ask him anything? I huff and continue my pursuit of the Abjuration sign up stand, and am relieved to see it in a quiet, dark room off to my left.

I enter the room, and a girl with glittering blue eyes raises her head from her hands perched on top of the stand. As she lifts her head, I realise it is the blonde from this morning that was in the bathroom with Dexter. She seems to realise at the same time I do—her sparkling eyes widen, and my heart races in my chest. I notice the light blue highlights in her hair, made more visible by the sun streaming through the window she sits against.

"So you're interested in Abjuration?" she says slowly, wrapping a lock of her hair around her fingers. Her voice is soft but sure— a gentle, sweet melody.

I nod, my cheeks flushed.

"Only a few people have been in here today… I don't suppose you'll bring some friends?" She looks up hopefully.

I wonder if she gets a commission from this, or is just really into Abjuration. I've got to admit, I expected the person manning the stall to be less… delicate. More like the mysterious guy who knocked me down earlier. The lessons aren't exactly known for being soft and sweet.

Pollo has told me about the numerous Keepers the Sanctum has had to send home due to various injuries caused by 'accidents' in Abjuration. He even said that one time, a water sprite launched itself at a student who was trying to take it down during class, and the poor Keeper lost an arm. Pollo doesn't take Abjuration, but I'm not going to let his stories stop me. Even though I have no doubt they are true.

"Uh… I don't really have any friends yet," I respond to her question truthfully.

She thrusts the sign-up sheet into my hands. "Well, here's a start then. I'm Navari. Water House. First Year." She smiles sweetly at me, blue eyes glistening like rippling water.

"Reyna," I reply, scribbling my name down on the sheet next to the Monday morning class.

"I'll see you around then, Reyna," she says warmly.

I return the expression and turn my back, walking to sign up for the four remaining classes I need to fill my schedule with.

"And hopefully not in the bathroom next time!" She giggles as she calls after me.

I meet up with Prisma and Dexter for lunch back at Earth House. The boys are sitting at one of the long tables in the common area where Head Quill gave his welcome speech last night. Dexter runs his hands through his dark hair as we approach with our lunch. He smiles in greeting when he sees Prisma and I approaching. I still feel uneasy about Prisma after the initiation last night, but I do believe she was just trying to look out for me.

"What classes did you choose?" Dexter asks us all. I filled my schedule with the enchantment class I was eyeing earlier, as well as divination, evocation and, of course, abjuration.

"I can't believe you're seriously going to take abjuration. What a waste of time," Prisma says, poking at her bowl of pasta. "What do you need protection from? There has been no threat to Keeper kind for over a hundred years. Vinmoor hasn't even attempted to invade us for centuries," she continues.

Vinmoor, an expansive mass of land South-East of Aspacia, was the last civilisation to dare attack our lands hundreds of years ago. Their hunger for land and power ultimately wasn't strong enough to take down all four Empires. Especially when we joined forces and became a united, impenetrable front.

"I know, I just find it fascinating. And besides, I've heard there are things in the forests inside the Sanctum more terrifying than any threat outside of it," I reply, trying to be as vague yet convincing as possible. I don't need Prisma, or anyone knowing the reason I feel the need to protect myself. The true feeling of being powerless. The reasons I can't sleep at night.

Last winter, my mother and I were on the brink of starvation. The crops had long died off in the harsh winds and icy frosts that plague the Earth Empire at that time of year. We were huddled near the fire in our small, one bedroom shack, our teeth chattering against the chilly winter outside. The last of the logs were burning away in our rusted fireplace, and my mother sat in her usual armchair staring at the wall, it's paint peeled off long ago.

All we had eaten in two days were the scraps of radishes and carrots I pickled in thick, sweet vinegar earlier in the year. My stomach grumbled as I turned to my mother, wearing the same vacant stare she has had plastered on her face ever since father left. She was getting more frail with each passing day, and the lack of food certainly wasn't helping. I knew she still had it in her to love, but I hadn't seen my mother for a long, long time. She was a shell of a woman, withered away by sadness and grief at the loss of her husband. It was as if he were dead.

I decided I needed to do something, anything, to save us. Pollo wasn't going to be of any assistance; he was back at the Sanctum for his second year. I needed another way, and I needed it fast.

There was only one person who could help me. I didn't have any other relatives I could rely on—Mother must have family in the Air Empire, but she never speaks of them. So, in the dead of night, I took a horse from a neighbouring farm, left my small village, and rode day and night until I reached the Royal Palace.

I remember approaching the looming gates like it were yesterday: massive golden arches stood tall above me as I approached on my half-dead horse. I stopped at the guard tower and requested to see my father, but the gruff Royal Guards wouldn't let me into the palace grounds. I couldn't give up when I'd come so far. This was my only hope, my only chance. I had to keep trying.

I decided to sit outside the palace walls until they let me see him. I sat there for days, barely surviving on the small amount of food and water I'd brought with me, and constantly worried someone would come and drag me away.

On the third day, just when I was about to give up, a man wearing a dark cloak thrust his hands through the gates, holding a small cloth bag. I couldn't see his face—only the light of the moon let me know he was a man at all by his tall, muscular figure.

"Take it," the man commanded, throwing the bag towards my frail, half-starved body.

I crawled towards the bag and opened it. Inside was a pool of gold coins. More than enough to keep my mother and I fed for the winter. I turned back to the gate to thank the man, but he was gone. To this day, I don't know who the man was. Was it my father? Or just a kind stranger? I knew he was my saving grace, but I wasn't pleased about it. I now owe someone a debt—one that I know I will never be able to repay.

I snap back into reality as Dexter flicks me softly on my hand, making me drop my fork. He grins playfully and gives me a questioning look, as if to ask, 'Are you okay?'

I put an enormous, fake smile on my face and nod, however I can tell he isn't convinced. Prisma and Dexter still sit around discussing their classes, and I find I have the same divination class as Prisma, and evocation with Dexter. I'm glad to know I won't have to face those two classes alone. Maybe I will see that Navari girl in my abjuration class. If she isn't too busy in the bathroom.

5

The rest of the day passes us by quickly, and in the evening we set ourselves up in the Central Gardens to watch the sun go down over the cliffs. Small groups of students lay scattered on the soft grass around us, also enjoying the last of the sun.

I am grateful for the pair I now sit with—I'm not yet sure if I can call dorm six my friends, but they have been nothing but welcoming so far. Prisma sits with her back facing us, staring out at the setting sun. Dexter sprawls on the picnic blanket next to me. I lay back, looking up at the pinky-orange sky. Moments later, Dexter lies so his head is next to mine.

"Do you ever wonder why you were chosen?" he says. I stare at him questioningly, unsure what he means. "Why were we so unlucky to have Keeper blood in our veins? If I were born a mortal, things would be so much different," he says softly.

"Unlucky?" I raise an eyebrow.

"I can't help but feel that with a simpler life, without power, without the Sanctum, I'd be happier." A shadow falls over his eyes, and there is something swimming within them that I can't quite grasp.

"I guess I've never thought of it that way," I reply. "I know what you're meaning though. Sometimes, I think I might as well be a mortal," I say, lifting my head to look at him instead of the sky. I don't know how, but Dexter seems to already know of my missing powers. He's known from my very first day, when he saved me from falling to my death at the initiation.

He smiles softly, and says, "There are other ways to be powerful here. You will find your power one day. Until then, I've got your back." He grins up at me reassuringly.

"I only wish I had your faith. I've never felt more disconnected, more weak," I confide in him.

"Reyna… you are stronger than you know. I can see it in your eyes."

My cheeks flush a deep shade of pink, and become even more flushed when I realise they have. I wasn't expecting anyone to actually be nice to me once they found out my situation. I was fully prepared to fight this battle on my own, but it is nice knowing he has my back.

Eventually, the sun moves behind the sea on the horizon and the sky goes dark. We take it as our sign to head back to Earth House.

"I'll catch up with you guys later," I say to the group. I plan on heading to Air House to find Pollo and confront him about the initiation. I won't allow my brother to think he's getting away with the way he acted last night at the initiation.

My blood boils at the thought of him standing next to Wex, laughing over the terrified faces of the first years they forced off that cliff. I'm more than happy to give my brother a piece of my mind, and if he knows me at all, he will be expecting me.

Prisma and Dexter agree, thankfully without asking what I'm up to, and I watch as they leave the Central Gardens. Dexter gives me a wink over his shoulder as he walks away.

The path from the Central Gardens to Air House is lit only by purple lanterns gleaming on the sides of the dirt trail. The night air whips my hair around my face and bites at my exposed legs. I knew shorts and a shirt were a bad idea, but the sky was full of sunshine earlier. I approach the tall front door to Air House, marked by the purple cloud insignia. I'm not sure whether to knock or go inside, but I don't want to risk another run in with Wex.

I decide to check the handle and, sure enough, it's unlocked. I head inside and am about to ask a tall, curvy girl with friendly eyes if she knows what dorm Pollo is in, when I hear his voice behind me.

"Rey. I'm surprised you came here," Pollo says. His expression is the same as last night, a knowing smile teasing at his lips as they form into a grin.

"We need to talk," I say to him, and he motions me to a purple sofa in the corner of the common room.

The room is a reflection of Earth House's one, yet everything is in hues of purple. The sofa I sit on is plush and covered with decorative pillows, positioned by a tall window. I watch as the trees outside sway in the wind, and a large raven perches on a low-hanging branch.

I'm not sure my initial plan of having a calm and collected chat will go down so well. I can feel my blood boiling with rage and betrayal.

Pollo brings over two glasses of red wine from God knows where, and places them on the small table in front of us. There has never been an age limit on alcohol in Aspacia, but we have never been rich enough to afford such luxuries. I'm not sure I'll take a liking to it anyway—I've seen what happens to those who overindulge. They end up doing things they don't want to do, with people they don't want to see again.

Pollo plonks down beside me, facing me and crossing his legs over like he is completely at home in this place.

"So. I'm guessing this has something to do with last night? You know, you weren't very nice," he mocks. I feel my temper burn under my skin, but I push it back down. *You came here for a civil discussion to find answers, Reyna. Don't let him stir the pot.*

"Yes," I begin. "I wanted to say sorry for the way I acted, the things I said. Obviously, I don't wish for you to 'never speak to me again.' Although surely you understand why I said it," I say, urging my voice to sound as sincere as I can make it be, given his teasing. I know that if we don't sort this out right now, he will continue bringing it up for months.

He raises an eyebrow.

"You were trying to kill me. Can you really blame me?" I ask.

He laughs a booming laugh in response, slapping me on the back and throwing his head back. How is this funny?

"I shouldn't have come," I say angrily, standing.

He pushes me back down. "It's all good, I get it. I just didn't think you'd barge on into Air House, track me down and attempt to apologise. That's not usually your style," he begins, and I remember our quarrels as children on the farm back home.

We would fight tooth and nail for the last piece of bread, for the bigger shovel. I'd always win, but I know that's because Pollo would tire of my stubbornness—I'd never back down, no matter how hurt I'd gotten. No matter the cost. And I'd certainly never apologise.

"Relax, Reyna, you were never in any danger. You really think I wouldn't tear the whole Sanctum apart just to keep you safe? I made an air bubble below the cliff, under the sea. If you fell, you'd have landed in it and risen right back to the top of the cliff. You'd have known that if you stuck around," he says, and I stare at him in shock.

There was never any danger. He played me like a fool.

"Why didn't you tell me you'd found your power?" Pollo says, eyes searching mine for the truth.

I explain to him about Dexter helping me and he nods, looking as disappointed as I felt when I realised it wasn't me who had saved myself from the crashing sea below the cliff.

His eyes meet mine, testing the waters between us. "You know I've got your back," he continues. "I would never hurt you, you are my blood. You can't let anything that happens here let you forget that. Don't you remember my warning?" he asks.

I nod, remembering his final warning to me yesterday: *not everything is as it seems.* I thought he meant there would be physical illusions lurking in the buildings or some crap. I now understand that the manipulation of the Keepers themselves can be much more dangerous.

"Here." He thrusts the glass of wine into my hands. I hesitantly take a tiny sip and he laughs again.

"Come on, lighten up a bit. You're officially one of us now, and you've more than earned your place. Even the freshies who didn't save themselves from the fall off the cliff last night get to stay. We just know who the strongest of you are now," he states matter-of-factly. I guess that makes sense—in a sick, messed up kind of way.

I take a long swig from the glass, the liquid feeling nice on my throat that's dry from the wind on the walk here. The wine burns at first, bitter against my tongue, but as I have more... I can see why people drink it. I feel a buzz moving over my body almost immediately. This stuff must be stronger than I thought.

We continue chatting into the night. Pollo tells me Wex has been selected by Head Windance of Air House to sit in the student council this year. A jolt of revulsion tingles down my spine as I picture that asshole being given even an inch of power over the happenings at the Sanctum. It might not have been a truly dangerous act he forced me into last night, but the smile on his face, the taunting laughter that came from his lips... Wex definitely enjoyed watching us squirm.

"Speaking of the devil..." Pollo trails off, glancing over my shoulder.

I turn around, and as I do, a firm hand is gripping my shoulder. I look up and sure enough, there he is. Rolling my eyes, I shrug Wex off as Pollo grins at him and invites him to join us. He clearly seems to think my apology and forgiveness extends to Wex. It doesn't.

Wex runs a hand through his sandy blond hair, smirking down at me with purple eyes full of danger. His jeans are slung low on his hips, and his tight shirt doesn't leave much to the imagination.

"I was actually just about to go, it's getting late," I say, eager to leave.

"That's too bad," Wex says disappointedly, dropping into a sofa across from Pollo and I. "I'm sure we'd have a lot to chat about." He winks at me. I shoot him a stare filled with disgust, and stand up to leave.

"Do you want me to walk you back?" Pollo asks. I dismiss the gesture, saying I'm looking forward to a solo walk. "Be careful—you never know what lies in the shadows here," he warns. Ugh, another warning.

"Don't worry, Rey, we will have to catch up another time," Wex says, beginning to stand. "Oh and Pollo? I'm sure she'd be able to fight anything in those woods off," Wex says, a half grin on his face. "After all, she can shoot those vines like a pro. Isn't that right, Reyna?"

I take a deep breath.

He knows.

6

Walking through the Sanctum at night is oddly calming. The leaves rustle in the countless trees along the path, and the moon's light illuminates the pale grey bricks of the buildings. I decide to go the long way home, around the back of the Sanctum instead of straight across to Earth House.

I'm keen to explore, and don't feel like going to bed anytime soon. I rarely find sleep until early in the morning, anyway. Nightmares plague my slumber, so I try to avoid it all together. They began when my father left, and only got worse when Pollo did too. They are the same each time: I am staring at myself in the mirror, and in place of my green, bright eyes, are hollow pits of darkness.

Black eyes stare back at me, and I watch my unfamiliar reflection grin a wicked smile.

Then I wake up.

I walk through a forest of tall trees, similar to the ones Prisma led me through the night before. Noises of the forest sound around me; scuttling and twigs breaking from small animals and birds. Well, that's what I tell myself is the culprit for the noise. I walk until I am in the

North-East corner of the Sanctum's grounds, the buildings out of sight, and I hear some sort of rippling coming from a clearing ahead.

I walk towards the sound until I find a large silver lake shining under the light of the moon. It is truly gorgeous; I am in awe of the stillness of the water as it glistens as if it were made of the stars themselves.

Around the edge of the lake lie a few scattered, medium-sized rocks, perfect for perching on. I walk over and sit down between two, with one also at my back so I am unseen from the path I came in from. I'm trying not to think about what might lurk in the shadows—I've heard the stories, listened to the warnings—so I can't help but be cautious. Especially out here all alone past midnight.

I push the shadowy thoughts from my mind and reach out my hands. I practice calling my power to me by focussing on the short blades of grass around me. For the smallest fraction of a second, I think I feel something. But nothing happens—the grass remains the same.

I give a frustrated sigh. Why can't I do the one thing an Earth Keeper should be able to do?

A Keeper's power is natural—like an extension of their hand. From the time they are born until the day they die, their power lies beneath their skin. Children wield it with ease from the time they're able to walk, and by the time they are eighteen, they are ready to go to the Sanctum to learn to control it. So where is mine?

A rustle sounds in the distance to my left, but this time I can't dismiss it as a small animal. It is too loud—too big. And getting closer. Twigs snap, and I hear heavy footsteps quickly approaching. Whoever or whatever this is, they are walking with intent and purpose, maintaining a steady pace.

I duck my head back behind the rocks, hoping that whoever is arriving won't see me. At least until I see them first. I reach down and place my hand on the hilt of my dagger, tucked into my waistband as always. The footsteps slow, and I allow myself a quick peek.

A shadowy figure emerges from the tree line and I recognise the man instantly: it's the arrogant jerk who knocked me down at the class selections. I can't deny that I'm intrigued: why is he out here all alone at this hour?

Although, I suppose he could ask me the same thing. I make sure I am unseen and sneak another quick peek out from behind the mossy rock. I recall his piercing amber eyes, now covered by the darkness of the night. He stares out into the strange, glistening water for a few moments, and I have to hold back a gasp of horror as I realise his shirt and hands are covered in blood.

He tears the bloodied fabric from his chest and throws it into the lake, revealing his chiselled torso. His body shines under the moonlight and I can't help but stare more closely. Raising his hands towards the shirt now floating in the water, he sets it alight with a sudden blaze. It disappears under the surface, a small puff of smoke in its place.

I watch from the cover of the rock as he holds a small flame in the palm of both hands, burning away the blood until he is clean. The man doesn't seem to be in any pain; his body is free from any injuries. My eyes widen as I realise the blood wasn't his. Where did it come from, then? A wave of dread washes over me—*who* did it come from?

He shoots a small orb of fire straight from his hands and hovers it above the water. The orb flickers against the dark sky, twisting and turning, a magnificent flicker of warm colour. He grins, pleased with himself, and throws the orb into the lake.

In the distance, a fizzle erupts where the fire meets the water, simmering as the light disappears. He lifts his hands again, this time more slowly, and shoots a more controlled, smaller orb from his palms out above the lake. He shapes it so it forms a serpent, then a dragon, then a butterfly.

I'm watching the fire change and mimic the animals' movements so intently that I don't notice the presence behind me until it's too late.

"You know, it's rude to spy on people," a deep voice that could only belong to the man I saw at the water's edge moments ago booms down at me.

I rise, but not quickly enough as he grips both of my wrists and spins me so I am facing him.

"I wasn't spying," I spit out at him, furiously trying to detach my arms from his hands. How dare he?

His only answer is a grin as he releases one hand and reaches out to wrap a lock of my hair in his fingers. Damn it, if only I still had my hand on my knife. He stares into my eyes so intensely that I can't help but look away, and finally releases his grip on me after what feels like an awkward eternity.

"You wouldn't be the first." He laughs, condescendingly shaking his head as if I'm a curious child who's been caught stealing candy.

I narrow my eyes, maintaining my furious stare. He doesn't seem the slightest bit annoyed, despite his actions. He smiles playfully, then releases me all together and takes a step back. I immediately flick my hands to my sides. I don't have any power, but I'm counting on him not knowing that.

"Go ahead," he says with a laugh. Crap. At this rate, the whole school will know by tomorrow. If they don't already. I never intended to keep it a secret—it's not an offence to attend the Sanctum without power. Well, I don't think it is. However, the unprejudiced respect from everyone was nice whilst it lasted, when they assumed I had power just like everyone else. I lower my hands and roll my eyes, crossing my arms tightly against my chest.

"What do you want?" I reply, trying not to think about the bloody state this man was just in. Or his shirtless body in front of me.

"I didn't think anyone would be out here so late. I come here all the time and never bump into anyone," he says.

"You call sneaking up on me and attacking me 'bumping into someone'?" I ask furiously. He smirks a one-sided smile.

"How did you even know I was here?" I continue.

"Your perfume," he answers. "You smell like lilies." Damn Keeper senses. I bet he could smell my favourite floral scent from a mile away. I roll my eyes in annoyance.

"And if you call that an attack... you're in for a rude shock when classes start. I'll see you around," he says. He strolls away, back through the trees in the direction he came from. I know for a fact that I don't want to see this guy around.

Annoyed and finally tired, I head back to Earth House along the dark, twisted trail. When I arrive, I trek the stairs up to dorm six. Sure enough, Dexter is sitting in his usual armchair by the window when I arrive.

"So... this is becoming strange," I say to him with a grin.

"What? I just like the night time," he says in response. He motions for me to come and join him and I sit in the chair next to him.

"How is life at the Sanctum treating you so far? It's day two for you, and you haven't died or been seriously injured yet, so I guess that's a win," Dexter says.

I remind him that did almost happen.

"Oh yeah… sorry." He gives me an awkward glance.

"I've had the strangest night," I say, keen to change the topic from the initiation. I tell him about the lake and the strange encounter with the mysterious guy.

"Hmm… Fire Keeper, hey? There's a few people that could be, but from your description it sounds like you met Hayden Radford," he says with a sour look on his face. "You're better off avoiding that guy. I've been here with him for two years, and don't know anything about him. He seems… private. Like he's got something to hide."

"Trust me, I don't plan on making his acquaintance again. He wasn't super likeable," I say, meaning it. I had no intention of surrounding myself with unpredictable people like him, let alone one's covered in blood.

I wish Dexter goodnight and head to bed, and decide to leave my door slightly ajar, just as he did last night. An invitation.

But either he doesn't notice, or doesn't care, because ten minutes later I am still sitting in my darkened room alone. I guess whatever he has going on with Navari is more serious than they made it seem this morning. It's two o'clock in the morning, and officially my first day of classes at the Sanctum. I spend the early hours of the morning as I usually do: bundled into a tight ball under my covers, keeping myself awake as long as I can. Until the nightmares begin.

7

I wake with a jolt, my body sweating and my mind reeling. I can't remember whatever darkness plagued my dreams last night, but I already know it was the same as always. Maybe it has something to do with all the power around me now. I just hope I don't go back to screaming during them like when I was younger. That would be an impressive addition to my already crumbling reputation here at the Sanctum.

I hurry to get ready, realising my first abjuration class begins in only thirty minutes. Being a night owl means I'm not an early riser, or a morning person. I drag my brush through my tangle of hair, throw on a comfortable outfit, and scoop up a piece of toast on my way through the common area—but then double back to grab a coffee. I have a feeling I'm going to need it for my first day of classes. The bitter liquid scalds my throat as I quickly slurp it down, before checking my schedule. I see my class is in the Academy building across the campus, near the Fire House. By the time I make it across the bustling campus, it is eight o'clock. Just in time.

I enter the golden Academy, trailing through the glimmering corridors until I reach a small room at the back of the building. I realise it's the same one that the sign up for this class was in, although this time there are about a dozen desks and chairs facing a chalkboard at the front of the room. Relieved to see I'm not the last person to arrive, I take a seat at a desk in the back row. As I slide into my seat, I notice that sitting next to me is Navari, the friendly girl from the sign-ups.

"Reyna, right?" she says, greeting me with a warm, genuine smile.

"Hey," I say, giving her a rare smile. I'm grateful to see a semi-familiar face here. "There's not many desks—I guess you weren't kidding when you asked me to bring some friends," I say, scanning the desolate space around me. I count that six other desks have been taken, making a grand total of eight students in the class so far.

"Yeah. No one really takes this class. It's seen as a waste of time," Navari replies, flicking her almost-white hair over her shoulder. Looking more closely, I can't help but awe at how gorgeous she is. Her long, slender body sits daintily in her chair, and I wonder why she hasn't brought her own friends to the class. Surely she is drowning in them.

Then, as if she'd somehow guessed my thoughts she says, "I don't waste my time with unimportant people. I'm not keen on being weighed down by frivolous girls who only care about what's on the cover of Enchanted Magazine. You seem different, though. Like you actually have standards."

I smile, but can't help thinking that if she knew me, the real me who works on a tiny farm back in Earth Empire with a poor family and no power... she wouldn't be so willing to sit beside me right now. It's girls like her that made me give up on making friends in my village.

But I feel the same way about Navari—she's different. She's not what I thought she was that morning in the bathroom. I curse myself for judging her too quickly and hope things aren't already doomed between us.

Two more students shuffle in, and I recognise Wex as he takes a seat near the window. He is wearing dark sunglasses, no doubt to hide a brutal hangover, and wears a dark expression. He catches me staring and rolls his eyes, turning away. Ten more minutes go by, and there's still no sign of a professor to actually teach us. My eyes dart around, but none of the other students seem phased.

"Is it normal for the professors to be late?" I whisper to Navari.

"How would I know? This is my first class too," she says in a hushed whisper.

A few moments later, a giant gust of wind rushes through the small room, causing notebooks and pens to fly off desks onto the floor. I look around in a panic and find a shadowy figure in the doorway.

A young woman, drenched from head to toe in water, stands alone at the entrance to the room. She slowly moves forward, and as she comes into the light more, I realise something isn't right about her. She has a blue hue to her skin, and her dark eyes are wider than any I've ever seen. As she takes small, slow steps, she drips a trail of water behind her that seems to be endless. She wears a skirt of seaweed, and her wet, red hair hangs revealingly over her chest. When she reaches the middle of the room, she pauses.

Then, from the corner of the room, a scalding blaze of fire shoots out towards the woman. I scream in horror, jumping out of my seat, but Navari grabs me and holds me down.

"Just watch," she says, seemingly less disturbed by the attempted murder rolling out in front of us. Maybe she is used to such creatures in the Water Empire, but for me, this is new.

The woman, now engulfed in a trail of flames, flashes a set of sharp fangs and lunges forward, shooting her long talons towards the culprit. But she is too late. A cloud of steam emits from her body, and moments later, it lifts and she is gone. The only sign she was ever there is the remaining steam lingering above where she was standing. I look to the corner of the room where the flames had come from and sure enough, there stands our resident Fire Keeper from my adventure to the lake last night.

I knew he was powerful from the way he wielded the flames so easily at the lake, but to disintegrate this… *thing* right in front of us without a trace? I make a mental note to keep out of his way.

"That was quite impressive, well done, Mr Radford. Take a seat," speaks a booming voice now standing in the doorway where the woman had just stood. I guess Dexter was correct about the identity of the man at the lake. Hayden slides back into his chair, and I curse myself for not scanning the faces of my classmates more carefully earlier.

"Mr Radford, can you please remind us what that creature was?" asks the woman in the doorway, walking towards the front of the room. She exerts power, pacing between the desks with a stern stride.

"A Fideal, ma'am," Hayden replies, blowing on his knuckles where some smoke is lingering.

"And why did you use fire against it?" the woman asks.

"Fideal are dangerous water spirits. If given half the chance, that bitch would've dragged one of us out to the nearest water source and drowned them. So I fizzled her out," he replies, showing zero interest on his face although he'd just 'fizzled' someone out.

"Very good." The woman is now unpacking her things at the front of the room.

"I've heard that Professor Windance loves to make a spectacle in the first lesson," Navari leans across and whispers to me. I recognise the name from my conversation with Pollo yesterday—Head Windance is the Head of Air House.

I wonder how many year levels are enrolled in this one class. If abjuration isn't popular, maybe this is the only class available for it and is open to each year. A darker thought washes over me: what if Navari and I are the only first-year students? Head Windance confirms my dreaded thoughts when she walks over to us.

"Welcome to Abjuration. You'll learn a lot in my class if you keep your heads down and pay attention." She speaks to everyone, but her eyes lie only on me.

Head Windance is perhaps the least friendly, most unsmiling woman I've ever laid eyes upon. Her short, dark hair frames her ominous features, cut just past her jawline. I notice every student has turned to where her eyes linger— to me— and my cheeks flush red. Head Windance gives me a look up and down, then turns her back and waltzes to the front of the room once again.

"As most of you know, I don't believe in textbooks. Abjuration is the practical art of defending yourself from the monsters that lurk in the shadows of our world, and theory can never fully prepare you for the real thing. From here on, all lessons will begin in the Blackwood Forest at eight o'clock sharp. Don't be late," she says in a commanding tone.

"The Fideal was but a taste of what's to come. You'd do well to learn as much as you can about their kind, especially if you plan on competing in the Royal Tournament in approximately two weeks' time," Head Windance finishes, and her hint isn't lost on me.

Pollo has told me all about the Royal Tournaments the Sanctum holds each year. It is a test of strength and skill, and is basically a guaranteed ticket to becoming a Royal Guard. The Royal family only selects the most powerful, determined Keepers to join their ranks and protect their lives, and so, the Royal Tournaments began. I give Navari an electrified smile, and she returns the gesture, her blue eyes swimming with excitement.

"Class dismissed," Head Windance finishes, her intense stare landing on me. "Miss Arrington, a word, please."

I hang back as the rest of the class exits the room. Before she leaves, I promise Navari that I will catch up with her later in the week to study and learn everything we can about Fideal. We agree to meet on Friday in the Central Gardens.

"Miss Arrington. I couldn't help but notice the way you and Miss Wickers reacted when I mentioned the Tournament," Head Windance says as she walks over to where I remain seated at the desk.

I nod once, noting the stiffness of her back and the blankness of her stare.

"The Sanctum is a small place, as I'm sure you're aware," she continues, "and I can't help but hear the rumours that pass the lips of my students." I think I know where this is going. I take a deep breath and await her next words.

"You have no power, is that correct? No elemental ability?" she asks.

"Yes, that's true. But I—"

"No." She cuts me off, placing both of her hands atop the desk. "You will not enter the Tournament. Do you hear me? It causes enough casualties as it is, and you'll be signing yourself up for a guaranteed, painful death."

"But I can fight. And I'm smart. Maybe I could—"

Her hand goes off, cutting me off with a condescending look.

"Don't even begin to think you will ever be fit to be a Royal Guard, Miss Arrington. The sooner you realise that, the sooner you can move on with your life. Take a botany class, or spells. That way you will be able to actually make something of yourself, and it won't have to cost you your life."

"But I don't want to be a farmer. Or a gardener. Or a baker or a teacher. I want to be a guard for the Royal family. I know the rules of the Tournament, and anyone is allowed to enter," I say, trying to maintain a calm demeanour in front of the stern woman before me.

She laughs, her shoulders shaking with the force of it. She begins to walk away towards the exit, adding, "Don't say I didn't try to warn you."

I pack my notebook away, not that I particularly needed it this lesson, when I am interrupted. Hayden casually swings his legs over the side of my desk as he sits on it with a thud. Why won't this guy leave me alone? I look up at him and feel a flutter of rage, a remnant from last night's misadventure.

"Can I help you?" I snarl, glaring across at him, and my eyes are met with his smug, half-smirk expression. His amber eyes stare into mine intensely.

"Hey, butterfly. Just a tip for you—only powerful Keepers can take down a Fideal by themselves. You'd be better off taking her advice. Go back to the pile of dirt and crap you crawled out of, earthie" he says, then slides off the table and leaves the room before I can come up with anything to come back at him with.

Butterfly?

I can't believe the nerve of him. He doesn't even know me—he shouldn't pretend to know if I am strong or not. I don't wield air, fire, water or earth, but my mind is sharp and my blade even more so. My father made sure of that by training me to fight. Before he left.

I haven't had to fight a monster before, though. Creatures like the Fideal are few and far between in Aspacia, and the worst things we have back in the Earth Empire are the garden gnomes who steal our freshly grown harvests.

I take a deep breath, wash Hayden's taunts from my mind, and finish packing up my things. I head to the Central Gardens to read over some course outlines before I head to my Evocation class later this morning.

$$8$$

I walk into evocation class and immediately note the number of desks. There are several more than abjuration class this morning, which I can only take as a good sign.

"Welcome, everyone," says a man from the front of the room. I recognise him as Head Vespertine from the end of summer ceremony on the weekend. I swiftly take a seat in the back row. A few moments later, Dexter arrives and takes the seat next to me.

"How was Abjuration?" he asks.

"Well… it was something."

He grins at me with a knowing smile. "Maybe that's why no one—" But I cut him off with an icy glare. I can't hold it for long, and we both laugh. Head Vespertine clears his throat.

"Let's begin. Most of you are in your first or second year here, so I will start with the basics. Pull out your textbooks—" He stops speaking when someone enters the room. Prince Theon roams the rows of desks before finally choosing one in the middle. Probably so everyone gets a splendid view of him and his perfect golden hair, I think to myself.

"Welcome, Prince Theon," he exclaims, checking his attendance sheet. "I didn't think you were enrolled in this class. I'll get that fixed up for you."

The prince nods approvingly.

"As I was saying, take out your textbooks and turn to page twelve. Evocation is the art of calling forth spirits to provide information. Today, we will learn how to use a Ouija board to summon spirits. Anyone who doesn't have their own can borrow one." He motions to a stack of old, worn boards at the front of the room.

I get out my textbook and Dexter hands me a board he's gotten from Head Vespertine. I look at the shiny, black surface. Each letter of the alphabet and numbers 0-9 are printed on it in fine cursive writing, as well as two circles containing 'yes' and 'no'.

"We won't be actually using them today unless you are third year or higher, but first and second years feel free to check one out. Familiarise yourselves, but I will show you the ropes." Head Vespertine shows us how to set up the board, as well as what to chant when trying to summon a spirit.

"These are a load of crap," Dexter whispers to me, struggling with his board despite being in his third year.

Grinning back at him, I put my planchette on the board, lightly laying my fingers on top. Immediately, a wave washes over me, almost like I feel when I am attempting to use my power. I can feel the hair on my arms straighten, and a shiver runs down my spine. Before I know it, the planchette moves.

"H, E, L, L, O," I whisper the letters as my fingers move across the board.

"Miss Arrington! I said we are NOT using the Ouija today!" Head Vespertine booms across at me.

"I—I didn't mean to, I swear. It just started—" My hands are yanked from one corner of the board to the other.

"D, A, R, K, N, E, S, S." I glance over the letters. *Hello darkness?*

Head Vespertine is standing over my shoulder now, his eyes wide and arms crossed tightly against his chest. "I see…" he trails off. "Well done, Miss Arrington. It seems your gifts would be better suited to practice at a third year level next class," he says.

When I glance up, I notice Prince Theon staring at me from across the room. His intense gaze burns into mine as we enter yet another staring competition. I'm forced to break the eye contact when Dexter yelps as his board sets alight.

"Crap," he mutters.

A girl near us shoots her hands out towards Dexter's board and produces a stream of water that extinguishes the small blaze. We turn to each other and shrug.

"I guess I'm going to need more practice." He laughs. I give him a look of pity—he's been practicing for two years already and here I am, acing it on my first go.

I decide to stay behind after class to speak to Head Vespertine.

"Sir," I ask him, "is what I did today… normal?"

"Ah yes, Miss Arrington. Quite normal for someone with a few years at the Sanctum under their belt. But different students have unique talents, and it seems you may have found yours. Most first years can't manage to even summon a spirit, let alone have it speak to them. Do you know who it was? Usually if a Keeper has lost someone close to them to the spirit world, they may try to reach out," he asks, his amber eyes gleaming as if he's found his newest project.

"No idea… is there any way to find out?" I ask hopefully.

"Unfortunately, no. A spirit only reveals their identity if they wish to."

Waiting for me in the doorway of the evocation room is none other than the prince himself.

"That was quite impressive," he says, blocking my path.

"Thanks," I mutter, trying to get past. Should I bow or something? I don't know.

Head Vespertine has now left the room through the back exit, and it is just the two of us alone in the empty classroom.

"What's the hurry? Most girls would kill for some time alone with me," he says with a grin.

"Trust me, I know. But no, I'm not 'most girls', thank you," I say as politely as I can muster.

"Wait, your name… it's familiar. Do I know you somehow?"

"No, I don't think so," I reply. "I've got to go now—"

"Wait! That's it. You're Commander Arrington's daughter. I knew I'd heard the name before."

"Yeah," I stammer, keen to leave this conversation.

"Sorry to hear his power doesn't run in your veins," he says with a smirk. "But no matter. When you fail to become a Royal Guard, I'd be more than happy to have you guard me personally. All night long," he says with an insinuating, disgusting wink.

If he weren't so crude, I might actually think about it. I wouldn't mind a distraction from my life right about now, let alone a super handsome, royal distraction… but no. He is repulsive, and who knows what kind of trouble he has in mind.

"I'd sooner guard a garden gnome," I retort disgustedly.

He gives a grin, and suddenly, the man in front of me is nowhere to be seen. In his place lies a fat, little creature with a pointed blue hat and white beard, exactly like the gnomes back in the Earth Empire.

"God damn royal power," I mutter to myself. Before the prince could realise his mistake of shrinking himself and leaving the door unblocked, I sidestep the gnome and exit the room.

Maybe I should've stepped on him, I think darkly to myself as I traverse the corridors of the academy. That would save me the temptation.

I walk as calmly as I can back to my room. Well, my first day of classes wasn't a total failure. I sit down on my bed in a slump when a knock sounds at my door. Prisma pokes her head through the door before entering without waiting for permission. She sits next to me with a thud. "How was your day?"

"Well, it was all right until—"

"Hang on," Prisma eyes a folded piece of paper on the small wooden table in front of us. She reaches out at the same time I do, but she manages to snag it first. Grinning, she peels apart the paper and begins to read:

"Dearest Prisma and Reyna. I await your presence in spirit. Don't keep me waiting. Love D."

Prisma rolls her eyes whilst I mull over the words.

"There's a bar called Spirit we usually go to, in Pineside, but you definitely can't wear that," she says, eyeing my outfit consisting of jeans and a sweater.

The closest—and only—town near the Sanctum is named Pineside, after the dense pine tree forests surrounding it. The Sanctum lies on an island to the west of Aspacia, and relies on Pineside to supply food and other resources to the school. Pollo and I came past it on the way here last week, but besides that, I've only heard tales of its beauty. I guess I'm going there today.

Prisma tells me to dress up, so I walk to my closet and pick out my comfiest pair of pants and a long sleeved top. My hair is semi-behaving itself today, but I sweep it into my usual high ponytail. Glancing briefly into the mirror as I walk by, I head into the small sitting area of dorm six to wait for Prisma. After what feels like an eternity, she struts out of her room looking like she should be on the cover of *Sparks Magazine*. She is a vision in a short dress and high heels. Her straightened, crimson hair falls to her shoulders, and the deep blue of her dress brings out her gleaming eyes. But when my eyes meet hers, they are narrowed in my direction.

"I thought I told you to dress up," she raises an eyebrow as she trails her eyes over my unkempt hair and fraying shirt. Sighing, Prisma beckons me into her room with a jerk of her head and her hands on her hips. She stomps in and slams the door behind us, then forces me into a small velvet stool in front of a mirrored vanity. She doesn't say a word as she gets to work on my unruly hair, brushing and braiding away until it is somewhat fashionable.

"Stand," Prisma commands, and I do as she says for fear of the consequence. Who knows what getting in the way of Prisma and her masterpiece will entail. She flings hanger after hanger from her closet onto her plush bed, and before I can wonder why her room is so much more luscious than mine, she squeals in delight.

"Close your eyes," she says, but I look at her with an eyebrow raised. "Trust me, Reyna."

Reluctantly, I do as she says, and am shocked to feel her fingers unbuttoning my pants a moment later.

"Uhh, I can do that myself," I say.

"Hurry up then! Dexter is surely wondering where we are by now. I didn't factor this into my getting-ready-routine!" She huffs as I slide off my pants and tug the frayed shirt over my head, trying not to be self-conscious in front of this goddess of a woman. I try to peek as Prisma slides a silky fabric over my head and down my body, but she waves her fingers over my eyes after scowling at me. Moments later I'm forced back into what I assume is the velvet stool.

"And just one finishing touch…" she swipes something over my lips and eyelids. "And voila! Stunning!" I can hear her step back, as if to admire her work. "Open your eyes, Reyna."

When I look into the mirror in front of me, I can't help but open my mouth in shock. This person doesn't look like me. Her lips are too red, eyelids too dark, hair too neat. Prisma has dressed me in the most exquisite green silken gown, and even managed to get a corset on me despite my struggles. Taking a deep breath in, I turn to her and she winks.

"That's more like it," she says, trailing her eyes up and down my body. "Who knew you were hiding that under those baggy sweaters. Let's go."

A few Earthies eye me hungrily up and down as we walk down the Earth House stairwell, and I curse my mother for the more desirable traits she passed on to me. I'd much rather sink into the surrounding walls than be the centre of attention.

83

9

We leave our dorms and I notice Prisma is leading us towards Air House.

"Why are we going this way? The gates are the other way," I say.

"And what are you gonna do when you get to the gates? Walk all the way to town? Come on, I know an Air Keeper that owes me a few favours." Prisma leads the way to Air House, and when we arrive she knocks heavily on the door. A man with purple eyes and scruffy, blond hair opens it.

"Eric. We need a ride to town," she says pointedly, motioning to me with a jab of her thumb. This is not where I thought this was going. The man rolls his eyes then grins, eyeing us both up and down.

"Hurry up, we don't have all night. Maybe next time I'll invite you, too." Prisma winks at the man. Eric holds his palms out towards us, and a purple orb forms between them.

"Hold my hands!" Prisma calls out to me.

I do as she says, and as soon as our fingers touch a blast of strong wind is shot from Eric's hands straight at us. It lifts us and sends us in a whirl of air spiralling up and over the forest. I scream out but my voice is lost in the rush of air. Prisma laughs from beside me, throwing her head back and exclaiming at the view below us. I don't look down until we land, our feet both safely on the ground.

"Travel by whirlwind. It's not the most graceful, but it sure is fun. All you've got to do is think of the place you want to go, and the wind will carry you there," Prisma exclaims happily.

Now I know why she needed an Air Keeper. I have no doubt I look like I've had an accident with the blow-dryer, so I run my hands through my hair to fix it as best I can. Somehow, Prisma's red locks are hanging just as they were before we left the Sanctum.

I take in my surroundings: it seems as though we have landed right in the middle of town. I am in awe at the different cafes, shops and bars that litter the winding streets. Prisma grabs my hand again and leads me along the brick path, until we stop in front of a run-down building with a sign out front that says 'Spirit'. There are decaying wooden boards on the windows, and the small array of plants by the doorway are withered and dead.

"I thought you said I'd need to dress up for this place," I questioned Prisma, eyeing the dishevelled 'bar' outside the car.

"Trust me," she replies.

The sun is about to set over the hills, and an eerie air falls over us. Prisma waves her hand at a small grate on the door as we approach, and two eyes peer back at us. Prisma holds out her hands, cupping them in front of her. Before my eyes, she produces a pure white lily from nothing. The grate closes, and there is a clunking sound before the door swings open.

Prisma nods at the man behind the door. He wears dark grey overalls and a flat checkered cap, which he removes from his head as we enter. I now see that his ears are pointed where mine are round, and realise he is an elf. I have had little experience with their kind, but my father often speaks of them in his letters.

When King Zale needs to make deals with the Elf Kingdom to keep peace, they send a party to speak with the king. Elves are selfish, unfriendly creatures with short tempers, so I make a mental note to stay on this one's good side. Prisma slips two five-dollar bills into the elf's hat.

"Thanks, Tanyth." She smiles sweetly at the elf.

"Welcome to Spirit," Tanyth says in a low voice. I nod at him and follow Prisma into the dark hallway in front of us.

A thick smoke assaults my lungs, the scent sickly sweet. As we walk, we pass other elves and Keepers, noisily chatting along. We reach another door at the end of the hallway and Prisma pauses, eyeing my hesitant expression.

"I said trust me. This is why." She pushes the heavy door open and the sight before me is one I'll never forget. Plush chaise lounges scatter a darkened room populated by dozens of Keepers. A dance floor is in the far corner, as well as a bar stocked with every colour liquor one can imagine.

I feel uneasy; had I really agreed to coming to this place without knowing exactly what I'd walk into? I don't even know these people properly yet, let alone why they are being so friendly to me.

"Let's dance!" Prisma screams, grabbing my hand and pulling me to the dancefloor: a crowded, small space in the corner of the room. The dark atmosphere clouds around us as bodies push up against me and I feel claustrophobic.

"I'm going to get a drink," I yell into Prisma's ear so she can hear me over the music. She motions me to the bar and waves me away, beginning to dance with the surrounding strangers. I head to the bar and sit on a stool with a huff.

"I'll get a red wine for the lady, and a whiskey for myself," says a familiar voice beside me to the bartender. Crap. I really should be more aware of my surroundings before choosing a seat next time.

"What are you doing here?" I glare at Hayden Radford, three already-empty glasses in front of him.

"It's the first day of class. Of course I'm here," he replies smugly. "I didn't expect to see you, though. You don't seem the type."

"What's that supposed to mean? You don't know me."

"Evidently, I do," he says as the bartender places a glass of thick, red wine in front of me. How does he know what I like?

"I don't take handouts from creepy men at bars."

"Creepy? I'm the least of your problems here, butterfly." He grins. "See those guys over there?" He motions to a spot where five shady guys are sitting on the lounges. They each have a girl in their laps who look totally infatuated with the men, but they pay the girls little attention. "Fifth-years. Someone should probably expel them from their enchantment classes."

I watch more closely and I realise the girls have a glistening haze to their eyes, as if they are in a trance. Enchanted.

"That's disgusting," I gasp, feeling sick to my stomach with rage. I immediately move to go over there and help them, but Hayden grabs my wrist.

"I wouldn't. What are you going to do, face a bunch of fifth-years with your one day of magic knowledge? Bad move, butterfly."

"You realise that's not my name, right?" I glare at him. He shrugs, as if to say 'I don't care'. He downs his whiskey before moving my glass closer to me.

"Like I said, I'll pay for my own drinks," I say sternly.

"Trust me, you've already paid for it in my books. That little outfit is payment enough." He smirks, looking me up and down.

Yuck. I roll my eyes at him. But if he is giving away free drinks, I'll bite. I down the entire drink as quickly as possible and stand. I don't plan on spending any more time sitting here with him. Turning my back, I walk back to the dance floor.

Prisma is still there, jumping up and down to the music with an enormous smile plastered on her face. I feel a tap on my shoulder and I whirl around, ready to tell Hayden to piss off. But the face that meets my eyes is Dexter's, smiling down at me with a slightly confused expression.

"Whoa there, it's just me," he exclaims, holding his hands up and laughing. I sigh in relief at the sight of him, thankful it's him.

Dexter wears a tight, black suit, with a few of the buttons of his shirt undone. "You seem disappointed to see me," he queries, eyeing my surprised expression.

"Not at all, I just thought you were… someone else."

Dexter takes my hand and leads me to the dance floor, next to where Prisma is dancing. Another woman joins her now, her brunette hair swinging as she dances with Prisma. She holds her by the waist as they sing along to the music. Dexter catches me eyeing them.

"That's Sapphira." he says with a grin. "She's Head Windance's daughter. Not super friendly, but Prisma likes her so we deal with it."

I nod as he continues. We move in time to the beat, not touching but very close to it. Our bodies sway in time, and a thoughtful gaze takes over Dexter's expression. He is hard to read. I can never tell what he's thinking, but I'm hoping it's something similar to what is on my mind.

He is looking exceedingly handsome tonight. I notice the way his shirt hangs over chest, the way his green eyes gaze into mine. His powerful arms wrap around my waist gently at first, testing the gesture, before pulling me in against his firm body. My head feels slightly light, and I'm sure the wine has begun to make its way into my system. His fingers trail through my hair and to the back of my head, lingering there as we dance in the shadows of the club. I feel my cheeks blush, and I hope Dexter can't see their traitorous shade of pink under the glowing lights.

Do I actually want this, or does it just feel nice to be wanted? I can't help but think this through a million times in my head. I don't really know this guy.

The warnings from Pollo flash through my mind as Dexter spins me so my back is against his chest, his hands on my waist again.

Nothing is as it seems. Pollo's voice carries through my thoughts.

Does that mean this is too good to be true? I think back to all encounters with Dexter. It was Dexter who picked up my books. Wiped my tears after the initiation. Opened up to me during our picnic. I give in to the feeling of his body on mine, letting him sway against me to the music. I notice Prisma and Sapphira across the room, and when she finds my eyes, Prisma gives me a wink.

When Dexter spins me around and tries to place his lips on mine, the wave of uncertainty rushes over me again and I gently push him away.

"I don't want... I want to take it slow," I say, unsure if I was really hearing the words I was speaking. My whisper of a voice catches me by surprise, and I realise I am out of breath.

Here I am, a super-hot guy about to kiss me, and all I can think of are Pollo's warnings. When I raise my gaze from his chest to his eyes, Dexter gives a small smile. He is obviously trying not to look too disappointed, but he is graceful in my rejection.

"It's okay, we got a bit... carried away," he says with a smirk.

"I've gotta use the restroom," I say, keen to leave this increasingly awkward situation. He nods, and I head off in search of the ladies' room.

I'm walking through the crowd when suddenly a firm hand is on my shoulder, forcefully pushing me forward. I try to resist, but the strength of whoever has their hands on me is too great. I try again to plant my feet as firmly into the floor as I can, digging my heels in against the wooden planks. But it is no use.

There's a muffled grunt as my attacker continues pushing. I panic when I realise I am being pushed towards the back entrance to the club. I could scream, but no one would hear me over the music, and it's too dark for anyone to notice.

At this point, I'm relying on Dexter finding my dead body after he realises I've been 'in the restroom' too long.

We burst through the door and out into a small alley behind Spirit.

"What the hell do you think you're doing?" I yell, whirling around now that the hands are off my shoulders. My rage grows immediately when I realise who has forced me outside. I should've known.

"Hayden?" I stare at the tall man with an increasingly furious expression.

"I could ask you the same thing, butterfly. What are you doing?" He stands a few steps away from me, his body language oddly calm, although I can tell he is trying to wrangle some sort of fury inside of himself.

The moonlight shines on his face, highlighting his amber eyes in the darkness. The alley is empty, only the rodents hiding in the dumpsters would be witness to anything happening. It's moments like these I am thankful for my father's training. He believed that complacency was as dangerous as a blade, so he did everything in his power to keep me sharp.

Before he left us, that is. We would run around our backyard with wooden swords before he had to move away. I remember the day I finally was able to outsmart him and strike him in the leg. He wasn't even mad at me, just proud.

"What makes you think you can just force me into this creepy back alley? You obviously suck at picking up girls, but this is a whole new low." I want to hit him where it hurts, throwing verbal jabs left and right until he explains himself.

"You need to stay away from that guy."

"Who, Dexter? You're joking, right? The only guy I should stay away from right now is your whiskey drinking ass." I yell at him.

He pauses thoughtfully. "Wait here," he says with such command that my body instantly obeys without consideration. He goes back inside, and returns a few moments later with another red wine in hand. "Drink."

I weigh up my options. If he had done something to it, no one would find me in time to help me. Although from the expression on his face, I'm worried if I don't obey and drink, something even worse will happen. I snatch the drink from him, bringing the cup to my lips, then pause. Hayden gives me a flat, menacing look as I slowly take a tentative sip. Tastes normal to me, but you never know.

"Now that you've got something in your mouth, you might actually listen to me." He grins suggestively. I give him a stare filled with pure hatred. "Dexter Fallon. He's bad news. Stay away from him," he repeats himself.

"Why should I believe anything you say? You're the one dragging me into an alley in the dead of night."

He gives me a cold stare, like there's more to say than what he's telling me. "He isn't like—" Hayden is cut off by the sound of the door slamming open.

A massive vine shoots from the open space at Hayden. He quickly retaliates with a ball of fire aimed at the vine, and it disintegrates into nothing. Another vine shoots from the doorway, circling Hayden's body. He falls to his knees with a thud.

I make use of the time I have before he burns the vines away and runs inside, slamming the door in his face. I run straight into someone standing in the doorway, and when I look up, I realise it's Dexter.

"Thank God," I say, hugging him tight. My body is trembling from both the cold air outside and the intense situation I'd just escaped.

"I've got you. I've got you," he murmurs into my hair, holding me against his chest.

I don't particularly feel like returning to the dance floor after that, so Dexter and I take a walk around Pineside. Pulling out my phone, I shoot Prisma a quick message telling her my whereabouts, and she sends me a winking face in return.

"Are you all right?" Dexter questions me as we traverse the empty streets of the small town. "If that asshole hurt you…" he begins, and I can see the fury burning behind his eyes.

"I'll be fine," I say, not wanting him to storm back into the bar and find Hayden. Who knows what he would do?

We walk the streets until we eventually find a quiet, grassy spot facing a large river. We sit apart from each other on the grass and take in the silence, only broken by the ripples of the water in front of us.

"What did he want?" Dexter asks with that difficult-to-read expression of his. It's like a mix between concern and… something else.

"He warned me about you. He said to stay away from you," I answer, gazing up at him. His eyes flash with something that looks a lot like fear, then he returns to his usual blank expression.

"Did he say why?" he asks, and I shake my head. "That guy has had it out for me since the day we both started two years ago. I don't know what I did to get on his hit list, but if he comes after you again, I'll make him sorry he ever talked to you."

10

On Friday morning, I meet Navari in the Central Gardens as promised. She sits on a white bench, resting her head in her hands as she scans the contents of perhaps the fattest book I've ever seen. I hoped that because Navari is also in her first year at the Sanctum that she wouldn't make me look stupid, but I abandon that thought the minute I see her endless scrawling of notes and piles textbooks stacked around her.

"Reyna!" she greets me with a warm smile and pulls me in for a hug. My body stiffens, not expecting the gesture. She pats the spot next to her on the bench, and plonks one of the books in front of me.

"So I've been to the library a few times since our last class. And there is a lot to know about Fideal," she says.

"You're not kidding," I say, scanning the piles of books. "How are we supposed to read all of this?"

"Well, that's the thing," she says, and I look at her more closely. Her usually bright, wide eyes have purple bags under them, and her blue eyes are bloodshot. "I already did. I couldn't put them down, there's heaps of interesting stuff in here, and—" she says, but I cut her off with a raised eyebrow and grin. She pauses, before her face lights up with her usual warm smile.

"Leave me alone." Navari laughs, turning the page of the book she has entranced herself in. "Like I was saying before I was so rudely interrupted—" She winks. "—there's so much stuff in these books that the information contradicts itself. Some books say Fideal can be drowned, some say they can't. I don't know how I am going to beat one with my power. But for you, they all say Fideal can be buried by earth," she says.

"Navari, I—" I try to begin explaining myself, but I'm not sure where to start. She obviously hasn't heard the rumours, as so many other pairs of ears apparently had. She looks up at me from her notes, eyes expectant and waiting.

"I don't... I don't have any powers," I manage to say eventually. "I can't wield earth. Or any element, for that matter."

Navari pauses, her eyebrows raised and lips pursed. I'm anticipating her to bag me out, to tell me how stupid I am for even coming here to the Sanctum in the first place, let alone wanting to compete in the Tournament. But she doesn't say any of that.

"Okay... that's okay. We will just have to figure out another way." She says sweetly, and I am relieved to find not even one hint of pity on her face. It is refreshing compared to the sorrowful looks of sympathy usually thrown my way when people find out. It makes me like her even more.

"I'll do some more research. There has to be something else. A weakness, perhaps—"

"I'll figure out a way. Let's just focus on you for now. Did you find anything else useful for water Keepers?" I say, trying to turn the attention away from myself.

"No, but I did find something else," she says. "Fideal love the smell of salt. Centuries ago, they would wait where the salt water rivers meet the oceans for sailors to drag under the water. Nowadays, the Fideal have become lazy—they take up residence anywhere frequented by people. For example, the Westgrave River," she says, and I have a feeling I know what she's getting at before the words leave her mouth.

"I won't know if water works for sure or not unless we actually test it out. I want to try it on a real one," she says, the excitement and fear mixing together on her face.

"Are you sure? What about the rules? We aren't allowed to practice our power without supervision," I say, unsure of how Head Montero would react to one of her own stepping out of line.

"That's why we go in the dead of night. Deep in the Blackwood forest. No one will see us," Navari says. She sits facing me now, legs crossed at the knee and hands clasped in her lap.

"Give me a week to work through these books, then we can meet up to practice," she says.

"Fine. But you better be sure about this," I say uncertainly, and I swear she almost physically jumps with joy.

It's nearing the end of my second week at the Sanctum and I've come to realise that besides evocation, I have absolutely no luck in my classes. I can't seem to enchant anything, summon my power or even manage a simple incantation. I'm getting impatient, and beginning to listen to the part of me that worries that I will never find my power. It's already been years since it was supposed to form, and I still can't even wield anything more than a small child can.

Actually no, in most cases, they wield more than I do. All my life I've been trying not to lose hope—to push through the feelings of self-doubt and the cruel words of the people in my village. But maybe they are right after all. I sigh as I sit alone in the Central Gardens, my study notes spread in front of me like an endless maze of useless information.

I like coming here—the feeling of the luscious grass beneath my feet and the sun in the sky usually brightens my mood. I am still waiting for that to happen. I've found a nice spot tucked away in a quiet corner under a willow tree with long, flowing branches. I slam a heavy textbook closed and lie back in the grass, surrounded by the swaying leaves that move with the breeze through the gardens. The smell of freshly cut grass and wildflowers fills my senses, and I watch as the fluffy white clouds travel along the open sky above. Until I am interrupted.

"Maybe you're more in touch with the earth than you think," a male voice says from somewhere close. I sit up to find Dexter's smiling face, his hands full with a wicker basket and a decent sized box.

"What's all this?" I ask, as my stomach grumbles.

"You've been down here all morning—I figured you could go with some lunch and good company," he says, and my eyes dart to my watch. Two o'clock.

I didn't realise I was starving until the sweet smell of fresh pastries and bread fills my nose. Dexter laughs as he sees me eyeing the basket, and he places it beside me, unstacking the box from on top. He passes me a deliciously crisp pastry with jam, and one of the Sanctum's famous baguettes that I've been eating almost daily.

I grin as I take an enormous bite, getting jam on the corners of my mouth. Dexter laughs once more, reaches a tender hand to my cheek, and wipes away the sauce, before sucking his thumb clean. I scrunch my nose at him, but he stares back at me with bottomless green eyes.

"What?" I ask, trying to keep a cool and calm facade as my heart almost jumps through my chest.

He opens his mouth to speak, but pauses. "I was just thinking of something stupid. Don't worry about it," he says, and I swear I notice his cheeks turn a slightly deeper shade of pink.

"No, what is it? What were you thinking?" I basically beg.

"Fine… if you really must know. I was thinking about the next time I touch your lips, I want it to be with my own." His words wash over me like warm honey, and suddenly he isn't the only one blushing.

I drop my gaze, fidgeting with a long blade of grass as if it were interesting. "What's in the box?" I quickly ask. Anything to change the subject.

Dexter empties its contents onto the grass, revealing a shiny, marble chess set.

"I thought you could go for some entertainment, too. Do you know how to play?" he says, setting up the pieces carefully atop the board as it sits half-sunken into the grass.

"Yeah, I'm all right," I lie. I am in fact more than all right. I used to play chess with my father before he left, and he was a relentless teacher. He never let me win, and I would whine about it every time.

On the same day I first struck him with my wooden sword, I also beat him in chess for the first time. He joked that I'd become the provider for our house. If only he knew that a few years later, that would become true.

"Black or white?" Dexter asks, placing the final piece on its square.

"Black." I always made the same choice. My father tried to get me to explain it, and I never could. I refused to play with him unless I could be black.

"Okay… there, ready. I'll start," Dexter says, and the game is afoot. He moves with tactic and skill, parrying his pieces between the squares with deadly precision. He takes out my pieces one by one, but he's made a few mistakes that will cost him the game.

"Don't worry, I'll go easy on you next time," he says, moving his knight to put me in check. I grin. He still believes the game is his for the taking.

"You've left your king open," I say, finalising my deadly plan of attack by sliding my pawn into the winning square.

"Checkmate," I say, grinning up at him. Dexter's mouth falls open, and he stares back at me with widened eyes.

"You played with your most powerful pieces, forgetting the masses of others at your disposal," I say, trying to give him some tips without coming across as condescending.

"They're most powerful for a reason. Why bother with the weak ones?"

"There's more of them. They're underestimated, especially when you use them together." I noticed that he moved around the board crashing into anything he could, using his queen and rooks to dominate.

"But they're useless. One powerful piece is better than having ten weak ones," he says a little too intensely, and I get the feeling he isn't talking about chess anymore.

"As you can see—" I gesture to the chess board. "—that is not the case." I smirk, and he creases his brow.

"Again," he says, resetting the board. I sigh and help him, claiming the black pieces once more. We play five more rounds, each time Dexter requesting a rematch when I obliterate him.

"I give up. You're clever, Rey. You could teach me a thing or two." He places a soft hand on my thigh and I smile.

We pack away the chess and head back to the dorm to settle in for the night. Dexter takes his usual place sitting in the armchair by the window, and I sit across from him.

"Why do you always choose the black pieces? White gets to go first," he asks me, and I have to ponder the question for a moment.

"I like it more. It feels… right to me," I say, honestly not sure why I am drawn to the colour. "I get to watch your first move and decide how I want to play from there. Really, it's an advantage to go second."

"That's a bit dark," he replies with a laugh. "You're too sweet to be saying such morbid things." I consider his words for a moment, but then a realisation hits me.

"Light is not always good, and dark is not always evil."

11

On Friday night, I go to meet Navari in the Blackwood forest when the moon is at its highest in the sky. I walk along the winding dirt trails from Earth House to the forest as a lone raven circles above, and I can't help but shudder as I remember Pollo's warnings about the things hiding in the shadows.

Navari wears tight black pants and a sports bra, her white and blue hair glowing in the sun. We walk together until we reach a sizable stream in a clearing in the forest. It seems to run through the forest in each direction as far as the sea, and I guess that it cuts across the whole of the island from north to south.

"It's called the Westgrave River. Home of the Fideal, among other creatures," she says, poring over one of her numerous notebooks. She rummages through her bag, revealing pens, paper, and a jar full of… are those olives? Bags hang under her eyes and I suspect she spent the night in the library yet again, scraping together any last scraps of information she could find to help her today.

I look into the river and notice the sparkling current flowing down and out towards the ocean. It seems calm, although I doubt what lies beneath the surface will be the same.

Navari lays a napkin by the riverbed, then piles on some black olives and douses them with a salt shaker she removed from her bag.

"Delicious," I remark sarcastically. She gives me a nervous grin, and we wait for the Fideal to reveal themselves.

We wait for half an hour, chatting about our lives back home. Navari has eaten nearly half the olives, and I begin to suspect that has something to do with the lack of Fideal appearing from the river.

"There!" Navari excitedly whispers and points to a small ripple forming at the side of the river.

I watch as a head emerges, piercing grey eyes staring directly at us. This Fideal is completely different to the one from abjuration class the other day; she has long, blonde hair, and is covered in what seems to be the whole river's worth of weeds and kelp. Navari leaps up from the ground, ready to test her powers on the creature. Its blue skin seems to shine with the slick, shiny water of the Westgrave River.

"I'll go first," she says cautiously, as she hesitantly steps towards the creature.

She raises her hands slightly by her side, readying her power to attack. The Fideal is now fully emerged from the river, leaving a trail of dripping water as she slowly steps towards us.

It isn't fast, but I know it will wield some sort of power, given the chance.

Navari lifts her palms higher, and the Fideal attacks with a scream. It opens its mouth wide, revealing two sets of sharp teeth in place of what used to be a pretty smile. It lunges forward, easily closing the distance between her and Navari.

Navari calls out as the Fideal goes to strike forward again, releasing her power from her hands and lifting an enormous wave of water from the river. Navari wraps the water around the Fideal so it is completely submerged whilst still standing on the river bank.

The Fideal screeches as she loses her footing, frantically trying to claw her way towards us with long talons that have emerged from her fingers. The bubble of water surges around the creature, twisting its blonde hair in the pull of the water.

Navari flashes me a smile as I stand to the side, my heart beating frantically. But she shouldn't have taken her eyes off the Fideal.

It lunges towards me, closing the distance between us in an instant, and I prepare myself for impact. I scream as it plunges its claws into my thigh, piercing the skin of my upper leg. It removes its claws and eyes me hungrily, lifting its hand to swing back at me once again.

Before it gets the chance, a massive blast of water knocks the creature away with a jolt. Navari is there, standing between me and the Fideal. She gives me a fearsome look, her brows furrowed and shoulders squared. I've never seen her this strong, this menacing before.

Once it regains its footing, the Fideal charges again. Navari pounds it down once more with a long, forceful stream of icy cold water, then turns to me with helpless eyes.

"I can't kill it! I thought I knew how but… but look!" I glance at the Fideal again and sure enough, it wasn't showing any signs of drowning despite being submerged by Navari's power.

I grimace as I stand, the pain shooting through my leg as blood trickles down into my shoe. Limping over to stand next to Navari, I raise my hands just as Navari did moments ago. It may be foolish, but it seems like our only hope. No one else knows we are here. Nobody is coming to save us.

I can do this. It's now or never, and if my power doesn't show itself... I won't have to face the shame of it anymore. I dart my palms out towards the creature, still entangled in Navari's wave, and feel something shift within me. Like something is scratching at the surface of my skin, needing to be let out. The searing pain in my leg grows, and I throw every single ounce of energy I have into this. I need this to work.

A dark, hollow feeling comes over me, and I watch as a smoky stream of darkness flows from my palm to the Fideal. It shrieks in horror as the mist makes its way over to the creature, and forces itself down the Fideal's throat.

I feel an undeniable surge of power shooting through me, shaking me to my core, but I've never felt more in control in my life. I don't know what is happening, but I continue to shove my hands in the direction of the creature until it is no longer breathing. My heart beats faster and faster with each breath as I try not to let the shock of what's happening take over.

The Fideal's limp body now lies on the river bank, and the shadows retract themselves into my hands. I turn to Navari, who is hesitantly taking a step away from me, her eyes wide and hands at the ready.

"I..."

"What did you do?" she asks, her shocked voice nearly at a whisper.

"I don't know," I say, staring at my palms as I try to control my breathing. What was that? It definitely wasn't earth.

"I've never seen anything like it," Navari says, looking a little less terrified of me this time. She stares at me, terrified, but eventually walks over to me. I guess she was making sure I'm not going to wildly spout darkness again. Navari rummages through her backpack, pulling out a small, white container.

"Sit down," she commands, and I find a tree stump to perch on.

My leg aches as I bend it on the way down. Navari brings over a small first aid kit and begins dressing my wound. I didn't realise how deeply the Fideal's talons had pierced my skin: three large gashes run down my thigh, slicing through my flesh and the jeans with ease.

"You're going to need to go to the infirmary, but this should stop the bleeding for now." I smile at her gratefully, even when she is pushing against the wound, causing me searing pain.

We slowly stumble along the empty trail back to the Sanctum at an excruciatingly slow pace. Navari is struggling to support me, but she keeps her arm under my shoulders all the same. My sock is completely drenched in my own blood and I begin to feel light-headed. Whether it's from the sight of the blood, or from how much I've lost, I can't tell. Just as we reach the edge of the forest, I collapse in a heap onto the dirt. The world around me goes dark as I see a tall figure running towards me.

"She's waking up!" called an excited voice I recognise to be Navari's from beside me.

My eyes struggle to open as I try to come to my senses. A bright, unfamiliar room surrounds me. Heavy footsteps are approaching, and I force myself to sit up.

"Easy there, Reyna. Relax," says a man, now next to me.

I realise I am in a large, extravagant living room, lying down on a green velvet sofa. A jolt of pain ripples through my leg and I remember what happened.

"You lost a lot of blood," says Navari, her face now hovering above mine. Her brows are furrowed into a concerned look, and her white hair has splotches of red.

I reach out and touch it. "Oh… sorry," I say, realising I stained it with blood.

"You don't need to apologise for bleeding, Reyna." She smiles softly.

"That Fideal got you pretty good. You're lucky it wasn't worse. You two must be super brave or super stupid to go after one on your second week of classes," an unfamiliar male voice says.

I realise with a start that I know exactly who it is. I turn my head slowly, and sure enough, to the left of me stands Prince Theon himself. He stands over me, peering from my face to my leg to my face again.

"It's good to see you again, Reyna," he says knowingly. I flash back to him turning into a disgusting gnome the other day and nearly lose it. I fight a smirk.

Navari turns her head to me, confused at his words. I have yet to mention to her the strange run-in I had with the prince after our evocation class. His golden eyes flash with entertainment as his gaze trails past the no doubt viscous wound on my upper thigh.

His stare lingers for a bit too long on my exposed skin. A warm flush settles into my cheeks as I realise I am sitting in the prince's house in my underwear.

"The prince found us just as you collapsed," Navari explained. "I didn't want us to get into trouble for killing the Fideal without supervision." She pauses, and I make a mental note to thank her later for not mentioning the strange outburst of darkness I shot from my palms. "The prince kindly suggested we bring you back here," she offers as an explanation.

"Where are we?" I ask.

"Welcome to my home. Well, it's home at the Sanctum, anyway," says Prince Theon.

I inspect my surroundings: from the view out the window, we must be a few floors above the ground, and a couple doors lead off into other rooms. He must have the entire floor to himself. His bronze hair is swept to the side, and I realise he is shirtless. My eyes linger for a bit too long on his chiselled torso, and he notices.

"Don't worry, I had to take it off. It got... dirty," he says.

Damn it. Whilst I was unconscious, I somehow managed to bleed all over Navari's perfect hair, as well as the heir to the throne's shirt.

He must've seen my flustered expression, and a low laugh escapes the prince's lips. Navari looks more than happy to be here in his presence, when all I can muster is a small, "Thank you."

She gives me an icy glare, then says, "Sorry about her, your highness. Please let us know how we can repay you. Reyna and I are thankful for all you've done for us today and maybe, if it's not too much to ask... could you not mention it to anyone? We don't want Head Windance getting wind of this." She smiles shyly.

The prince and I both grin at the unintentional air pun Navari just made. She is oblivious to it, and I wouldn't be surprised if she—oh wait, there she goes. Navari drops into a graceful curtsy, keeping her head low. The prince gives an amused look.

"Please, stand. There's no need, and your secret's safe with me. As for payment... if you're ever feeling lonely, now you know where to find me," he says, winking at her.

I snort in disgust and their eyes turn to me. It wouldn't shock me if Navari decided to take up his offer despite whatever she has going on with Dexter.

I slowly swing my legs over the side of the couch and glance down at the wound on my leg. I gasp as I notice the immaculate line of stitches binding the deep gashes together. The bleeding has stopped, and all that's left of the blood remains in my sock. Prince Theon sees my surprised face.

"I've sewn up my fair share of injuries." His eyes darken, as if he is reliving a memory inside his head. I wonder what he could be thinking of. As a prince, he wouldn't need to dirty his hands with anything so mundane as first aid. Unless he regularly found helpless girls to be in his debt.

"Navari, can you please get me a towel from the room on the left there?" he asks, and she obliges, heading out of the room. He quickly turns to me. "I find it fascinating that you were able to stand up at all after the Fideal scratched you," he begins. "I've heard about you, and your lack of power. You're very lucky Navari was there with you. You're even more lucky to be alive considering a Fideal's claws contain a hallucinogen intended to render your mind useless. That's how they got sailors in the old days to comply so easily." He looks at me accusingly, but I just shrug.

I genuinely have no idea why the Fideal's venom didn't work on me. "I guess I was lucky."

"Yes," he agrees, his dark stare meeting mine. "Very lucky indeed." He stares me down with narrowed eyes, but I have no answers for him.

Navari re-enters the room and produces a blue towel, which the prince thanks her for and takes.

"Come back here in seven days and I'll take out the stitches."

I nod in agreement, thankful for his help but wary of his intentions.

"Here." He hands some grey sweatpants to me. "Yours got ruined. You can have these."

"Thank you, your highness," I mutter.

His eyes meet mine intensely and he says, "Call me Theon. And next time, stab it in the heart the first chance you get." He eyes the bulge at my waist where my knife lies, hidden by my shirt.

12

"I can't believe that just happened," Navari squeals as we sit together in the Central Gardens the next morning.

We chose a spot under a luscious willow tree, out of the hustle and bustle of Keepers going to and from classes. A large, black bird flies overhead, and the wind blows a pleasant, cool air around us. My mind is still reeling, but I think back to that blue towel the prince made Navari go get.

He didn't even use it. He must have wanted to speak with me alone.

I pull a sandwich out from the brown paper bag Navari snagged from the dining hall, and cringe at the sight of the too-tight pants Navari lent me. I threw mine out— they're no use to me with three giant gashes in them.

Navari chats about the happenings of this morning. We severely underestimated the Fideal's power, which nearly cost us more than a scraped up leg. I can't help but feel a rush of excitement when I think back to the way I fought against the creature. I should feel terrified, but I've never felt more awake. "Do you feel… different since arriving here?" I ask her.

"Different how?"

"Like something's finally awake inside you. Something strong."

"Hmm… not really." She shrugs, digging into her ham and cheese baguette. Must just be me then.

The tug on my power urges me to use it again. Urges it to be released. I almost feel like I can't contain it, which might become an issue considering we aren't supposed to be conjuring anything without supervision. But I push the thought to the back of my mind— there are more pressing questions at hand. Like *where the hell did that black smoke come from?*

I think back to the sheer power Dexter used at the club last week, and the way Prisma sprouted the white lily to get into Spirit. It must be more of a guideline than a rule—or maybe they just know how to get away with conjuring.

"Look… I shouldn't have suggested fighting the Fideal last night. I just wanted to impress you," Navari says, blue eyes staring up at me. She sits with her legs crossed, leaning back on the trunk of the willow. Her hair has two tiny braids hanging at the front, framing her delicate features.

"Impress me? Why?" I ask, unsure why anyone would feel the need to do such a thing.

"You're… different. And not just because of whatever the hell that stunt was you pulled back at the river. I like you," she says sweetly, staring down at her shoes.

"I like you, too. Just a shame the way we met," I tease, and she nudges me with her elbow and grins as we remember the bathroom incident.

"Did you notice on the way home from the prince's where exactly he lives?" she exclaims.

"I noticed it was an old building with a few stories, but I haven't been there before today."

"It's the faculty residence building. I can't believe they gave him a place there, although I guess he *is* royalty. Some of the professors are already forced to live in the Sanctum with the rest of us because of a lack of space at the faculty block." She smiles, a playful grin takes over her expression and I can tell she's thinking something controversial.

"Just imagine," she begins, "Prince Theon coming home late with his newest conquest on his arm, drunk and rowdy, and running into Head Vespertine."

I can't help but throw my head back in laughter as she does the same. I feel like I have someone here I can call a friend. Someone that will have my back, just like when we were fighting the Fideal.

The day has slipped away into darkness as the last remnants of the sun fade away over the sea. The cliffs in the distance stand tall, guarding the Sanctum from the expansive crash of waves below. Navari and I say our goodbyes and I return to Earth House with another wild day under my belt. Prisma and Dexter are already seated in the dining hall. I serve myself a plate of spaghetti and meatballs and join them, sinking into the chair beside Dexter. I notice a lack of noise in the room and look questioningly to Prisma.

"There was another attack," she says softly. My heart stops.

I recall the first attack that occurred one year ago. Cousins of the Air Emperor were killed brutally in their homes as they slept. There were multiple, extensive investigations, but nothing was found except for their bodies. An innocent Keeper family, gone in the blink of an eye. No trace of the attacker except one thing: an out-of-place strip of yellow fabric.

"This time it happened in the Water Empire. Same yellow fabric. Whoever it was murdered a whole family, like last time. They were apparently close friends of the Water Lord," Prisma continues.

A sullen silence lays over the room and I know already that the news has spread. The usually vibrant dining hall is less busy than usual, and only faint murmurs of the gossip can be heard.

No one speaks much after that. Head Quill advises us that we are safe here at the Sanctum, and that travel to smaller towns like Pineside is now prohibited. I clear my mostly untouched dinner into the trash and walk alongside my friends up to dorm six. It isn't until I am alone in my room that the full weight of what has happened hits me.

Aspacia is supposed to be safe; the Empires are at peace after a hard-fought war a century ago. Whatever is happening now scares me senseless. The two attacks seem related, they were both going after emperors' families. Whoever did this has a calculated plan, and I don't want to know what their next move will be.

My father told me stories of the great war that occurred between the four Empires long before our time. Before the Royals gained their throne. Tales of darkness, raw power, and death plagued my nightmares as a child, but nevertheless I'm thankful my father told me about it.

The war caused the Empires to become even more resentful of each other, more intolerable of their differences. Aspacia has been in a hard-fought peace for centuries, but I can't help but think how much more peaceful things would be if the Empires actually mingled with one another.

At the moment, interactions between Empires are only becoming more tense. My mother and father faced the daily ridicule of their marriage between two Empires, and Pollo and I were born into a world that would always see us as products of a partnership that never should've been forged.

I trained with Pollo before he left us too for the Sanctum. I'm not sure how I will practice here, but I'm hoping all the new skills I will learn will make up for it. Besides, I'm confident I won't lose my combat skills; they are ingrained into my being as a survival instinct.

13

The day of the first round of the Royal Tournament comes around quicker than I'd like it to. I've spent countless hours alone in the forest, dodging the taunting eyes of other Keepers, to practice with my dagger. My footwork is getting better, and I am getting quicker and quicker each day.

I don't want to get too self-assured, but I've seen the way Keepers rely on their powers to get them what they want. I've got the element of surprise here—they see me as weak, as a stupid girl without power. But little do they know, their underestimation of me could be their downfall.

I dress in black pants and a sturdy, leather shirt—the outfit I'd always wear when training with my father. Tying up my boots, I slide my dagger into my waistband, hiding it under my clothes. Dexter and Prisma walk with me through the winding forest to the giant arena the Sanctum staff have spent all week setting up.

The tall, makeshift walls of the arena are lined with rows upon rows of seats, forming a semi-circle closed by the Westgrave River. The relentless water runs rapidly off to the side, splashing as it laps at the bank. In the middle of the semi-circle lies the riverbank—a field of grass and small bushes dotted with wildflowers. It's beautiful. You wouldn't think that two dozen Keepers were about to shed their blood here.

I realise with horror that this first round of the Tournament must be the one Head Windance hinted at in our first Abjuration class. Navari and I's practice a few weeks ago certainly hasn't helped my confidence to face one. But I can't back out now.

Dexter walks next to me as we proceed to the sign up stand below the amphitheatre seating. Prisma finds a spot in the stands and waves madly at us, trying to get Dexter and I to make note of where she's sitting.

When we make it to the front of the sign-up queue, Head Montero stands behind a desk with a clipboard and pen. I see there are already perhaps fifty Keeper's names on the list. I scrawl my own name down in my messy handwriting, pretending not to notice the displeased scowl on Head Montero's face. She warned me not to compete in the Tournament, but she made one, small mistake in doing so. I'll just add her to the list of people I'm trying to prove wrong.

Dexter jots his name down below mine and we are given some basic protective gear, although there isn't much the Sanctum can provide us that could block out the various elements the Keepers here wield. We walk over to the large group of Keepers in the waiting area at the furthest point from the river. Navari meets up with us, clad in a deep navy outfit that brings out the blue in her eyes. She gives me a greeting hug. Her weak smile hints that she is nervous, but I can't imagine she would ever admit it. She's like me in that respect—a tough outer shell.

But whereas hers is made of sunshine and warmth, mine is an unyielding brick wall.

I spot some more familiar faces amongst the crowd—Wex stands with a few of his Air Keeper friends, whilst Hayden stands alone silently at the back of the crowd. I watch as a group of girls shoot him longing, lustful looks as he pretends not to notice. The only giveaway is the half-smirk constantly plastered to his face.

I shudder at the thought of ever finding that attractive, like the increasing number of girls crooning their heads to him. How could such a self-centred, arrogant man possibly be capable of anything remotely close to caring for someone? It doesn't seem likely to me.

We hang around for what seems like an eternity, anticipating the events of the first round, when a loud, brassy horn blares across the arena. The Sanctum Heads sit upon four elaborate thrones, each designed to correspond to their elemental power. They watch on from the middle of the stands, whilst the crowd quietens down in anticipation. Once every single Keeper is silent, Head Vespertine rises from his seat, and the other three Heads follow suit.

"Welcome, students and staff. We are more than honoured to once again host the Royal Tournament on behalf of the royal family. We have produced some of the finest Royal Guards Aspacia has ever seen, who have the honour of serving and protecting those most important to our nation's continued survival and peace," Head Vespertine's voice booms across the arena, his face stern and shoulders squared. He wears an amber robe embroidered with Fire House's emblem—a swirling, detailed flame.

"There will be three rounds in total, with only one spot to be claimed by the worthiest of you at the end. Today's first round will be announced by Head Montero of Water House," he says.

Head Montero steps forward into the light of the blazing sun, high in the afternoon sky. "In round one, Keepers will demonstrate their ability to wield pure strength and power to overcome any threats that they may face as a Royal Guard. Today, you will be partnered up to fight and kill a Fideal. These creatures are pests, infesting the sparkling waters of our beloved Westgrave River. Do not fall for their beauty." She motions to the rapidly running river in the distance. "Only one of you from each pair may succeed and move on to the second round. Whoever delivers the fatal blow will be declared champions. If neither of the pair succeed in killing the Fideal, you will both be cut from the Tournament," Head Montero says.

She begins pairing us off, beginning with Navari and a short, stocky Fire Keeper named Devin. Navari shoots me a nervous glance.

"You can do this. You have all the practice you need." I wink at her, and she offers a nervous smile in return.

"Keepers at the ready," Head Montero motions for the two students to stand on a white line painted onto the grass in front of the crowd of Keepers. With a swish of her hand, she somehow summons a Fideal that begins poking its head out from the river.

It isn't until the creature is fully emerged that Head Montero shouts, "Begin!"

Navari immediately runs forward, seeming to have found her confidence, and closes the distance between her and the creature across the grassy field. Devin, on the other hand, steps back, his face contorted with fear. Navari reaches where the Fideal stands in no time, and whips her hands up in a fast motion. She throws an enormous wave of water from her palms into the creature.

Whilst she shoots the endless stream, she brings another blast straight from the river itself. The Fideal screams, its red locks drenched and crazed. Navari makes use of the distraction she's caused by running from behind the creature and ripping something from its neck.

She grins as the Fideal screams, staring at the object in Navari's hand. Navari relentlessly continues the stream of water straight into the Fideal's face, and I notice the creature is turning more blue than usual.

A few moments later, it collapses in a heap on the ground. Dead.

Devin is standing exactly where he was before Navari took her first shot. His eyes are glazed over, and it is clear he had no intention of even trying to win this challenge.

"We have our first champion! Well done, Miss Wickers. Smart move taking the Fideal's locket. For anyone who didn't do their research—" Head Montero eyes Devin, "—a Fideal's locket is what enables them to breathe underwater. Without it, they are helpless to an attack from a Water Keeper. Miss Wickers, I suggest you hold on to that locket. It may come in handy in the future."

Navari gazes at the black locket in her hands with an excited grin. I assume she's done some more research since our last run in with a Fideal. Probably because of what happened.

The next pair is called— two names I don't recognise. A lean girl and tall boy step forward and I listen as Head Montero counts down.

I stand in silence as I watch the girl turn her back on the Fideal for only a split second. I watch as the creature slices through her from behind, its venomous claws digging into her.

The next pair is about as lucky as the previous one— a Fire Keeper and an Air Keeper go head to head, and it ends with a stray fireball to the chest of one of the competitors.

I feel a single bead of sweat forming on my forehead and quickly wipe it away. I can't let the shock of this overcome me. Not yet.

"Next up. Let me see… Miss Arrington and Mr Radford."

I stand, and to my dismay, so does Hayden. He gives me a wink as he joins me on the white starting line. She motions to the water as she did before, and another Fideal appears.

"Don't hold back, butterfly." Hayden grins.

"You can count on it," I hiss through my teeth.

"Begin!" calls Head Montero.

I charge forward, ready to throw everything I have at this creature. Hayden goes to one side of it, and I the other. We stand facing each other with the Fideal in the middle. I hastily search my surroundings for anything that might be useful to me. I don't have the luxury of a huge surge of power like the other Keepers, and I sure as hell can't rely on whatever happened last time I took down a Fideal.

My eyes widen in delight as I spot a long length of rope, intended to close off a portion of the grassy field. I sprint over and yank it from the posts holding it up, and wrap the thick length of it in my hands. I hastily knot it into a loop and run straight towards the woman-like creature.

Before the Fideal notices what I am doing, I dart around it in circles, twisting it's legs in the rope. It stumbles for a moment, before Hayden shoots out a powerful hand and burns away the rope, leaving nothing but the now freed Fideal behind. My heart sinks in my chest. I should've known.

"Thanks, but I'm not gonna need that," he says.

I try to keep my frustration at bay—I've got to stay level headed. *Think, Reyna, think.* I curse myself for not going to the library and doing some reading on Fideal with Navari. My mind immediately flashes to my dagger, and the prince's words from that day: *Stab it in the heart.*

Whipping the blade out from my waistband, I charge at the Fideal, slashing with deadly precision as my father taught me. I manage to plunge the knife into the creature's chest. It lets out a horrid scream and tries to claw at me, but knowing what those talons can do, I swiftly deflect the attack.

Yes! I was so caught up searching for the things I didn't have last time that I forgot about what I do have. I forgot about how effective a simple knife can be in a fight.

In the chaos and the thrill of the moment, I forget about Hayden until his shadowy figure is in front of me. His amber eyes gleam in the sunlight as he kicks me down—hard. His foot lands exactly where the gashes lie on my leg and I scream out in pain.

I feel the stitches strain against his heavy weight as he steps on me, and I am powerless. The pain is searing, it is too great for me to possibly fight back. Gasps sound from the rows of seats watching over us.

"Sorry, Rey, nothing personal." He grins in a way that tells me it most definitely *is*. How can someone be so cruel?

Hayden looms over me and stands with one leg on either side of my body. He lifts his foot again and pins down my wrist with it, then pries my dagger from my hand. I hear Navari and a few others yell out in surprise, unable to believe what they're seeing. Hayden turns his back and faces the screaming Fideal, now lying on the ground in agony from the knife wound.

I can't stay down, I think to myself. I have to be strong. *Be strong. Get up, Reyna.* I grit my teeth as I attempt to stand, but I can feel the blood seeping from a broken stitch through my pants. I look to the hundred eyes on me, including the four Sanctum Heads. I will not let them see me weak. I will not cry.

Gritting my teeth, I manage to swing a leg under my body and hoist myself up. Limping over to where Hayden stands, my mind races in search of a solution. I'm about three steps away when he spins around and shoots a wall of fire between us that blazes so fiercely I'm worried my hair will singe.

"Just stop, butterfly. I've already won."

I watch through the flames as he plunges my dagger directly into the Fideal's heart. The creature collapses, black blood spilling out from the two stab marks in its chest.

Hayden reaches down and snatches the locket from its neck, not bothering to wait for Head Montero's permission. He stares at me through the wall of flame so intensely that I can't help but turn away.

I am ashamed. I should've won. What would my father say? I will my face into a blank slate, devoid of any emotion. I will not let him see me hurt. I will stand tall.

Head Montero clears her throat and raises her brows at Hayden. He twists his hand and the fire is extinguished, leaving a line of black between us. I return to my seat next to Navari, grimacing in pain.

"Are you all right? How did he know about your wound? I swear, I never told a soul," she says.

"Trust me, I'm just as confused as you are," I say.

I chew my lip anxiously as Hayden stares over at me, tossing the locket between his hands.

"Well… it seems we have a champion! Mr Rad—" Head Montero is cut off as Head Quill leans over and whispers something in her ear. She breathes out a heavy sigh, before nodding.

Head Quill walks down the steps, down from the makeshift amphitheatre, and onto the arena grounds. He walks purposefully over to where the Fideal's body lies. Head Quill stands over the once menacing creature, examining it closely.

What is he doing?

He returns to his seat next to Head Montero in the stands, again leaning over to whisper to her. Her stare remains planted on me, an icy cold glare that sends a shiver down my spine. Just hurry up and tell me I lost. Let this be over with.

"Upon inspecting the body, Head Quill has found two fatal wounds directly in the Fideal's heart. It would be impossible to tell which one caused the fatal blow." My mind flashes to when Hayden stabbed the creature. Was it already dead? I can't recall.

"Miss Arrington, Mr Radford… as the challenge was to deliver the fatal blow, you will both be proceeding to the next round of the tournament," Head Montero says, rolling her eyes as if she can't hide her annoyance. Head Quill watches me from the stands, his face impossible to read.

Head Montero continues the round, and by the end of it, only twenty Keepers have been crowned champions. The bodies of the twenty Fideal are stacked up in the corner of the area, dragged by begrudging Sanctum staff out of the way. Five silver coffins are brought to the middle of the arena for the bodies of the Keepers who weren't so lucky in their fights today.

I can't help but feel even more grateful that all I got from my run in with the Fideal last time were scratches. Being forced to stand here and watch as they killed innocent Keepers only trying to chase their dreams is beyond terrifying. My stomach churns and my eyes water, but I know better than to let my feelings show. I will hide them until I am alone once more, and then, only then, will I give myself a moment to feel my sorrow.

"Round two will proceed in two weeks' time. You will not be able to study for it, but be prepared to show the extent of your power in a gruelling challenge only the strongest of you will survive." Head Montero's eyes wander to the now occupied coffins in the centre of the arena.

I can't watch anymore. I focus on the river, lapping at the bank in the distance with its sparkling waves. Just let me get through this Tournament. Let me live through this.

The crowd begins to disperse as a horn similar to earlier signals the end of the first round. I examine the twenty Keepers, the champions, standing around me on the floor of the arena. Towering muscle, lean, slender waists, eyes full of unyielding power… Navari stands beside me, eyes still hovering over the bodies on the field.

Dexter stands tall on my other side, following Navari's stare with solemn, bottomless free eyes. His hand falls to his side, and slowly entwines with mine as we stand silently, in shock of the events of today. I can't help but rethink my choices—is it really worth it? If this is only the beginning… I can't imagine what is in store for us in round two.

Hayden sits quietly in the corner, as if he isn't the least bit disturbed. He is surrounded by four slim, beautiful Keepers with full lips and dark lashes. I snort in disgust and turn away, folding myself into Dexter's strong arms. I press my head against his chest, and try to distract myself from the horror by listening to the rhythm of his heart.

And when I move my head to look into his eyes, I could almost swear the pace quickens tenfold. He manages a small smile as stares down at me, his green eyes full of sorrow.

14

After dinner, we all head up to dorm six to get some rest. I return to my room, sit on my bed, and breathe. There, in the solo darkness of my own space, I allow a single tear to slide down my face. I let myself have a moment, just a moment, to feel the sting of Hayden's actions, the hurt of my leg. The terror of the fallen.

When the moment is over, I wipe my tears and draw a deep, long breath. That is the last time I will cry over Hayden. If I stay out of his way, if I don't provoke him… maybe I will be okay here. Maybe I stand a chance and will be able to live out my dream after all. If I think it enough times, maybe I will convince myself it is true.

Slowly and painfully removing my jeans, I find the wound is worse than expected. At least three of the stitches are broken, and blood has come seeping from it once again. I sigh, slipping carefully into my nightgown and into bed. I nearly forget I left my door ajar—an invitation—when there's a soft knock at the door.

"Come in," I reply, sitting up.

Dexter enters the room. "Crap, sorry, I didn't mean to wake you," he says.

"No, it's okay. What's up?"

"I just wanted to check on you. I noticed we didn't get our nightly chat yet."

I smile, thinking back to the strange way he stays up late, sitting in the chair by the window of dorm six's common area. He approaches the bed, sitting tentatively on the end of it. He pretends not to notice that he's left his door noticeably ajar the last three nights, and that I've just returned the gesture for him.

"I'm okay, just tired."

"No, you're not. Why didn't you tell me you were injured in the first place? I would've helped… I could've tried to—" He stops, his brow creased in frustration. His gaze falls to my legs, still covered by my sheets.

He moves slowly, taking the blanket from them and gazing upon the large, red gashes on my thigh. I partly curse my nightgown for not being longer, but yet, I partly don't. He reaches out and strokes a soft hand up my leg, avoiding the wound. Looking into my eyes, he slowly, but surely, moves his face closer to mine.

"I was supposed to watch out for you," he says, almost a whisper.

"What do you mean?" I ask, confused.

He takes a long, deep breath, staring at me with green eyes alive with the lantern light. "When you got here, when I learned you have no power… I told myself it was my job to protect you. To watch over you. You just seemed so helpless and… I had to do something to preserve the smile you gave me the first time I saw your face. To save the girl I knew I wouldn't ever want to take my eyes off of," he says slowly, now sitting back.

I stare at him with narrowed eyes. I feel my walls going up as they always do when someone tries to get close to me. When someone tries to get me to be vulnerable.

"Why?" My voice is a soft whisper against the wild night outside.

A storm is brewing, throwing the tree branches against my window and the pelting of rain almost sideways as it falls from the sky.

Dexter sweeps a stray strand of hair from my face, meeting my eyes with a soft glance. "Because, Reyna. Since you've arrived here… you're all I can think about. I even had dreams about you, damn it. Dreams that…" he begins, but seems to decide against it.

I'm glad for his pause because I jump in. "But what about Navari? You two are—"

"She's a great girl, that's for sure. But no, we were never together. Just having fun," he says quickly. If what he is saying is true…

"I don't even know you," I say, realising though I've spent a lot of time with this man, I know hardly anything about him.

"Ask me anything. I'm an open book," he says.

"Okay… where in the Earth Empire are you from?" I ask.

He pauses, fidgeting with his hands. "My father is Emperor Velynn of the Earth Empire."

I can't help but gasp audibly at what he's saying. Emperor Velynn is a soft, blond man who looks nothing like Dexter. He lives in his manor in the Earth Empire, rarely coming out or making public appearances.

"Honestly, I'm surprised you didn't know. I don't advertise it or anything, but you know how rumours are in this place." Yes, I know exactly how rumours are here. Thanks to them, everyone knows how powerless I am.

"Thankfully his traits didn't carry over to me," Dexter continues with a wink, but all I can manage is a blank stare.

My mind can't rest. Thoughts of what Dexter just told me, as well as memories from the first round of the Tournament swirl through my mind like a hurricane. Dexter must sense it too, because he moves his firm body so it's pushed up against me, and I lean my head on his broad shoulder.

"Reyna... if it's too much, you can always resign from the Tournament. No one will think any less of you," he purrs softly in my ear, his hand trailing through my hair.

That's easy for him to say. No one would ever question his power, his ability. His strength. He will never know what it's like to have your willpower be the only thing keeping you alive through a treacherous winter. He will never know the feeling of your body withering away from starvation, with your sheer determination being the only thing left that forces one foot in front of the other to go and find food.

"That's true, they wouldn't think less of me. But only because they don't think anything of me to begin with," I say, my gaze still plastered on the wall.

I've become used to the way other Keepers stare at me. I don't know why I thought it would be any different at the Sanctum. Their eyes are either full of pity or repulsion. Even my own father's eyes were constantly brimming with sorrow before he left us. But his sorrow wasn't for me—it was for him. For the ridicule he faced for being my father.

"They don't know you. You don't need to prove yourself to anyone —you're enough. They don't know that you are so much more than your power." Dexter pauses, and lifts my chin with a soft finger.

His deep green eyes meet mine, and it is like he is gazing into my very soul. He is right, they don't know me. But that is purposeful. I don't want anyone to get close enough to me to actually know me. The last time I let someone in, he kissed me on the cheek and abandoned me. I haven't seen my father in ten years.

"You are beautiful, Reyna. From the moment you walked into dorm six, you haven't left my mind. Not even once." My chest becomes as heavy as a brick. To think it is even possible for someone to find me beautiful… especially someone as kind as Dexter.

Without powers, I've never been considered beautiful by anyone. Even my own mother sighed as she brushed out my hair as a child. Her voice is a constant echo in my head: *Maybe one day you'll find your powers. Maybe one day you will be beautiful.* I begin to consider that maybe Dexter is right. Maybe I don't need to compete in the tournament—all it will do is show everyone the worst sides of myself. It will show them the things I don't have, instead of the things I do.

Dexter tilts my chin with his fingers, angling my face towards his until our lips are practically touching. And then, with a sudden rush of movement, they are.

He kisses me hard, pushing his soft lips against mine. I've never kissed anyone before—not like this. Dexter takes the lead, running his hands through my hair. A shiver runs down my spine. Is this what it's meant to feel like?

I follow his lead, matching his rhythm and pressing my hand to his chest. I feel my heart thumping, my pace quickening like a flood through my body. My breathing deepens, my lungs are filled with the sweet scent of him. Cedar and cherries.

I can feel him grinning beneath my lips as I gently tug on his. Eventually he pulls away, his eyes falling to the ground.

"What's wrong?" I ask.

"Nothing, I just… really like you, Reyna. I hope I'm not rushing you," he says.

"No. That was…" My thoughts flash back to the way we danced that night in Pineside, our bodies pressed together, the heat of the cramped bar… and I am instantly regretting not doing that sooner. "That was perfect."

He grins, then stands from the bed. Dexter reaches down and lifts me up, and I circle my hands around the back of his neck.

"I don't want you to get hurt. Why don't you resign from the tournament? I can go on and win it for us both. We could have a good life, you know."

I pause for a moment, considering the thought. But no. If this were to be my future… I won't resign myself to becoming a lonely woman waiting for her husband to be disbanded from the Royal Guard, withering away from grief like my mother. If Dexter wins, that is exactly what I'd become.

"I'll think about it," I say, knowing full well I've made up my mind about this, but not wanting to disappoint him.

He carries me over to the door, his hands clasping my thighs, and puts me down softly. He pushes me up against the cold, wooden surface, his lips meeting mine with another long, deep kiss.

"I've got to get some rest, it's getting late. But I'll see you tomorrow?" he says.

I nod, and open the door. He trails his hand through mine as he walks away.

I throw myself back on the bed, mind reeling with what Dexter has told me. Why didn't he tell me he's the emperor's son? He acts so... casual. I would've thought Head Quill would make a big deal out of it, like the Heads do with Prince Theon and Princess Vera. Unless Dexter asked them not to... I find myself caring a bit too much about the situation and curse myself for letting my walls down even the slightest bit.

Since my father left us, I'm the one who's had to be strong. Had to be there for my mother and even Pollo at times. And when the winter wind was too powerful for them to stand the chill, it was me who went and got firewood for our small, iron fireplace. Pollo would complain, and Mother was no use, so I gave up asking for help.

I know why I don't let anyone in, why I vowed to never have a family of my own. Why I won't give anyone my heart the way I gave it to my father. It will just get broken into a million pieces.

But Dexter... he is the sun on those freezing nights. He is there to kiss the broken parts of me until they don't hurt anymore.

I go to sleep eventually, even more confused than I was before my chat with Dexter.

<h1 style="text-align:center">15</h1>

It's a windy, miserable Saturday. I sit in my room, staring out at my view of the pine forest bordering the Sanctum. The second round of the tournament is in one week's time, and, to no one's surprise, my powers are still nowhere to be found.

My lack of power is only becoming more prominent in my classes. I've been itching to use whatever came out of me weeks ago with the Fideal, and believe me, I've tried. But nothing happens. No matter how long I sit in my room staring at my palm, *willing* the power to come out of me, I'm always left disappointed.

I need to go somewhere where I can practice for the Tournament. Somewhere alone. I pack a few supplies into my small, black backpack: my notebook, a sweatshirt, some food and water.

I reach Silver Lake an hour later, my breath heavy as I trek through the mud and rain covered earth. As I approach the water's edge, I gasp and nearly lose my footing. I can't believe this: Hayden is here. Again. He sits with his back to me, facing out to the water. He doesn't seem to care that he is being drenched by the rain. I begin to back away slowly.

"Too late, I already heard you," he calls out to me. So much for some time alone. I slowly step out from the shadowy tree line and approach him.

"Come to clear your head too?" He smirks at me.

"Clear it of what? All the annoying shit you do?" I really shouldn't provoke him, but I'm curious to know what makes him tick. He finally turns to face me, his expression strangely serious and complex before turning to a half smirk.

"Oh, so I annoy you, do I?" He smirks. "Butterfly, if only you knew. Come, sit," he beckons me over.

I know I said I was going to stay out of his way, to not remind him of his seemingly irrefutable love of annoying me, but I can't stop myself as my body moves towards him. I am too curious for my own good, and there's something about him… Something that deep down, I know I won't be able to stay away from.

He has a special talent for making my blood boil, my temper rage under my skin. I approach him cautiously, sitting down on a rocky spot a fair distance away from him. He notices my hesitancy and laughs.

"You have nothing to fear from me, Rey." He scoots his body closer to mine.

"I seem to recall differently," I say, thinking back to the Tournament.

"Did you ditch that guy yet?" he asks, his face suddenly an icy stare. I open my mouth to respond with some witty retort, but he cuts me off. "Nah, what do I care? You can mess around with whoever you want. Just don't say I didn't warn you."

I think back to Dexter last night, the things he told me about his family and who he truly is. A warm feeling takes over me when I think of him, like butterflies rising in my stomach. I realise I'm staring off into the distance when Hayden stands to leave.

"Wait," I say before I can stop myself. "Just wait. Please." I'm not sure why the words come out of my mouth, but I need to know one more thing before he goes.

As much as his presence makes me nervous, I feel certain I can make it to my knife before he can raise his hands to smite me down with fire. As he stands there looming above me, his wet hair sticks to his face. His white t-shirt is now see-through, but I pretend not to notice.

"Whose blood was on you the last time we were here?" I ask through the downpour, the question rolling off my tongue.

My lips quiver as I sit here in the pouring rain, staring up at this dark, handsome man who admittedly scares the crap out of me. He glances at me over his shoulder, a smirk forming at the corner of his mouth. Turning his body back towards me, he walks over and sits down, closer to me this time.

"Well, butterfly… that information would require something from you in return. A trade. A truth for a truth." His eyes dare me to refuse.

I weigh up my options. I don't have secrets to hide, but at the same time, I like that he doesn't know much about me. Every word I say to him feels like I'm giving him some sort of knowledge, and I'd rather keep him as a stranger… But I'm so desperately intrigued by this man that I need to know.

What are the odds he will ask the right questions that expose anything important anyway? Besides, I've always been a skilful liar.

"Fine, but you first," I agree.

"What do you think of the Prince of Aspacia?" he asks quizzically, his smug expression now difficult to read. I wasn't expecting him to ask *that* of all things.

"Prince Theon? Why do you—"

"The point was to answer the question, not ask me a new one," he says.

"Fine." I roll my eyes. "His reputation isn't stellar, and I've heard more about his extravagant social life than I'd like to know. But it's almost like there's another layer to him. He seems... complex," I answer, satisfied with my reply.

"Complex?" Hayden prompts.

"Hey, it's your turn to answer my question." I grin, and he lets out a huff of air. "Whose blood was it?" I repeat myself.

"You're going to have to be more specific, I have my fair share of blood on my hands—" I cut him off with a cold stare. "Fine," he says sternly, gazing out over the lake once more.

He pauses for a brief moment, his face a blank stare.

"It was Wex Brennan's," he finally says.

Wex's? I mean, I know he's an asshole, but I didn't think other guys saw it too. A memory flashes before my eyes of Wex in our first abjuration class this week. The dark shades he wore... I just assumed it was to cover a long night of drinking and overindulgence.

But if what Hayden says is true... I remember going to Air House that night to see Pollo. Wex was there in front of me less than two hours before I ran into Hayden at the lake the first time. Whatever had happened, Hayden must've made his move whilst I was walking to the lake.

"Why?" I demand.

"Nope, your question quota is up. Unless you're willing to trade another truth?" he taunts, eyeing my leg where under my jeans my wound from the Fideal is. Where he kicked me, ripping open the stitches. A shiver runs down my spine at the memory.

I consider his proposal, but no. I can't risk him asking the wrong questions for a second time. I've gotten my answers, and I'm definitely not going to get any practice in with Hayden here to watch. I pick up my bag and stand.

I glare at him, walking away through the rain, as he calls out to me:

"You are more dangerous than you know, butterfly. You don't need anyone."

After my run in with Hayden last night, I don't feel much like practicing. It is a Sunday afternoon, and the clouds still hug the sky with no intention of clearing anytime soon. Back in my room, I try to dig deep inside myself in search of whatever clawed its way to the top that day by the Westgrave river. I haven't felt anything like it since, and I haven't had many opportunities alone to try. It felt so right, so true, when the power was coursing through my veins. It clicked inside me, begging to be released. I just haven't found how to do that again. There's a light knock at my door, and Dexter pauses before coming inside.

"Hey," he says, staring directly at me. I've been avoiding him since last Saturday night; since I found out who he is.

Whenever I've seen him around in the common room or in class, I can't help but fear speaking to him. Because I know if I do, I will let him in. And I don't know if I can handle that kind of heartbreak again.

"You've been... distant lately. I just wanted to check you're okay." He stands tall in the doorway, running his hands through his short, dark locks. I nod and give a weak smile in return. I can't muster much more enthusiasm for him right now.

"I've just been busy with study and class," I reply.

"I—" he begins. "Look, Reyna... I know you're probably mad at me. I know I overstepped—"

"Don't begin to pretend to know how I feel," I say, the emotion finally rushing out of me, perhaps a bit too harshly.

Dexter seems taken aback, and I begin to regret speaking. Because now I'm going to have to explain myself.

"You're right. I have been avoiding you. But not for the reason you probably think. I wanted to talk to you so badly, to tell you I feel the same way... but I'm scared, Dexter. I can't be hurt again." The tears are rolling softly down my cheeks before I even realise I'm crying. "I just can't."

"Reyna, look at me." He moves so he is standing in front of me, holding my face in his hand. "I won't hurt you. You are safe with me. All I want to do is protect you."

"Do you promise?" I say in between a heavy sob. Damn it, it seems when there's a crack in the wall, the whole thing comes crumbling down.

"I promise you, Reyna," he says, and softly presses his lips against mine. He stares up at me, his green eyes full of love, and kisses me again, harder this time.

His hand still rests firmly on my leg, just below the Fideal scratch. He stares at me, his eyes a question in need of an answer. I watch the way his shirt clings to his chest with each steady breath he takes, and I begin to feel a warm flush in my cheeks when I realise I've been staring too long.

"I'll be back," he says.

What? Why's he leaving? I try to hide my disappointment but he is through the door and back in front of me before I can actually be sad about it.

"I believe this is rightfully yours." He reaches out his hand towards me, and in his palm lies a black locket. Just like the ones the Fideal wear.

"How did you… Is this…" I stumble on my words, unsure how Dexter obtained such a thing.

"Yes. I figured you deserved it more than he did."

"He… Hayden?" I ask.

He nods once in response.

"How did you get it from him?" I whisper, not wanting to know the answer to my own question.

"I could make up some lie and say I tracked him down and fought him for it. But no—he found me earlier and gave it to me. Asked me to give it to you."

"Was that all he said?"

"Yeah, and he didn't hang around long enough to let me ask any questions, either."

I glance down at the locket, still in his hand.

"Here." He motions for me to turn around, and he gently brushes my hair aside. Reaching over my shoulders, he hangs the pendant from my neck. It sits just below my throat, and I turn to the mirror to see it more clearly. A polished, black stone, with a small silver button on the side.

Dexter still sits behind me. I feel his breath as he leans in and softly brushes his lips on my neck, the slightest touch sending tingles down my spine. Looking up at him, I begin turning around when he pulls my waist against his, so I am now sitting in his lap.

"When you say you 'look out for me'… do you watch me all day long?" I whisper curiously, my breath heavy from his touch.

"No." He laughs softly into my hair. "Although I wish I could." He brings a gentle hand up to caress my cheek, and I feel my heart beating faster in my chest. "Just as much as I can. I've got to attend classes too, you know. My father thinks an emperor's son should *be dedicated to his education*. If I slip up even the slightest bit… I'll never hear the end of it. He will personally ensure I study until my eyes bleed." He laughs, and I smile tentatively, unsure whether he is serious or not.

"The Sanctum is safe, but obviously there are times when I should've been there for you and wasn't." He glances down to where the gash in my leg is hiding under my pants. He reaches out to softly trace it with his finger.

I wonder if things would've played out differently that day if he were there lurking in the shadows. If he were there, if he stopped the attack, I wouldn't be in this pain. I never would have had to endure Prince Theon's wandering eyes and menacing smile.

16

The following week passes me by in a blur. The gloomy weather seems as though it is here to stay, so there isn't a lot we can do besides hang out in our dorms.

I spent my Sunday cuddled up in dorm six's common room, sitting on the sofa by the fire with Dexter. We talked for hours about our lives before the Sanctum. He spoke about his father, and why he is so secretive. The other emperors splash their faces and personal business all over town, throwing their agendas down their citizen's throats. But Emperor Velynn feels that it is his duty to handle the politics and business of the Earth Empire, not to concern himself with frivolous things such as fame.

Dexter speaks of his father with admiration, and he seems like a man who takes care of his family. I note that Dexter didn't mention his mother or any siblings in the hours we talked for. There must not be anyone in Dexter's life besides his father, and I am too nervous to ask him about it.

I wasn't aware the emperor had any family, but I now realise that is just how he wanted it to be. Keeping business and personal affairs seems like a smart way to go, and my respect for the Earth Emperor only increases. I think of my mother back home in our small village. Before I left for the Sanctum, I made sure that the summer harvest would last until I could return again at the end of the year.

Students at the Sanctum are allowed to travel home for the winter break and certain holidays, but only if they can afford the cost of getting back home. And Pollo and I cannot. Luckily, our harvest was fruitful this summer, and there was even more food than my mother would need. I carefully pickled some of the vegetables so they would keep without going old, and sowed some new seeds into a small patch right outside our front door so it will be easy for Mother to pick the carrots when they grow. I somehow doubt she would even make it from her armchair in the living room most days, though, let alone out of the house at all.

Today marks two weeks since the Fideal attack, which unfortunately means I need to go see Prince Theon again to have my stitches removed. I've been dreading this ever since the last time I was there: he makes me uncomfortable. His kindness disgusts me—he wields it like a shield to hide the dark actions he is capable of. I can't help but remember the things my father told me about in his letters, and my cheeks flush with rage. His intentions are clear—he's stitched me up, and now I owe him. We both know it.

"Are you sure you don't want me to come? I've met the prince many times before because of my father. I know how to talk him down," Dexter asks me as I lay next to him in my bed. He has been by my side almost every minute of each day this week, and I can't help but feel grateful for his presence.

I don't want to let him fully in yet, my guard is definitely still up, but maybe… maybe this could actually be real.

"I'll be fine. And besides, I'm sure you'll be waiting for me outside, anyway," I say with a wink.

He softly tackles me back down onto the bed, putting his hand between my head and the pillow. I run my fingers through his dark hair, noticing the way his green eyes dance in the early morning light. I don't want Dexter to come with me to see the prince because I can't help the way my eyes narrow with rage when I see him. Or the way my skin feels like it will set alight with fury when he looks at me.

I don't want Dexter to see me that way—it could be taken wrong. Treason is something taken very seriously here in Aspacia, and I don't want Dexter to think I have any reason to not like Prince Theon. Especially as the emperor's son. I know he will be able to read me like a book—so no. I have to go alone.

I walk along the winding path from Earth House to the staff residences. About ten minutes later, I arrive at Prince Theon's door. Knocking twice, I wait for an answer. None comes. I knock again, and wait. I hear a voice from within approaching, and the door swings open. Prince Theon stands in front of me, wearing nothing but a thin white towel slung low on his hips.

"Hi," he says casually, as if he couldn't care less that he'd opened the door half naked.

"Who is it?" a female voice calls from within his room. Crap, I hadn't thought to check somehow if he had company.

"Umm. Hi. I can come back if this is a bad time," I say awkwardly.

"Nonsense. Come in," he commands.

I awkwardly shuffle inside, chewing my lip anxiously as I take a seat at his dining table. Footsteps approach from another room and I brace myself for a run in with the prince's latest conquest.

The girl turns the corner, and I realise I was wrong. Princess Vera smiles sweetly at me as if she were genuinely happy to see me.

"Is this Reyna?" She turns to her brother, swishing her soft brown hair over her shoulder. He nods in affirmation. "Theon's told me *alllll* about what happened last week with the Fideal. You poor thing!" Her voice is like honey, and I can't help but think how fitting it is for this gorgeous girl in front of me to be born a princess.

The way she moves is elegant yet she is sure of herself, and her features are delicate and kind. I glare at Theon, who promised not to tell a soul about what happened. Obviously he had, and my mind flashed with the memory of Hayden kicking me down during the Tournament, right where my wound is.

"Looks like someone couldn't keep his royal mouth shut," I say through gritted teeth at him, probably sounding as hostile as I feel.

Princess Vera's jaw drops at my nerve, but to my surprise, Theon's face lights up and he laughs. Which pisses me off even more.

"Can you just get this over with?" I scowl at him.

"Well, Reyna, you've actually come at the perfect time considering Vera is here. You should actually be thankful to me for telling her about your little... mishap the other day," he says pointedly.

"Why should I be—"

"I'm sure you've heard of Vera's celestial abilities," Theon says, gesturing to his sister.

I briefly recall my father mentioning that the princess could heal any wound with her power. I nod, annoyed that he's actually making a decent point here.

"Maybe if you drop the snarky attitude for a second, Vera might be able to help you out. You have to ask her nicely, though." He winks at me and my blood boils.

"Nonsense. She needn't ask. Come here." Vera gestures to the green velvet sofa I am all too familiar with from my last visit. I sit back on it, about to lift my long skirt to reveal the wound, when I remember the prince's presence.

Before I can say anything though, Vera swiftly shoos him away to a different room, giving me some privacy and a knowing smile.

"There you are. Now, show me what I'm working with," she says in her soft, sweet voice. I lift my skirt so my left thigh is revealed, showing the three deep gashes the Fideal left, along with the stitches—some broken—that Theon had given me seven days ago.

"Okay, okay… not as bad as I thought." She smiles. "I've seen a lot worse, I promise."

I wonder whether she has to use her gifts much. I can imagine that the unsteady peace between Empires has caused some conflicts she has had to tend to, and I feel a twinge of empathy for the princess. She must recognise the concern in my eyes, because she gives me a weak, saddened smile.

"This shouldn't hurt, but it might feel warm for a minute." She reaches and places her hand so it is hovering above the wound. The princess closes her eyes, and a bright, golden light spreads out across my leg. A warm, cheery sensation takes over me. Not just physically, but my mind is warmed by the light, also.

A moment later, the feeling is gone. I stare down at my leg and sure enough, it is as though there was never a wound there in the first place. The skin is as good as new, and perhaps even a bit brighter. I'm lost for words as I look up at the princess, who now sits across from me on the sofa, as if what she did was nothing special.

"I... thank you," I stumble, not sure how to thank someone for a gift so special.

"My pleasure. I cleared up the infection that was starting there, too. Why didn't you come sooner? Those broken stitches must've been a killer," she asks.

It is jarring to hear a Princess speak so casually. I definitely wasn't expecting her to be so friendly and likeable. Her words hit me: infection?

"I didn't know it was infected," I say.

"Oh, yeah, it was a nasty one. Probably because of the broken stitches and new bleeding. What happened? Did you bump it or something?"

"Yeah, something like that." She gives me a look that suggests she knows I'm hiding something, but thankfully doesn't prod into my business. I'm surprised she doesn't already know—she must not have been at the Tournament. Must not have seen Hayden's cruelty. I couldn't be bothered explaining the Hayden situation to her, and don't want to bring it up right now.

"You know, I don't usually freely offer this, but you seem like you might be so reckless as to need it. If you're ever in need of my services again, come straight to my dorm. It's above Theon's."

"Thank you, Princess," I say, grateful for her generosity.

"Call me Vera," she says. I guess the royal children have a thing for rejecting being called by their titles.

"Theon! You can come back now," she calls.

He emerges from the other room, seemingly annoyed to have been ushered away. "You know, sister, it's not like I haven't seen Reyna's legs before." He winks at me.

I shudder in disgust, and Vera scrunches her nose at him. It's funny seeing them together: they're exactly like regular siblings would be. I think of myself and Pollo, our playful fights but natural instinct to protect each other.

A part of me that I've pushed deep, deep down wishes that he was there to protect me when I was watching my mother wither away after he left for the Sanctum. But no, I decided long ago that those thoughts were selfish, and useless. Pollo deserves to be here, no matter the price.

"I better be going—thank you again, Princ—" I stop myself. "Thank you, Vera."

She smiles in return and walks me to the door whilst Prince Theon stays seated in the living room. "You know," she begins in a hushed whisper, "he talks about you often. Every time he does, his face lights up. Mostly with fury, yes, but also sometimes I think I see something more."

I stare at her in shock, not knowing that such a cruel man spent actual time speaking of me.

"Bye, Reyna. I'd say stay out of trouble, but I'm sure I'll see you again soon." She laughs, eyeing my leg.

I return the laugh, which admittedly slips out without my intention. I bid Vera goodbye, and head to the Central Gardens.

17

I meet Dexter in the Gardens, who no doubt has been trailing me since I left Theon's dorm. We lay next to each other on the rug, the wind a soft breeze against my cheeks. The sky is clear of clouds for once, and a large, black bird flies overhead.

Dexter rolls onto his side, smiling down at me with a soft expression. His hand trails lightly over my shoulder, his other resting at my waist.

"What's your family like?" he asks curiously.

I have to stop and think for a moment because they're all so different. "My brother is my best friend. We know each other like the back of our hands, and he is the most loyal person I've ever met. Even if he is a pain in the ass. I'd do anything for him." I smile, thinking of Pollo's teasing ways. I need to make an effort to see him more, but I know we are both busy with Sanctum life and classes.

"My father is a guard for King Zale. He writes me all the time, though. And was always teaching me new things about the farm. He taught me how to fight." I unsheathe my dagger from my hip. "He gave me this." Dexter eyes the blade as it shines in the sunlight.

"That's…" he begins, but decides against it. Whatever he was going to say seems important, because a dark wave comes over his features.

"What is it?" I press him, eager to know more. If he knows something about my knife…

"I've seen it before. In a library book. The swirling pattern, the dark handle… I'm sure it's the one. I can show you," he says.

I agree and we immediately head to the large library building behind Air House. I've never been there before, and when I arrive the sight of the sheer mass of books astounds me. I've never seen so many in my life, let alone the enormous stacks upon stacks of them madly populating the space.

Dexter leads me through rows of books that are all stacked on top of each other. Two smiling librarians greet us as we walk through the isles, their skin a light green colour. I look to Dexter and he explains.

"Nymphs. They offered up their service to the Sanctum after their home in the Earth Empire was invaded. After the Royal family forced out any creature that wasn't of Keeper descent," he says, and I gasp.

I thought we just didn't have many creatures like that in my Empire —not that they were forced away. I wonder if that has anything to do with the growing prejudices within the Empires regarding splitting up the Keepers based on ability. If a hatred so large was left to run rampant across Aspacia… A shudder runs down my spine.

The enormous building is straight out of a dream: the wooden banisters on the roof are painted with scenes from Keeper history, showing each Empire as representations in swirling colour. I look up at the green, flowing design high above me, showing the first Emperor of the Earth, his power swirling around him in a green haze.

I've heard the stories of how centuries ago, Aspacia was united. Keepers lived amongst each other, no matter what their abilities were. They were at peace, not having to constantly be in fear of being invaded, or worse—falling in love with someone of the opposite ability. The intricate paintings above are truly beautiful.

Finally, we stop in front of a stack labelled *SWORDS OF ASPACIAN HISTORY*. Dexter pauses, and I wonder how anyone would be able to select a book from this library without the stack above it toppling over. The books pile high on top of each other, and if one were removed it would surely come crashing down.

My thoughts are answered, though, as Dexter swishes his hand, and the stack parts exactly where he intends it to. He holds the books up with whatever spell he has used, and pulls out a black, hardcover book from under them. The rest of the stack falls back into place, as if nothing were taken from within.

"Here," he says, passing the book to me.

I take it, and immediately my hands are pulled to the floor. Okay, it is a lot heavier than I expected. Dexter chuckles and helps me up, and we place the book on a small reading table nearby. He sits down on a sturdy, wooden chair, and scoops me into his lap. He circles his strong arms around my waist as I slide the book in front of us.

I notice that the lantern light changes to green as we sit down. Maybe to show the space is occupied? Or to show we are Earth Keepers? I'm not sure, but Dexter doesn't seem to notice or care.

I flick the book open to the contents page and search in the dim green light, although I'm not sure exactly what for.

"Shadow Reaver," Dexter says, and his eyes darken.

I turn to the page titled Shadow Reaver, and find an exact replica of my dagger painted into the book before me. It's dark handle engraved with swirling designs, with an intricate lily flower stamped into the silvery metal blade.

This makes no sense. Where would my father have gotten my dagger? I read the page and find it was previously wielded by an Aspacian Prince—Prince Jordan. He was the son of the king who, at the time, led the war that ultimately divided Aspacia into its four Empires.

I reach down and feel my blade sing beneath my touch. The blade was lost in the war, but rumour has it that it will one day be returned to its land of making.

"What does this mean?" I turn to Dexter, hopeful he has some answers, but he only shrugs.

"Prince Jordan betrayed his father's command in the War for Aspacia. The king wanted him to lead a battle troupe into lands occupied by soldier's families, and the prince committed regicide because of it. He killed his own father to save hundreds of innocents," he says solemnly.

I look at my blade, and wonder if this small dagger was used to kill a King. If something so small could do something so mighty, how did it end up in my hands?

I sneak out later that evening to try and finally get some alone time to try and find my powers once more, whatever they may be. I need to know what I am, what I can do. If I am worthy of my place here at the Sanctum, and ultimately, as a Royal Guard.

I decide against going to the Silver Lake again—I don't want to risk running into a certain Fire Keeper there for the third time. Instead, I decide on the Blackwood Forest. It should be dark enough by the time I get there that no one will bother me. I pack a few things into my bag and swing the window open. I don't want Dexter following me tonight—things could get messy if other people are there in my way.

The window looks out across the Sanctum, and I can see the sun setting behind the ocean in the distance. I step carefully over the ledge, my toes only just fitting on the small step beyond the window.

Quietly closing the window behind me, I shimmy along the ledge until I can go no further then grab onto the wooden lattice clinging to the mossy bricks. The thick vines that have grown upon the lattice make it easy to climb down the remaining five stories, though I am sure not to make a sound.

If the wrong person glanced out their window at the exact moment I pass… they'd be sure to report me to Head Quill for breaking the Sanctum's rule number one: *no one out after nine o'clock*. When my feet silently touch the dirt below, I jog over to the forest entrance, saying a silent thanks for making it down the six story building in one piece. A thanks to my father, for teaching me such useful skills, even if it were years ago.

I stick to the shadows, making sure I'm not seen. Breaking rules isn't high on my agenda, and I'm sure the Sanctum Heads won't be pleased by a first year running off into the woods at night to practice unsanctioned magic.

I make my way deep into the woods, until I am surrounded by nothing but tall trees and the onset of darkness quickly falling over the forest.

I stand in the middle of a small clearing, and begin. Raising my hand, I try to wrap only the smallest tendril of my power around my mind. I envision the black smoke I saw come out of my palm the other day. It swims in my mind, and will it into existence and… nothing.

What am I doing wrong? I was making progress since the day it happened, but now I'm thinking it is the exact opposite. Perhaps in that moment I was so desperate, so terrified by the Fideal about to drag Navari and I to our deaths, that I somehow used up the dusty remains of whatever power I once had. But no. I can't give up. Not when this means so much to me and my family.

I try again, holding my palms out. I think back to how Prisma sprouted the white lily out of her hand that day in Pineside at the bar. She did it so easily, as if it were nothing more than a passing thought.

I concentrate with all my might, visualising the small flower, and close my eyes. When I open them, I'm not exactly surprised to see the exact same result. Nothing.

Why is this so difficult? I begin to question myself. Do I even belong here at the Sanctum?

If I can't find my powers, there is no way I will ever be a royal guard. The palace would never want someone so unreliable and weak guarding the royal family. I sit down on the lush grass with a thud, crossing my legs and holding my head in my hands.

I sit there for a while, trying to decipher what I could possibly do in this world without powers. Maybe I am doomed to work on my family's small farm forever, using only my hands to labour away. But I can't resign myself to such a mundane life. I won't allow it, when my dreams are so big.

A new wave of motivation rushes over me, almost like a warmth the stems from my very core. When I lift my head from my hands, the grass all around me is covered with white lilies.

They spread through the entire stretch of the forest floor around me, going on as far as my eyes can see and into the dimming light. They glow under the light of the moon, now rising in the sky over the Sanctum. I almost scream in excitement. I jump into the air and hold my hands over my mouth.

Something catches my eye in the dark corner of the forest to my right. I turn my head, trying to track down whoever or whatever is there. I hear a twig snap to my left this time, and I jump to my feet.

Every single one of Pollo's warnings crashes into me about the creatures that lurk in the forests here at the Sanctum. My palms begin to sweat, and my heartbeat quickens. I hope whatever is hunting me in the shadows can't hear the thumping in my chest.

Squinting into the darkness, I watch as a shadowy figure slowly approaches from the shadows. It emerges slowly and is difficult to keep a track of, as if it is made of the darkness itself. My hand quickly moves to my dagger, tucked into my waistband as always, and I rush behind a tree. A few moments pass by, when a chilling, gravelly voice calls out to me.

"Reyna Arrington, reveal yourself. You face no harm if you do as I say," the voice says, sending a shiver down my spine. There is absolutely no way I am giving away my position to whatever lurks in the shadows.

"I know you're there, cowardly hiding behind that tree. Reveal yourself, girl, or I will level the forest to find you," the haunting voice continues, and I decide not to question its ability to do so.

If power were carried in voices, this one could destroy the whole world. It doesn't sound human; its tone is too low, and its words are somehow carried by the shadows themselves over to me.

The forest is now fully darkened, and the moon sits in the middle of the sky above. I know I can't hide here forever, I will have to move eventually when the grace of darkness leaves the sky. If I'm going to make a move, I'd prefer it to be on my own terms. I reluctantly step out from behind the tree, dagger at the ready by my side. My knuckles whiten on its hilt as I step forward, into view of the creature. I can see it now, only a few steps away from me, under the light of the moon.

"What… what are you?" I stammer out, trying to remain as calm as possible in its foreign presence.

Every ounce of my effort is going into keeping my shoulders squared and my back straight. I will not let it see me cower, no matter how much I feel like it. It looks as though it is made of the shadows themselves: it wears a dark, hooded cape, its skin wrinkled and grey. The creature's bony fingers extend towards me, beckoning me forward.

"Come here, child. Let me see you." Its voice is something out of a nightmare, and I won't soon be forgetting the way it seems to only kiss the ground with its feet, as if it were floating on the darkness surrounding it. I step forward, in an attempt to seem confident and calm. I am not.

"Hello, darkness," the voice says, and I instantly recognise the words from my evocation class. It was what the spirit called out to me using the Ouija board.

"I am the Nightbrood, sentinel of the Shadow Isles. I have been summoned to you, Reyna, daughter of the Earth," it continues, the gravelly voice floats over to me, mere steps away now from the creature.

"Why?" I will my voice to sound calm, hiding the sheer terror I am feeling beneath it. The Nightbrood looks ancient, and speaks as if it were from another time entirely.

"It is your birthright. Your destiny." My mind travels back to Head Quill speaking of the dark forces at the Sanctum—perhaps this dark creature has found a girl alone in the forest in the dead of night to feast upon.

"How can I trust a thing you say?" I question the creature, my voice becoming steadier with each word. It begins to speak, but stops when it's sullen eyes land on my arm.

"You carry the mark, from the Prophecy of the Void." The Nightbrood sounds shocked as it squints at my arm, where the small, circular birthmark sits upon my skin on the inside of my wrist. It is made of two circles overlapping, in an unnaturally round curve.

Before I can stop it, the Nightbrood reaches out and touches it with a long, spindly finger. As soon as it comes into contact, my birthmark lights up as if it were somehow awakened by the touch. One of the circles glows as if it were made of light, and the other sings with darkness—as if it had been solidly tattooed with one touch.

Dark and light, together in one perfect circle. I snatch my arm back, shocked by the glowing mark. I've had it all my life, but never thought much of it. Who would? Although, my mother has always noted how strange it is to have such a perfect circle naturally born onto my skin.

I stare at the creature, its words rushing through my mind as I try to make sense of them.

"The prophecy of what?" I ask, one of the many questions I have.

"The Prophecy of the Void," the Nightbrood repeats. "My lady won't be pleased..." it says, and although it is difficult to read its expression, for a moment I swear I see a glimpse of fear cross its dark features.

"Centuries ago, a prophecy was written that would shape the world as we know it." The creature pulls a yellow scroll out of the folds of its dark cloak and begins to read from it. "*The end of a reign will be caused by a girl of the same name. Shadows lurk beneath her skin, a halved circle upon it; she is the ruler of the shadows. She is darkness itself.*"

"A girl of the same name... What does that mean?" I murmur.

"I think you already know. Your powers are missing, yes? They have been dormant since you were born. Have they arisen here? Being exposed to such a significant site, with such magic surrounding you... Have they?" the Nightbrood asks.

I nod reluctantly. "Once," I say, thinking back to the shadowy wisps that left my hands that day.

It simply nods, gesturing for me to continue unravelling the story when it raises one greying eyebrow.

I think the words from the Prophecy over in my head. *The end of a reign, a girl of the same name...*

"Reyna," my own name escapes my lips, and the Nightbrood smiles.

"I'm glad to see you have your wits about you. You're going to need them," it says. "You are the key, Reyna Arrington, the key to end all wars. If you can handle the tests in front of you, you will rise."

"What tests?" I ask, my mind spinning. I feel lightheaded. The Nightbrood avoids my question and continues.

"You need to come here, to the Shadow Isles. Complete the Rising and unlock your full power. As for the Prophecy of Shadows... do not mention it to a single soul, especially in the Shadow Isles. It is not safe." The Nightbrood is so close to me now that I could reach out and touch it. Not that I'm going to. I nod.

"Swear it, darkness, swear it to me. You will not whisper one word of what you feel when you undertake the Rising Ceremony when you arrive in the Isles to anyone. Otherwise I will leave you here in this godforsaken Sanctum of hopeless dreams to rot, never knowing your true destiny," it says.

I can't help but feel that this is the moment I've been waiting for my whole life. The moment I finally find out who I am truly supposed to be. There must be more to this life than working on the farm until I'm skin and bones. So I nod once more, and swear myself into the silence the Nightbrood requests.

"I'm sure you can figure out a means of transport. Come alone, darkness. As soon as you can. We are waiting for you." The creature immediately leaps upwards into the sky as dark as itself, and flies away on the set of enormous, magnificent wings once tucked in at its back.

One particular part of the Nightbrood's words are left ringing in my head.

We are waiting for you.

159

Golden as the Night

18

The Shadow Isles are a small, deserted series of islands off the North West coast of Aspacia. They only consist of barren, desolate landscape and tall, unforgiving cliffs. I've read in textbooks that those who dare to sail there, never return. I shudder, my mind rushing with all the possible ends I might meet if I go.

I lie awake back in my room, tossing up whether to listen to the Nightbrood or not. My body is tangled in my sheets as I toss and turn, unable to even close my eyes. If I do travel to the Shadow Isles, the consequences could be worse than death, if the dark rumours of the Isles are true.

But if I don't go, I may never fulfil the Prophecy of the Void, and may never know my true power. I think back to my practice before the Nightbrood came and interrupted. I have no power, no clear path, and no true home. I will always be an outcast in the Earth Empire—the worthless girl who never found her abilities. I will never be able to work as a Royal Guard if I don't learn whatever I can about the shadows inside of me.

So, in the darkness of my dorm room, I decide that I must travel to the Shadow Isles and face whatever lies there waiting for me.

The only way I know of that could possibly transport me across the sea to the Isles is travelling by whirlwind, just as Prisma and I did when we went into Pineside. Luckily, I know an Air Keeper that would do anything for me, and hopefully won't ask too many questions about where I'm going.

I arrive at Air House bright and early the next morning, banging on the door relentlessly until I am let in. A small, brunette man answers the door.

"Which room is Pollo in?" I ask, making it clear I am in a rush.

"Umm, you really shouldn't be—" he begins, but I shoot him an unnerving look that clearly carries as much weight as I intend.

"Four. He's in dorm four. Fourth floor, second room on the right."

I smile sweetly at the boy, as if I hadn't just intimidated my way in. I step past him and make my way up the stairs. I hear hateful whispers of Air Keepers as they pass me. *"Don't leave any dirty marks behind, Earthie" and "I smell rotting fruit."* I am used to the remarks, but that doesn't stop me from staring them down as they pass. I can't help but wonder what it would be like if Aspacia were united once more, as it was centuries ago. Would there still be so much prejudice between Empires?

When I reach Pollo's room, I don't bother knocking and head straight inside. I immediately regret it. I realise my mistake when a muffled voice yells at me before I see two bodies on the bed, one hiding away under the covers.

The other one sits up, daring me to stare... shit, this isn't even Pollo's room. I immediately lurch myself back out the door, slamming it behind me. Crap! What was I thinking? I curse the boy who gave me inaccurate directions. I press my body to the wall outside the room, completely embarrassed by what just happened.

Moments later, Wex emerges from the room wearing a loose hanging robe, shutting the door behind him.

"Hey, Rey. I knew you'd make your way back to me eventually. Would you like to join us?" He winks at me mockingly, and I shoot him a look of disgust.

"I'd rather burn in the pits of the Fire Empire. Where is Pollo's room?" I scowl.

"Aw, little sis needs her brother. What for, babe?" His eyes light up as he taunts me, clearly enjoying my state of confusion.

"None of your goddamn business," I snap. I go to walk away and find someone with accurate directions this time, but Wex steps in front of me and blocks my path.

He grabs me by the arm, hard, jarring me back against the wall. "I said," he continues, "what for Earthie?" He just isn't going to let this go, is he?

"I need him to transport me somewhere," I reply, not giving him the whole truth.

"Oh yeah? Well, I've got bad news for you, Rey. Pollo sucks at traveling by whirlwind. He's flunked every class since our first year. I, on the other hand, am an expert." He inspects his knuckles, as if that's something impressive.

I consider his proposal for a brief moment. If I got Wex to do this for me, I wouldn't have to endure all the questions Pollo is bound to ask me. And by the sounds of it, I might not even end up in the Shadow

Isles if Pollo tries to do it. I'd rather not end up whirled to the ends of the country, stranded in the middle of the ocean.

"Why would you help me?" I ask, curious to see what kind of ridiculous price he is expecting me to pay.

"A date. A nice one, too. Dinner at a restaurant. One time offer, no returns, exchanges or rain checks. And I want it *before* I whirl you." His purple eyes smile at me smugly, fully aware of how irritating he is. I weigh up his offer.

"Your friend in your room isn't enough company for you?" I taunt, and he shoots me a glare of daggers. "Okay fine. One date in exchange for one whirlwind, with no questions asked."

"Deal." He holds his hand out for me to shake, but when I place my hand in his, he brings it to his mouth and plants a disgusting, sloppy kiss on the back of it.

"I'll pick you up at seven tomorrow night. Wear something… purple." He winks at me, and I make a note not to wear anything even remotely close to the colour. He finally releases my arm, and heads back into his room to resume what I interrupted. I make a swift exit before I hear anything I don't want to.

"I don't think you two should go alone," Dexter says.

I went to find him as soon as I made the deal with Wex. Dexter sits in the Earth House common area, laid back in an armchair. He pulls me onto him, so one of my knees is on either side of him. He can't follow me tonight, wherever Wex takes us. I don't want anyone knowing what I intend to do, especially Dexter. I know he will try and stop me. And besides, I am more than capable of protecting myself from the revolting Air Keeper.

"We'll be fine, I promise." I told him Navari and I will be hanging out at the library tomorrow to study for our abjuration exam, then I'll be staying at hers for the night. He seems to buy it.

"I don't know… I suppose I have some studying to get done, too," Dexter says, and I excitedly see that I'm winning this.

"Great! We will just have to make up for lost time when I'm back." I wink at him, and he pulls me in for a long, slow kiss. His lips taste like honey; he is a ray of light in all the confusion before me.

"Ugh, get a room, you two," Prisma calls out to us, making her way over to the sitting area.

I pull away, but Dexter pulls me back in and I can't suppress my giggle. Prisma makes a gagging noise, and when we finally pull away, Dexter shoots her a playful glare.

"So, Reyna," Prisma says, keen to change the topic. "How's the power going?" I give her a look that is all the answer she needs: it's not 'going' at all.

"By the way, when did this happen?" Prisma says, waggling her finger at Dexter and I.

"She couldn't resist me." Dexter winks, and I slap him playfully on the knee.

"Honestly, it just sort of happened," I say, and Prisma sticks out her tongue in disgust. I can tell she is happy for me though. Her eyes smile through her teasing, and she is always giving me encouraging looks when she thinks no one else is watching.

"We better go," Prisma says, eyeing her watch.

I stand, Dexter giving me a quick peck on the forehead, and the two of us make our way to divination class across campus at the Academy.

Last week in divination, Head Montero taught us how to read tea leaves. This week, she has us focusing on reading runes to answer questions and show us our future paths. I sit beside Prisma, my small bag of rune stones in front of me.

"Remember, to correctly wield the meaning of the runes, you need to think of a question and focus on finding an answer," Head Montero says, her blue eyes shining in the golden academy light. "When you are ready, think of a question you'd like to know, reach into your bag, and draw out one stone. We will work up to drawing out more."

I'm not sure what to ask when I have so many different questions running through my mind. I watch as Prisma digs into her bag, pulls out a rune, and grins cheerfully.

"I knew it!" she exclaims.

"What did you ask?"

"When will I see Sapphira next? I got 'Nyedis'—the night stone. So maybe tonight? I suppose it could mean any night..." She sighs, staring off into the distance.

I get a feeling that this is a load of crap, but I try to keep an open mind. I dig into the bag in front of me. *What do I need to bring to the Shadow Isles?* I think the question over and over in my mind until I feel a stone that is warmer than the rest. Plucking it from the bag, I see it is the 'Üruz'. Strength. If I am to believe the runes, any hope that this would somehow be an easy mission is gone.

It's exactly seven o'clock on Saturday night and I stand by Navari's dorm room door, tapping my foot. She's out at a party, and I didn't want anyone to see the likes of Wex Brennan showing up on my own doorstep. I don't know why I was expecting him to be on time, but I stand here annoyed nonetheless. I put on a pair of black jeans and a simple, black top—the least purple outfit I could think of, and not too fancy that he will get the wrong idea. I'm going on this date purely to get what I want out of Wex—nothing else.

A few moments later there's a loud knock at my door. I unlatch the lock I installed—a very hasty job, but it will do—and swing the door open.

"Hey, babe." Wex stands in the doorway, looking me up and down. "That's not the outfit I requested." He stares at me, eyes lingering on my body in all the spots they shouldn't be. I glare at him and push through the doorway, keen for this night to be over with.

"Where are we going?" I ask.

"I thought I'd take the liberty of showing you a taste of what my whirlwinds can do. We're going to Pineside."

My mind rushes to the memory of Head Quill forbidding us to travel beyond the Sanctum due to the increasing attacks between the Empires.

Wex must see the concern on my face, because he says, "Don't worry, Reyna. I won't let anything bad happen to you."

I roll my eyes. It's just like Wex to be that cocky, though, so his words are expectedly stupid.

We stand in dorm six's common area, and I pray no one else emerges from their rooms and sees me with him. Especially Dexter, who I lied to about being at Navari's. He is due to return home from his study group at any moment.

"Let's just get this over with," I say, my voice clearly annoyed.

Wex grins, takes my palm in his, and we are off. Somehow, being indoors wasn't an issue for his whirlwind. It feels stronger, less chaotic than Eric's—the Air Keeper Prisma talked into transporting us last time. The air rushes around me in a gentle hum rather than a disastrous crash of wind as Wex and I fly through the air.

We soar over the Sanctum, and I see the Silver Lake, the tall pines of the Blackwood Forest, and the Westgrave River cutting through the landscape. The night air is chilly against my bare arms, but the feeling only brings me joy. I can't believe things like this actually exist, and that Air Keepers can just take off whenever they like.

I bet Pollo curses himself for not being able to do this. Wex trails his eyes over me, and a flicker of joy crosses his stern gaze. I truly hope Dexter isn't somehow 'watching over me', because the way Wex's hand holds me tight against his firm body isn't something I imagine he'd be okay with.

We eventually drift down to a small patch of grass outside Pineside. The lights of the city are astonishing in the darkness of the night: the small town only grows more beautiful. Wex tries to take my hand again, but I snatch mine away.

"That was fine for the flight, but don't get the wrong idea. I'm only here because I have to be," I snap at him.

"That's fine, babe. But I have to warn you, you'll want my fingers all over you before the night's end." I shudder in disgust at the thought of a man like Wex ever touching my skin. Part of me wishes I'd asked Dexter to come along tonight, after all, but I quickly shake the thought away when I remember what that would mean. I can't have him knowing about the Shadow Isles, the Nightbrood, the Prophecy… any of it.

We walk the streets of Pineside in silence. Wex attempts to make friendly conversation, but I refuse to let him talk me into complacency. We stop in front of a romantic looking restaurant with an exuberant variety of scents wafting from its door.

"You know, I was thinking something more casual would—"

"Don't be silly. I doubt you'll ever agree to a date with me again, especially if I take you to some casual diner joint. I plan on making the most of our time together," he says, and I sigh. This is going to be a long night. I swing my small bag filled with only the most essential supplies over my shoulder and head into the restaurant.

We are welcomed by a small, female elf with reddish-brown hair and a friendly, sharp-toothed smile. She directs us to a booth in a quiet corner of the restaurant, and I sit on one side. To my annoyance, Dexter slides in right next to me.

"There's plenty of space over there." I motion to the other side of the table.

"Trust me, babe, I know. But what's the point of the booth then?" He winks at me, and I busy myself with the menu. The smiling elf comes back, and I order a plate of meatballs. Wex gets the pizza.

"Why did you ask me on a date? Surely there's something more desirable you could've asked for. Money? Study notes?" I pause, then snakily add, motioning to his clothing, "Fashion tips?"

He smirks across at me, daring me to continue my string of insults. His eyes suddenly darken, his smirk increasingly cunning. "You know, Reyna, I can't think of anything I'd prefer than this date. I love watching you squirm whenever I mention anything even the slightest bit crude. It's hilarious."

"That is not even one bit true," I huff in annoyance. The waiter brings our meals, and I am glad for the distraction. But it doesn't work. Wex pushes his pizza to the side and continues.

"Sure, I could've asked for some dirt on your brother, or maybe even for some suggestive pictures of you to flash around campus." He smirks, and I curse myself as my cheeks go bright pink. I take several deep sips from my wine, hoping he will leave the topic alone.

"See, there you go again. I can't even mention a photo of your own body and you get flustered. I bet you've never even seen a man naked before, let alone done… other things." He trails his hand up my arm that's resting on the table.

I nudge him away and attempt to scoot to the furthest spot on the seat possible. He turns to me and stares me dead in the eyes. His face has become serious, his teasing smile from seconds ago gone.

"You're practically begging to be touched, babe." He stares me down, eyes darkening as he moves them across my body.

I busy myself with my meatballs, not wanting to engage in this conversation with him. I don't understand how my kind, caring brother can be friends with him, when Wex is the exact opposite. He puts a finger under my chin, raising my face in line with his. I glare at him, trying to muster as much courage as I can in this moment, but I am beginning to feel dizzy. He slides his hand into my lap, caressing my thigh, moving higher and higher…

"Stop," I command, but he doesn't listen. My hand goes to my dagger, but to my horror, it's not there. My head feels heavy, like a fog has come over my mind.

"Looking for this?" Wex grins as he removes my dagger from his own waistband, placing it on the table in front of him. "I snagged it on the ride here. I've got to say, I'm surprised you have the guts to carry it. You need to be careful with sharp objects, little girl. The damage you could accidentally do with that..." Wex grins at me, and I feel as though the walls are caving in.

My eyes are heavy, and I can't even muster a scream. He continues moving his hand higher, until it can't go up any more. He brings his other hand over, pinning down my wrists as I attempt to struggle against him. I stare around frantically, hoping someone will see, but no one does. The quiet corner of the restaurant is too dark for anyone to notice.

I realise with horror that Wex planned this. He must've asked for this exact table, to do these exact, sick things to me. What did he do to me?

I muster all the strength I can manage, and ram my head into his the way my father taught me. It hurts, but not as much as it hurts him.

"You're going to regret tha—" He is cut off by a loud crack.

I manage to turn my head and realise the noise came from a chair being thrown across the room. It was in the path of the man furiously storming towards us. A man who… Hayden.

"What the fuck did you do to her?" he demands, my eyelids failing me as I begin to lose consciousness. He grabs Wex by his shirt, ripping him from the booth next to me. Wex eyes my hand instinctively as I take a deep sip of wine.

"You fucking spiked her drink?" Hayden snatches my glass from me and throws the contents onto the ground.

I watch drearily as he slams a hard fist straight into Wex's face, sending him reeling backwards. Wex sends a powerful rush of air towards him, but Hayden is faster. He dodges the blast, and sets fire to the shirt on Wex's back, causing him to run frantically into the men's bathrooms in search of water. Whatever Wex put in my drink has taken full effect, and I can no longer keep my eyes open. It feels as though someone has given me a safe, warm space inside my head to rest for a while.

"Reyna, stay awake. Stay with me, butterfly. You're all right. You're safe. It's okay—" The last thing I see before the world fades to black is amber eyes staring down at me, and a firm hand keeping my head up.

19

"Hey, take it easy," a soft, male voice echoes down to me, and I realise I've been asleep. I open my eyes with a jolt, and find Pollo's caring face looming over me. I sit up in a panic.

"Whoa, whoa. Reyna. Just sit," he says, resting a hand on my shoulder.

I take in my surroundings: I'm sitting on a pink velvet sofa, identical to the one in the prince's dorm room. As I scan the room, I see another figure in the kitchen, scrubbing away at something in the sink.

"Vera?" I manage to whisper, and she smiles at me as she fills a teapot with water.

"I knew I'd be seeing you again, but this soon? I don't know whether I'm happy to see you or feel bad that you're here," she says, her soft voice carrying from over in the kitchen.

I guess this is her dorm then. But why am I here? There's a knock at the door, and Hayden lets himself in without waiting for a response. He eyes me on the sofa, his gaze intense and difficult to read.

"I can't believe Wex did that to you. I'm so sorry, Rey. I should've known, I should've been there," Pollo says, his eyes full of concern.

I remember bits and pieces of the events from last night. The restaurant, the drink, Wex's hands… and Hayden madly destroying the restaurant to reach me.

"How long have I been asleep?" The windows let in bright, sunny light from the forest outside.

"Nearly three days. It's Tuesday Morning," Pollo says with pity in his eyes.

Three days? The question lights my eyes in fury. That means…

"The Tournament." I hang my head in my hands, massaging my temples. I've missed the second round. Pollo places a heavy hand on my shoulder, a gesture filled with empathy and sorrow.

Wex had not only betrayed my trust and my permission, he had stolen any chance of my future being bright. I rise, sitting on the sofa and staring off into the distance, a blank gaze crossing my features. The realisation hits me like a runaway train: I've lost my shot at becoming a Royal Guard.

My body feels as though every last drop of energy has been drained from it—as if every single piece of hope I once had is gone. There is no other way that someone like me would be able to achieve such a thing. I will be forced to work on the land forever, fighting for scraps with the rest of my poor, poverty-stricken village. I jolt up suddenly, a thought crossing my mind.

"Where's Dexter?" I ask, suddenly realising how worried he must be. Why isn't he here? He knows how much the tournament means to me.

"He's back at Earth House. I went and told him, but he seemed to think you had enough people here to watch you," Pollo answers.

That makes sense, I guess… I just thought he would want to be here. To be the one to wipe my tears when I found out.

Vera brings me a piping hot tea in a delicate, pink cup. "Hayden sat with you for three days straight. He wouldn't budge, even to sleep. I finally convinced him to get some food just now, and that's when you woke up." Vera smiles at me, taking a seat beside me on the sofa.

Hayden rolls his eyes from the doorway as he leans casually on the counter. Three days? I've slept for ages, but have never felt more awake. If he's been next to me for three days, he missed the tournament too.

"What did he do to me?" I ask quietly. I feel sick to my stomach as I think about all the possible things Wex could've done without my knowledge that night.

"I got there before that creep could do whatever he had planned," Hayden says slowly, staring at the floor, his low voice booming across the room, "but judging from how long you slept, he probably used nightshade in your drink."

"Hayden brought you straight to Vera, and she used her powers on you. Otherwise, you'd be much, much worse off than you are now. Nightshade can paralyse Keepers permanently, and if you take enough, it can kill you," Pollo says, a dark expression on his face.

"Why was Wex…" I begin, but then the understanding of the situation fully sinks in.

He wasn't trying to kill or hurt me. What he had planned was perhaps even worse. I slowly sip the tea.

"Don't worry, that one's fine," Hayden motions to my cup.

Vera slaps him on the shoulder and scowls, a look that I didn't think I'd ever see cross her perfect face. The motion is strangely familiar, and

I wonder how close the two of them are. I wouldn't in a million years think they would be friends, let alone speak to each other. Vera is soft, loving and kind, whereas Hayden… not so much.

"Sorry." Hayden shrugs, looking back to the floor.

I know I shouldn't, but a small laugh escapes my lips before I can stop it. Damn this man for having the same dark sense of humour as I do. Pollo gives me a disapproving glance, clearly not amused by Hayden's joke. I scan Hayden's face and notice a small reddish smear across his cheek, and realise this is the second time I've seen him with Wex's blood on him. He must've truly been at my side for days—he hasn't even showered.

Eventually, Pollo and Vera have to go to class. Judging by the position of the sun in the sky, Hayden and I have already missed our morning abjuration class in the Blackwood Forest. I'll have to make up some excuse for Head Vespertine next lesson.

"Reyna, I know you're really into making rash choices lately, but please, stay and rest a bit longer. The place is yours for the day—I won't be returning until tonight after my classes," Vera says, and I appreciate her generosity. I'd much rather spend the day alone here, away from distractions and no doubt a mountain of questions from my friends in dorm six. Dexter knows where I am, he knows I'm safe.

Vera and Pollo leave, Pollo giving my arm a reassuring squeeze as he goes, and it's just me and Hayden left in Vera's large dorm room. One moment, he's standing at the kitchen counter, the next he's sitting on the armchair across from me. He stares at me in a way that tells me he has something to say, but he seems to decide against it.

I don't care why he stayed with me. I don't care that he missed the tournament. Whatever reasons he has, I don't want to know. All I know is that he is in front of me right now and I don't know what to say.

"You should go," I say to him, wanting to be alone to rest and perhaps somehow re-strategise my failed plan to travel to the Shadow Isles.

"I know, I will. I just need to know something first," he says, and I look at him questioningly. His eyes linger on my left leg, where the Fideal's claw marks used to be. Where he'd kicked me down.

"Why were you there with him?" he asks, his stare now burning into me from across the lounge area. He sits with one leg crossed at the ankle, lounging in the chair with his arms over the back of it. I was worried he was going to ask that.

"I needed something from him," I reply, as vaguely as I can manage.

He gestures for me to continue, raising one brow in question.

"It doesn't matter anymore. It obviously didn't work out," I finally say. If I told Hayden my plan, I imagine he would go and tell Head Quill I intended to travel outside of the Sanctum and break the rules. Or worse—punish me himself.

"Tell me, Reyna," he commands. My name sounds strange on his lips—he usually calls me a different one. "I need to know what was so important that you willingly went to dinner with Wex Brennan of all people. I thought you were seeing Dexter Fallon? Speaking of, where the hell is he?"

"I am—seeing Dexter, I mean. I'm sure he has good reason for not being here, and it's none of your business." I try to keep a level head, but there's always something about the dark-haired man before me that sets my mind alight with a burning rage. I hesitate before continuing. "I needed Wex to travel me by whirlwind. Pollo can't do it, and he wasn't going to ask questions." I eye Hayden as if he should do the same, but I can see more questions forming on his tongue the minute the words leave my mouth.

"Go." I point towards the door, and motion for Hayden to leave.

"I quite like it here actually," he says. He's made himself comfortable on Vera's armchair, draping himself over it like it belongs to him. I sigh and realise he won't be leaving without a fight, and there's not enough strength in me right now to beat him, especially without my…

"Here." He holds something shiny out towards me, and I instantly recognise my dagger. I'd know it anywhere; it's intricate swirls on the hilt look like dark clouds.

"How did you…" But I stop, because I already know the answer. He must've taken it from Wex on Saturday night. My mind flashes to the heavy punches Hayden laid into the guy, and I wince.

"Don't worry, I was more gentle than I should've been. He will be fine… once his nose heals." Hayden chuckles, and I can't help but feel relieved. Wex deserved the punishment he got. I'm just annoyed I couldn't be the one to carry it out.

"Why were you there?" I ask, suddenly curious.

"I don't believe I owe you any truths, butterfly. Your half-truth about the whirlwind doesn't count, when you haven't told me where it is you want to go so badly. And from the look on your face, I'm guessing you'll never say." He grins a knowing smile.

"Maybe you'll be more honest with me if I help you out."

What he does next is not in any Keeper textbook, not in any tale from history.

Hayden Radford stands up from the seat, extends his hand out in front of himself, and releases a small puff of air from his palm. He smiles down at me as he creates a larger wind that lifts the blanket away from my body, and my cheeks flush red as I realise someone's changed me into my nightdress. The black, lacy one.

He smirks as he eyes my body and I feel completely naked, despite being covered by the thin slip of material. My body is thin and muscular, but angled in all the wrong places from starvation. It is beginning to fill out though. Some of my curves are coming through—probably from the three meals a day situation here at the Sanctum. The way he looks at me… it's as if he is seeing an elaborate piece of art for the first time. I can't help but squirm beneath his gaze, like a wild animal on display.

Damn it, I let this man distract me yet again. The wind coming from his hands… Did he just wield air? Hayden is a Fire Keeper. I gawk at him in confused shock, but he simply grins.

"Wow, butterfly, I don't think I've ever seen you this quiet," he taunts, but despite him I can't think of anything to say. "I was born this way, with multiple elements. So I was thinking, if you need a whirlwind so badly, maybe I can make one for you. My price is much, much smaller than Wex's, and I promise you won't end up with a steady dose of nightshade in your system." He grins.

Born with multiple elements? That is unheard of. I wonder why he keeps it hidden—surely a man this arrogant would be flaunting his powers all over the Sanctum. But I guess some things are more powerful as a tightly held secret.

I stand, suddenly feeling empowered again. I may not have any power—well, none I can rely on—but Hayden has made a potentially fatal mistake. He gave me back my dagger.

"What's your price?" I ask. I don't want to force this from him, but I will if I must. If his price is too high, there are higher prices he will have to pay in return.

"Oh, butterfly, it is but one simple word," he taunts. "You have to say please."

I roll my eyes, suspicious of his motives here. Why would he offer the very thing I want for so little? But beggars can't be choosers, and I'm running out of options. I'm glad to see my enchanted bag slung over a chair, still intact from Hayden's rampage in Pineside.

I begin rifling through it for some clothes, and head into the other room. This one must be Vera's very pink, very frilly bedroom—it is filled with gorgeously girly furniture, a canopy bed and a closet of the most dazzling gowns I've ever seen. I eventually tear my eyes away from the assortment of shoes and makeup, and get changed into my usual black jeans and a sweater. I rake through my hair with my fingers, leaving it in flowing locks at my side, and make sure my bag is securely strapped over my shoulder.

When I return to the living room, Hayden looks me up and down with a wicked smile. I straighten my back as I approach him, showing that I mean business.

"Fine." I walk over to a space free from furniture. "Please." I spit.

"Well, since you're being so polite." Hayden smirks, walks over, and takes my palm in his.

I swear I can feel his power vibrating under his skin, just like I felt mine that day. His amber eyes glow like the fire he wields so effortlessly, and I'm taken back to the day I met him at the Silver Lake, where he moulded the flames into different creatures. It was almost like a work of art—the way he moved the blaze to shift with the animals as they moved through the air. Clearly having another ability doesn't mean his power is divided between both fire and air. He must be just as powerful, if not more, than a fire and air Keeper combined.

His eyes lock with mine, relentlessly unyielding to my guarded gaze. I'm taken aback when Hayden reaches up slowly, hesitantly, and brushes a hand against my cheek. He swiftly removes it as fast as it was there, but the lingering warmth where his fingers met my skin remains.

"Are you ready?" he asks, clearly trying to distract me from his gesture.

I nod and prepare myself for the inevitable barreling wind about to course over my body. His hands grip mine firmly, and I concentrate on the maps I've seen of Aspacia showing the Shadow Isles in the North West corner. It's difficult to picture a place I've never been to, but I'm hoping my focus on the map and the name of the place will be enough to get me there in one piece.

Hayden's whirlwind is lighter, crisper than Eric's. Even more controlled than Wex's. It embraces me in a demanding, yet controlled rush of wind, circling my body in a seamless motion.

Hayden says something softly that I can't quite catch before my feet leave the ground.

I rise upwards, watching as my body soars higher and higher, carried once again by the soft caress of the whirlwind. Once I am above the clouds and the ground below me is gone, I allow myself a moment to breathe.

I can't believe I'm actually doing this. Heading to a foreign land using magic from my enemy because of the words of a monster... it doesn't seem like the smartest choice now that I'm hurtling through the skies as fast as lightning. Hayden's whirlwind is relentless, faster than anything I've ever experienced. But the longer I am in the air, the more at home I feel, and the more I can feel a type of... tug. Like something is pulling me towards it. If the Shadow Isles are truly part of my destiny, maybe the pull comes from my fate itself.

20

The clouds part and I soar towards a dark island, surrounded by a misty fog that is too dense to see through until you are past it. This must be it. The Shadow Isles. I land on a rocky cliff, high above the treacherous sea below. The remnants of Hayden's whirlwind whip around me.

I probably should've mentioned to Dexter where I was going. But if all goes according to plan, I'll be home before he even knows I'm gone.

A rustle sounds from the bushes to my left, and the Nightbrood stands tall in front of me, as haunting as ever. It beckons a spindly finger at me, gesturing me to follow it. Without a word, we walk through the thick, dead forest above the cliff. It's different to the Blackwood Forest back at the Sanctum; no leaves populate these trees, they are dark, tall towers of decay. The forest floor is muddy, it clings to my boots as we traverse the non-existent path.

I lay my hand on my dagger, cautious and prepared for any oncoming threats, but the Nightbrood presses on into the dark, shadowy wilderness. I notice we are moving downhill, perhaps towards the ocean.

"Where are we going, exactly?" I ask, but the Nightbrood meets my question with a cold glare, its face shadowed by the dark cloak clinging to its bony frame. *Of course,* I think to myself.

About an hour later, we arrive at a small clearing. I go to step forward, but the Nightbrood extends its arm in front of me.

"Wait, child. Look carefully at what lies before you. Find the way," it says, voice thick and croaky.

I scan my surroundings once more, and catch a glimmer of light through the masses of tree branches. I move towards it and the Nightbrood nods in agreement. I guess this is the way then. Moving towards the light, more and more are appearing, to the point where eventually a whole town appears right before my eyes. It lies at the bottom of an enormous, cascading waterfall, surrounded by high cliffs.

My eyes widen in shock: The Shadow Isles are deserted. No one lives here. But obviously, the library books were wrong. The glimmering city is no myth; it stands before me in all its glory.

"Welcome home, Reyna." The Nightbrood says.

Home?

We walk on though the brick pathed streets, and I notice the people of the city all have one thing in common: their eyes are black. My own green ones search through the litter of people as if they are searching for something amiss, but these people seem to pose no threat. They are hanging out clothes to dry, children play in the front yards of their home. Men and women sit on front porches sipping tea. Everything seems perfectly normal, and I can't help but feel my heart warming at the sight. There is no yelling, no punishments being inflicted in the town square. Everyone here seems content, as if this town is a separate, untouched corner of the world. The buildings here are made mostly of sparkling black stone, and enormous leafy oak trees line the pristine streets.

"Where are we?" I ask, but the Nightbrood continues leading me through the city.

People's heads turn to us as we walk past. At first, I think it is because of the haunting figure of the Nightbrood, but then I realise they are all staring at me, placing both of their hands over their hearts.

I have a feeling my questions will have to wait as we approach a tall towered building with a gorgeous, elaborate garden in front of it. It seems like some sort of palace, although I note the lack of gate or guards, and was built directly beside a great waterfall. As we approach the enormous wooden door, it is swung open, revealing a tall, young woman inside the building.

"Welcome, Reyna Arrington of Earth," says the woman. "My name is Hanniah. I am the Empress of the Shadow Isles, ruler of Amaris." The woman has blonde hair cut in a sharp line at her shoulders, and wears a small wreath made of black leaves upon her head. She wears all black, and I feel content with my own outfit choice of the same colours, although where I wear jeans and a sweater, she wears a sleek, revealing gown that hangs low on her chest. I'm not sure whether to bow or shake her hand, so I just nod and smile.

"All will be explained. Come."

I follow her, and the Nightbrood waits outside. Hanniah walks through the large building full of black decor. Everything is black: the stairs, the picture frames, the curtains. Luscious velvets and heavy stone tiles are everywhere. We eventually reach a room with two black sofas and a coffee table. I can't help thinking how obscure it is that such normal types of furniture are in this strange place.

"So." Hanniah takes a seat on one of the sofas, and I sit across from her. The building's staff close the doors behind us, and we are alone. "I'm glad my Nightbrood found you with ease. I hope he explained the importance of you coming here, Reyna," she says, her black eyes sweeping over me.

"But why—"

"You are special, Reyna. More valuable than you know. Aspacia is in disarray. Are you aware of the attacks? The beatings?"

I nod, recalling the discussion I'd had at the Sanctum only days earlier. I think back to the public punishments inflicted in the Town Square back home. "For crossing the borders, you mean?" A fury burns within me, more fuel being added to the flames each second. This is my country, and I am helpless to it turning on itself.

"Yes, and more. Keepers are frowned upon for having children with those from other Empires than their own, but King Zale is making it his mission to strengthen these laws. If he has his way, he will ensure absolutely no marriages or children are born out of a Keeper's Empire. Any existing bonds will be broken. Children ripped from their families, lovers torn apart. And if they don't comply… Well, you've already seen the beginning. The beatings will look like a warm embrace by the time the king has finished what he's started. He wishes to keep Water, Air, Earth and Fire Empires strictly separated, and will go to any destructive means to make sure of it."

I take a second to process her words. If what she's saying is true… My brother and I are in danger. My mother is in danger.

"What about here? Are the Shadow Isles safe?" I think of the dozens of families, the kind, black eyes smiling at me as I passed them earlier.

"Yes, we are fine for now. My ancestors made a deal with the Royals a long time ago. If they allowed us to stay here, an untouched, peaceful civilisation in the Isles, we wouldn't go to war with them. The Royals didn't like the Shadow Keepers running rampant across the country with their 'dark magic'. The rest of Aspacia forgot about us, and that's exactly the way we like it."

"Shadow Keepers?" I ask.

"Yes, Reyna. There is another element, one forgotten by time. In the past, we were outlawed due to conspiracies and superstition. The world thought we were inherently evil. That the shadows running through our veins came from some dark power, and that we would be the doom of Aspacia. I'm sure you've seen by now that is not the case."

I recall walking through the town this morning. How friendly the faces were, how peaceful everything seemed. Things are beginning to add up, but there is still one important part Hanniah has failed to mention.

"You still haven't told me why exactly I am here."

"Oh, yes. I'm sure you've noticed your Earth powers are missing," she questions, and I nod. "That is because you were never an Earth Keeper. You were made for more, Reyna. Your mother is a Shadow Keeper, but the rest of her story isn't mine to tell." She pauses, looking away through the tall windows.

"But… her eyes," I question. Hanniah walks me over to a large mirror, and swishes her hand in front of my face. I watch as my green eyes change to purple in the blink of an eye, and back to green with another swish of her hand.

"A simple enchantment. Don't believe everything you see, Reyna. Tomorrow night, we will remove the blocking spell your mother cast on you to suppress your powers, and Rise, as per your birthright. You will become a Shadow Keeper."

One of the palace staff, a small elf with greenish skin, leads me to a room full of dark furniture, and a four-poster bed fit for a queen.

"There should be everything you need for the Rising Ceremony tomorrow night. Until then, you may explore the Palace as you please, or go into town. Just be ready at seven tomorrow," the small elf says before closing the door.

I sit alone with Hanniah's words flooding through my mind. It's as though pieces of a puzzle are finally fitting together. My mother's sorrow, my absent power, my preference for the dark. I stare down at my all black outfit, and wonder if somehow I already knew. There's no way I could've known about the Shadow Keepers here in Amaris, but I've always felt out of place in the Earth Empire. Like half of me was somewhere else.

A wave washes over me that can only be described as relief; as though years of worry, struggle and famine are rinsed from my soul. I look at the clock on the wall, with sculpted dark roses ringing it, and see it is five thirty. My drab outfit is damp and muddy from the journey here, so I remove my clothes and boots, laying them in a neat pile on a black velvet armchair.

I think about what Hanniah said about Aspacia being separated into its Empires. It is how it's always been—we do what we can within our own Empires to sustain life and build our communities, and the Royals ensure everything runs smoothly. I know firsthand how important the roles of the Royals are: my father dedicated his life to their safety so that they could continue protecting and watching over the Empires. I planned to do the same, but if what Hanniah says is true… how could I work for someone who uses physical force and intimidation to get people in line?

I wanted freedom from my village, from the farm. But now… I don't think I will find that freedom by becoming a Royal Guard. Not when Keepers aren't free to walk between Empires, or marry for love and not for the sake of their ability.

It is the end of a long day and I am sick of trying to sort through the new information running through my mind. I decide to make my way into the bathroom and run a long, scalding hot bath. To my delight, there is a bottle of bubbles atop the bench, and I dump the entire contents into the boiling water.

I peel my clothes from my body, heavy with the mist of the ocean and the mud from the walk to Amaris, and slide my aching body into the bath. I let my dark hair flow around me as I sink into the bubbles and let the water wash away my worries. I lift my hands from the water, inspecting the dirt caked under my nail beds, and the rough calluses from years of shovelling dirt on the farm. I may not be an Earth Keeper after all, but my hands definitely look like one's.

After what feels like an eternity, my body is clean and refreshed, though my mind remains heavy and crowded. I dry myself off and make my way to the closet. A lacy, black nightgown, similar to my own back at the Sanctum, has been laid out on the bed for me. I slip it on and slide under the covers, hoping to find some sort of reprieve from the constant chatter in my mind.

As usual, it takes me hours to fall asleep. Just when I am about to finally close my eyes, Hayden's words from earlier finally reach me, as if he sent them on the wind itself. The words I wasn't able to hear when he sent me flying away on his winds.

"Be careful, butterfly. Fly home to me."

I awake to the smell of breakfast, an elaborate spread of meats, bread and fruits, placed on the small table across the room. Upon further inspection, I find a hot jug of thick, black coffee. Thank God. I dress in the simplest gown I can find in the overflowing closet, which admittedly is far from simple anyway, and brush out my knotted hair. It hangs by my side in loose waves, framing my soft features as always.

I spend the rest of the day walking through the Palace the elf suggested. It is made of endless corridors with elaborate paintings, all framed in thick, black frames, and rolling carpets made of black velvet. I walk through dozens of hallways and rooms before lunch time, all beautifully appointed with the most dazzling furniture and luscious decorations. Although everything is so gorgeous, I can't help but feel the Palace is missing something.

After lunch, I figure out exactly what it is: people. There are lots of staff manning the kitchens, cleaning the countless bathrooms and hanging clothes out to dry, but nobody else. I don't even see Hanniah as I make my way through the Palace. I begin to wonder if perhaps she lives here alone. If she has any family, they certainly don't show themselves to me before the day is over.

After lunch, I make it my personal mission to track down the library. I have always loved the feeling of being in the presence of endless books, and Hanniah's collection does not disappoint. Shelves upon shelves of books line the walls of the library, making the room we met in yesterday pale in comparison to this large space.

Multiple sliding ladders hang over the shelves, and I take in the scent of old pages filling the room. A dark green sofa sits in the middle of the space, and I settle in for the rest of the day, reading about great wars and loves, monsters and histories. If I spent every day in here for the rest of my life, I still wouldn't know all of the knowledge these books contain. I make it through two fat books before it is time to get ready for tonight.

The Rising Ceremony Hanniah spoke of looms over me like a dark cloud. I am beyond excited to unlock my powers, but fear what may occur tonight. I've been trying to distract myself all day, but I can no longer block out the fear growing inside me. What if it doesn't work? Or even worse… what if it does?

Back in my room, I remove the gown from earlier and go to the wardrobe and choose a black gown. It's gauzy layers of tulle fall to my feet, and it is dotted with tiny white pearls. This expensive, high quality gown is so not what I'm used to, and I'm already plotting how best to move quickly in it if I need to make a break for it. The small elf comes back and helps me with the corset, and part of me dies inside.

"What is your name?" I ask. She stares at me blankly, astounded, as if she weren't anticipating my curiosity.

"Sioni, Lady Arrington." She smiles at me as she tugs on the corset strings. My chest screams at me, and I wonder how much trouble I'll get in if I just don't wear one.

"Sioni... what exactly happens at the Rising Ceremony?" I ask, and she motions for me to sit at the dresser.

She begins arranging my hair into delicate braids atop my head, leaving the rest to fall at my waist. "My apologies, Lady. I'm not sure. We've never had one before. Well, not for centuries, anyway. It isn't often that a Shadow Keeper isn't raised here in the Isles with the full knowledge of the power within them. Your mother did right by you and your brother, even if it meant hiding you away from the Shadow Isles until you were old enough to return here yourself," she says with a soft smile.

I don't understand what Sioni means. Why would my mother keep me from this? The years of torture from not only the other children, but from myself, for being powerless...

"I see... Sioni, I don't mean to pry, but what else do you know about my mother? She never told me anything of the Shadow Isles," I say, trying not to sound desperate as my voice catches. I feel betrayed that my mother has kept this side of her life from me for so many years, and I had to find out about it for myself. She wasn't even the one to tell me.

"She fell in love with your father when she was twenty, when she travelled to Aspacia to trade goods with the Earth Keepers. Shadow Keepers are a treasured secret, yes, but we need to get certain materials from the other Empires to survive. Your mother never intended to fall in love... but here you are. She couldn't reveal who she truly is to anyone, not even your father, as all Shadow Keepers swear an oath before they are allowed to travel. She chose to stay in the Earth Empire with your father. She chose love," Sioni finishes, a gleam of happiness in her dark eyes.

The woman Sioni speaks of is a mystery to me; my mother is a shell of a person, full of sorrow and pain. I can't picture her as a travelling Shadow Keeper, protecting her secrets at all costs. Even from me.

Sioni finishes with my hair, and I stand and gaze into the full-length mirror. The face staring back at me is more sure, more confident, than I have ever seen myself look before. The black contrasts with my fair skin, and I feel… desirable. Important. Sioni catches me staring in shock.

"You're beautiful, my lady. Here, the finishing touch." She stands on a stool beside me and places an intricate wreath upon my head, similar to Hanniah's.

It is formed of twisting, black leaves, encrusted with shining black gems that match the pendant around my neck. I almost forgot I was wearing the Fideal's black locket that Hayden gave me, but it sits below my collarbones as if it were meant to be.

21

Sioni leaves me alone to finish preparing myself for the ceremony. A loud banging noise comes from the window, and I jump. I wait, and it happens again. Walking to the tall window, I part the heavy black curtains and peer out into the darkness. There, floating on a cloud of air, is Hayden Radford himself. He hovers there, grinning at me from the darkness—his amber eyes daring me to stare.

"What are you doing here?" I hiss.

"Fully recovered from the nightshade, I see?" he teases. I scowl and quickly usher him inside my room.

"You seriously think I don't know where my own power goes? I tracked you, and when I found you were coming here… I wanted to, uh," he stumbles on his words, and I glare at him furiously. "I wanted to find out for myself what trouble you've gotten yourself into. Nice place." He scans the room. "Could go for some colour though. This is a bit drab." He walks across and plants himself on the bed, settling in.

"You can't be here! Go back to the Sanctum. You know where I am, now go," I demand.

"Nah, I think I'll stay for a bit. This place is nicer than I thought it would be. You know, considering it actually has people." He lies back on the bed, and my rage builds up inside my chest.

I know Hanniah will be furious with me for bringing him here. Even though I didn't. This place is a secret from the rest of Aspacia, and I've led a rogue Fire Keeper here. Well, Fire and Air Keeper, apparently.

"Get. Out. Now!" I fiercely whisper, not wanting anyone walking past the room to suspect anything is amiss. "Go! You can't be here!" I throw a pillow at him. It lands more softly than I intended on his chest.

"Oh, I see... so that's how you wanna play this." His tone is concerning, and I wait for whatever he's going to do next. He grabs another pillow off the bed and throws it directly into my face. The wreath on my head tilts to the side from the impact. My fury grows as I throw my hands into fists by my sides.

He eye's the Fideal's locket around my neck. "Such a rude little thing. Didn't even say thank you," he says, gesturing at the necklace. "You're welcome, you know," he continues, and I snatch it from my chest and throw it at him.

"Take it. I don't need your pity. I'm sure I'll win it back from you fair and square one day," I hiss, and I hope he fully, truly hears the words I intended.

I will win fairly, whereas he did not. He throws it right back at me, grinning a teasing smile. I scowl at him as he goes to grab another pillow from the bed. Before he gets the chance to throw it, I charge forward. I misjudge the weight of my heavy gown, tripping slightly, as I ram my fists into his chest. He dodges them with ease, throwing me down onto the bed beside him. I am up again before he can make his next move, grabbing my dagger I'd concealed in the folds of my dress. Thank God for pockets.

I jump on top of him, pinning him down to the bed by tucking his wrists under my knees. I grin wickedly as I trail my knife along his chiselled cheekbone, pondering what exactly to do to him.

"You know, Reyna, you are just full of surprises." Hayden grins, eyeing my blade. "But so am I." He bucks up with his hips, catching me off guard, and rolls us over so now he's the one pinning me down. He grabs my wrists and pries my blade from my hand.

"This feels all too familiar," I snarl at him, breathing heavily.

This is exactly the move he made the last time he stole my dagger during the Tournament. He grins, and I know he's remembering it too. He throws the dagger across the room, and it stabs into the wall. I realise too late my dress has ridden up, and Hayden's eyes fall to my exposed thigh. The spot where the Fideal clawed into me. He doesn't seem the least bit shocked to see the wound is gone, the one I know for a fact he knew about.

"That day… I shouldn't have kicked you down. It was a dirty move," he says, his tone suddenly soft. My mouth opens in shock: did he just sound… remorseful? He covers my leg with my dress.

"I didn't know you were capable of regret," I say, still angry, but the feeling is dimming.

There is a brief knock at the door, and it bursts open without warning. My head spins back to Hayden, but he's vanished. His weight lifted off my body without me even noticing.

"Everything okay?" Hanniah says from the doorway, confused expression taking over her features. I lay alone on the bed, my back pressed into the plush covers.

"Yes, sorry. Everything's fine." I don't need her knowing Hayden had followed me here, especially when the Nightbrood specifically told me to come alone. Where the hell did Hayden go?

"Are you ready?" Hanniah asks, and I nod, adjusting my wreath.

We walk out of the room, twisting and turning through what seems like an endless maze of hallways, until we reach a dark, wooden door that is bigger than the rest. Hanniah unlocks it, and when it swings open, I realise it has led us straight underneath the waterfall behind the palace. A glass dome protects us from the cascading water, hitting the top of it with a steady rhythm. It's like being under water, but without the calm stillness of it.

"This is a sacred place. We haven't gathered here for centuries, so excuse the dust."

We approach a large, brightly lit cavern, filled by a large crowd of Shadow Keepers. They sit on seats carved from the cave itself, lining the walls with hundreds of dark eyes. Lanterns light up the room, suspended from the roof of the cave. The Keepers rise as Hanniah and I walk in, and we stand together on a platform made of dark stone in the centre of the cave.

"Welcome, beloved citizens of the Isles." A roar of applause thrums through the cave, making the lanterns shake above us. Hanniah raises her arms high above her head. "Before you stands Reyna Arrington, Daughter of Shadow. Lost to the Earth Empire, today she reunites with us and unleashes her true abilities. Let the Rising begin!" Another loud roar rushes over the crowd, their hands clapping furiously with joy.

Hanniah speaks softly to only me now. "Reyna, you need to step into the light." She gestures to my right, and I notice the stream of light being let into the dark cave by a hole in its roof, despite the darkness of the night outside. The light is strange: it almost glistens as though specs of the sky itself are entwined with it. I glance at Hanniah hesitantly, and she takes my hand.

"It's going to be okay. I promise." She gives me a genuinely kind look, her black eyes smiling at me. I give a nod to reassure her, and myself, and step slowly towards the light, hoping my faith in this doesn't betray me.

I reach out and place my hand into the light streaming into the cave, and I immediately know it's going to be okay. A wave of belonging rushes from where the light touches me; the same feeling I felt when I first saw the city of Amaris. I step fully into the light, letting it embrace me and fill my body with the feeling. The light is almost tangible.

I open my mouth to speak, but I am slowly lifted off my feet—a dark fog swirls around me, beginning at my feet and travelling upwards. I realise that the hole in the roof is gone, and along with it, the light. I begin to panic as the darkness creeps its way up my body, but relax when I notice it feels as good as the light. No. It feels even better. It's like my senses are awakened; a darkness inside of me opens up and devours the block on my powers. I can feel it in my veins, in my mind, in my very soul.

My head is thrown back as the final parts of my body are enveloped by the darkness, and it is as though the rest of the cave disappears—as though I am inside my own mind. Flashes appear before me, and my mother's smiling face forms in the shadowy mist.

"Mother?" I reach out to touch her, but the image washes away as my fingers trail through it.

My feet touch the ground once more, and I'm not sure if I was floating for minutes or hours. I can hear the audience murmur around me, and I realise I'm not aware my eyes are closed until I open them. Silence spreads like a thick mist over the Shadow Keepers. Even Hanniah is staring at me in awe. I already know what they see without having to look into a mirror. A girl with black eyes. The audience bows to me as I stand where the light once shone, nothing left but my darkness in its place.

"From this day on," Hanniah announces, smiling at me, "you will be forever known as Reyna, Keeper of Shadow. You are home, Reyna. You are one of us."

I don't know what to say, so I just stand there, trying not to act like a complete fool.

"It's all right, we know it's a lot to process. As I told you earlier, you are more than you know. You belong here—it's in your blood. Let's get you back to your room so you can think this over," she says kindly.

I appreciate her understanding of my need to process this, because I am about to pass out from all the eyes on me, let alone what just happened.

When I walk back into my room, the first thing I see is my dagger still lodged in the wall from when Hayden threw it earlier. I realise I totally forgot he's here somewhere, and swiftly slam the door behind me. In a frantic rush, I try to tidy the room, putting the pillows back on the bed and hoping Hanniah didn't take notice of the mess when she came to collect me.

"Hayden?" I whisper, scanning the large space. Where could he possibly have gone? My question is answered, as he steps through the window, still open from his first entrance.

"Hey, butterf—holy shit," he says, staring at me. In my panic, I forgot about my eyes. "What the fuck, Reyna? That's why you came here?"

"It's not like that. My mother, she's a—" But I stop myself. "I don't have to explain myself to you, especially when you've done nothing but avoid my questions."

His eyes are wide, as if searching my face will somehow provide the answers he seeks. He stands by the window, his muscular figure blocking out the light from the moon outside.

"Truth for a truth?" He grins.

"Fine." I think carefully about what exactly I want to ask him. "Why did you really come here?"

"I already answered that before."

"Yes, but you lied. I can tell," I say. Being a great liar myself, I know the signs to look for. It was a dead giveaway when he averted his eyes and scratched his chin earlier.

"Fine." He rolls his eyes. "I needed to make sure you were safe. I've heard the stories about this place." His answer surprises me.

Why would he give a damn if I'm safe or not? All he does is torment me.

"My turn," he says. "You already know my question, I believe it's the same as yours." I hesitate, but I owe him an honest truth. I may be a great liar, but I don't break my word.

"Well… I recently—very recently—learned that my mother is a Shadow Keeper," I begin, noting that he doesn't seem surprised at all by the Shadow Keeper's existence. "And so am I. I just needed to have my powers awakened in a Rising Ceremony. My mother put a block on me as a child to protect me. To protect Amaris." I think back to

Hanniah and I's conversation in the living room earlier. She wasn't keen on offering up my mother's story, but there were some details I needed to know.

Hayden stares off into the distance, as if needing some time to process what I'm saying. "So… your powers. You weren't powerless. You just were never an Earth Keeper," he says, as if trying to understand it for himself.

I nod. He sits down on the bed, deep in thought, and I can't help but wonder why he is putting so much of his time into this. I wish he'd just fly home and torment someone else.

I need to make a plan—what are my next steps going to be? If I go back to the Sanctum now, I'll still be the outcast, just *because* of my power, not the lack of it. If I stay here, I'm afraid I may never leave. This gorgeous city has grown on me in only one day, and I've never felt more at home than I immediately feel here. I settle on a third, slightly more risky option. I need to know the truth about my brother.

"Hayden?" I sit on the bed beside him. "I need to ask you for one more favour." He raises his eyebrows and I sigh. "Please."

"Oh butterfly, you're so polite. What can I do for you?" he says teasingly.

"I need to travel back home. To speak with my mother."

"Fine, whatever." He lets out a sarcastic sigh. "But this time I'm coming with you. I need to see how this ends, I'm getting too invested in your pathetic adventure. It sickens me."

I slap him on the shoulder, surprised by the grin on my face.

"Now?" he asks.

"Now," I confirm.

He takes my hands in his, and the soft whir of wind stirs around us. Crap. I should've used my truth to ask him more about his random double abilities. Too late now—we are soaring out the window and into the sky. I watch as Amaris disappears below us, and feel a twinge of sadness to see it go, although I know I will be back as soon as I can. Hayden moves his arm so it hugs around my waist, and I can feel his firm body against mine as we fly through the sky.

22

We reach my small village back in the Earth Empire in no time at all. Hayden's whirlwind is fast—faster than I thought. With the help of my directions, we land directly outside my small, run down house. My cheeks blush—wherever Hayden is from, I can't imagine it being more dismal than this. I try not to let my embarrassment show, and I open the front door.

"Mother? It's me. Are you home?" I call out, but there's no response. I walk, with Hayden trailing me, into the living room. I notice the untidiness before the smell, and my embarrassment only grows. I spot my mother sitting in her usual armchair, staring out the window.

"I can wait outside, if that would be easier," Hayden asks, and I hastily agree.

"Mother?" I ask again, and she turns to me. Her eyes open slightly wider when she sees me, but she says nothing. She takes me in, staring at me for what feels like an eternity. I still wear my wreath and black gown, and I know she's already noticed my black eyes.

"Reyna...you came back." Her voice is soft, as if she hasn't used it since I left. It feels like months ago, but in reality I've only been gone a few weeks. She looks worse—as if she had hardly eaten any of the food I'd prepared for her. Her dark hair hangs limply at her side, and her skin is so pale it's almost translucent. Her bones jut out of her body unnaturally, and I nearly double over from sorrow. But I don't. I have to be the strong one, as always.

"Mother, I need to ask you something," I say.

She motions for me to sit on the sofa beside her, and I do. "You've been there. To Amaris," she says, eyes widened, and I nod.

"Hanniah told me some of it, but she said she wouldn't tell your story for you."

"Hanniah always was a weak woman," she says, surprising me. "You've come to ask about Pollo," she continues. Her tone suggests a history with Hanniah that I cannot begin to understand. I feel that if I asked, I would be sitting here all night listening to whatever story my mother is hinting at. But I won't bite, not when Hanniah has been nothing but kind to me since arriving in Amaris.

"Yes, Mother. If you're a Shadow Keeper, and Father is an Earth Keeper… where does Pollo get his Air abilities from?" I ask.

She pauses for a moment, toying the question over in her head. "Pollo, my sweet boy. He has his father's gifts," she says slowly. "His name is Elwin Dayarus."

I stare at her in shock. *Isn't that…*

"The Emperor of the Air Empire, yes," she finishes my thought for me. "I met him when I was trading with the Air Empire for the Shadow Isles. It was my first time in Aspacia—I thought I'd fallen in love. Instead, he turned out to be a horrid man. I didn't tell him of my pregnancy, and to this day, he doesn't know. I met your father a few months later, when I was trading again, and he took Pollo on as his own. And then a few years later, we had you."

"Why did you stay? Why not just go back to the Shadow Isles?"

"I did it for your brother. I planned to stay, forgo my powers and enchant my eyes, so he could one day attend the Sanctum, and get the education he deserves. He wouldn't have those opportunities in the Shadow Isles—we don't know enough about Air magic. And then I met your father, and my decision was fully made. I knew one day you would return there, I just wanted… I wanted to be the one to take you."

I turn my mother's words over in my head. My brother isn't my full-blooded brother. "Does he know?"

"No, Pollo can't know. I made a vow not to share the secret of the Shadow Isles, of Amaris, with anyone. Not even your father," she says quietly.

I can't imagine how difficult it must have been for her to swear off ever using her powers again, and to hide such a big secret about her past from the man she loves most.

I remember Hayden waiting outside, and realise the time. "Mother, I've got to go. Please, eat some of the food I made you. It's in the kitchen still. Please, Mother. Please," I practically beg her, to which she offers a small smile. I know she won't do as I ask. I begin heading for the door, when she calls out to me.

"Reyna. I hope one day you will be able to forgive me." She doesn't give any further explanation, but I already know what she means. And maybe one day I will be strong enough to forget the years of gruelling labour and emotional torture she put me through. But forgive? I don't think I will ever be that stupid.

Hayden whirlwinds us back to the Sanctum without any more questions or insults, almost as if he could sense the lingering feelings of resentment my mother brought out in me. We land outside Earth House—the green light shines dimly against the mossy brick walls of the building, the intricate fern leaf stamped onto the stone by the doorway.

Before I left, my mother showed me the enchantment she uses to hide her eyes. I make sure to do the same to mine, and they are back to their usual green before we land. It feels like an eternity since I've been here, but in reality it has been two days. Two very, very long days.

"So. I guess I'll see you round, butterfly. I think your nickname is even more fitting now," Hayden says, but I grab his arm before he turns away.

"Don't you dare tell anyone, you hear me? Or you'll find my knife lodged in your throat," I threaten him. I can't have the Shadow Keeper's secrets running rampant across the Sanctum. That would not be a very good way to show them my gratitude.

"Don't worry. I'm sure anyone I'd tell would stop listening as soon as they hear it's about you, anyway." He walks away, and I watch him go, hating the way my eyes unwillingly follow his muscular figure down the path.

"Reyna!" a different voice calls out to me from inside Earth House. Before I even see him, Dexter has his arms around my waist, hugging me close from behind.

"Where were you? Pollo told me you were attacked!" My mind flashes back to Wex and the bar on Saturday, a distant memory. "He told me you were at the prince's. I thought you would be fine there, but I should've come to see you."

"Yeah, you should've," I say, pushing past him and beginning the six-floor ascent to my room.

A rage I had forgotten about refuels me, and I know I'm going to find it hard to forgive him. How could he just leave me there without checking on me? I thought he cared about me more than that. I know if the roles were reversed, I'd tear down the Sanctum to be with him. Yes, I was fine, but what if I hadn't been so lucky?

"Reyna, I'm sorry. What else can I do to make it up to you?" he asks, trailing me as I walk. I turn to face him, staring him dead in the eyes.

What else? He really thinks 'sorry' is enough?

"Dexter..." I begin, knowing everything is about to come flowing out of me like a tap turned all the way on. "Why do you want to be with me?"

"I love you," he replies. His words hit me with a force so great I have to physically take a step back. No one has said those words to me for a long, long time.

"But why?" I press, and he takes a moment to think. An excruciatingly long moment.

"You... I need to look after you. You give me someone to protect, to watch over. I want to be that for you, want you to know I'll be the strong one."

"What makes you think I'm not strong?"

"Of course you are. But I... you know it, Reyna. Don't pretend you don't. You and me could be happy together. You'd have a nice, safe life with me. You could spend your days at home as you please," he says, pleadingly.

I can't help but feel maybe Dexter is what I've been searching for all long. Someone that can help me knock down the walls I've built so high inside my mind. To help me love and be loved again. He's tempted me into at least trying to talk this over some more.

"Can we… Can we go somewhere private? Your room?" I ask, not wanting to continue this conversation where half of Earth House can hear us.

"Actually, let's go to your room. Mine's kind of messy at the moment," he says, a bit too quickly.

"I promise you, mine's just as bad. Come on, I don't mind. I thought you wanted to fix things," I say slowly.

I don't want to go to my room. Don't want to see the traces of my memories from home in the belongings I brought. Not now. I continue up the stairs, with only one more flight to go until level six.

"Reyna, let's go to the Central Gardens. They're nice this time of night," Dexter says.

"What? It's nearly midnight. It will be cold and dark," I say, pressing forward up the last few steps to dorm six. I walk past my door towards Dexter's down the hallway, and see that it is slightly ajar.

"Reyna, wait. Just—" he begins, but it's too late.

I'm standing in Dexter's doorway, face to face with a half-naked girl sitting in his bed. I've never felt so betrayed, so humiliated in my life. The brunette stares at me with widened eyes, scrambling to cover herself with the sheets. Her hair is a mess, and her lips red and swollen. It is now clear to me why Dexter didn't want to talk in his room. He stands in the hallway, looking at me with a horrified expression.

"Reyna, just hear me out. It isn't—" Dexter begins, but is cut off when I hold my knife to his throat.

I stare him down with eyes so intense, for a moment I'm afraid their true colour has somehow slipped their enchantment. He holds my gaze, clenching his sharp jaw and raising his hands slowly in surrender.

"I broke my rules for you. I never let anyone in—I thought you were different," I say, putting all of my effort into keeping my voice steady despite the sound of my heart tearing in two. "But no. I was wrong." I press my knife more firmly against his neck, and I can feel his racing heartbeat through the handle of my blade. I notice shadowy tendrils beginning to escape my palms, and pull away before he has the chance to notice.

I will not be talked down into submission by the likes of him. Dexter holds his hands up in the air, backing away slowly. I stare him down until he moves out of my way, and I storm past him to my room, slamming my door behind me.

I should've known better than to fall for a guy like Dexter. My mind floods with his words, his actions, everything he has done since we met… and then it hits me. Dexter has never truly loved me. If he did, he wouldn't see me as some weak housewife that he only uses to inflate his sense of self-importance. He will never see me as the person I want to be, would never allow me to become anything more than a damsel in distress. I'm sure the shadows have slipped fully from my body by now, but the state I'm in doesn't allow me to care.

I would have to spend my whole life waiting for him to come home from God knows where with God knows who, just to be belittled and manipulated. As soon as Dexter knew I was being looked after by someone as powerful as the prince that day after Wex's attack, he decided he wasn't needed. But I want more than protection.

I want someone to lift me up when I'm down, be the wind at my back when I'm already winning. To be the loving face to come home to no matter how good or bad our days were. I remember the vow I made years ago to never have a family of my own, and it is cemented inside me like a stone.

Dexter's actions have only stacked bricks on top of my walls, blocking my trust and ability to love even more deeply inside my mind. Whereas he is scared of the darkness, I greet it like an old friend. It sits alongside me and helps me rebuild the walls I began to break down, adding another layer of brick.

I stand with my back pressed against my door, eyes closed and heart beating fast in my chest. I try to hold back my tears with so much concentration that I don't realise Hayden is sitting on my bed.

"So I was thinking about your little trip to the Shadow Isles," he says, before turning to see my now reddened face and shaking body. His jaw clenches, and his eyes search mine as I try to wipe away the tears that managed to fall despite my attempts to conceal them.

"I'll kill him." Hayden's spine straightens as he stands to cross the room.

"Wait!" I say, grabbing his wrist as he tries to push past me.

"What did he do? Actually, I don't care. Either way, he's dead." Hayden's eyes burn with fury, his deep voice filling my small dorm room.

"Please, it isn't worth it. Just go," I plead.

"He can't just…" Hayden runs his hand through his hair. "I told you this would happen. I fucking told you! But no, you had to go and spend your time with the likes of him. You had to go and fall for him."

"Hayden, please." I stare up at him, my eyes begging.

As much as I want him to storm into Dexter's room and beat him to a pulp, I don't want the hassle of dealing with the trouble it will cause. Or of Dexter thinking I've sent my guard dog to finish what I couldn't. Hayden's arm stops resisting my grasp on him, and eventually he takes a small step back.

"Why do you even care?" I ask, raising my eyebrows, my cheeks still damp.

"I don't," he says quickly, turning his eyes to the floor. "No one can torment you but me, butterfly. I won't have it."

I roll my eyes at him, crossing my arms tightly against my chest. "Why are you here?" I ask, my voice a hollow whisper.

Hayden sighs and sits back on the bed, his muscular figure crashing down onto my crisp sheets. "Like I said, I was thinking about your little trip to the Shadow Isles," he says slowly, clasping his hands in front of him.

"So you've come to rub it back in my face? I won't hear your taunts about my family. Just leave me alone," I say, not even bothering to question how exactly he got in here. I am furious at the nerve of him. Do I seriously need to get a lock for my windows too?

"I saw you literally fifteen minutes ago. Get out of here!" I say, trying and failing to keep my cool. I am so not in the mood for his bullshit.

"And there's something still unclear to me," he says calmly, ignoring me, which only makes me madder.

"I don't care! None of it is your business."

"Ah, sweet little Reyna. But you see, I've made it my business." He grins and I want to smack it right off his stupid, smug face. "My question is this: what can you actually do now you're all jacked up on shadow power?" I roll my eyes. I force myself to forget about Dexter for a moment when I realise he has a point.

"First of all—" I glare at him. "—like I said, it's none of your fucking business. And second of all—" My face drops. "—I don't know." Maybe if I hung around longer instead of whirling off to see my mother, Hanniah would've shown me how to use my new powers.

"Well, that's quite the dilemma, isn't it? If only there were someone who does know. Someone super smart. Handsome. Sexy beyond belief." He grins again, and my curiosity peaks. I raise my brows at him, keeping my arms crossed against my chest.

"And who might that be?" I say, full well knowing he is talking about himself.

"I know a thing or two about Shadow Keepers. And I can't explain to you how I know. So if I'm going to help you, you can't ask me about it. Deal?" he says, looking extra comfortable on my bed. I scowl as he lifts his feet—shoes still on—onto my clean blankets.

"Who says I want your help? I find it hard to believe you'd just do this for me out of the goodness of your heart."

"Well actually, I wouldn't be. There's something I need, that only you can do. It's kind of perfect, actually."

"What is it?"

"Someday, I'll call to cash in my favour. Until then, I'll help to train you." I weigh up his offer. The only other way I can think of to get to understand my power would be to go back to the Shadow Isles. But that would mean missing days of class, and having to find another Air Keeper to whirlwind me. And seeing as apparently they can track their winds, it's too risky. I don't want to bring another unwanted guest to such a special, secret place. I hate that he is my best option right now, and he knows it.

"Fine. But I call the shots. I want to practice? You better be there," I say, making it clear who's in charge.

"You're on, butterfly. And by the way, I know a good place to start."

23

I meet Hayden at the Silver Lake at eight o'clock the next morning. I'm not particularly looking forward to it, but it gets me out of my dorm for the day. Away from Dexter. It's proving harder than I thought it would be to remove my heart from his hands, but I have to. He will never be strong enough to care for it.

I have no idea how I'm going to continue sharing a dorm with him. Maybe I can put in some sort of request to Head Quill to change rooms. I make a mental note to speak to him when I get back to Earth House this afternoon.

When I get to the lake, I'm not surprised to see Hayden standing at the water's edge, gazing out into the distance. I can't help but wonder what goes on inside his head. He can be so harsh, so cruel. But trouble never looked so goddamn fine.

I'm almost tempted to run up and push Hayden into the clear, icy depths, but decide against it. I need to be civil; he's here to help me. Well, for now, anyway. I have no idea what 'favour' he was talking about last night, but I figure that is a problem for future Reyna to solve. Besides, I need all the help I can get right now.

"Took you long enough," he says, and I roll my eyes.

We both know I'm exactly on time. He turns, and I see something brewing his amber eyes. I'd rather not at this time in the morning. They taunt me from where he stands, and I can tell he is up to something. Suddenly, he whips out his hands and throws an enormous wall of flame between us.

"What was that for?" I yell across the blaze.

"We may have a deal, but that doesn't mean I'm putting myself in the direct line of your new power. This is to protect me from whatever reckless shit comes out of your palms."

Fair enough, I guess. I've never had any power before, let alone used it. I don't really count that one accidental time, either.

"Scared of me?" I smirk at him.

"Oh, butterfly," Hayden rolls his eyes. "I've never met anyone so scared to be themselves. Even with this new power being thrust upon you, I doubt you will ever have the grit to use it properly. So no, *I'm* not the one that's scared of you." He takes a small step forward towards the flame, arms crossed over his chest.

"You should be able to cover yourself in shadows. It will seem as if you aren't even here," he calls to me.

"How do I even start?" I ask, having no clue what the first step might even be. I've read all the books, done all the theory in attempts to get my Earth power to the surface, but nothing has prepared me for this moment.

"Feel it beneath your skin. Your power calls to you, you just need to listen," Hayden calls. I try to do as he says, focusing on the whir of power beneath my skin, trying to find that feeling I felt in Amaris.

A small, dark wisp of shadowy smoke forms in my palm. I glance up and see Hayden staring at me in awe, unsure how to react. He remains silent as I will the shadows to swirl around me, until they cover every surface of my body.

"Holy shit," Hayden says under his breath, and I notice he is no longer looking at me. His stare lands a little ways off to my right, and I realise he doesn't actually know where I am. He can't see me.

"All right, that was faster than expected. Now show yourself and we can move on to the next thing," he says, but I have no intention of doing that. I slowly move, walking along the shore of the lake, until I reach the end of Hayden's fire wall. Slipping around it, I circle back around, this time on his side. I swear I see his eyes change to yellow for a split second, but the thought washes from me as he grabs my wrist.

"Nice try," he teases, his hand still gripping mine roughly. I shake him off and step away.

"How did you see me?" I ask.

"Next, I want you to try something more difficult. This might not be so easily mastered," he says, completely ignoring my question.

He twists his hand, and his wall of fire is gone. I guess he's realised that it won't help protect him when I can disappear. He sits now, facing the Silver Lake once again, motioning me to sit beside him. When I do, he turns so we are sitting directly facing each other, and I hate that I notice how handsome he is. It's not the first time I've noticed the way his dark hair sways in the light wind, or how his jaw clenches when he is deep in thought.

"So. This will involve getting inside my head. If you can actually do it, I'd appreciate you not digging too deep. I've got walls up, an enchantment I keep in place to protect me for this exact reason, but we don't know how strong you are yet," Hayden says, suddenly serious for once.

I can't help but think about how he knows so much about the Shadow Keepers, to the point he would continuously enchant his mind to protect himself from their abilities. But I told him I wouldn't ask. I can't help but feel as though until I came to the Sanctum, my life was very sheltered. I'd never seen creatures such as Fideal, never had to deal with enchantments or spells. It was just me, my shovel, and my family. But now I know better.

It is as if my power knows exactly what to do without any prompting from Hayden this time. The whisper of shadow appears in my palm again, and I begin sending it towards him.

"Are you doing it?" he asks.

"Can you not see this?" I say, gesturing to the tendril of smoky shadow sitting in my palm.

"No, that would defeat the purpose of the shadows. Only you can see them. It is only when you wish for them to appear to others that they do so."

I nod slowly, and continue sending my shadows into his mind. They move slowly at first, but then it is as if they are being pulled into his mind through his ear. I feel my eyes turn into a blank stare, and then everything is dark.

In the shadows, I can see flashes of images, and I instantly realise they are memories. Hayden's memories. Some are blanked out—they must be the ones he has blocked me from seeing. But others… I watch as a young Hayden is outside, alone in a luscious garden.

He is perhaps ten years old, and wearing dirty clothing. His left eye is swollen, and his lip is bruised. He sits amongst the bushes, as if he were hiding from someone, crouching down and holding his breath. I watch from a distance as I hear a deep, bellowing voice coming from somewhere across the garden, and I hear Hayden whimper softly.

Then, I am sucked away from the image, back in the black void that is Hayden's mind. I know I shouldn't, but I can't help thinking of the blanked out memories he has hidden away. Maybe they will tell me why he is so cruel. I reach out for one, wondering if I am strong enough to break his walls, and when I touch it... I've never experienced such pain.

The feelings that rush out of the memory are darkly intense. Guilt, fear, shame... I can't see anything, but the feelings stay with me as I snap back out of his head. I can't take it anymore. My eyes flutter open, and Hayden is above me. I feel something wet, and realise my nose is trickling blood. I sit up and swipe it away, still shocked by what I just did.

"What did you see?" Hayden asks, his eyes panicked and wide. He takes off his shirt and gently wipes my bleeding nose with it.

My eyes linger on his chiselled stomach, chest, arms... this isn't the time, Reyna.

"Who is the man?" I ask, my voice almost at a whisper.

His jaw tightens, and he pauses a moment before answering. "My father. Is that all you saw?" he demands, hovering over me threateningly.

"Yes. I saw you as a child, hiding in a bush with a beat up face. A man's voice called out, but I was sucked away after that," I say, and it's not a complete lie.

That is all I saw, but I won't soon be forgetting the things I felt behind his walls. He lets out a breath and hastily stands up.

"What happened to you?" I ask, but he turns away.

"You only know a part of me, butterfly. The part I let everyone see." He looks across the lake as if he were in deep thought. "We're done for today," He finally says, and begins walking away.

I am left sitting there at the lake's edge, my blood smeared on my face, thinking about what could've caused the bruises. What could have caused the terror Hayden is hiding.

I walk back across the Sanctum, headed to divination class, when Vera spots me in the Central Gardens. She crosses the lawns, trailed by a few other girls, and gives me an excited wave. I don't know why I didn't expect that her friendliness towards me would extend to public situations, but she greets me warmly all the same.

"How are you feeling?" she asks, and I realise she is talking about the nightshade. Laying on her couch seems as though it was weeks ago with all that's happened in between.

"Fully recovered," I say, giving her a convincing smile. It's true, I don't feel the hazy residue the nightshade left in my body, but different types of pain have taken its place. I look to the floor.

"Reyna—" she begins, sounding as if there's something she needs to tell me, but something catches her eye. Her eyes dart over my shoulder and across the gardens. I turn, and see Theon standing with his arms crossed, leaning against a stone pillar. His cold, sharp eyes are narrowed, returning Vera's stare.

"Sorry—I've got to go." She abruptly walks over to him, and I notice the worried expression on both of their faces.

They are too far away for me to hear, but whatever they are saying, they are trying to keep a secret. They hide their mouths with their hands, speaking in hushed whispers, then Vera turns her back to me and the bunch of girls she was with. Theon remains looking my way, his brow furrowed and his mouth drawn into a concerned line.

I couldn't focus in class, all I know is I need to tell Pollo what I know about our mother, and what has happened to me. He is the only soul I can trust with the Shadow Isle's secret, and I feel a twinge of annoyance that a certain Fire Keeper had to find out for himself already. I wait for him in the Blackwood Forest, sitting by the Westgrave River as it rushes by in an entanglement of ripples. The forest around me is still—only a single black bird flies high in the sky above me. I check my watch—Pollo was supposed to meet me here ten minutes ago. Where is he?

A rustle comes from the bushes in the distance, and my hand reflexively moves to my dagger at my waist. I let out a sigh of relief when I realise it's exactly who I've been waiting for.

"Hey. Sorry I'm late, I couldn't get away without having Wex be suspicious. I had to wait for him to leave first."

"You're seriously still hanging around with that guy?"

"No, but he's my dorm mate. I have no choice. Trust me Reyna, if it were up to me, after what he did to you… he wouldn't see the light of another day," he says solemnly, his mouth a fine line on his face. He takes a seat next to me beside the riverbank, sprawling his legs out in front of him. "What was so important we had to meet all the way out here?" He gestures to the dense forest around us, and I think back to the half-hour trek it took me to get here this afternoon.

"I needed somewhere private. We need to talk," I say, my serious stare locking with his violet eyes. "It's about Mother."

"It's finally happened, hasn't it?" He stares off into the distance, and I can hear his breathing get heavier.

"No, no, she's fine. I went and visited her the other day and she is definitely worse, but still alive." I go to start telling Pollo about what has happened, but I don't know where to start.

So I tell him everything. Instead of explaining the facts-only, summary version of the story, I allow my words and thoughts to jumble together into the confusing, tangled mess that the story truly is. I tell him about the Nightbrood finding me in the forest, and why I went to see Wex. I tell him about Amaris, and Hanniah, our mother, the Rising Ceremony… all of it. Even the parts about his own, buried truth. Then, with a swift flick of my hand, I remove the enchantment from my eyes, allowing my newly blackened irises to see the light of day.

At first, he says nothing. He ponders over the information in his head, and I worry that he might explode. He looks up at the now dimming sky, watching the pink clouds move along in the air.

Finally, he speaks. "You know, I'm the best whirlwind maker the Sanctum has ever seen."

"Seriously? That's what you decide to say? I just tell you your father isn't your real father, that your mother belongs to a banished land… and you're wanting to maintain your reputation?"

"No. That's not it. If you'd come to me, if Wex hadn't lied about me not being able to transport you… you never would've had to go through that with him. I should've warned you, should've somehow stopped him before he ever had the chance to touch you." His words slam into me, and I realise his question had nothing to do with assuring me he's powerful… and everything to do with reminding me how much he loves me.

My brother is a loyal man, perhaps to his own detriment, but I won't soon forget the look on his face at this moment. When he speaks of what Wex did to me, his eyes are taken over by a burning fury as fiery as the pits of hell.

"It's okay, Pollo… truly. He won't ever be able to hurt me again," I say softly, and he wraps his arm over my shoulder.

And I know what I say is true.

This power within me is dark, heavy. It creeps along under my skin like a scratch that needs to be itched. But it is invigorating—I feel as though I could take down all of Aspacia with the snap of my fingers. We sit there in silence for a few moments before Pollo pulls away. He stares into the cloudy water of the river, contemplating everything I've said.

"So what exactly can you do?" he asks after a long while. Instead of telling him, I decide to show him. He watches me as I feel my dark eyes narrow in concentration, and I produce a whisper of shadow in the palm of my hand.

Then, I circle my body and become the shadows themselves. He can't see me; to his eyes, the space I once sat is nothing more than a contortion of darkness, hiding the truth. His eyes awaken, and he smiles a surprised grin. I reveal myself, returning the gesture.

"I can also go inside people's heads. See their memories, hear their thoughts. And feel what they feel." I shudder at the memory of Hayden's tortured soul, the darkness and pain he keeps locked away, hidden to everyone including me.

"I'm still the most powerful in the family," he teases.

"Not by a long shot. Check this out." I stand, and show him the trick I tested on Vera today without her knowing. It was quick, subtle enough for her not to notice anything was amiss, and I don't feel so bad about doing it because I was testing a theory. If I can get inside people's heads, see their thoughts and memories... who is to say I can't input some... suggestions of my own?

Staring deeply at Pollo, I envision him standing up and putting his hands above his head. Moments later, he does exactly that.

"What the fuck?" He grins, but I can tell he is nervous. I make him jump up and down, touch his toes, and then sit down again, before releasing my grip on his mind.

"I think the shadows have some sort of sway over people's minds. More than just reading them. It takes a lot of concentration, but I can feel my power growing." I think back to my training with Hayden, and begin to understand why he didn't show me this part of my power. If he even knows about it. I decide not to mention it to him just in case.

Besides, I don't plan on using it very often—it feels like a total violation of privacy and a non-consensual invasion of someone's body. I'm beginning to understand why King Zale thought of Shadow Keepers as such a threat to the rest of Aspacia, although during my time in Amaris, I didn't see anyone else using such power. Maybe there are limits. Or maybe... no. I push the thought away before it forms. It can't just be me. Pollo's face is still aghast in shock, but there's something behind his eyes that tells me his is with me, that he is on my side.

"One day I will go back to Amaris and train with the Shadow Keepers. One day I will return to my true home."

I make my way back to my dorm, keen to get some rest after a day that feels like an eternity. I manage to fit my key in the lock through dreary eyelids, and open the door to find Prisma sitting in the common area. She has her feet up on the coffee table, a pile of study notes on her lap and a pen in her mouth. Her face lights up when she sees me, dropping the pen onto her lap.

"Hey! You're home late. Everything okay?" she asks, her green eyes wide. I shrug, and she motions for me to join her, patting the sofa next to her. "Come on, please? I could go for a distraction. Or maybe some help… this Evocation work is absolutely mind-numbing." She smiles at me, and as much as I want to roll into bed and have the day be over with, I settle in beside her on the green sofa.

"Let me see," I say with a grin, pulling some of the notes she's taken onto my lap. Her writing is seriously messy; I can't even read the endless cursive scrawl she's dotted all across the paper. I raise an eyebrow at her.

"Sorry… my hand can't keep up with my mind most of the time." Her cheeks flush, and she swaps the notes in my hand for a heavy library book titled *The Art of Evocation: A History*. "Listen, Reyna… I know I'm not always there when you need me. But I just want you to know that I've got your back." Prisma looks up at me, and I know immediately she must've somehow heard about what Wex did. Perhaps what Dexter did, too.

"I'm sorry, I didn't mean to pry. But it's difficult when half the school is gossiping about one of my friends. Is it true that Wex drugged you?" Prisma says, and I decide I need to tell her the whole story. The true story, despite what she might've heard from countless mouths around the Sanctum.

I tell her about the date, the nightshade, Hayden beating Wex up, and Vera's healing. I tell her how Hayden sat with me for three days, and how Dexter didn't visit me even once. I leave out the parts about why I went on the date, though, as well as anything to do with the Shadow Isles. That part of the story remains only mine.

"Wow… I'm so sorry, Rey. I've been such a shitty friend. I should've visited you, should've done something—"

"You couldn't have known. It's okay," I say, and truly mean it. I didn't expect her to be there, to find me in Vera's dorm. It is nice to know that she cares, though.

"You're here for me now. That's more than Dexter ever gave me," I say, feeling my resentment bubble up inside me. I don't bring up the girl in his bed—I can't without becoming a blubbering mess.

"I can't believe he knew where you were and didn't even bother to see you. What an ass," Prisma says, her brow furrowed and fists gripped into balls, a temper as fiery as her hair building beneath her skin. I nod at her and shrug, not wanting to bring up the heartbreak any further.

"But Hayden on the other hand… I didn't know you were into Fire Keepers," she says with a wink, and I push her playfully in the side.

"Not in a million years," I say.

Hayden is secretive and cruel. I'd rather not have him cross my mind if I can help it. Even though sometimes I can't. These days, wherever I go, he seems to follow.

"So to read runes, you're going to need to know these symbols," I say, handing Prisma the list of runes in the massive book I'm still holding, clearly wanting to move on from the topic.

She raises an eyebrow at me, but I pretend not to notice. She sighs and grabs the book, scanning the list I pointed out.

24

I wake to a loud, sharp knock on my door. A quick glance at my clock tells me it is eight o'clock in the morning. I groan as I slip on my fluffy slippers and robe, and shuffle in a half-awake daze over to the source of the knocking. This better be important. I slide the lock bolting my door shut, and crack it open a few centimetres.

A pair of green eyes loom down over me from the entrance, on the stern face of an all too familiar man. His dark, greying hair is neatly styled with a whisper of it curling above his forehead. My heart freezes in my chest. What does Head Quill want? He's never personally knocked on my door before, let alone at this hour of the morning.

"Reyna. Apologies, I know it's early, but this simply cannot wait. Can we talk?" He motions to the plush sofa in the dorm six common area just past my doorway.

I don't think I'm really in the position to deny him, so despite my frazzled hair and fuzzy slippers, I nod and join him outside. He sits opposite me on the dated wicker armchair that Dexter would sit in on my first nights here. The memory rises up like bile in my throat and I push it deep, deep down again.

My eyes meet Head Quill's in a questioning stare, before I break it and search for the floor once more. He is nothing like Head Vespertine —he has been nothing but kind and sincere since I met him. But Head Quill still holds a demanding presence shrouded in power, and I have never been one to rise up against authority.

He leans forward and places his elbows on his knees before speaking. "As I'm sure you're aware, the third round of the Royal Tournament is to be held today at noon," he begins.

I nod, unsure why he is rubbing salt into my wounds. I didn't even attend the second round, let alone successfully complete it. I'm not a competitor anymore.

"It has been brought to light very recently—this morning actually, that your absence from round two was beyond your control. Not to mention illegal. One of your fellow classmates approached me this morning, demanding you and Hayden Radford be reinstated in the Tournament. This student wishes to remain anonymous, but between you and me, she has an honour as solid as stone.

"Whilst I was less than happy about being awoken at such an ungodly hour this morning, your friend told me everything that happened. That Wex Brennan drugged you with nightshade and Mr Radford assisted you in recovering. I've just been over at Princess Vera's dorm to confirm the story, and she gracefully confirmed everything. Mr Brennan has been disqualified from the Tournament due to using a banned substance to harm a student. So if you'd still like to—"

"Yes!" I jump up in joy, unable to contain myself. Is this truly happening?

Head Quill eyes me with raised eyebrows, but I can see a small grin forming at the corners of his mouth.

"I mean, sorry. Yes, sir. I would love to." This is a dream come true. My chest swells with excitement—maybe my dreams aren't completely shattered after all. The feelings of hope I've tried to muster and keep for my whole life rush back inside of me, and I feel like I've been pulled out of a deep, long slumber.

Head Quill nods, and says, "I expect to see you with the other competitors at twelve noon, then. Meet us in the Blackwood Forest for the final round." He stands from the armchair, walking towards the door. "Oh, and Reyna? Don't be late." I nod. He can count on me being there. I will make my father proud.

The tall pine trees sway in the wind as I follow a long stream of students deep into the Blackwood forest just before noon. I am grateful for my practice sessions with Hayden—if he hadn't shown me how to use my new gifts, I wouldn't have anything to bring to whatever the third round is today.

The winding dirt path eventually disperses into an arena not unlike the one from the first round, although the amphitheatre of seating is rounded into a full circle. I enter through a small door at the side and am ushered by Sanctum staff to another room just for competitors.

The small, barely lit room before me lies underneath the stands, full of the remaining Keepers in the Tournament. I scan their faces, mostly vaguely familiar from the first round, and am glad to see Head Quill has been true to his word—there's no Wex in sight.

Unfortunately, he also came through with his promise to reinstate Hayden. He sits across the room from me atop a large wooden chest, surprisingly alone. The usual trail of girls he attracts is nowhere to be seen, and I realise they must've gotten out in the second round. I scan the room once more and count—one, two, three… there's only eight Keepers here, including myself and Hayden.

I'm not surprised to see Navari laughing with another girl in the corner of the room, as well as Dexter off to the side with a permanent scowl plastered to his face. His eyes meet mine but I immediately break the gaze and walk over to Navari. I'm not in the mood for him and his sucking-up.

"Hey, where's everyone else?" I ask her, and she gives me a small, sad smile.

"This is it. The rest were eliminated in the second round." A dark shadow crosses over her eyes as she speaks of the previous round, and I make a note to ask Pollo more about what it was. By the look on her face, it was even more gruelling than the first.

"I'm so glad they let you back in. What that asshole did… I hope I never run into him because I doubt I'd be allowing him to hurt anyone ever again." I've never seen Navari with such rage in her eyes. It is as if they are dancing with a blue blaze. And I feel as though I've never related to anyone so deeply before.

Although she may not seem it on the outside, she is one of the strongest, fiercest people I've ever met. She is a true warrior, and would make an exceptional Royal Guard if she wins this. I begin to wonder if it means as much to her as it does to me to win—when my thoughts are interrupted by the brassy horn signalling the beginning of the round. We are ushered out of the room into the sunlight in the middle of the field encircled by the arena's seating, pushed forward by gruff Sanctum guards in greying uniforms.

I eye the two, sharp swords crossed at their backs, and can't help but feel a flutter of envy mixed with excitement. That could be me if I win this. But even better. A Royal Guard.

I raise my hand over my eyes, shielding them from the beaming sun above us, and look to the stands. A large section is reserved for the four Sanctum Heads, and next to them sits none other than King Zale himself. He wears a long, golden robe that glistens in the sunlight, his greying blond hair doing the same.

Atop his head lies the Royal Aspacian crown—a dazzling entanglement of jewels, each a different colour, to represent the four Empires. I can't help but scoff as I once again realise the depths of Aspacia's forgetfulness—as I know there are five. And today, they shall all be reminded.

The king is seated next to Head Vespertine, wearing a cold, blank expression on his ageing face. When the horn finishes blaring, Head Vespertine stands and takes his position next to the microphone. I stand next to Navari and the female she was speaking to earlier— Wrenn I believe, and the other five competitors stand in a line next to us, facing the Heads and the king.

"Welcome, Sanctum students and staff, to the third and final round of the Royal Tournament. Please join me in welcoming with the greatest honour, our Royal Majesty, King Zale," Head Vespertine's voice booms across the arena and a loud roar sounds from the crowd of Keepers, all clad in their House colours with pride.

"Our King is here today to ensure the Keeper chosen to guard him and his family is truly worthy of the position and can be trusted in life and death situations. Fifty of you entered this Tournament months ago, and now only eight remain. You have been asked to deliver the fatal blow in round one, to follow strict orders in round two—"

I look to Navari, who gives me a small, sad smile at the mention of the previous round.

"—and in round three, you will be given the ultimate and perhaps most honourable task yet. Royal Guards are trusted with their power, their obedience and finally, their wits. That is why in this round, you are to fight amongst each other until your competitors either yield, or meet their deaths." Head Vespertine smiles a wide, sickening grin, as if he actually finds joy in commanding grown adults to brutally harm each other.

The faces around me are filled with fear and shock. But that isn't the most worrying part, no—some of my fellow competitor's faces are returning Head Vespertine's wide grin. Including Dexter.

When I turn to Navari, I see she has smartly done just as I have—her face is a blank, emotionless slate, although I doubt beneath it she is feeling as calm as she seems. The crowd above is murmuring, some of the Keepers are shouting in outrage and even some in joy. They came for a show, and a show is exactly what the Heads and the king are going to give them.

Suddenly I am not so grateful to Head Quill for allowing me back into this no doubt bloodbath of a round, but I know that the road to true power was never going to be easy. I need to stay determined—to remember who I am and what I came here to do.

The eight competitors are directed to different areas, and when I look around I notice we are evenly spaced out around the circular arena. I stand upon a golden, square plate that marks my starting point. The rest of the arena is completed devoid of anything. No objects or plants, or anything that could be used as a weapon are anywhere in sight. Just the eight of us, staring with determination and fear at each other across the arena.

"The last Keeper standing will be the champion of the Royal Tournament this year. Make your House and your Empires proud." Head Vespertine glances at Hayden and another girl as he speaks, and I realise he is not so subtly rooting for them to win as the Head of Fire House.

I pay closer attention as I take in the people around me and realise there are two Keepers from each House left in the Tournament. Well, that's what they all think. Little do they know, I am not and never truly was an Earth Keeper. I am too far below the crowd for anyone to likely notice, but I whisper the short incantation to remove the enchantment covering my black eyes. Now there is nothing but the true, real me standing here, ready to take on one last round.

The brassy horn sounds once, then twice, and on the third blast, we are off. I decide to remain in my area, feet plastered to the golden starting plate. My competitors don't know what I can do, what power lies beneath my skin, so they're bound to underestimate me and leave me alone. For a small while, at least.

Except for Hayden. I scan the area, but am relieved to see him charging towards a stocky Water Keeper instead of at me. They clash their elements together in a cloud of steam—water spilling over his fire, extinguishing most of Hayden's relentless blaze. But I know better than to expect that to take him out.

Hayden surges towards the guy with a second, even larger blaze, and it surrounds the man with a hiss as his water evaporates into thin air. I guess water doesn't always beat fire, and I marvel at the sheer mass of power Hayden commands. His face is determined but shows no signs of fatigue as he moves in on the water keeper.

The man, who is clearly exhausted and his powers spent, holds his hands up in surrender. Hayden grins and begins to turn his back, but the Water Keeper sends an enormous wave of water straight towards Hayden. But he saw it coming. Hayden somehow manages to dodge the wave, and shoots his own towards the water keeper, made of an unrelenting fiery blaze. It moves from Hayden's palms to the man in a matter of seconds, and as soon as it comes into contact, the man is reduced to nothing but ashes.

A pile of black dust lies where the stocky Water Keeper once stood, and Hayden marches forward to find his next victim. His expression is difficult to read, but I doubt he takes any pleasure in killing for sport. He must truly want to become champion, no matter the cost. Just like I do.

I hear a roaring scream as a lithe, female Air Keeper charges towards me. I had been so busy watching Hayden that I forgot to watch out for myself. She runs towards me with such determination, cutting through the air with such speed as if she is using her power to be the wind at her back.

This is it. This is what Aspacia has forgotten. This is how they will remember. I feel my power bubbling under my skin and know exactly what I need to do. No wrapping myself in shadow today, no mind tricks.

Today, I'm going to use the last thing Hayden showed me before the third round. And I bet he is now regretting it.

I hold my palms in front of me as if I'd been doing it my whole life. The shadows begin to swirl in my hand, second nature and instinct taking over me just as Hayden and I practiced. I let the dark whips of shadow spill over my palms, falling to the floor soundlessly. I allow every single eye in the stands to see them, to bear witness to my power. And although this isn't the best way to get Aspacia to accept Shadow Keepers, it is my only choice. They will see my power. They will burn for what they've done to my Empire.

The girl continues towards me at a tremendous speed and I realise it is Wrenn, the Air Keeper Navari was chatting to earlier. Oh, how things have changed in the span of twenty minutes. The once smiling, giggling girl, now has a expression on her face that is so furious it could bring an Empire to its knees. Her blonde hair whips around her, moving with the wind she's created, as she raises her palms at me. Her eyes only widen when she looks to my own palms and notices the pool of darkness I've created.

I can't help but think how low and pathetic it is for her to come charging at me when she suspects I am powerless. I hope that when I raise my palms at her, she realises I am the opposite. She shoots a blast of air directly towards me before I get the chance to fire, knocking me back into the wall behind me. My body aches from the impact, pain searing through my back where I landed. But I will not fail. I will not yield.

I stand as quickly as I can manage, grateful that no bones seem to be broken, and send my shadows flying towards Wrenn. They twist and turn as they stumble over each other in a sprawling expanse of darkness, before eventually meeting their target.

Wrenn screams as I reach my shadows around her throat, circling it tightly. I grip her with my power, tightening it more and more. I pray she surrenders soon—I don't want her death on my hands. But I will show no mercy in front of the king. If she were a threat to the Royal Family and I were sent to kill her, I need to be able to control my emotions. No matter how difficult that may be.

I squeeze tighter and tighter, lifting her from the ground in a shadowy haze. By now, the majority of the crowd's eyes are locked on us. A silence ripples over the arena, and I know it is because of what they are seeing. Before the Nightbrood approached me not so long ago, I had never heard of Shadow Keepers or the abilities they possessed.

The students watch on with widened eyes and opened mouths, unable to believe what they're seeing. I steal a quick glance at the king, whose face is still contorted into that blank, emotionless slate from earlier. If what Hanniah says is true, he already knows about the Shadow Keepers. He doesn't seem one bit surprised to see one in front of him, in the tournament of his making.

Wrenn's face is turning blue and any attempts she has made to fight back have been useless. Her body hangs limply, suspended in the air by my shadows.

She is only moments away from death when she says in the tiniest, strangled whisper, "I surrender."

I immediately lower her down to the ground and retract my shadows back into my palm. Her body hits the ground with a loud crack. She lies there, still as a statue, and I begin to worry I let go too late. Long, painful moments go by, but eventually she extends an arm out from under her body and lifts herself up. A team of medics in grey

Sanctum guard uniforms comes running out from one of the small doors dotted on the sides of the arena.

They give me a wide-eyed stare that says 'stay the hell back', and lift Wrenn's barely breathing body onto a stretcher. They carry her back through the door to safety. I can't help thinking if that were me, I wouldn't feel any sense of relief. I would only feel like a failure. I will never surrender.

I push the image of Wrenn's broken body from my mind. I need to focus. I need to win. I see Dexter in the opposite corner of the arena, taking down a male Air Keeper as though he were made of glass. Dexter lifts the earth from beneath the man, then dumps it back on top of him. I gasp as I realise Dexter has just buried someone alive. Without giving any chance for him to surrender.

Rage takes over my entire body, bubbling beneath my skin so deeply that I feel it make its way onto my face. I don't usually let my emotions show, but this... an act so heartless, so despicable could never go unnoticed. Or forgiven. I know exactly who my next target will be.

There's no point in staying in my starting space now—everyone in the crowd and in the arena has seen what I can do. I make my way past the screams of battle, marching in a purposely direct line straight at Dexter. I ball my fists at my side, preparing my shadowy power beneath my skin. He deserves to pay. And, unlike the Keeper he just soullessly buried, he deserves no mercy.

His green eyes meet mine when I am halfway across the arena, and I grin a dark, wide smile meant only for him. I flare my hands, feeling the shadows trickle between my fingers as I approach Dexter, not slowing my pace even for a moment. He stands still, his eyes twinkling as if I were only there for his entertainment. But I can promise him this

—the only one being entertained by what I'm about to do will be myself.

I swing my arm up in a sharp, sudden movement, and shoot a wall of shadows directly at Dexter. The darkness spreads rapidly, a stream of dark, smoky whispers, just as I had done to Wrenn. But this time, I'm shooting to kill.

Dexter is unfortunately quicker than I anticipated, and returns the shot with a flick of his wrist. He shoots thick, green vines directly at me, and I only just dodge my legs from being tied up with them. I can't help but remember the last time I saw him use those vines. But that was different—at Spirit bar, he did it to save me from Hayden. This time, he's trying to save himself. And I won't go down easily.

I try again, shooting a thicker, wilder stream of shadows towards him. They meet their mark. He screams as I trickle them through his ear, directly into his mind. He scratches at them, trying to brush them away, but I am unrelenting. And I have a plan.

I don't bother to read his mind—I don't believe I'll care for whatever dark thoughts or memories he has in his evil head. And I don't imagine I'll be at all surprised.

Instead, I reach inside and plant memories from my own mind inside his. The ones of us together, from my eyes. The ones where I truly loved him, cared for him, wanted him. I want him to feel how I felt. Want him to feel as heartbroken as I am. I push in the feelings of happiness, trust, love, and all of the other spectrum of great things Dexter made me feel before he tore my heart in two.

And then, when his eyes are full of love when they gaze into mine, I circle my shadows around his neck.

"Reyna?" he says, his eyes searching mine for an answer I won't give.

To anyone watching from the crowd, this would seem like an attack from only the outside, just on Dexter's body. But what I've done is much, much worse. What I've done is something he is more than deserving of. The look of betrayal, of pure heartbreak in his eyes is something I will never forget.

I want him to know the pain I know. Feel exactly as I did when he did the same to me. I know exactly what he is feeling right now—I made him love me, and then tore it all away in a matter of one minute.

I hold him in the air, my shadows tightening around his neck more and more each moment. The screams around me are washed away by my sheer determination. I am powerful. I am strong. And I am the Darkness, just as the Nightbrood whispered to me all those months ago through the Ouija board.

But I am torn from my own gust of power when a blast of fire singes my back.

25

I whirl around, thrown from my murderous rage, to see Hayden storming towards me. I run my arm against my lower back and sigh in relief to feel only my clothing has been burned.

"You're about to see firsthand, Reyna, that you need me more than you ever could know." Dexter glares at Hayden, tightening his hands into fists at his side. But I know better.

Hayden sends another ball of fire, and I brace myself for an impact that never comes. The fireball soars past me, straight into Dexter's chest. He screams in agony as the flames burn away his shirt, then lick at his skin with an agonising kiss. Despite the pain, he grins through clenched teeth.

"If you truly cared about her, you never would've reduced her to the pile of ash you're about to become." Hayden's voice is an unrelenting growl as he glares at Dexter, who is attempting and failing to fight off the flames. My eyes widen as I realise what Hayden means.

"I surrender! I surrender!" Dexter yells through his sobs, and a medic team rushes out from a side door, just as they did for Wrenn.

A man with blue eyes dressed in the grey guard uniform shoots a soft, steady stream of water at Dexter, extinguishing the flames. When the smoke has cleared, I can see his chest is scorched and his skin is blackened. I force myself to look away. I have no doubt Dexter's father will be disappointed in his son's surrender.

I turn around, planting my feet firmly into the dirt ground below me, as I face Hayden once and for all. When I scan the arena, I see there is no one left standing besides the two of us. My mind flashes to Navari—if someone hurt her… My brows furrow and my fists clench. I don't know what I'd do if Navari didn't make it. She is stubborn, yes, but hopefully not to the point where she didn't surrender. But like I said earlier, she is just like I am.

"Isn't this fitting, butterfly? The two of us at the end. Who would've thought you'd make it this far? I guess you've got me to thank for that," Hayden sneers at me, standing mere feet away. He is covered in blood, his hair wet from the water keeper's attack. His amber eyes search mine, but I won't give him anything. No sign of emotion or weakness to use against me.

My mouth remains a thin line, and I make certain he can see my black eyes directly. Part of me wants to wrap myself in shadows and hide until he gives up. But I know that is the coward's way out. That will not please the king, who watches on intently from his seat in the middle of the stands.

"I guess we should've known it would come to this," I say through my teeth. I step towards him, readying my power in my palm once more.

He does the same—I can see the fiery haze he holds in his hands, flames licking his fingers. We circle each other, just as we did in the first round. I wonder if somehow Head Montero knew it would come down to us when she paired us to fight the Fideal. If somehow she knew we would meet our matches in each other.

I decide I can't be the one to wait for him to make the first move. I take another step forward, and shove my hands towards Hayden. Shadows come spiralling out of me with a greater force than ever before. If I am going to beat him, I'm going to need to muster every last piece of strength I can. My mind flashes to the way he reduced the water keeper to ashes with a simple wave of his hand, and I try not to shudder.

My shadows roll over each other in a smoky clamber of darkness, clawing their way over to him. They circle his legs tightly, climbing higher and higher up his body. I try to secure his hands, but I am not fast enough.

He sends a giant bird made of flame over to me, just like the one I watched him create that first time at the Silver Lake. I watch as it soars through the space between us, mesmerised once again by its beauty. It's feathers, made of the flame itself, light up as bright as the sun as it moves towards me. The bird is nearly upon me when it changes: it morphs into a large serpent, it's fangs bared and heading straight for me.

I don't manage to dodge the enormous snake of fire in time—it darts at my wrists with a singe, forcing my shadows to retract from Hayden's body. I scream as the flames lick at my skin, burning my wrists with its reptilian form. As soon as my shadows have fully disappeared, the serpent retreats back to Hayden. I examine my wrists —thankfully they're nowhere near as badly burned as Dexter's body was. I glare at Hayden as he stands unharmed across the area, and raises his hand. Instead of pouring flame from it, he beckons for me to come to him. And I do as he asks.

I won't give him the opportunity to defend himself this time. I can feel the crowd's eyes burning into me from every angle, especially the golden eyes of the king himself. I charge towards Hayden, shooting my shadows towards him and circling his body once more. They plunge into him and knock him over onto the ground before he can react. I pin each of his hands to the dirt with my shadows, and climb on top of him, one knee on either side of his strong body.

"You're quick, butterfly," he growls, furrowing his brows. "But you forgot one thing."

I raise an eyebrow at him questioningly, but realise my mistake a moment too late. He never got rid of the serpent.

I feel it's presence behind me, before it is there biting into my neck with a piercing blaze so hot I think I might pass out. Hayden slides out from under me with ease, watching as the serpent of flame singes my skin over and over again. The pain is almost unbearable—the serpent is relentless and I am at its mercy, too weak and pained to muster any power to fight back.

I'm sure my back is beginning to look a lot like Dexter's chest by now—it's fangs of flame shooting into my skin and singing it where it circles me. I am nearly engulfed by the flame, my body aching and my mind racing for a solution. I cannot find one.

"Surrender, butterfly," Hayden says.

I shake my head violently despite the pain. I promised myself. I will never surrender.

"Surrender," he says more forcefully this time. A command. One that I will not follow. "Reyna. Please. You're killing yourself," he says.

"No," I whisper.

My mind races frantically for a solution, an idea, anything. But I am in too much searing pain to use my power. I'd rather die than give up. And in this moment, I know that belief will be my end. I feel as though my power has completely faded, and my body will not be able to stand let alone fight if I somehow got out of this. No, this is my time.

And I know I've gone down with a fight. I think of the king's golden eyes watching on, and hope he sees how powerful I really am. I think of Pollo, no doubt in the crowd somewhere, watching his sister burn to death. And I think of my mother, all alone back in the Earth Empire, having to go on with one more burden on her soul. Is it worth it?

Before I can answer, before I can even consider surrendering for the sake of my family, the flames retreat. Through scalded eyes, I see Hayden retract his power, the serpent becoming nothing but a trickling remnant of flame. And then it is nothing. Hayden closes his palm around the last of the flames, and raises his hands above his head. I will never understand why the two words leave his lips:

"I surrender."

And the world goes black.

I wake in the Sanctum's infirmary, the scent of medicine and blood thick in the air. My eyelids sting when I open them, but not as much as I expected. I guess I passed out once Hayden surrendered at the Tournament. Around me I can see a dozen other beds, some filled with familiar faces from the third round earlier today.

I am more than relieved to see Navari lying in the bed next to me. She is covered in thick, red welts, as though she had been wrapped up somehow. She gives me a weak smile, and glances down at me to what I expect is the carnage of my burned body. But when I follow her gaze, my eyes are met with a simple, white robe and my undamaged skin. I lift my hands to my face, turning them over in amazement.

"You know, I'm always happy to help you, Reyna. But seriously, you need to stop needing me," a soft, familiar voice says from above me.

I'd been so concerned with examining the room, I didn't notice Vera smiling down at me. Next to her is Pollo, and on the other side of my bed stands Prisma.

"I didn't think you'd lend your skills to the infirmary's needs," I say, but immediately want to take it back.

Of course she would. She is kind, caring and everything that a good doctor would possess anyway, and it shouldn't have surprised me to have her here caring for me once more.

So I shake my head, and say, "Thank you. Once again."

Vera simply smiles her gracious, dazzling smile, and strokes a soft hand gingerly through my hair.

"You were amazing, Reyna. Why didn't you tell us what you could do?" Prisma asks, and I turn my head to her. She seems genuinely concerned, and I begin to think maybe I've wrongly judged her intentions towards me. She may be self-centred, but she is a true friend. Someone I can trust to turn up, to be there for me when I need her most.

Unlike things ever were with Dexter. As the thought crosses my mind, I find myself searching the infirmary ward for him, but he is nowhere to be seen. Maybe he's in a different room? Or maybe…

"It didn't really matter. And I promised…. Someone that I would keep it a secret. I guess it's well and truly out now, though," I say, thinking of Hanniah and Amaris. I would never put Amaris at risk by speaking of its existence, but what's the point of having these powers if I can't use them? I think it's better to beg for Hanniah's forgiveness than ask for her permission.

"I thought I was going to lose you," Pollo says, sorrow crossing his angled features. He will deny it if I ask, but I can tell he must've shed tears when Hayden had me pinned down. His eyes are bloodshot and sunken, but the smile he wears now shows his relief.

"Never," I say, and I mean it. If there's one person I can truly trust in this world without fear of being let down, it's him.

My brother has never let me down, and I can't believe how close I came to doing that to him. I didn't realise until that last moment in the arena—and now that I'm seeing Pollo's pained, tear stained face—how stupidly wrong I'd been. If I let myself die out in that arena, it would break him. He'd never be the same. A wave of shame takes over me— my own selfish desire and pride led me to believe I was nothing without winning the Tournament and becoming a Royal Guard.

But when I look into my brother's eyes, I can now see there is so much more to living than proving myself to people who don't matter. I now know, within my own heart, that I am worthy, with or without my newfound power. I am worthy, because of the people around me. And I am worthy of loving myself, exactly as I am. And with Amaris, with the life my mother has given to me, I know I won't have to spend another day farming the land in the Earth Empire for people who ridicule and taunt me endlessly.

Who knows, maybe I'll return and show them what I can do now.

"You won, Reyna. Hayden surrendered. You won the Royal Tournament," Prisma says excitedly, beaming down at me. I'd almost forgotten about that part.

"The Sanctum Heads want to meet with you and Hayden when you're up and about again to discuss your victory. They said—" Vera begins, but she is cut off when I jump from the bed, feeling more than ready to go and meet the people delivering my fate. The thing I've wanted for so long seems only a fingertip away. "I'll take you there, it's on my way anyway," Vera smiles, and we head out of the infirmary towards the staff residences.

The last time I was in this building, I was in Vera's dorm room with Hayden when he swept me away to the Shadow Isles for the first time. Vera leads me through hallways I've never been in, winding in different directions and paths until I'm sure we've entered a maze rather than the staff residences.

Eventually, she stops at a large, double set of wooden doors labelled *'Meeting Room'*. She knocks on the door for me before walking away, leaving me waiting alone outside the looming doors.

I hear heavy footsteps coming closer from the other side, and the door is swung open by a striking female in a purple gown. Head Windance's purple eyes find mine, her chiselled cheekbones stiffening as she smirks down at me and beckons me to come inside. The meeting room has a large, oak table in the centre, with ten chairs surrounding it. Four are occupied by the Sanctum Heads, and in another sits Hayden Radford himself. Vera did say that he would be here, but I can't help the feelings of shock and pure hatred that wash over me.

This man tried to kill me, burned me and caused me excruciating pain. He stares at me with a blank expression as I slide into the dark wooden chair directly across from him. I want him to be trapped in my eyes. Feel their wrath as I stare him down.

"Well, now that we're all here. We need to discuss the matter of the Tournament champion. Miss Arrington, as you may recall before you passed out, Mr Radford here surrendered." Head Vespertine turns to Hayden with a look so hateful I'm worried he might actually set alight. I can imagine that a Keeper from his own House surrendering in front of the king isn't something the Fire Head is particularly pleased with. "The four of us have discussed the results with King Zale, and he has had a fair bit of input regarding the champion of the round."

I await his words eagerly. What does he mean? I didn't think there was much that was up for discussion—with Hayden having surrendered, I'd won. Even if I was about to do so myself... no one has to know that part.

"The king was not pleased with your powers, Miss Arrington. Shadow Keepers have been outlawed for centuries, and the king does not trust one to be on his Guard." Head Vespertine's words hit me like a crashing wave, washing over me and soaking my skin with a heavy, lingering disappointment.

"What do you mean? I won. Fair and square," I say, trying to grasp what is happening.

"Miss Arrington. You will not be joining the Royal Guard. In your place, the king has personally requested that Mr Radford travel to the Royal Palace and resume training."

I almost can't comprehend what Head Vespertine is saying. I look at the faces of the other three Heads, but they offer no solace. Even Head

Quill doesn't have a single ounce of emotion on his usually warm, caring face. I want to scream. To tear down this room and everyone in it. But I don't. I force my wrathful power to contain itself, and instead glare directly into the eyes of the man across the table from me.

"And if I refuse?" Hayden asks, his question ringing around the room like a ringing bell.

Why would anyone refuse this? It is an honour. The most well-renowned position in all of Aspacia for those not of royal or empirical blood. I tilt my head at him, to which he gives me a small, unreadable smirk.

"Well… then we would have to discuss it with the king again. But I assume the role would go to our third place champion." Head Vespertine's words run through my mind and I realise he is talking about Dexter. Hayden seems to realise it at the same time as I do, and he nods in understanding.

"Well, in that case. I accept," Hayden says.

He has stolen what is mine. What I rightfully won. I can't contain the rage within me any longer, and I have shadows rolling from my palms upon the table before I even realise what I'm doing.

"Miss Arrington. Stop." Head Montero's voice shakes me back into reality and I quickly retract the shadows.

There is nothing left for me in this room. No matter what I do, I won't be able to change their minds. And besides, it's not their minds I will need to change—it's the king's. And if his prejudices run as deep as Hanniah says, he will never allow me to join his ranks. I should've seen this coming. Should've known I would never be able to get what I truly want. I rise from my seat abruptly, scraping the legs on the stone-tiled floor, and storm out of the room, making sure to slam the door as loudly as I can behind me.

I've spent the last few days holed away in my dorm room, not wanting to speak or hear from anyone, not even Pollo. He has slid numerous notes under my door, trying to get me to let him in, but I leave them unopened where they land. I can't face the rest of the Sanctum, not even my own brother. Not when I have failed at the one thing I've worked my whole life for.

Why was it so easy for my father? He didn't even win his Tournament when he was at the Sanctum, he was chosen later in life by the king himself. But then again, he is a physically strong man with more Earth power than anyone I've seen. He's definitely given Dexter a run for his money. The thought makes me giggle, and I realise it's the first time I've smiled since I woke up in the infirmary.

At that moment, everything was perfect. I had achieved my dream, I had three smiling faces surrounding me. But now, I've never felt so hollow. So numb. Even when I refused to feel the emotions instilled in me all my life, when I'd push them down and use them as a layer of brick to add to my walls, I wasn't as low as I am now.

It is the loud, consistent knocking at my door that finally gets me out of bed.

"What?" I yell through my door annoyedly.

"Sorry. I can come back another time. I just thought—" Navari is cut off when I swing the door open and throw my arms around her.

"Uhh, hi," she says, her face contorting with confusion. "I didn't think you were the hugging type." Navari laughs as I release her. She looks me up and down, taking in my tear stained cheeks and wild tangle of hair. She opens her mouth to speak, but I beat her to it.

"Are you hurt? What happened to you in the third round?" The questions come gushing out of me and it isn't until I saw her face that I realised how much I've missed her.

Navari is wearing the blue of her House, her streaked hair in a high ponytail atop her head. Her delicate features smile back at me. She steps into my room and I shut the door behind her as she collapses onto my bed with a thud.

I sit down next to her and raise my eyebrows, waiting for her answer to my question.

"It was horrible, Rey. Truly horrific," she begins, glancing to the floor and fiddling with her skirt. Navari tells me about how she surrendered to a Fire Keeper when she came up behind her and singed her entire body.

My mind flashes to the excruciating pain Hayden inflicted on me. To the blistering, burned skin on Dexter's chest. And I understand exactly what pain she must've felt in those moments.

"There is no shame in that. None at all. You'd be stupid to give your life rather than realising you've lost. I know that now," I say, the words like an anthem in my mind.

I've done a lot of growing in the last few days, and I've realised that becoming a Royal Guard is not a cause I'd be willing to die for anymore. Navari nods slowly, continuing to pull at a rogue thread on her blue checkered skirt. She twists it in her fingers as she slowly lifts her eyes.

"I heard what happened. I'm so sorry, Reyna. I know how badly you wanted to be a guard. The king is an asshole for discriminating against you like that," she says, and I can't help the small smile that crosses my face. I've never heard her speak like that, and it is refreshing to hear her say the words I feel.

"It's okay. I have bigger plans anyway," I say, and when the words leave my lips, I know it is true. My path now leads me to the Shadow Isles. To Amaris, my people. My home. She smiles at me knowingly.

"Navari… what did I miss in the second round? I've never asked, and every time it's mentioned…" I cut myself off, unsure of how to ask her to tell me something potentially so painful. She takes a while before answering, and I'm worried her skirt will be nothing but a pile of thread by the end of this conversation.

"It was horrible, Reyna. I don't have words for the things I saw. The things I had to do." Her eyes water, but she looks up and blinks the brimming tears away. "The challenge was to obey orders, as a Royal Guard would need to. They made us slit the throats of our friends. Of fellow students. I was ordered to kill a first year. The way she stared at me, her purple eyes were…" Navari stops, holding back the tears. "But it was all an illusion. Once my sword found its mark, the girl turned to dust. I've barely slept since then. Every time I close my eyes, I see hers, and am reminded of the cruel lengths I'd go to to get what I want. The darkest parts of me smile back in my nightmares, the part willing to kill innocents in the name of my dreams."

"Hey, it's okay. You didn't know," I say, trying to console her.

"Exactly. I didn't know it wasn't real, and I still cut her throat. And I know I'd do it again if it meant I wouldn't have to return to my dismal life in the Water Empire." Navari's eyes are full of pain, and I understand.

Because I know I would've done the exact same thing. Without the promise of becoming a Royal Guard, I thought my life was bound to be meaningless. But I was wrong.

A loud knock at my door interrupts us, and Prisma yells from the other side. "Quill's called an official Earth House meeting. It's not optional. You'd better come, Rey. It sounds important." Navari and I look at each other, before I call back to Prisma.

"Fine. Give me five minutes," I say, rising from the bed.

Navari does the same and moves towards the door.

"Hey, everything will be okay. I promise. If you ever need someone, you know I'm always here," I say to her. She gives me a weak, appreciative smile before pulling the door shut behind her.

I scramble to get changed out of my oversized t-shirt and dressed into the nearest clothing I can find. I pull on a pair of black pants and a grey knit sweater, rake through my hair, and attempt to rub the mascara from under my eyes. I check myself in the mirror quickly—I look like hell. But I couldn't be bothered to fix it. I slide the lock on my door open, and follow Prisma down the stairs to the Earth House common area on the ground floor.

Head Quill has all of Earth House gathered together in the room, and he stands at the front of it on the small step where he made his welcome speech all those months ago when we first arrived.

I sit with Prisma on a soft, green sofa, and am surprised to see Dexter standing in the opposite corner of the room. It is as though Hayden's flames never touched him, and I realise that Vera must've used her powers on others from the Tournament. Dexter glares at Prisma and I across the crowd of Keepers between us, but I stare straight ahead and pretend not to notice. I couldn't care less about Dexter and his broken pride right now. I've got my own to manage.

"Due to recent increases of instability in the Empires, myself and the other Sanctum Heads have had to make the difficult decision to send all students home for the winter break four weeks early," Head Quill's loud voice booms across the large room, and there are gasps from the Earth Keepers around me.

"I'm sure you've heard the rumours. Things are becoming increasingly worse all across Aspacia: prejudices grow, and the divide increases. Keepers are becoming more aggressive and are posting the blame to each other. It is no longer safe here—whilst this unease across our land continues, we cannot trust our students not to turn on each other. Please pack what you need, and be ready to return back to your homes tomorrow morning. This is not optional—no one will remain here at the Sanctum until things are settled in the Empires."

His words rush over me, and the understanding hits me like a brick wall. The attacks, the punishments... they are getting worse. So bad that they have to send us home. This must be what Vera was trying to tell me earlier before Theon called her away. She was trying to warn me.

"You expect us to return and fight with our families?" a girl asks from in front of me.

"Hopefully there will be no fight at all. The Empires shall find peace again, but until that day, the Sanctum will remain closed. Go, be with your loved ones, and pray for the safety of Aspacia. We are going to need all the help we can get." Head Quill steps down from the small step at the front of the room, and exits the building.

I'm back in my dorm room, packing away the belongings I'd brought to the Sanctum with me mere weeks ago. How things can change in such a short amount of time. The open window allows the dark of the night to trail into my room. It doesn't scare me anymore—somehow, I am drawn to the shadows, as if my power sings out to the black sky above.

A sudden realisation crosses my mind. One that has been swimming in my subconscious for years. The nightmares. I always see myself with black eyes in them. What if they were never nightmares after all, but predictions? I couldn't have known until the Rising Ceremony, until my eyes really did turn black. I had no need to fear the dark, no need to be jolted awake at night by my own screams. The shadows were always there in my mind, blocked away behind the firm walls my mother built to protect me. I just didn't know it.

I am startled from my thoughts when a loud knock pounds firmly at my door. I hear heavy footsteps pacing outside, and I pause. Maybe if I pretend I'm not here, whoever is there will leave. Another even louder knock sounds. What if it's Dexter? I don't think I'm ready to—

"For fuck's sake, Reyna, I know you're in there, I can small that God awful lily perfume from a mile away. Open this goddamn door now," Hayden's low voice booms from outside my room, startling me to my feet.

I slowly approach the door, hesitant to let the obviously crazed man behind it in. Unhooking the lock, I creak the door open just wide enough to see Hayden's frantic state: he peers through the crack I've opened, running a rough hand through his dark hair. His eyes are bloodshot, as if he hadn't slept since I last saw him days ago.

He barges his way into my room, which feels even smaller now that this tower of muscles had forced his way into it. I lock the door again, and when I turn around he is pacing back and forth across the small space.

"Didn't feel like using the window this time?" I tease, and he shoots me daggers with his stare.

"Reyna, this is important. There's something you need to know." His eyes are widened as he stands still. He squares his shoulders and furrows his brow.

"The king is coming for Amaris."

26

Immediately I begin packing a bag full of clothes, supplies, books and anything else I think I might need to bring with me to Amaris. I need to return there. I need to warn Hanniah and the Shadow Keepers. Now.

"When?" I ask, trying not to choke on my strained voice. It is hard having something to care about, and even harder when it is threatened. Hayden closes the space between us with a few steps, and grabs my shoulders.

"Reyna. Breathe." I hadn't realised how hard my breath is filling my lungs, or how flustered my face is.

"When," I repeat, slowing my breaths, my words more of a demand than a question this time. The most powerful man in Aspacia is threatening the one bright light in my life. My one chance at a future that actually means something. A future that is actually mine.

"In one month's time. The king is rallying the emperors to strike. They are building armies, Reyna." He seems genuinely worried, a look I have never seen on him before. I didn't think he cared about anything. His amber eyes shine in the moonlight, wide and tired.

"I have to warn them," I say, resuming my packing.

"I know. That is why I came," he says.

"And I assume you'll want to come with me?" I ask. I saw the way he eyed Amaris when he thought I wasn't watching him. He was completely awestruck by the dazzling lights in the reflection of the cascading falls. The town that hums with life despite everything its people have had to endure.

"No. I can't this time," he says, and I sense genuine sorrow in his usually teasing voice.

I am about to ask how he possibly knows about the king's plan, when he leaps through the window and carries himself down the six stories to the ground on a breath of air. He pauses at the bottom, staring up at me with intense amber eyes, then disappears into the darkness. Whatever he knows, he has heard from someone important. As for how he knows it… he seems to know a lot of things I can't explain. There are many things that confuse me about that man, but I know his words are true. He has never lied to me before, even when it hurts. I am not about to begin questioning his truth now. Not when my true home is in danger.

"Pollo!" I bang loudly on his door. I ensured I had accurate directions this time. I'm not going to make that mistake twice. I raise my fist to knock again, but the door is opened before my hand comes into contact with the solid wood.

"Reyna? Are you okay?" Pollo stands before me in loose sweatpants and a t-shirt, rubbing the sleep from his eyes. His wavy hair is tousled and it is clear I've woken him from a deep slumber. I step inside the room.

"Reyna, it's four o'clock in the morning. This better be good—"

"He's coming for Amaris." The words gush out of me as soon as Pollo latches the door closed.

He pauses, processing what I've just told him. "He?"

"The king. And the emperors. And their armies." I sling my heavy bag of belongings onto his bed, and begin rifling through his drawers and tossing his clothes into another bag.

His face sinks and he helps me pack. He grabs a large, yellow envelope off his desk and tucks it inside the bag. Within five minutes, we each throw our bags over our shoulders, hold each other's hands, and visualise Amaris. Pollo's whirlwind is even more precise, more gentle, than Hayden's as tendrils of air wrap around my body. He lifts us into the air, out his window and we soar off into the night.

Hanniah sits in the dark living room that we spoke in the last time I was here. Pollo and I sit across from her, and he gawks at every inch of the space. The walls are lined with elaborately carved bookshelves, made from tall wooden planks. The matching sofas are a luscious black velvet, an intricate swirling metal design holding them up from underneath. Hanniah flicks her sharp, blonde hair over her shoulder, her age only visible within her eyes. They are as deep as the ocean, as black as the night sky. She is dressed in one of her usual dark gowns, with her legs crossed daintily at the knee.

"We knew this day would come." She sighs under her breath after we tell her of the king's plan. She sips on hot tea in a black, dainty cup, swishing the liquid in her mouth before swallowing.

"Zale Rhanes has always felt threatened by the Shadow Isles, because it is something he cannot control. He has dishonoured the deal between us before, in smaller, insignificant ways. But this... this is unforgivable. This is war," Hanniah continues, her voice stern and emotionless.

"Hanniah... we need to move the people of Amaris somewhere safe. We need to—" I begin, but am cut off.

"Oh dear, sweet, Reyna. I have absolutely no intention of running from this fight. Not when I know we can win." She smiles a wicked grin, and I raise my brows in question. There are nowhere near enough Shadow Keepers to take on the Aspacian armies alone, no matter how powerful they may be.

"Have you been discovering your powers?" she asks me quizzically.

I pause, uncertain of how much to share. My promise to the Nightbrood rings in my ears: Do *not mention the Prophecy of the Void to a single soul, especially in the Shadow Isles. It is not safe.* My eyes flick instinctively to the exposed skin on my wrist where my birthmark lies: two overlapping circles so perfectly geometrical they don't seem natural.

Hanniah must take my silence as a 'no' to her question. "If only you hadn't run off so quickly after your last visit. We were going to show you how to—" But she trails off, staring at the shadows I hold perfectly in my palm.

I shape them now, so they lift high above our heads. I contort them into animals, just as I once saw Hayden do to flame. A dragon, a stag, and finally, a butterfly. It's wings spread out across the room, made of grey shadows.

"I see… what else can you do?" she prompts, and I tell her everything. I'm not breaking my promise to the Nightbrood—it only asked that I don't mention the Prophecy. So I tell Hanniah everything else. I tell her how I can wrap the dark around my body, how I can leap into minds. How I can whisper sweet nothings into people's heads and they follow my every command.

"Reyna… I—" She pauses, deep in thought. Her eyes narrow, as if she is weighing up a decision in her head.

"I would never use it to hurt anyone. I've only used it to practice," I say, voicing my innocence.

"No, no, it's not that. You are more powerful than I thought. Most Shadow Keepers train for years just to be able to cloak themselves. But you—you figured it out alone. And more." She sounds so impressed, so proud, that I decide not to mention Hayden's help—that I didn't figure it out alone. That would only arise questions that I don't have the answers to.

Pollo and I stand to leave and return to our rooms for the rest of the early morning hours to finally get some sleep, but Hanniah stops us.

"Wait. This came yesterday. It's from the palace. I haven't opened it yet, but now, with the information you've brought me… it may be more important than we know. Open it." She slides me a large yellow envelope, identical to the one Pollo packed in his bag earlier. I run my finger along the red wax seal, stamped with the royal emblem: an open eye with a flower as the pupil, and tear the envelope open. Reaching inside, I pull out a letter on thick, glossy paper, and realise upon reading that it is an invitation:

Dear Empress Hanniah and her Empirical Court,

You are honourably invited to join the Royal Family for their renowned Annual Winter Solstice Ball.

Please RSVP in no later than one week's time.

Regards,

The Royal Family

The date attached to the invitation states the ball is due to be held in two weeks. According to Hayden, that is two weeks before the king plans to attack the Isles.

"This is perfect," Hanniah says, and I can see a plan forming in her mind. "We aren't usually invited, but everyone who's anyone will be there. And now, we have all the pieces we need to make our move."

I raise an eyebrow at her in question, and she grins a smile that darkens her entire face.

"Reyna. You will accompany me to the ball. Once there, we will take something so important from the king that he will have no choice but to stand down for good."

"What does your letter say?" I ask Pollo, a curious expression on my face. We both sit in the room Hanniah gave him, across the hall from mine in the Shadow Palace's visitor wing. The dark interior is only brightened by the morning light trickling its way inside the room.

"It's an invite to the palace, also. But not for a ball." He hands me the yellow envelope, and I read the contents:

Pollo Arrington,

Your educational achievements have been duly noted by the Royal Family. You come with shining recommendations from your Heads at the Sanctum. Please join the king for a meeting with other selected candidates for the Royal Council.

Regards,

King Zale

This makes no sense. What could the king possibly be wanting Pollo on his council for? I mean, he is a smart guy, but not top of his classes or anything. The look on Pollo's face is just as sceptical as mine, and it is clear he doesn't understand either.

"Are you going to go?" I ask. If he does, he would be siding with a man plotting against my home. If he doesn't… he might miss his shot in life.

"I haven't decided yet," he says, snatching the letter back from me.

I nod, and slowly stand to return to my own room.

"Reyna? How long are we staying here?" he asks as I stand in the doorway. His expression is difficult to read.

"Well… we can't go back to the Sanctum. And if we go back to Mother, we won't be able to help Hanniah and the Shadow Keepers," I say, mulling my options over in my head. "I'm going to stay here at least until we go to the ball. You—you can go home if you wish to."

"I'd never abandon you like that," he says, and I know it's true.

Morning light streams through the window, and I realise the dark curtains I closed last night are wide open. With no need for the enchantment here, my dark eyes freely scan the room around me. It is the same one I stayed in last time. A fancy bathroom is attached to it, and it is furnished with only a few things: the dark wooden closet I used last time, a long, chaise lounge made of—you guessed it—black velvet, with a small coffee table next to it. A dressing table sits below the window, accompanied by a plush stool. The bed envelopes me in its plush blankets and soft pillows, and I can't help but feel I could get used to this. A soft, tentative knock raps at my door.

"Come in," I say, thinking it is probably Pollo, but the small elf that comes inside is the complete opposite of my brother.

"Sioni," I say, and she smiles warmly in greeting.

"Good to see you again, Lady—sorry, Reyna." She places a tray of tea on the coffee table and begins fussing with the pillows on the lounge.

I realise she must've come in when I was asleep and opened the curtains. My hair is swirled in crazed patterns on my head, and I note how well I rested last night. No nightmares in sight. Maybe my theory about what they mean is true.

"Hanniah is waiting for you in the dining room for breakfast," she says, beginning to select some clothes from my closet for me. To my relief, she chooses a pair of black pants with lots of pockets and a leather tank top, accompanied by a pair of sturdy leather boots. She sees me eyeing the outfit with delight.

"What? It can't all be ballgowns and corsets." She winks. "Besides. Hanniah has plans for you today that you can't wear a dress for." She motions for me to sit at the dresser, and begins brushing my mess of hair until it is knot-free. She creates two long braids atop my head, plaiting my dark waves down to my waist.

"What exactly will I be doing?" I ask.

She hands me the clothing she chose for me, and I get changed. I glance at my reflection in the mirror and can't help but like what I see. I look powerful. Strong. The leather top cinches in at my waist, and I realise there is a sheath on the waistline of my pants for my dagger. It is as if these clothes were made for me—they're much more my style than a corset.

"Hanniah is waiting for you in the dining hall," she repeats her words from before with a sly grin.

Sioni leads me to a room with an enormous, long table, with three people seated at the far end. She motions me through the door, then closes it softly between us. I walk forward, having to squint at the people before me to see who they are. Pollo is digging into a plate of bacon, eggs, toast… everything you could ever want.

My mouth waters hungrily at the sight of the food, and I realise I hadn't eaten dinner last night. Usually hunger doesn't begin until the second day, as it had all those times before in my village, but I guess my body has grown accustomed to three full meals each day.

"Apologies, we began without you. Someone—" Hanniah eyes Pollo in distaste. "—couldn't wait another moment."

I grin as Pollo eyes me sheepishly, before turning to the other Keeper at the table. A man who seems to be around Pollo's age sits back in his chair, his heavily muscled figure leaning against the dark wood of his seat. He looks at me with dark eyes and grins.

"Reyna, this is Carter. Commander of the Shadow Army, and—" She pauses, taking a deep breath. "—my brother."

I eye the two siblings, but am unable to find anything they have in common besides their age. I'd perhaps think they're twins if it weren't for the stark differences in their features. They catch me staring, and Carter smiles.

"We have different mothers," he clarifies with a grin, giving me the impression this is something commonly questioned about him and his sister.

Hanniah's locks are undoubtedly naturally blonde, her sharp features almost jarring against her dark eyes. But Carter, he has auburn hair and a softer set jaw, still strong but not as prominent as Hanniah's.

"Our father was a Shadow Keeper in the palace guard here, and my mother was the Empress herself."

I note that Hanniah talks in past tense. What happened to her parents? She mentioned the king had broken his deal with the Shadow Isles before—did something happen?

"If you're going to accompany me to the royal palace for the ball in two weeks' time, I need to be able to rely on you to ensure my safety. Carter will remain here to watch over the Isles, so I will need someone with powers such as yours to defend me if need be. You will train with Carter each day until the day of the ball. In the afternoons, you are free to explore Amaris, but your mornings are his," Hanniah says, her stern voice cutting through me with her power.

I slowly nod in agreement, trying to hide my disappointment. I was looking forward to exploring the city and my powers alone.

"Pollo, you will spend your mornings with me. I'm sure your abilities will come in handy with the mountain of paperwork I have to do each day as Empress." He grins, and I can tell he would be more than happy to take up her request. He has always had an eye for detail, and maybe he did better at the Sanctum than I originally thought.

The Commander turns to me, and I have no doubt he is seeing only what I show on the surface: a weak, fragile girl with new found powers greater than she can manage. Little does he know, I've been training to fight since I was a child, and my immense power is my newest weapon. He eyes the dagger strapped to my hip as I take a seat and serve myself some breakfast. His eyes don't leave me until breakfast is over—I can feel the heat of them trailing over me like a hawk.

28

We stand in the freezing cold as Carter lectures me on hand to hand combat skills. I barely hear his words as he speaks, which I imagine is something he is not used to. I can't help it, though—the forest around us is breathtakingly beautiful. It lies atop the cliffs surrounding Amaris, and is covered in a thick, powdery snow. Winter has truly arrived, and I couldn't feel more at peace in this newfound home of mine.

Except when Carter slaps me across the face.

"What was that for?" I yell at him, clenching my fists at my side in fury.

"Rule number one: never get distracted." He grins at me, a few steps away now. He is gorgeous in his battle leathers—an outfit similar to mine with dark, embroidered swirls on his shirt.

"Again," I challenge, determined not to let him strike me down once more.

I move my feet quickly as my father taught me, staying light on my toes to anticipate and doge any attacks Carter throws at me. He goes to strike me right in the middle of my chest, but I manage to dodge it, side stepping to the left with ease.

"You're quick. That's good. Use that to your advantage," he says with a grin, obviously trying to hide his own embarrassment that I'd just outsmarted him.

He goes to throw another punch, but I let my shadows envelope me in darkness and jump out of the way. He spins around, unable to see me, and rakes his hand through his hair.

"Reyna. We agreed—no magic. You need to be able to do this without it. The palace will probably have enchantments warding against your powers, blocking them inside the walls to protect the royals."

I huff in annoyance—how am I going to learn to master my powers further if I'm not even allowed to use them? I drop the shadows and stare at him with a cold, icy glare, hoping it pierces right through him, but he only chuckles softly to himself. A new motivation rises within me—to smack that smug smile off his face.

I step to the left, and we circle each other from a distance. Carter steps forward, I step back—it's almost like a dance. He no doubt has tremendous strength and skill, but I know I am faster than him, and he knows it too. He goes to throw a punch, but I quickly duck under his arm, and swipe a leg into both of his, sending him toppling into the snow. I turn my back for just a moment, and he is there, holding a knife to my throat.

"Rule number two, little girl. Never turn your back," he says darkly, and I roll my eyes, pounding my fists against him. It is no use—he is much bigger than me, and my edge of surprise is now gone.

"You know more about this than I thought," Carter says as we descend the hundreds of stairs leading back down to the city after we finish our practice for the day.

"My father taught me," I say between heavy breaths. I may be skilful, but I'm a lot less fit than I thought. I guess my months at the Sanctum left me complacent to my training. My father would be disappointed.

Carter eyes my dagger, just as he did at breakfast this morning. He sees me watching him, and goes to say something but stops himself.

"What is it?" I ask.

"That dagger, it… can I see it?" he asks, dark eyes sceptically dancing over the blade as I hesitantly hand it to him. He inspects it for a long moment before handing it back and turning away.

"What's wrong?" I say, remembering what Dexter told me about the blade's story. Shadow Reaver. The blade that the prince from centuries ago used to kill the king.

"Have you learned of the blade's lineage?" he asks, and I nod. "Shadow Reaver was forged by Fire Keepers centuries ago, and the Dark Prince that wielded it was a Shadow Keeper. A bastard son born from the queen's betrayal."

Dexter left that part of the story out. Carter's eyes glaze over, an emotionless expression taking over his face.

"I don't know how you ended up with it, but it seems fitting it found its way to you. It is said it sings out to those in need of it," he continues, and I think back to when my father gave me the blade. When he thrust it into my hand before leaving for the palace all those years ago.

In the afternoon, I walk with Pollo through the streets of Amaris. The full weight of what my mother had to leave behind hits me as I gawk at the snow-capped shingled roofs and laughing children. I am grateful for my mother's choice, to look out for my brother, but damn. It must have been hard knowing that all this was waiting back in Amaris. I wonder if she has family here. If *we* have family here. I make a mental note to ask Hanniah later.

We trail the cobblestone paths of the city, watching the Keepers go about their daily lives. I wonder if they know what danger impedes on them. I decide it is best if they don't. To disrupt this peace would be a crime in itself.

Pollo stops at a shop selling large, detailed maps of Aspacia, the Shadow Isles, and even the lands beyond. His eyes trail over one of the Sanctum, and I can tell from the glint in his eyes how much he misses it already. He gives me a sadden smile, and I make a note to come back and somehow purchase it for him.

Hanniah gave us a small allowance for our troubles and for Pollo's work with her. It isn't much in most people's eyes, but the golden coins in my hand are more than I've ever held in my life. When we approach a small store selling an assortment of spell books, cauldrons and potions, my heart feels as though something is calling my name. I walk into the store and notice how dusty it is—as if no one comes in here anymore.

An old, frail man sits behind the counter, welcoming Pollo and I in. Pollo stops to chat with him, but I continue down the rows of shelves and random items, following the tug in my chest. As I approach the back of the store, the feeling stops. In front of me, a lone, dusty book lies on a shelf. When I pick it up, it seems to sing beneath my fingertips.

It is made of black leather, with the words '*Shadow Magic: Spells, Potions and Enchantments*' embossed on the front in golden, cursive writing. I'm not sure why, but I return to the counter and buy the book from the old man with three shining coins. I tuck it in my enchanted bag, and it falls to the bottom of it with a loud thud.

We arrive back at the Shadow Palace in the late evening, and attend dinner with Hanniah and Carter. As we consume copious amounts of meats, salads, breads and wine, I can't help but think about how lonely Hanniah and Carter must be. I haven't seen anyone in the Palace other than the staff, and I make a note to ask Carter about it at our next practice.

After dinner we return to our rooms, settling in for the night. I fall into a deep slumber, devoid of any nightmares once again.

For the next week, I train with Carter each morning, working on my combat skills. He seems impressed with me, but I can't wait to use my powers in a fight. He promises that we will move on to that 'when I'm ready.'

Please. I'm ready now.

I explore a different part of town with Pollo each afternoon, on the other side of the river dividing Amaris.

When I return to my room after dinner, there is a man in dark clothing waiting there for me. Hayden. I quickly close the door behind me, hoping no passers-by in the hallways saw him. He lies sprawled on my bed, his head resting on his hands.

"Why am I not surprised to see you?" I ask, sick of him showing up unannounced and uninvited.

"Just thought I'd check in and see what you've done with the information I gave you, butterfly. It's been a while since we spoke," he says casually, as if we are discussing something as simple as study notes, not the threat of war.

"I've told Hanniah. We have a plan. So thank you, but you can go now." I hiss through clenched teeth, trying to keep my cool. If someone were to find him here, all my hard work would be ruined. They'd never trust me again.

"Are you sure that's what you want?" he asks with a half-grin plastered to his cold, unyielding face. He locks his eyes with mine, and I refuse to be the first to look away. "I'm surprised you had the guts to actually return here and tell the Empress. It would've been much easier to return home to your sorry excuse of a village."

"Sometimes, Hayden, people choose to use their power instead of running away," I say with a sigh, realising I am unintentionally hinting at the plan Hanniah and I formed earlier. The Shadow Isles will fight for our freedom, not run and hide. "I don't expect you to—" I am interrupted by his tall figure swiftly walking over to mine.

Hayden stands in front of me now, eyes wild. "Say that again," he pleads, clenching his jaw.

I shoot him a confused glare, not knowing what part of what I just said he is talking about.

"My name. You've never called me by my name before." He towers above me, amber eyes locking with mine. He is so close I can see the fire burning beneath them, dancing in his irises. "You are infuriating, impossible to like. You hide yourself away up in that dark mind of yours so no one can touch you, but I see you for what you really are. A scared, lonely girl with too many daddy issues to count." His words hit a bit too close to home.

My brows furrow and I go to slap him across the face, but he sees it coming. He grabs my wrist, hard, and pins it to the wall over my head.

I'm not going to allow myself to be this easily defeated. I raise my knee, and shove it right where I know it will hurt him most. He releases my wrist, grimacing in pain, as I run across the room to put as much distance between us as possible.

"You think I'm infuriating? Get a mirror, Hayden." I silently curse myself for saying his name once more. "You're no better than I am. How many times have we fought, talked, argued, and I still hardly know anything about you! You are nothing but a pathetic liar with more secrets to hide than anyone I've ever met. And trust me, I've met my fair share," I yell at him across the room, no longer caring if Hanniah herself burst in and shot the cruel man in front me of down.

"You have no idea what it's like to be me. Don't pretend to know about things that you don't, Reyna. Have you ever thought about why I don't talk about my life?" he yells across the room, his deep voice almost shaking the windows.

My mind flashes to when I was inside his head: the scared, bruised little boy. The demanding father. A sweep of concern washes across my face.

"I—" I begin, but he cuts in.

"Don't. Just don't. I don't need your pity. It means nothing. *You* mean nothing," he says, almost as a whisper. Almost as if he is trying to convince himself instead of me. His tone does nothing for the look on my face, which only seems to make him madder. He comes at me again, grabbing me by the waist and throwing me over his shoulder.

"Put me down!" I scream, punching my fists against his back with all my strength.

He doesn't. I realise with horror he is heading for the window. I need to do something, and I need to do it fast. Wherever he is planning to fly me to… I don't want to find out. I lash out with my power and sink the dark shadows straight into his mind. What I find overwhelms every part of my body.

I move past the walled up, blanked-out memories he keeps guarded, not ready to face that pain again. I press on, navigating flashes of images, until I see it. Stashed away, in a dark, distant corner of his mind, Hayden keeps a bundle of memories. As if he is trying to forget them, to repress them, hide them. But they still linger. I watch on with horror as I realise they all have something in common.

Me.

I watch the first time we properly met at the Silver lake, him covered in Wex's blood. I watch as he deliberately bumps into me on class selection day, just so our eyes could meet. I feel the sheer fury in his blood the time he saved me from Wex at the bar. When he taught me about my powers and let me into his mind… I watch on through his eyes, feeling all the things he felt in those moments. There's something else: I watch myself through golden bars as Hayden reaches out and places a bag of golden coins in my hands. This makes no sense. He was there that day at the palace?

I snap myself out of there as soon as I realise what this means. Why else would he tie these memories together and shove them to the deepest, darkest corner of his mind? This betrays everything I thought he was to me, everything I thought he felt towards me.

Somehow, I manage to reach up to my waist and pull my dagger from its sheath. I don't hesitate before plunging it into his back. If my power isn't going to help me now, my combat training will. He lets me go, screaming in agony as he rips the blade from his skin. But he doesn't yield.

I go to run, to scream for help, to lift my arms in defence, but… I can't bring myself to move. My eyes are wide with the memory of what I saw in his mind, and my mind spins with what this means. I am frozen in place with shock. Hayden must notice the look on my face, as he slightly lowers my blade in his hand.

"What did you do?" he asks me. Somehow his voice sounds even more furious, more deadly, when he is whispering. His chiselled jaw locks in place, his glare made of ice. If he wasn't mad before, he certainly is now. Blood trickles down his hand from where he pulled the blade out of his back.

"I—you gave me no choice! I had to do something," I reply, but he doesn't listen.

He moves towards me slowly, purposefully, as if he is possessed by something greater than himself. I never intended to use my powers this way, to infiltrate his privacy, but I wasn't exactly going to allow him to carry me out the window.

"What. Did. You. Do," he repeats his question in the same low growl. His body is so close to mine that I don't dare to move. He can already tell when he looks into my eyes that I know the truth. I know why he hates me, why he makes every moment with him infuriatingly painful. Why he runs his hand through his hair on the rare occasion he smiles at me.

Then he attacks. In between slashes of my dagger, he yells at me, curses at me, as if I am the thing he hates most in this world. I know now that is just another one of his lies, and maybe he's even convinced himself it is true. I dodge his attacks, cursing myself for letting him get my dagger once again. He tries with deadly precision, and I remark at his skill. He has obviously been trained by someone with extensive knowledge on the topic. No amount of library books could make him move with such determination, such assured confidence. I remember what Carter taught me.

Using my speed, I circle my shadows around me as fast as I can, and tip-toe to the other side of the room.

"Damn it, Reyna, don't pull that shit! You speak of power, of not running away. Face me and fight," he demands, but I have no intention of doing as he says.

Just as I can tell he has no intention of fighting fair. He paces back and forth across the room, eyes wide and searching for me without any use. I stay silent, pressed to the cold, black wall behind me, wrapped in my shadows and out of sight. I stay there until he has given up searching for me, and sits on the bed in a heap. His broad, strong shoulders slump, and from where I'm standing, I can see the pained look on his face. I don't dare to move.

"I tried to fight it, you know. The things you saw... I could feel you in my head. I know exactly where you went in there, what you saw. I just wanted to hear you say it, because then maybe it would be real," he begins, his voice suddenly soft.

He sounds almost... pathetic.

Regardless of his stupid feelings, I'm not about to let him render me useless so he can carry me straight through that window like he attempted to moments earlier.

"I tried to fight it," he repeats, but this time I don't think he is talking about me being inside his mind. He sits back, arms extended behind him, and I can't help but drink him in. I have always found him extraordinarily beautiful, but that was a difficult aspect of him to focus on when he was constantly messing with me.

"I—you do things to me, Reyna… things I've been trying to ignore for months," he begins, and I creep forward in the protection of my shadow, my eyes on my dagger he left on the bed next to him. If I could just reach it…

"I didn't want to come here tonight. I was back home, perfectly happy, until those stupid memories resurfaced and hit me like a pile of bricks. I contemplated coming here for days, fighting with myself, but I lost the battle. I couldn't stay away. Why do you do this to me, butterfly?" His deep voice is soft now, and his gaze turns to the roof above.

I'm so close—so, so close—to reaching the dagger beside him. My fingers are inches away from it when he reaches out and grabs my arm, giving a wicked smile.

"Lilies," he says, and I curse myself for being so stupid.

That's how he found me at the lake all those months ago. Of course my perfume would give me away now. He only said those things to make me think he'd let his guard down. I'm a fool for thinking his feelings for me would ever be genuine in that way. He slides the dagger away and pulls me on top of him on the bed. I reveal my invisible figure, realising my facade is over.

"Hayden… I—" but I am cut off by his lips crashing into mine.

He kisses me hungrily, greedily, and as the shock wears off I can't help but moan against his mouth. The only other man I've kissed before is Dexter, but that doesn't even compare to how this is making me feel. It's like an explosion has gone off within me—like I am finally awake and smashing down my walls. His hands dig into my waist, exploring the skin exposed by my small shirt.

I know I shouldn't want this.

He is Hayden Radford, the guy who constantly belittles, harasses and hurts me. But I can't help myself. His tongue swipes over my lips as he stands and lifts me, hands moving lower as he walks me over to the wall I was hiding in front of moments earlier. He pins me against it, pushing his body against mine. I grin beneath his lips, and he must feel it, because he suddenly rips himself away.

"Fuck!" he yells, dropping me to the ground. I only just manage to catch myself and avoid crashing down onto my ass. He storms across the room and throws the pillows from the bed. I stand there against the wall, not sure what to say. My heart beats heavily inside my chest.

"I didn't mean to—I—I should never have come—" he begins, but this time, it's me that cuts him off.

I stare him down, eyes beaming with fury. How dare he just come in here, pin me down, and let emotional havoc loose on my mind. And to think I was just beginning to enjoy myself, to believe his intentions were true… I raise my hands, bringing shadows into my palms beside me. I feel my eyes darken, feeding on the anger inside.

"Go," I demand, my voice as dark as the shadows around me. This time, Hayden is smart enough to do as I say. His eyes widen as he re-buttons his shirt, which apparently I had undone in the midst of our passion. Hayden turns his back, and jumps out the window, into the night. I watch through the darkness as he carries himself away on a cloud of air, presumably back to the Fire Empire.

I flick my wrists and the shadows stop, sucking themselves back inside me. Letting out an audible sigh, I get changed into my black night dress, and slide under the covers, not bothering to fix the pillows strewn around the room once again.

As I close my eyes, I delve deep inside my own mind this time. And there, in the darkest corner, pushed right to the back, is an almost identical bundle of memories of my own.

29

The following week passes me by in a blur. I am getting stronger, faster and more powerful thanks to my training with Carter. After dinner, I've been studying the book I bought in town, *Shadow Magic: Spells, Potions and Enchantments.*

Each night I tackle a new page in the book, discovering a variety of different spells and enchantments that rely on and use my Shadow magic itself. I just hope that everything I've been doing is enough to prepare me for what lies ahead.

Before I know it, it is the day of the Winter Solstice Ball to be held at the Royal Palace. Sioni is helping me get ready after I ran into her in the hallways on my way to meet the others. She looked me up and down once, and didn't even bother to hide her laughter.

Ushering me back into my room, she swapped the plain, simple skirt and bodice I'd chosen for an elaborate black and silver dress made from a silky fabric. I put it on, and it hangs low around my breasts, not leaving much to the imagination, especially when she squeezes me into a corset over the top. I ensure my dagger is strapped to my thigh under the gown when I realise, sadly, there's no pockets this time. I sit at the vanity as she brushes my hair. She braids tiny pieces of it to frame my face, but leaves the rest loose, letting it fall in its natural waves to my waist.

"Sioni," I begin, and she smiles at me in the mirror's reflection. "What happens if I fail tonight? If I can't do as Hanniah asks me?" What she wants me to take from the king… it's no easy task.

"Then you tried your best my dear. But you should have faith. I do." She smiles again. "I've seen what you can do. Hanniah wasn't exaggerating when she told you how powerful you are. In fact, she probably didn't quite exaggerate it enough." I nod at her in thanks, hoping her reassurance is enough.

Pollo and I meet Hanniah and Carter in the large living room. They sit on the plush sofas, chatting away over cups of tea, as if they aren't even the slightest bit nervous about travelling to the Royal Palace. Of course Carter is staying here, but Hanniah mentioned she hasn't had to leave the Isles in his charge before, and she seemed worried about his inexperience.

Pollo has decided to stay here in the Shadow Isles with Carter, watching over Amaris, until he is expected at the palace two days after the ball. Hanniah agreed that it would be suspicious for him to arrive with us, seeing as he isn't even a Shadow Keeper, and that he was personally invited by the king such a short time after the event.

"Now, Reyna. No one has seen the Shadow Keepers for decades, besides your little stunt at the Sanctum last week in the Tournament. Be prepared for the looks and perhaps hatred that comes with that knowledge," Hanniah says, and I realise I hadn't even thought about protecting the secrecy of Amaris whilst we're at the ball. "As far as they know, we are a race of very few Keepers, living in the harsh conditions of the Isles. They cannot know about Amaris, otherwise the thousands of Keepers here are at risk. Do you understand?"

"Yes," I reply.

"Good. Let's go."

I hug my brother and Carter goodbye, and sling my enchanted bag over my shoulder. Hanniah adjusts her dark wreath upon her head, and she leads me out to the expansive gardens behind the Shadow Palace. The gardens here are as magical as the people of Amaris themselves. Luscious trees encircled by wild flowers and long, untamed grasses sway in the breeze as we walk through the gardens. A small stream flows through the middle of it, running off the great waterfall above.

I feel at home here, like I am back in the rugged wilderness of the Earth Empire. The sun streams through the gaps in the leaves above us as Hanniah comes to a halt in front of me. A large meadow of daisies knitted into thick green grass lies before us, stirring with life. Insects flutter by, and butterflies land on the flowers around us, kissing their petals. Until they are scared away.

Something rumbles in the distance—a loud, ominous sound assaults my ears and my senses scream for me to run. I look to Hanniah, but she stands there, both feet planted on the ground, as calm as ever.

"Reyna," she begins, looking in the direction of the deep, grumbling noise. "Meet Averyll. Harbinger of Darkness."

I watch as the sun disappears behind a towering shadow, as a mass of flesh and teeth moves towards us. I take a step back, my hand finding its way to my blade, as I watch the creature come into full view in front of Hanniah and I.

"It's a…" I start, but Hanniah finishes for me.

"Dragon. The last of her kind, and feared by all that know her. Averyll has lived in the Shadow Isles for centuries, and has serviced the emperors before me with valour. She is mine to command." Hanniah points to the creature's eyes, and I recognise the blurry sheen thrown over them.

Enchanted.

Just like those girls at Spirit Bar in Pineside all those months ago.

I try to refrain from showing my disgust on my face. How could Hanniah keep such a magnificent beast trapped with a curse so cruel?

"She will transport us safely to the Royal Palace and back," Hanniah says, and I look more closely at the beast.

Averyll has crimson scales so dark they are almost black. She spreads her enormous wings out, tipped with a claw at the top of each of them. She is truly terrifying. But glorious.

I follow Hanniah as we walk over to the beast, carefully trailing behind her. I may have this newfound, unyielding power, but I'm not about to take my chances with the likes of the enormous dragon in front of me. Hanniah motions a hand towards Averyll, and it lays its wing flat against the ground for us to climb on. I look into the dragon's eye as I climb onto it's back, and can't help but feel bad for the control Hanniah has over it. It is almost as though I can sense the beast's longing to fly as it pleases, wherever and whenever it wants. Hanniah climbs daintily along Averyll's wing and up to nestle herself atop the beast's shoulder blades. Despite her heavy gown, she is as graceful as a swan. When I climb up, on the other hand, it is not the same story. If anyone were watching, they would've no doubt gotten a good view of what's under my dress.

"Hold on," Hannah calls out to me, and before I know it we are jolting forward as Averyll takes off from the ground. Her magnificent wings flap loudly beside me as we soar higher and higher, leaving the dazzling city of Amaris behind.

Averyll lands on the luscious green grass outside the palace walls with an enormous thud. My mind is still swirling with the beautiful landscapes we encountered on the bumpy journey here: a sea so blue it reminds me of Navari's eyes, rivers running through the Water Empire in every crackled direction, and flocks upon flocks of wild birds as we approached land once more. As we continued inward towards the palace, the green luscious landscape grew more dense with forest and wildlife.

I stand now with two feet on the ground, and shudder as I recall the last time I faced the tall, golden gates before me. This time is different, I remind myself. This time we are invited. I can't help but wonder if I will see my father today. A rush of excitement washes over my body. I haven't seen him since the day he gave me my dagger. The day he left us. I try to push the thought away. I'm not going to let anything ruin my focus today.

Hanniah and I dismount Averyll, her more gracefully than I, and the beast gives me a long stare before thrusting itself into the open sky above and soaring out of sight. Hanniah and I approach the golden gates, and she produces the letter the king had sent. The guard looks at us sceptically, but lets us in nonetheless. A shimmering wall shows itself as the gates open, and as we step through, I realise the power that usually hums under my skin is silent. I test my magic by opening my palm—but nothing.

"It's the block I told you about," Hanniah begins to explain. "Whilst we are inside the walls of the Royal Palace, these wards will render us powerless." I don't bother telling her that I've learned to be powerful in other ways that don't require magic.

"Only the Royal Family themselves are able to wield their magic within these walls," Hanniah continues, and I nod in understanding.

As we walk the golden path towards the towering palace, I notice other Keepers mulling about the gardens. I get glimpses of their eyes— water, earth, air, and fire. And now Shadow. I hold my head up high as we press on, not allowing their glaring stares to bring me down. Some faces are friendly, welcoming, but others… I guess the prejudices the king is fighting so hard to maintain run deep within those in power.

I catch Elwin Dayarus' eye as he stands amongst his consort of Air Keepers, and give him a wicked, knowing smile. The man that left my mother alone to raise my brother. Pollo's true father. He looks back at me, and I grin knowing that I've caused the look of shock on his face, even if he has no idea who I am.

My extravagant gown is no match for the detail and beauty of the one Hanniah wears. She lifts it slightly as she walks, the tulle and lace dragging ever so softly along the pavement. I know for a fact that my hair is windswept and knotted, but I press on with confidence nonetheless, making a note to run my fingers through it to flatten it out once these prying eyes are off of me.

We reach the palace, and two guards on either side bow before opening the tall, oak doors. I notice the swords crossed at their backs, and their heavy helmets covering their faces. If my father were here tonight, he would see me long before I saw him. Although I'm wearing a mask of my own—made from deception and a blank stare.

We stride through the doors, and the sight before me is astonishing. The large ballroom is filled with Keepers from every Empire, all of high status. I recognise a few of the emperors that are particularly fond of splashing their faces across newspapers, and their families.

A terrible thought strikes me: what if Dexter is here? My eyes find the Earth Emperor sitting in the corner of the room at a beautifully decorated table, and I sigh audibly in relief when I see Dexter is not amongst the crowd surrounding him.

The high ceilings of the room are adorned with golden sculptures, with dazzling long curtains on each wall. Tall windows look out on the palace gardens. The room is decorated with millions of snowflakes hanging from the ceiling in celebration of the winter solstice, although one can hardly tell it is the season here at the palace. The air outside was warm, with no hint of snow in sight. It is beautiful, yes, but I immediately miss the Shadow Isles and the chilly, glistening streets of Amaris.

Hanniah clears her throat next to me, and I realise I've been gawking at the ballroom for too long.

"We need to go greet the king," she says, and I raise my upper lip in protest. I really would rather not face the man threatening my new home. I'm afraid I won't be able to handle myself.

King Zale and his family sit at the top of three large steps, looking out across the room. The line waiting to greet him seems to have cleared, so Hanniah and I walk over. I make an effort to keep my strides long and even, exuding the image of the confident woman I am so desperately trying to be in this situation. As we get closer, I notice

Theon and Vera on either side of the king, sitting on small golden thrones.

"Hanniah. It's been a long time. You look ravishing as always," King Zale booms down the steps to us, and we both curtsy in respect. Well, fake respect.

The king's full figure sits upon a larger version of Theon and Vera's thrones, wearing an enormous golden crown encrusted with four stones. The red, blue, purple and green gems shine in the light of the ballroom, one for each Empire. All except one.

"Your Majesty," Hanniah says, deepening her bow. When she raises, her face is plastered into an emotionless smile. "Thank you for your invitation tonight. What a wondrous ball you've thrown." She gestures to the room around us, brimming with Keepers.

"Of course. I thought it was about time for the Shadow Isles to show its face in our country. And such a beautiful one, for that manner," he says, and Hanniah blushes slightly. Now that's an emotion you can't fake. She must partly feel honoured to be here after all. "Oh yes, I remember you from the Tournament. What is your name?" he asks, gesturing to me with a fat hand entangled in jewellery.

"Reyna Arrington, Father," Vera answers for me, smiling excitedly. At least there is one kind face in this den of vipers. Vera doesn't seem phased at all by my newfound home amongst the Isles, unlike some of the other wicked faces here tonight.

"Arrington? Now, why is that name familiar..." the king pauses, stroking his greying beard. "Oh yes, that's right. Your father's a valiant and noble guard, Reyna. You should be very proud of him, as I'm sure you are."

If I were standing here six months earlier, I would be grovelling at the king's feet, telling him of my dreams to join my father as a Royal Guard. But not now. I cannot afford such naive dreams anymore. Not when I know they are twisted with lies and deception—with the murder of innocent Keepers.

"Thank you, your majesty," I respond, mirroring Hanniah's emotionless smile from before.

"As for your power... well—I'm sorry to hear of your misfortune." He laughs, as well as the guards surrounding him on the steps before us. It takes every single ounce of strength in me not to lash out at him, to unsheathe my dagger and throw it into his chest—but I know that will end with my slow, painful death. I nod once in return.

"Too bad really. I would've *personally* welcomed such a striking young woman as a member of my guard," he says suggestively, and I have to repress the physical revulsion I feel. "Enjoy the Solstice, and save a dance for me." He winks at Hanniah, and we turn back towards the festivities behind us. Circular tables line the edge of the large room, such as the one the Earth Emperor is sitting at. When I allow my eyes to gaze over to where he sits for the second time this evening, they stop in their tracks.

"What is it?" Hanniah tugs on my arm, but I dismiss it as nothing. The last thing I need right now is to make a scene in front of the man I used to love.

Dexter sits with his father now, sipping on a glass of thick, red wine. Although I don't like the way we left things, I don't feel particularly fond of going over there to make amends. Besides, what he did can never be forgiven.

The last of the sun goes over the hills looming over the Palace, and people begin to dance. I watch as emperors and their families, guards, children, and other high ranking officials partner up and swing each other around in the centre of the room. The music playing is happy and bright, keeping a lively beat under our toes. Hanniah grabs me by the hand and pulls me to the dance floor, where she leads us straight into the middle of a traditional Aspacian line dance. I twirl from arm to arm, trying to remain balanced on my two left feet, as I grin up a storm. I know I need to remain focussed but… this is more fun than I've had in a long time. I am swapped between arms once more, and now stand in the arms of a familiar face.

Prince Theon smiles down at me, and I can't help but feel guilty. My mission tonight will hit the palace where it hurts, and I'll be sorry to see him caught in the crossfire. But it must be done.

He places his hand firmly on my hip, taking my hand with his other, and spins me around the room in time to the music.

"I wasn't expecting you to be here tonight," he says.

"Well, how could you? I didn't actively advertise my new power on the front page of the Aspacian Daily." I grin sarcastically, to which he laughs a genuine laugh. He is not making this easy for me.

"Your home is beautiful," I gesture to the dazzling ballroom.

"Not as beautiful as you look in that dress." He looks me up and down. Seriously? I need to get away from this man right now before I change my mind about Hanniah and I's plan.

"Please excuse me, where is the bathroom?" I ask, and he points me in the direction of one of the hallways leading off to the left of the room. I smile graciously and make my exit.

In the bathroom, I splash my face with cold water. Focus, Reyna. He is a monster, just like his father. Don't fall for his traps—he only wants one thing from you.

When I feel ready to return, I go off and try to find Hanniah amongst the crowd. When I finally spot her, she is still dancing in the arms of the Air Emperor I last saw her with. She is a really good actress; her smile is plastered on her face with no intention of leaving. Elwin swings her around and they laugh. I feel sick, knowing what I know about that man.

I decide to find a quiet place to sit when a hand extends down to me. I know exactly whose it is before I even look up.

"Dexter," I say, an accidental scowl crossing my face.

He is not going to blow this for me. "Reyna, can I have this dance?" he asks, green eyes staring down at me where I sit.

I consider saying no, but then see the eyes of those nearby trained on us and decide against it. It would make me look bad, make the Shadow Isles look bad, to be seen denying an emperor's son a dance so rudely. I grudgingly take his hand and he leads me to the dance floor, the music turning to a softer, slower tune.

"You've been busy," Dexter says, his eyes staring into mine, taking in my newly darkened features.

I nod in response, not wanting to say anything that might implicate myself.

"Reyna, I never meant to hurt you, please try to understand," he begins grovelling, his face full of emotion and regret. It disgusts me.

I try to remain polite, not wanting to cause a scene for the increasing number of eyes now trained on us, but this is going to be difficult. If I thought simply wearing a black gown to the palace would cause a scene, I certainly wasn't prepared for the shock that would fall over the room when I danced with someone in green. Keepers here are mingling only within their own Empires— groups of each colour stand closely together in different corners of the room, and a bunch of blue-clad Air Keepers nearby us turn to stare.

"You just needed to give me another chance, and you would've seen that all I ever wanted to do was protect you," he continues.

"You'd sooner have me be your stay-at-home, child bearing wife than let me have any sort of free will," I whisper as harshly as I can manage whilst maintaining a smiling face.

"Would that be so bad? Look where your free will has gotten you. You will never know the comforts of family. The safety of being protected by a man who would do anything for you. Of never needing to endanger yourself with the likes of any threat at all. Don't you see Reyna? I love—"

"Don't you dare. You never loved me. If you did, you wouldn't want to own me. To diminish me of everything I want, everything I am," I say, trying to remain calm. "I'm sorry that you were never truly loved by anyone, and it made you cruel."

Dexter opens his mouth to speak, but is cut off just in time by a tap on his shoulder. Behind him stands a tall, dark figure. I'd recognise those amber eyes anywhere. I've never been happier to see Hayden Radford in my life.

"May I steal her for a moment? I believe your father is calling for you." Hayden smiles, and Dexter gives him a cold glare, before making his way to the table the Earth Emperor sits at in the far corner.

A flash of doubt crosses his eyes before he leaves, and I know that he is only giving me over to Hayden for fear that his father really is calling for him. How I ever fell for such a power hungry, yet completely powerless man, I'll never know. Dexter is at the mercy of his father's word, and would do anything he says to impress him.

"What are you doing here?" I ask in a surprised whisper as Hayden pulls me in by the waist, seamlessly resuming the dance. He must be more important in the Fire Empire than I thought.

"I have my ways," he says with a wicked grin. "You're lucky I resisted my urge to kill that monster as soon as I laid eyes on him."

"He's not a monster, not really. He's just a man," I say, realising it's true.

People are capable of acts worse than the things we are told about in horror stories and fairy tales. The words they say, the things they do, are particularly evil because they are real.

"I wasn't expecting you to be here either. I guess we are both higher on the royals' invite list than we knew," Hayden says, his face unreadable as always. I reach my hand past where it circles the back of his neck, until it finds its mark at the top of his back. I press down, but to my surprise, he doesn't even flinch.

"I see your back is healed."

"You mean from the literal knife you put in it? Yeah, it is. But next time, you should really aim for my front. It would be less… cowardly." He grins tauntingly and I roll my eyes, moving my hand back to rest behind his neck.

"Hanniah brought me. She says I am powerful, and she wanted to guarantee her protection," I say, not wanting him to get the idea that I actually mean something to the Shadow Empress. And I'm not entirely sure I do.

"Reyna… I wish—I wish you weren't here right now. It's not…" he begins, clearly trying to piece together whatever it is he wants to say. It is as if he is putting together a puzzle in his mind, putting only the pieces of the truth he wants to tell me together. "It's not safe."

"What do you mean? The Royal Palace is one of the safest places in Aspacia, except maybe the Sanctum."

"Not tonight. Just convince your Empress to leave. Now. You've shown your faces, you've accomplished what you wanted. Now leave." His eyes look at me pleadingly, as if this would mean more to him than anything he has ever asked of me. He reaches his hand in front of me, and in the space between us, he holds a small flame.

My eyes meet his in shock. "But isn't—" I begin, but am cut off by the brassy notes of a cornet blasting through the ballroom. The music stops, and I see that the king has raised his hand, physically pausing his audience. I recall his power to pause time and think maybe he actually has.

But no, when he clears his throat, it is clear he is making an announcement. A silence spreads across the room, no one daring to interrupt the king.

"Welcome, everyone. Thank you all for coming tonight to celebrate this wonderful Solstice with us. We open our home to you, and I personally hope you are enjoying your evening. But the festivities have only just begun."

Hayden removes his hands from my waist and runs his fingers through his hair. He looks to the ground, amber eyes avoiding my dark ones at all costs.

"I would now like to invite each of the emperors to the stage. All five of them," he says, looking towards where Hanniah stands across the room. Each of them make their way to stand at the top of the steps, beside the king.

"As you know, we have gathered to celebrate the Winter Solstice. But there is one more thing we are celebrating tonight. The Empires are at an uneasy peace, and I intend on consolidating it by any means. We do not need to be at odds with each other when we can simply stay out of each other's way. I intend to watch over the Empires and ensure this separation is successful and fully maintained. So tonight, I ask each of you—" He looks to the emperors and empress. "Will you stand with me in the fight for peace?"

Gasps fill the room. No one was expecting such a public proposal from the king. What he is asking is more than his words themselves say. He wants to know who will stand by him when he goes to war.

First with the Shadow Isles, then with anyone else in Aspacia with hopes of speaking to anyone from another Empire ever again. Who will stand with him when he separates Aspacia even further? I stare up at Hanniah and already know what her answer will be. At least I hope I do. I hope she hasn't gotten too close with the Air Emperor she was dancing with. That he hasn't gotten in her head. I pray she remembers the threat the king made to the Shadow Isles, that she remembers exactly who her decision will affect.

A line of guards all in golden armour make their way between the crowd and the stage, making clear they will use any means necessary to stop anyone trying to intervene. I stare at their faces, covered by golden masks, their swords at their side. Is my father one of these guards before me?

I stand in the middle of the crowd, looking on as best as I can between the heads of the shocked Keepers surrounding me. Hayden is no longer at my side—where did he go? Is this what he was trying to warn me about?

The Fire Emperor steps forward, a tall, muscular man with fiery hair and a strong set jaw.

"The Fire Empire will join your cause, your majesty," he says, his booming voice filling the room.

The king smiles and nods, and honestly I'm not surprised by the Fire Emperor's choice. The Fire Empire has always been the strictest regarding maintaining a heavy border and a zero tolerance rate for cross-Empire marriages.

"Let our children be pure and our minds focussed," he continues.

"Thank you, Rhudien. Your Empire is most powerful and will be a great asset to Aspacia," the king says, and the Fire Emperor moves down from the step, joining his consort past the guards.

"Kallas," King Zale says questioningly, and a man in a blue suit steps forward. His brunette hair falls over his face in ripples, his eyes as blue as the oceans he rules.

The Water Emperor stands before the king, and says, "No, your majesty. This is not the way to find peace. Water Empire will not stand with you."

An audible gasp comes from the shocked crowd around me, and the line of guards tighten their defences.

"Very well," King Zale says, and in one swift movement, the closest guard raises his sword and brings it crashing down on Kallas' neck. The sharp blade pierces his skin, slicing his head straight from his body. At first I think the scream is coming from my own lips, but when I reach a tentative finger to touch them, they remain closed. Instead, the wailing continues from the back corner where Dexter and I were dancing what felt like hours ago. Keepers dressed in blue cry out in outrage, in sorrow, in fear, until the king gives them a pointed look. They silence immediately. That is the power the king commands. The very same power he abuses.

If this was the punishment for disagreeing with the king... My thoughts rush to Hanniah. She stands on stage, trying to stay calm as the body of the Water Emperor lies in front of her, thick, red blood coming from the stump of his neck. The three remaining emperors stand helpless to their dead counterpart, devoid of any weapons or access to their magic thanks to the wards surrounding the Palace. I hear shuffling in the back, signalling what I'm sure is the sound of the remaining Water Keepers leaving the room.

"Velynn. What do you say?" The king extends a hand towards the Earth Emperor, and I have a feeling I already know the outcome. If Dexter's father is anything like him, he will cave under the king's command, even if it isn't his true belief. A weak man, with weak offspring. Velynn steps forward, and nods once.

"Earth Empire stands with you, your majesty." He bows a deep, long bow, then steps down past the guards, joining with Dexter and his consort. A smart move for a gutless man with absolutely no backbone.

That's two Empire's that have allied with the king so far, and one that has not. Elwin steps forward, Emperor of Air. "If we don't work together, we are a machine divided into its parts. Aspacia will stand no chance against neighbouring civilisations if they were to ever move against us. We need each other. So no. If death is my only option, I'd rather die a man true to his beliefs than live as a fraud." He glares across the room at Velynn, his words laced with ice.

My blood boils with the knowledge of what comes next. Perhaps I judged Elwin too quickly for his actions against my family. We share a belief, and maybe we would've been able to patch things up with Pollo. But no. The sword strikes into his heart and he lies dying on the floor, spluttering up blood. He gives a menacing grin before taking one, final, breath. I allow a single tear to leave my eye. For Pollo's sake. But I wipe it away before anyone can see.

A hand grabs my shoulder and I whirl around instinctively. The figure behind me is hooded, but I notice wisps of blond hair peeking out. "Theon?" I ask, my voice barely a whisper.

"Shhh, be quiet. Come with me now if you want to live," the prince says.

Little does he know he is just the man I've been needing to see. He pulls me by the hand and leads me through the crowd of terrified Keepers. They don't bother turning their heads as we slip past them. We walk through a long corridor, away from the ballroom, up some stairs and into a room Theon unlocks with a thin, golden key.

"Do you stand with him?" I face the prince, my words laced with venom. This is what I came here to do. It doesn't matter where he stands. But if he is with the king, this will make what I have to do far easier. He looks at me with pursed lips and his eyes dart away from mine.

"Do. You. Stand with him?" I repeat, more prominently this time.

He still doesn't answer. I'll take that as a yes. Either way, no matter what his answer was, I have a job to do.

"Is the door locked?" I say, trying to look as flustered and helpless as I can. It isn't too hard—I know what it's like to feel that way.

"Yes, Reyna, you are safe in here," he says.

I give him a wicked grin as I say, "You're not."

30

He looks at me, eyes widened with surprise at my words.

"What do you mean?" He hesitantly reaches for the sword at his hilt, and I allow him to. It won't be of any use.

"Oh Theon. What did you think was going to happen, your family allowing my Empire into their home. My Empire who has been so brutally separated from the world by your father. My Empire, who has to constantly be in fear of an attack. My Empire…" I trail off, staring him dead in the eyes. "…who despite all the shit you throw at it, is currently stronger than you'll ever know."

"Reyna, I'm not like my father. I promise—" he begins, but it's too late.

I call forth the darkness, surrounding him with shadowy clouds rolling around his body. My book of spells came in handy—it showed me how to surpass even the strongest of wards. I feel my power buzzing beneath my skin, relieved at its return.

"Why?" Is all he asks. I try not to look at his face as he begs for me to stop.

"I have to do this. For the Shadow Isles. For Aspacia." I wrap the darkness around his throat and contract my hand, making the shadows tighten.

Theon's golden eyes glare at me across the room, the hate in them astounding. I can see the light draining from him as he resists the pull of my shadows. He gasps for air, extending a pathetic hand out to me like I will offer him any mercy or pity.

Then it happens. His face begins to change. I've seen him transform a few times; once like the time he turned into a gnome in abjuration class, but never like this.

Never into another man.

I stare closely as his face sharpens, turning once rounded cheekbones into chiselled ones, once blond hair into black. Once golden eyes turn to amber and…. Oh my God.

It's him.

"Why would you do this?" I allow the grip of my shadows to ease the tiniest bit from around his neck. The man in front of me is no longer Prince Theon Rhanes. I am looking into the eyes of the man I despise most. The man in my bundle of memories.

"Hayden," I whisper, before regaining my control. This is just some sick, twisted game Prince Theon is playing to distract me, and I foolishly let it. I tighten the shadows once more.

"Wait… please," he calls out with a strangled tone.

I've had enough of his games, his torments, his betrayals. He needs to pay. My face flushes in anger as I prepare to deliver the final blow. He strains against the shadows, his muscular forearms pressing against the wall behind him as if that will help. Then, all of a sudden, he stops. He stops fighting.

He stares me dead in the eyes, and says, "I think it's time to call in that favour you owe me, butterfly."

How could Theon possibly know about our deal? About my nickname? The only person that knows would be…

"How is this possible?" I whisper under my breath, holding my head in my hands as I try to make sense of this all.

"It's me, butterfly. It's always been me."

"No. No, it can't be. You're messing with me. You must've somehow overheard us talking. Or…" My mind flashes with shock.

"What have you done with him?" He must have Hayden somewhere.

Theon somehow knew Hanniah's plan, and took Hayden to get under my skin. What he must've done to get him to speak…

"You still don't get it, Reyna. It's me." He reaches out slowly, but I tighten my grip on the shadows around him once more.

"Please, just let me show you. Please," he says, eyes full of emotion. He reaches out once more and takes my hand, then places it against his cheek. I can feel him let his mental walls down, his enchantments are weakened. He lets me in.

I travel through his mind in a shadowy haze, searching for anything that might give me the answers to whatever this stunt is the prince is playing. I realise with a start that this mind is familiar—I've been in here before. I twist and turn my way through flashes of memories until I find the ones I'm looking for. The blocked, blanked out memories once hidden by Hayden's enchantments are standing tall before me, free from any blocks.

I reach out and touch the swirling images with a tentative hand, and am sucked inside immediately. I need to know what's so secret

Hayden keeps hidden away from even himself. I am whirled through bright lights and the shouts of voices as I come to a halt in a bright, sunny room.

The golden detailing on the wallpaper, the luscious thick carpets and rich wooden cabinets… I realise with a start that I am inside the palace. A young boy who looks to be about eight or nine, sits in the corner of the room, playing with a younger girl with lovely long brunette hair. They pass sculpted pieces of wood between them, and I realise they are playing a game of chess.

The board is much more elaborate than the one Dexter used to teach me all those months ago—it is made of a solid, dark wood, adorned with swirling golden marks along its borders. The two children look up from their game, almost as if they are staring right at me. I take a step to the side, but their eyes remain where they first were, and I realise they are watching something behind me. No, not something. Someone.

I watch as King Zale moves towards the two children with a purposeful gait. He glares down at the two, and the girl shuffles back on the ground she sits on. Not the boy, though. He stands, meeting the king's furious gaze, squaring his shoulders and tilting his chin upwards.

"You left your shoes on the floor, Theon. Again," the king booms down at the child. Theon? How could this boy with amber eyes and dark hair be the prince? And if that's the king, the girl must be Vera.

"But, I… they're just in my room. I put them close to my bed, out of the way," the young Theon says, maintaining his emotionless face as solid as stone.

"How many times do I have to tell you? I don't pay the staff to clean up after the likes of you," the King booms down at him.

I look more closely around the room and realise it must belong to Vera. The pink ruffles on her bed match the decor in her dorm at the Sanctum. Clothes and toys are strewn all over the floor. The place is a mess.

Theon looks to the room around him also, and says, "But… Vera always—"

"This isn't about your sister. She is nothing but an irresponsible little girl. You know better," the king says.

Theon opens his mouth to speak again, but is interrupted by the swift, strong hand that smacks him across the face. Hard. The boy places a hand on his face as it grows redder by the minute. I see tears brimming in the corners of his eyes, but he wipes them away in a rush. Not before the king sees them, though.

"Real men don't cry. You've inherited all of your mother's sour traits."

"Don't speak about my mother!" Theon shouts, which only gains him an even harder fist to the stomach. He eyes the king with resentment behind those fiery eyes, and I can't help but feel I've gotten Theon entirely wrong.

We are more alike than I could ever know. The king swings his fists into the young boy until he lies on the ground, unmoving. Vera sits in the corner, mouth open, too shocked to even blink.

The king storms out of the room, and it is as if I am thrown with a force as powerful as those punches back out of Hayden's mind.

He stands before me, my shadows still encircling his tall figure. I've never seen him look so low, so defeated. Is this man before me truly

Hayden? He lifts his head, looking up at me with the same amber eyes of the boy from his memory. And I know I won't be able to carry out Hanniah's plan. I can't kill him. Can't hurt this fragile but deadly man in front of me, not after he bared his bruised and battered soul for me to see.

But how does he have the prince's memories? There is no other explanation. He is telling the truth.

"I never wanted to lie to you, butterfly." His voice is but a soft whisper in between deep, heavy breaths that I realise are my own. I pace back and forth across the room. What am I supposed to do now?

"He beat me. Every day. Until I was strong enough to strike him back," he says, a sadness looming behind his eyes. "Until I wasn't me anymore."

"All this time… all this time, you were him? You're the prince?" I try to wrap my head around what he is saying.

He nods once, slowly. My shadows have found their way back into my hands, not wanting any part in a crime so cruel. He goes to stand, and I take a step back. He moves towards me with purpose, until his face is right in front of mine.

All the twisted stories, all the things he knows that he couldn't possibly… that's how he knew about the Fideal's scratches. The Shadow Isles and the people of Amaris. He's lived in the palace his whole life.

"Which is truly you? Are you Hayden or Theon?" I ask softly.

"I've never lied to you, Reyna. Just didn't tell you everything…" he begins, running his fingers through my hair. "My mother was a Fire Keeper. My father has always resented me—I took after her looks and talents. His only gift to me was my power. My father chose my first name—Theon, but my mother chose my middle," he says, and I already know what that must be. *Hayden.*

"I created the blond, indestructibly cold prince to please my father. To stop the constant disproving looks. The sea of bruises on my body. But this here—" He motions to himself. "—is me. Truly me."

I can't imagine what changing yourself every day to please others is like. To change not only your appearance, but basically kill the person you are… I can't imagine the suffering Hayden must've been through.

"I decided to bring Hayden, my true self, to the Sanctum with me, shifting into him whenever I could. My father would never find out, he hasn't seen the real me since I was a child.

"At the Sanctum, I could be whoever I wanted to without the prying eyes of the palace back home. When we were younger Vera helped me create the image you know as Theon, and my father wholeheartedly approved. I modelled him after the son he always wanted.

"The son that looked like him, thought like him. And to both mine and Vera's surprise, he accepted this fake, made up version as his own. The beatings stopped when I was Theon, so I hid my true self as deeply as I could in my mind."

I think of the harsh, demanding presence Hayden puts out into the world. Never would I have guessed that his tough exterior was there to purposefully deflect the salt from the wounds he is trying relentlessly to heal.

"So that's why you can wield air," I begin to piece the puzzle together. Hayden nods, a small smile forming at his lips. "You can shift into an Air Keeper."

"Yes. But thanks to my mother, fire has always been my strongest power. It took me years to master it, as it takes most Keepers to do, and

I've only just learned how to whirlwind with air. As for water and earth... I haven't quite figured them out yet."

"Why did you bring me in here?" I ask, remembering his words from when he found me in the ballroom. *Come with me now if you want to live.*

"We both know what Hanniah is going to say to my father's question. I'd rather not stick around to see what he does to the rest of the Keepers out there once he's finished with the emperors," he says, fiery eyes full of sorrow. I hadn't thought of that. Every single Keeper the Water and Air Emperors brought with them is in danger because of their refusal to join the king. My eyes widen with the realisation.

"We have to help them," I say.

"So... you're not hellbent on killing me anymore?" He smirks. I can't believe he has the audacity to actually make a joke right now. I shoot him a glare made of daggers as I unsheathe Shadow Reaver from the strap on my thigh. Hayden's glance as I hoist my dress up to reach it isn't lost on me.

"You're absolutely insane, butterfly. But I will fight with you."

I grin at him as we march back to the ballroom. Hayden keeps to the shadows, and I wrap myself in a darkness of my own.

31

Hayden and I stalk the castle halls, making our way back to the ballroom. He keeps to the shadows, whereas I have my own. Together, we are an unstoppable force of fire and darkness. We approach the entrance to the ballroom, and I crane my head to try and hear whatever lies inside more clearly. No matter how hard I try, I cannot hear a single noise coming from the grand room.

"What now?" Hayden asks me. I haven't thought this through—if we storm into the room, it could be the death of us both. But if we try to sneak in, we might take too long to prevent the no doubt dire outcome the king has in mind for the rebelling Keepers.

"I'll go in first and see what it's like. If it's safe, I'll come back for you. Wait here." I shroud myself in darkness once more so I am invisible to the naked eye, and slowly open the tall wooden door leading into the ballroom.

Once it is open wide enough, I step through and close it behind me as quietly as I can. I silently thank my father for teaching me to be light on my feet and silent as the wind all those years ago. Although there is no need.

I scan the room and realise it is completely empty, save for the bodies of those the king hadn't spared earlier. The Air and Water Emperors lie lifeless upon the small stage area at the front of the room —their blood trickling down the steps. I try to avoid looking at them any more closely than I already had, and press on into the room.

The once busy dance floor is now nothing but an empty space with dusty footprints stamped onto the tiled floor. The tables bordering the room seat no one, and the stage itself is devoid of all Keepers. I let my shadows uncover me—there is no point now. Where did everyone go? I walk back across the room, less careful to be silent this time. That was a mistake.

Before I make it back to the door I entered through to get Hayden, I am stopped by a sharp knife held to my throat. A firm, male arm holds me against my attacker around my waist, the other continuing to wield the weapon upon me. I don't dare to breathe for fear of moving my skin against the blade. I was so, so close to the door. To getting back to Hayden.

"You're coming with me," a rough male voice says from behind me, breathing into my ear. The scent of cedar and cherries surrounds me, and I notice a familiar golden ring with a green stone on the hand clasping the knife. Dexter.

"Move and I'll finish what I started in the Tournament." Hayden appears from inside the doorway in front of us, his face unyielding and fiery as the surging power in his veins. Dexter tightens his grip on the knife at my throat and I stare at Hayden pleadingly. He could just leave me here, walk right out of this room to safety and not look back.

What does he have to lose? But no. He remains in front of me, fists clenched by his side with a gaze so murderous I wouldn't be surprised if Dexter dropped dead from looks alone.

"I said, don't fucking move," Hayden commands.

"Or what? As soon as you light that fire of yours, I'll cut her throat without a second thought," Dexter says, and although my back is turned to him, I can picture his cold, smirking face.

"Go ahead. Either way, you're dead," Hayden says, and my jaw drops in shock.

Surely he wouldn't… Dexter tightens his grip around my waist, and I see his muscles flexing as he holds me tightly pressed against his firm body.

"She sure is pretty. Maybe I'll just take what's mine, whether she comes willingly or not. I once told you we could have a good life together, Reyna. I stand by that. If you have to be in chains the whole time… well that's up to you, my dear," Dexter says beneath a snarling grin and I feel my repulsion grow even more immense.

"I can see it—me ruling over the Earth Empire, you being the loving wife I come home to each day," Dexter continues.

Whilst he is talking, Hayden's eyes lock with mine intensely, as if he is trying to tell me something. He looks from my eyes to my upper left thigh, then up again. Seriously? He's checking me out *now*?

I raise an eyebrow and he shakes his head the slightest bit, as much of a signal as he can give me without alerting Dexter, who is still blathering on about taking me home with him. Like there's a chance in hell I'd ever let that happen.

Hayden looks to my leg again, widening his eyes and trying to communicate something without words. I suddenly remember the heavy weight of my dagger, strapped to my upper left thigh under the folds of my dress. Of course. I give him a knowing smile, and slowly creep my hand down my leg. I have to get this right—if I move too quickly, Dexter will know. But if I don't move quick enough, he could stop talking and start carrying me off to wherever he wants.

My hand is at my leg now, trailing ever so slowly across my thigh. I pause for a moment as Dexter continues speaking.

"I bet you've gone and tainted my innocent girl, Hayden. You two sure spend a lot of time together. Maybe she isn't worthy of being my wife after all. But never mind, I'm sure she'd do quite nicely as a second option after I've had my fun with whoever I please."

I watch as Hayden's fury is no longer containable—his amber eyes flash with rage at Dexter's grotesque words. His hands flicker with the flames he carries within them, yet Dexter hasn't made his move with the knife despite his threats.

"I think you have to worry more about whether you're worthy of her rather than if she's worthy of you, you pig. You could live for a thousand years and still never figure out how to be a decent fucking person. Reyna is everything you are not, you will never be worthy of her. You are not worthy of the air you breathe." Hayden boils over with rage, the once small flames now a burning blaze of light in his palms.

I feel Dexter press the blade to my throat even harder, and a trickle of my blood falls down my neck. But it's too late—I've got a blade of my own now. I stab Shadow Reaver into Dexter's thigh as hard as I can, causing him to drop the knife he held me with. I grab it and sprint for Hayden, who shot an enormous ball of fire at Dexter the moment I left his grip. Hayden grabs my face in his hands.

"Are you okay?" he asks.

"Never better," I say, as we watch Dexter burn.

"How did you…" Dexter manages between muffled screams as he relives his torture from the last round of the Tournament. He doesn't finish, but I already know what he is going to say: *How did you use your power here?* I shoot Hayden a look as we walk away.

"You need to be more careful with your secrets. Any old nosy busybody could figure them out," I whisper with a wink, and he nudges me in the side.

Before we leave the ballroom, Hayden shoots a spout of water onto Dexter, extinguishing the flames burning his skin. Hayden gives me a dark look.

"I want him to remember. Death would be too kind," he says, and we exit the empty ballroom through a door across the room.

I open my mouth to ask where we should go, but I am answered by a high pitched, female scream flooding the hallway. It is filled with blood curdling terror, and I immediately know who it is. Vera.

Hayden doesn't stop running towards the sound until we reach a small, intricately decorated room that I recognise from when I was inside his head. It's Vera's room, from Hayden's memory of them as children. When the king struck him repeatedly.

The scream fills the room with a shrill presence, and I locate its source in the corner: Vera herself stands there, shaking and shielding her face from us.

"Please, stay back. Leave me be," she sobs through heavy tears.

"Vera, it's us. You're safe. You're safe," Hayden calls to her, and she removes her hands from her face, peering over at us with bloodshot golden eyes.

"You… Hayden." She runs up to him and throws her arms around his neck, burying her face in his chest.

"I thought… I thought he'd gotten you too."

"What happened?" Hayden pulls away and inspects Vera's arms, which are covered in large, red welts. She sobs, looking over to me in confusion.

"Why is *she* here?" Her voice is devoid of its usual soft, kindness. Instead, when she speaks to me, it is filled with pure, blinding hatred.

"Reyna knows everything, Vera. I had to tell her," Hayden says, but Vera shakes her head.

"You don't understand. It is her fault. She's the reason those poor emperors are lying dead in the ballroom." She takes a step back from me, pulling Hayden's hand with her, but he remains by my side.

"Vera, that was your father. You saw what he did," I say to her.

"He wouldn't have to have done that if you weren't…" She pauses, looking to Hayden for back up. "If you weren't the end of us all."

"What are you talking about?"

"Father came in here moments ago, before he…" Vera looks to her red arms, and I notice dark bruises are beginning to blossom under the red welts. "He told me what you are. What you will become. Hayden, you need to come with me." She tugs on his arm, but once again, he does not move.

"Vera, what did he do to you?" Hayden's eyes light with fury as he stares at her arms, but she ignores him.

"I should've seen it, should've known it was you. You are the one in the prophecy. You are Darkness herself." Vera's voice is a whisper.

In all the chaos of the last few months I'd nearly forgotten the prophecy the Nightbrood had sworn me to secrecy over.

My face turns to ash as Hayden looks at me, eyebrows raised. What does this mean? I can wield the darkness, I constantly feel the shadows turning under my skin.

But if I am darkness itself…

Hayden takes a small step towards his sister, unsure of me and my intentions. My mouth hangs open and I don't know what to say as they both stare at me from across the room.

"I don't know what this means. But I'd never hurt anyone who didn't deserve it, unlike your father. We need to get out of here. Where did everyone go? Please, Vera," I beg her, and she hesitates.

"My father was protecting the Empires, as he always has. He had to kill the two emperors for the sake of Aspacia. If they didn't unite with him…"

"If they did, it would be the end of everything! Don't you see? We cannot go on with the endless beatings, the separation between Empires based on power is pointless. We are stronger together, don't you see? Your father would have us stay within our Empires, never seeing the friends we make at the Sanctum, and for some of us, never seeing our family. If we just worked together, combined our power, Aspacia could be so much more." The words rush out of me, and I don't realise how passionately I feel about this until tears stain my cheeks. They flow in a stream from my eyes, but my voice remains steady.

"Reyna… he's stronger than you think. To stop him would be…"

"You've seen Amaris for yourself. We are stronger than anyone in Aspacia knows. Please, Hayden. Don't do this," I beg him to stand with me, as the king had done an hour earlier to the emperors. I don't know if I am prepared to carry out the consequences for denying.

Hayden looks at me with sorrow, his brow creased and shoulders slumped. I've never seen him look so… weak. So small.

"I—" Hayden begins, but is interrupted when the door to Vera's room flies open with a crash.

"There you are! Did you find him?" Hanniah stands before me, blood stained on her hands and face. My eyes widen at the fact she's still alive. I nod and point at Hayden, knowing he was about to force my hand anyway.

"It's him. It's always been him," I say to Hanniah, still pointing at Hayden.

He looks at me with pained eyes, my betrayal manifesting itself on his face. Hanniah looks between Hayden and I, then to Vera.

"We will have to kill them both, there's no time and she's seen too much. She will know we were in here with the prince," Hanniah says, and I realise she may be right.

Our original plan to kill Prince Theon, to take something from the king so great he will ache for years, will have to be changed.

Changed. That's it!

"Wait!" I call, just as Hanniah is preparing to fight Hayden, her shadows swirling in her hands at her side. She whirls around, looking at me with menacing black eyes.

"He will be more useful to us against the king if we take him alive. Back to the Shadow Isles." It's not an optimal plan, but it's better than watching them both die.

Vera is my friend, I couldn't bear to be partly responsible for her death—even if I'm not sure she will ever speak to me again. And Hayden… I don't think I could go on without him. Hanniah turns my words over in her mind, tossing up my plan, before finally turning to Vera and Hayden.

"Reyna is right. You will have to come with us." Hanniah rolls her eyes. "Reyna, do the honours."

I stare at them. "I'm sorry," I whisper. "Everything will be okay."

Hayden holds a burning ball of flames in his hand, aiming at Hanniah, but I am faster. I throw my shadows over them, blinding them with a thick layer of darkness. It coils around them both, blocking their vision, then I travel inside their minds, my words at the ready.

You must pretend I've commanded you. I won't make you do anything you don't wish to do of your own choice.

I whisper the words into their minds like a soft breeze. Vera nods in understanding, and lowers her hands. To Hanniah, she looks as if she is standing submissively at my mercy. Hayden is not so easily convinced. He looks through the shadows at me, eyes pleading with me as I am pleading with him.

Please, Hayden. Let me do this. Let me save you. Trust me.

His face contorts into the same blank slate as Vera's. Hanniah nods at me, pleased with my work.

Hanniah motions her hand and a loud roar comes from outside the window. The room shakes repeatedly, and I realise Averyll is waiting for us, hovering outside Vera's bedroom window. Hanniah flings the glass open, and leaps onto the dark beast waiting for us, motioning for us to follow. I shoot Vera a look, and once again speak to her through her mind.

It is your choice. If you leave with Hanniah, you will be safe in the Shadow Isles. I promise. If you stay here, you will have to continue facing the monster who wants to divide our world. The monster who marked you. The monster who has beat your brother senseless for years. Choose, Vera. Choose.

Vera takes a reluctant step towards the window, glancing over to her brother for any sort of reassurance. He provides none. She must choose this path herself. She takes a few more steps, until she is standing right at the window ledge.

"Hurry up! Reyna, make her do this quickly, we don't have long before the guards find us," Hanniah shouts at me through the open window.

The evening air whips around her, her hair flowing behind her head like a trail of golden leaves. Then, as if Hanniah's words had brought them forth, the door bursts open. A dozen Royal Guards storm into the small room, filling the tiny space with their towering bodies and sharp weapons pointed straight at me.

Vera shrieks and jumps forward through the window, safely making it onto Averyll's back. Hayden and I whirl around, facing the onslaught of men in golden armour surrounding us.

"Go!" I yell at Hanniah. The pain on her face is as icy as the snow on the mountains outside, but she whistles a shrill, high note.

Averyll lurches forward, and I watch as Hanniah and Vera fly off into the night sky, Averyll's giant wings causing the building to shudder beneath us. The guards cannot see that around the corner, from their view, their princess is being carried away.

A wide grin spreads across my face. We may not have gotten the royal prince, but the Shadow Isles now has the next best thing.

The princess.

32

"Good job, your majesty." One of the guards steps forward, and looks to Hayden, who has now transformed back into the body of the blond, false Prince. I can't wrap my round around it—should I call him Hayden or Theon when he's in this form? His blond hair is jarring against his golden eyes, especially now that I know the truth about who truly lies inside him.

"Hayden..." I whisper, taking a step back from the Royal Guards surrounding me, but he has joined their ranks. The man who spoke before glares at me through his golden helmet, his blue eyes stabbing into me like swords.

"Take her to the dungeons," Hayden commands without so much as glancing at me. He is impossible to read—his blank expression is harsh and cold. The typical face of a liar. I cannot fathom what would possess someone to be so cold, so cruel. I will not let him close enough to betray me again.

I begin to summon my shadows, but my hands are pulled back behind me, and my wrists shackled with a cold, heavy metal I don't recognise. It singes against my skin, and my struggle against it is no use. I try to shoot my shadows at those who dared to touch me, but I find myself powerless. Once again. My breathing quickens, my heart thumps heavily in my chest.

"They're made with nightshade. Don't even bother," the guard says to me. I can feel the slightest twinge of the familiar feeling of the nightshade against my skin. It is different this time to when Wex put it in my drink—it must not just be used to put a Keeper into a deep sleep.

Two guards grab my shoulders and push me forward, leading me out the door.

"Don't worry about your sister, my Prince. We will get her back. I swear it." The guard seemingly in charge speaks with confidence, his low, gruff voice muffled slightly by the helmet he wears.

Hayden doesn't answer him, just presses on behind us as I am marched through long, elaborate hallways, and down what seems like endless flights of stairs. The guards' grip on my arm tightens with every step we make, and I'm sure if I looked down, I'd find thick red welts on it. My mind flashes to Vera and her similar wounds—she had made the right choice to leave this place. To get away from her father and his devious plans.

Eventually we reach a dark, tiny room that smells of mildew and dust.

"This one will do, Roscoe," Hayden says to the Head Guard in an emotionless tone.

Roscoe roughly pushes me forward into a small, enclosed section of the room, with bars for walls and a small cement bench in the corner. When I turn my head, I can see straight through the bars into what looks like three more identical cells next to mine. The iron door is swung shut, and the guards leave.

Only one, tall dark figure remains looming outside in the dim light.

"Hayden. What are you doing?" My voice sounds pathetic. Weak.

"I had no choice, butterfly. It was either this or have them bring you to my father." He stands a few steps back from the bars I now hold in my hands, still shackled with the nightshade cuffs. "I want to help you, Reyna. You need to trust me, just like I did for you."

I pause, staring him down with thoughtful anticipation. "I like you better as a brunette." I grin through the iron bars at him. He immediately transforms back into the Hayden I know, rather than the body of the cold Prince Theon. He runs a hand through his dark hair, sweeping it away from his face.

"You have to promise me my sister will be safe. Promise me that, and I will help you escape," he says, and I nod. Vera's safety was never in question.

"Deal."

I spend what feels like weeks behind the cold iron bars of my cell, hidden away from the world. I have no idea what the king now plans for Amaris. Surely he wouldn't risk attacking whilst the Shadow Isles have his beloved daughter, but I wouldn't be surprised if he were readying his army as we speak. Wouldn't be surprised if he never truly loved anyone, including his lovely daughter.

I sit alone in the darkest corner of the small space, allowing the familiar feeling of being encased in shadows to take over me. Although this time, this darkness is created by the absence of light, not by my own hands.

A door slams closed as someone enters the dimly lit dungeon from down the hallway. Their heavy, determined steps approach my cell more quickly than I'd like, and I can tell whoever this is isn't the usual guard. They never come this late at night, and I've already been given my meal for today. The plate of mush the guards called 'dinner' lies untouched where they left it hours ago—I can't seem to muster any appetite after the things I've seen, despite my stomach growling hungrily.

I push myself closer against the wall, crouching to take up as little space as I can. As if I can somehow hide in this tiny cement-floored room. Pain blossoms from my bruised body, and I hiss in pain when I move too quickly.

"Reyna?" Hayden's voice calls out to me, and I sigh in audible relief. A pair of golden eyes peer at me through the iron bars, and his face comes into view.

"Why do you still pretend?" I ask, noticing his golden hair and soft cheek bones. This isn't his true face—this is the false prince he tried so hard to convince his father to care for. The prince his father loved more than his true son. Hayden's jaw clenches as he looks to the ground, and he runs his fingers through his hair.

"Just habit, I guess. No one knows except you and Vera. It has to stay that way. For now, at least," he says, his eyes now locking mine in an intense gaze.

"Why are you here?" I say. I haven't seen him since the day he brought me down here. I don't know how long ago that was—there's no way to keep track of the time in here.

"I said I'd help you. And I'm not as much of a liar as you must think me to be," he says. I stifle my rage — should I be grateful to him for letting me out, or blindly trying to gauge his eyes out for keeping me locked up for so long?

He fumbles with something in his pocket as he speaks, and reveals a long, rusted key. He holds a single finger to his lips, his eyes silencing my questions and soothing my nerves. Hayden fits the key into the lock, and slowly begins to open the door of my cell. I return his gaze with wary eyes—I don't trust him, don't want to go with him.

But I don't think I have any other option, besides waiting in this cell for the king to make up his mind on what to do with me. And I doubt that will be pleasant to say the least.

The door creaks slightly as he swings it open, and he moves his head to scan the hallway before him. I haven't heard any moment from the other cells whilst I've been down here—I must be the only person lucky enough to be held captive in the king's dungeon at the moment.

"Let's go, butterfly," Hayden whispers, his voice dark as the night.

I stand, closing the distance between us hesitantly. This is the man who lied to everyone for years. Who knows what else he is capable of hiding?

"You don't happen to have another key, do you?" I ask, weakly holding my shackled hands out in front of me.

The nightshade laced iron has rubbed against my skin from my countless hours of trying to escape the chains. The skin on my wrists is red and bruised, with dried blood covering their surface.

"If I do happen to have such a thing… what's to stop you from attacking me right here and now?" he creases his brow.

I contemplate the idea… But no. He is my only way out of here. Hayden knows his way through the castle, where and when the guards will be doing their rounds… my eyes narrow as I realise he is my only hope of making it out of here alive and unseen.

"You're just going to have to trust me," I say. I'm unsure why he would ever agree to that, but I don't have a better reason to offer.

To my surprise, he reaches forward and fits a small key into the lock of my shackles. They come off with ease, and his eyes dart to my bloodied wrists. I stretch them out, the feeling of finally being able to move freely putting a small smile on my no doubt dirty face.

Hayden seems to realise the state I'm in now that we are standing less than a foot apart from each other. He eyes my dirty dress that hasn't been changed in weeks, my matted hair with the lingering remains of the braids Sioni did for me when I was still in the Shadow Isles. I hadn't bothered to take them out—there had been other, more pressing things on my mind. Like my survival.

His eyes meet mine with a flash of pity, and I narrow mine even further at him. He breaks the stare, clearly unnerved by my tattered state and hateful eyes. I step past him, but then realise I have absolutely no idea where I am going. He sneers, pushing past me with a firm arm, and walks quietly towards the exit. It is late at night, and the guards are nowhere to be seen.

"Come on. The guards are changing shifts. We have about five minutes," Hayden says as he briskly leads me through the dungeon hallway, up several flights of cracked brick stairs, and into the main halls of the Royal Palace. I recognise the route we took from when Hayden led me to the dungeon as we press on, and I can't help but notice how strange it is that he is now the one to lead me out of the dark.

We keep walking until we approach a tall, golden door that stands out from the rest. It has gold, swirling patterns upon it, as well as a shiny, crystal doorknob. Hayden opens it and guides me inside with a strong push to my back. I whirl around, a frown crossing my face, when my eyes widen at the sight before me. The room Hayden has brought me to is breathtaking.

As my eyes scan the expansive space, I realise it must be his own. Dark green velvet curtains hang from the windows, letting in a bright stream of moonlight that bounces off the golden embellishments scattered across the room. A desk covered in letters, books and… are those diaries? I step towards the desk, but Hayden intercepts me.

"Don't even think about it," he says gruffly, and I try to hide my disappointment. To get my eyes on those pages would show me more than I could ever see in his memories.

"You look like shit," he says, barely suppressing his grin.

I scowl at him, although I know it's true. He points to a door I hadn't noticed on the far side of the room, and I walk across to what I realise is a sprawling, lavish bathroom attached to Hayden's room. My breath is ripped from me at the sight of the clawfoot tub alone, and I realise it's been weeks since I've bathed.

"Take your time. We can leave for the Shadow Isles in the morning. There's something I need to take care of first," Hayden says.

He pulls the bathroom door shut between us with a thud. I turn on the tap over the bath so that it pours almost boiling water inside. The mirror is my enemy at this point, and I make a point to avoid it as I strip myself of the soiled gown. I grimace as I recall it's once glamorous state—the silky dark fabric with shimmering silver streaks now ruined and tattered.

Despite everything that's happened, I would do it all again the same way if it meant saving Hanniah and Vera from a fate like this. Those weeks in the dungeon were… unspeakable. I've never been afraid of the darkness—it was the one thing in that cell that gave me any comfort. It was the light that made my heart freeze and my mind scream each time it visited me. It was the sign of the guards opening the door down the hallway, bringing me my meals. But they brought other things, too.

I've come to realise the hatred for my kind runs deep in the Palace— the guards would deliver my dinner with a side of closed fists and heavy boots kicked into my ribs.

My body screams as I slide into the tub, the weeks' worth of bruises now fully blossoming in purple and blue patches covering my legs and torso. I wash the layers of grime from my now frail, malnourished body, and the blood on my wrists comes off in flakes, staining the bathwater a crimson red. When I slide my head under the water, I close my eyes and retreat inside my mind.

If what Vera said is true… it's no surprise how many times I've been visited by darkness. As I lie submerged, I welcome it as a friend. And for just a moment, the weight of the world doesn't seem so heavy.

"What the… Reyna!" Hayden yells as he lifts my heavy head from under the water, his eyes boring into mine as I force them open through wet eyelashes. I must've fallen asleep in the bath. I cough up what feels like an ocean of water, my lungs stinging against the burn.

"You're so fucking stupid." Hayden glares at me as he removes his hands from my bare shoulders, dropping me back against the side of the bath. He is himself now. Dark hair and amber eyes, a chiselled jaw and unruly, raging temper. Yes, he is well and truly Hayden.

"I... I didn't mean to," I say, my voice only just audible as I splutter and cough up some more water.

It's only when I watch Hayden's eyes drop to below my face that I realise the situation I'm in: I'm sitting in the bath, with absolutely nothing but the dirt and grime to cover my naked body from his lingering eyes. His stare trails the bruises, the jutting ribs and marked wrists. And though his eyes are usually made of fire, I've never seen them burn so intensely.

"What did..." he begins, clenching his jaw. "I didn't know it was this bad." He looks to the floor, and I drearily try to cover myself, using up whatever strength I have remaining. I really should've eaten at least one of those piles of mush, but what can I say. I'm stubborn as hell.

"I tried to get to you sooner... I fought every day. I didn't give up, but they wouldn't even let me down there to speak to you," he says, looking to the floor. Of all the people in this world, Hayden is the last one I would want to see me this weak, but I can't fight the state my body is in anymore.

He reaches down between where my legs lie in the bath and pulls the plug. He passes me a plush, green towel from the rail and extends his hand to me. I struggle against my weight to stand, but my knees give out beneath me.

Hayden is quicker than I thought, though, and he manages to catch me before I collide with the ceramic basin, scooping me up in his muscular arms. He holds my towel-wrapped body against his chest as he carries me from the bathroom and sits me on the end of his bed. The mattress is the softest thing I've ever felt—it is as if I've fallen into the clouds themselves. Hayden sits behind me without a word, gathering my hair and gently drying it with a towel. I can't do anything but sit there in shock. This man, this unyielding, cruel liar, tenderly brushes through my locks, taking care not to pull on the knots.

"Get some rest. You're safe in here," he says, my back still turned to him. He rises, and I shuffle backwards on the bed.

My head finds the pillow, and I am at the mercy of my own tiredness. I lie wrapped in nothing but a towel in Hayden Radford's bed, but can't even muster the strength to demand something to wear before my eyes close once again.

33

My eyes flutter open to the light of morning streaming through the green velvet curtains of the prince's room. I sit up with a jolt at the memory of where I am. Of what's happened.

I leap from the bed although my body screams in protest, still exhausted and devoid of energy. Scanning the room, I sigh in relief when I find no trace of Hayden. He is probably off somewhere in the palace, which is no doubt bustling by now with a search party for yours truly. I doubt they will look in here—the king would never suspect his own son. Well, the version of his son he chose to care for. I realise that I am naked, the towel slipped off when I slept. This simply won't do—I need to find something to wear, and quickly. I shudder at the thought of Hayden's lingering stare from the bathroom last night.

A large closet full of elaborately adorned breeches and shirts, cloaks and jackets lies in the corner of the room. I rummage through it, carelessly throwing anything with gold on it to the floor. *If this is the colour of my new enemy, let it be as messy as this fight is bound to be.* Eventually, in the back of the closet, I find a pair of sturdy hunting leathers that I inch around my waist with a belt to make them fit.

I yank a dark green shirt over my head and examine my face in the bathroom mirror at last. I look gaunt, my cheekbones hollow, my eyes circled with dark bags. I look worse than I did before I came to the Sanctum. Like a ghost of the girl who only a month ago was sitting by the Silver Lake, discovering her power.

My stomach growls when I spot the plate of food Hayden must've brought for me while I slept. It is piled with pastries, eggs, bacon, and —to my relief—a giant cup of coffee sits next to it. I don't think I've ever eaten anything so quickly in my life—the food is gone in seconds and I feel a little better. I swish the bitter coffee in my mouth, scalding my lips as I sip deeply until that too is gone.

I guess now I should wait for Hayden to come back so we can leave… but my curiosity gets the best of me. I look to his desk in the corner, and to my annoyance, the diaries that were there yesterday are gone.

Where did he put them?

Walking around the large elaborate room, I check any place a book could possibly be hidden in. I search his draws full of jewels, behind the curtains, under the bed… but find nothing. I sit down on the bed in a slump, staring across the room in thought. Then, I see it.

One of the dark floorboards sticks up slightly. I scramble over to it in a rush, sticking my fingers under the board and prying it upwards. Under the floor, I find what I've been searching for. A stack of books and a box full of folded papers are hidden out of sight. I imagine that whatever these contain, Hayden doesn't want his father to get a hold of. Or me.

I can hear heavy footsteps in the hallway outside, rapidly approaching the room. I snatch up one of the papers, stuffing it into the waistline of my pants and placing my shirt over the top, and place the boards carefully where I found them. The door is swung open, and I hold my breath until I can confirm it is Hayden. I've stupidly left myself standing in the open for anyone who bothered to check in here to find.

Thankfully, the man who enters wears an all too familiar grin, his amber eyes finding me standing in the middle of the room. Hayden raises an eyebrow at me in question, and I give him a small grin in the hopes he can't read the suspiciousness of my face.

"Most of the ladies around here only wear gowns," he says, looking at my borrowed clothes. I try not to fidget as his eyes move past the spot on my waist where I'm hiding the papers.

"Are you ready?" he taps his foot.

"Are you seriously asking me that? You could've whirled me away weeks ago," the annoyance rolls off my tongue as I recall the weeks of torture I've endured. A pained look crosses his face.

"Like I said, butterfly, I tried." His eyes darken. "Now, if you'll stop your snarky comments…" He reaches his hands out to me, and I realise that he must be coming with me to the Shadow Isles. It makes perfect sense. His sister was whisked away on an enormous beast with the woman his father despises most—he wants to leave this place too.

I take his hands, looking up at him with hesitant eyes. He must sense my reluctance, as he raises an eyebrow at me.

"Why are you really helping me? Don't spout your typical bullshit answer this time," I say, removing my hands from his. "I need to know." He runs his hands through his hair and squares his shoulders, pausing before he finally speaks.

"This was never supposed to happen."

Before the confused expression can even reach my face, he grabs my hands and we whirlwind back to the Shadow Isles. To my home.

We fly at the speed of light, Hayden's hands on my waist to keep us together as we hurtle through the sky. I look at him, but his eyes remain trained ahead, avoiding my gaze. I've suspected it for a while, but to hear him say it... despite everything I've done, despite everything he's done to me, he loves me? I can't wrap my head around it.

I watch as the lights of Amaris show themselves, the buildings and bustling streets alive with the morning sky. As we whirl closer, I can see Shadow Keepers traverse the paths, tending to gardens and sitting at restaurants. I see the Shadow Palace looming under the towering waterfall, it's cascading waters glistening as they fall away into the river below. The black building is jarring against the falls, but somehow feels as though it is exactly where it is supposed to be.

Hayden whirls us to the entrance, and we are greeted by friendly guards in black armour.

"Reyna!" a man's voice calls out to me from my left, and I turn to see him running towards us.

Carter halts in front of me, pauses, then shrugs and pulls me tight embrace, the commander's strong arms hugging me against his chest. The gesture is unexpected, yet somehow comforting. Here is home, and here he is.

"Hanniah said you were done for, but I knew you'd make it home." He smiles down at me, and I return the expression.

It truly is great to be back here. Carter's eyes look to Hayden, and I suddenly remember his presence. I'm unsure how I could forget the towering man behind me, his hair tousled from the flight here. The fact that he wears no gold isn't lost on me either.

"Carter, this is Hayden," I say.

"I know who he is." Carter glares at Hayden, his black eyes intense and unwavering. Hayden does the same, and I stand awkwardly in-between the two men.

"Where's Pollo?" I ask, keen to break up whatever this is up. Carter eventually breaks his gaze, and Hayden gives a small, smug grin.

"He left, Reyna. After Hanniah returned with Vera, he decided to go home to the Earth Empire in case you showed up there," he says, giving me a sympathetic look. I make a note to get Hayden to whirlwind me there as soon as possible.

"Hanniah's inside with Vera. Your sister's quite a soldier, you know." Carter looks at Hayden with a smirk, to which Hayden balls his fists at his side.

"We are about to have lunch. You should join us," he says to me, then looks at Hayden over my shoulder. "You can come too, I guess."

We follow Carter inside to the dining room, standing around the dark wooden table. Hanniah walks in a few moments later, as radiant and regal as ever. She grins when she sees me, but does not seem half as excited as Carter did.

A slender woman in a flowing pink dress follows closely behind her. Vera. She folds into Hayden's arms, a single tear flowing from her eye, before making her way to me. I stand uneasily on my feet, unsure of where we stand, but she takes my hand in hers.

"Thank you," her honey-soft voice says as she looks into my eyes, and her words take me aback.

"Vera, I'm so sorry. If they hurt you—" I begin, but she cuts me off with a wave of her hand.

"It's okay. Truly. Actually, it's more than that. This place is amazing, Reyna. Hanniah and Carter have been nothing but welcoming hosts. Carter even taught me how to use a bow and arrow." She grins, and I sigh in relief. In those weeks in the dungeon, my mind replayed the image of Vera's horrified face as she jumped out of the window onto Averyll's back.

The look in her golden eyes… It was pure terror. I spent countless hours thinking over the possibilities that awaited her return to the Shadow Isles. Hanniah wanted Theon dead—what would she do to Vera? I'm honestly surprised to see her standing in front of me, very much alive and well. I wonder if Carter had anything to do with it.

We take our seats as lunch is served. I've definitely missed this. Piles of different meats, breads and salads are spread on the table, brought by the palace staff. My glass is filled with thick, red wine, and I barely resist downing the entire thing before Hanniah raises hers.

"I propose a toast," she begins, tucking her choppy blonde hair behind her ear. "To the future of Aspacia. We sit here today, two different sides of the same coin, with a common interest. We toast to a future that is bright, a future where we stand together. But above all, we toast to the darkness." We raise our glasses, meeting them together with a clink.

"Cheers!" Carter calls, giving me a wide grin.

Vera smiles brightly, and even Hayden manages a small smile as he raises his wine also.

After lunch I go back to my room, still exhausted from the weeks prior to coming here. I lie down on my bed, thankful for the plush mattress. Although it isn't as soft as Hayden's, it is a thousand times better than the floorboards I used to lie upon back home in my village. When I sit back up, I feel the soft jabbing of something against my waistband. The papers I stole from Hayden's room.

I remove it from the top of my pants immediately, and it isn't long until I realise it is a letter. The stark white page is filled with familiar, scrawling handwriting:

> dear father,
>
> it was a cold, snowY winter, the crOps didn't last long and oUr reserveS were low from a poor Harvest seasOn earlier this year. we made it throUgh, but mother becomes more and more fraiL each Day. i Bet at the palacE you get more food tHan you can eat. i can't wait to lEave this place and begin my life. can't wait to see you again. you haven't Replied to my last thrEe letters, but i know the king keeps you busy. please write me when you can. i hope you're okay.
>
> love you always,
>
> reyna

My heart stops.

The letter I am holding is the last one I sent my father before I left for the Sanctum.

My own handwriting stares back at me, along with the butterfly stamped into my stationary set from home. The one with the butterflies printed onto the corners.

I find my mind spinning and my feet propelling me forward and out the door—I need to find him. I storm through the hallways, not bothering to restrain the shadows that have slipped from my hands. My fury and confusion burn through me, through any rational thought I have in this moment.

I find Vera in the living room adorned with numerous black sofas and tall bookshelves.

"Where is he?" I demand, my voice full of anger.

She puts down the book she was reading and stands, taking a small step back when she locks eyes with mine. "I... I don't know. Reyna... wait, please," she says, but I'm already storming back through the door.

Where the hell is he? I walk past the palace staff, past guards lingering in the hall outside the room Hanniah must currently occupy. I don't imagine Hayden would be in there.

Eventually, I find myself outside, in the grassy expansive gardens behind the palace. The waterfall crashes down in the near distance, and I see him.

He sits at the edge of the garden on the steps, his back turned to me. I approach quietly, sneaking through the grasses with the stealth I'd learned all those years ago. When I am mere feet away, I see he holds a small butterfly made of flame in his hands, contorting its wings to flutter as if it were truly alive.

I attack. I unsheathe my dagger and hold it to his throat from behind.

"What is it this time, butterfly?" he asks, not sounding even the slightest bit phased by the blade at his neck.

With my free hand, I toss my letter into his lap, struggling to maintain control when all I feel like doing is breaking down.

"Where is my father?"

Acknowledgements

There are so many people I would like to thank for contributing to Golden as the Night in so many different ways.

First and foremost, thank you to my amazing partner Zac, for being a human bulletin board, search engine, and cheerleader. I wouldn't have had the confidence to pursue this to the extent that I have without your endless support and encouragement. Thank you for the months of putting up with my crazed excitement, self-doubt and giving advice. I feel as though this story is partly yours due to the amount of advice and ideas you gave to me, and I am forever grateful.

To Ellen, Abbey and Kim- my three honeybees. Thank you for always having my back and cheering me on with this project and every other one in my life. You all are my inspiration, my muses and my supporters, and I can't thank you enough! Your love of reading encouraged me to keep writing on the days I felt useless, and as well as on the days I felt on top of the world.

To my amazing editor, Belle Manuel, for contributing your thoughtful ideas and keen eye to my work when I was unsure it was even something anyone would want to read! Thank you for helping me through the editing process for my debut novel, and making it super easy and exciting.

Thank you Alice Maria Power for designing the STUNNING cover art for this book! I couldn't have asked for a more easygoing, lovely person to work with, and the end result is phenomenal. I still can't believe my book has a cover this gorgeous!

To Beck Michaels, for designing the cover graphics for Golden as the Night. You were a dream to work with and I'm so thankful to you for guiding a newbie like me through the process with ease. The end result is beautiful, I'm so glad we got to work together and look forward to what's to come in the future.

337